BLACK SUN

THE BATTLE OF SUMMIT SPRINGS, 1869

TERRY C. JOHNSTON

St. Martin's Paperbacks

BLACK SUN

Copyright © 1991 by Terry C. Johnston.

Cover art by Frank McCarthy.

ISBN: 0-312-92465-8

Printed in the United States of America

St. Martin's Paperbacks edition/April 1991

10 9 8

for my wife
Rhonda
who gives me a serene and safe place
to write.
More than inspiration,
she is my motivation.

It has been said that the Battle of Summit Springs was one of the few in history of the frontier which would measure up to all the requirements of the writers of western fiction.

—James T. King
*War Eagle—A Life of
General Eugene A. Carr*

The severe and well merited chastisement given these savages by General Carr in July produced the most marked effect upon the conduct of the whole Cheyenne tribe . . . the Cheyennes concerned have come in to Camp Supply and begged for peace, declaring they have had enough of War. It is believed . . . that there are no hostile Indians on the Plains of Kansas or Colorado.

—Major General John M. Schofield
Commander, Dept. of the Missouri
following Battle of Summit Springs

This battle ended Indian terrorism in Kansas and Nebraska. The savages had never before received such a stunning blow in any engagement . . . Considered as a complete success, the battle of Summit Springs takes rank with Washita Village; but in a broader sense it was of infinitely greater importance, as it forever secured to the white race the undisputed and unmolested possession of the Republican River and its tributaries.

—George Frederic Price
*Across the Continent with
The Fifth Cavalry*

The [Summit Springs] fight was the last in that section of the plains . . . Eight companies were in action, which makes it a major battle by Indian wars' standards . . . Summit Springs . . . was one of a very few of these fights that would satisfy Hollywood and the writers of Westerns. The cavalry charged with bugle blowing, a woman was rescued (and later married a soldier), the slaughter of Indians was large—as attested by a board of officers who counted the bodies—and the troops suffered no losses.

—Don Russell
*The Lives and Legends of
Buffalo Bill*

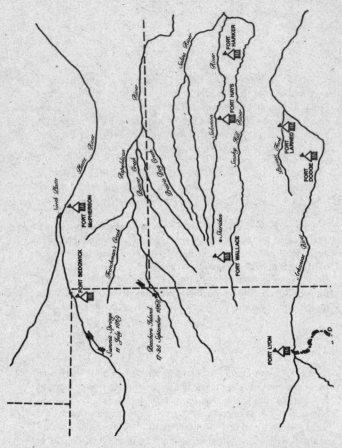

Map drawn by author from General Philip H. Sheridan's campaign field map, furnished by the Office of the Chief Signal Officer, War Department, Washington, D.C.

(graphics drawn by Victoria Murray)

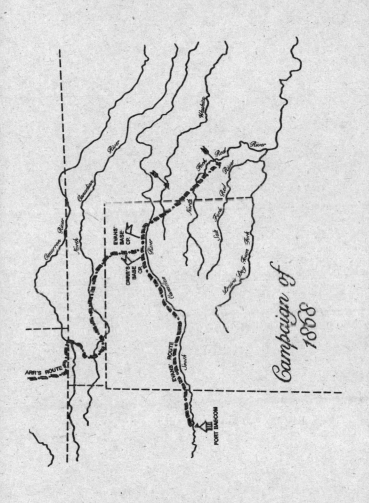

Campaign of 1868

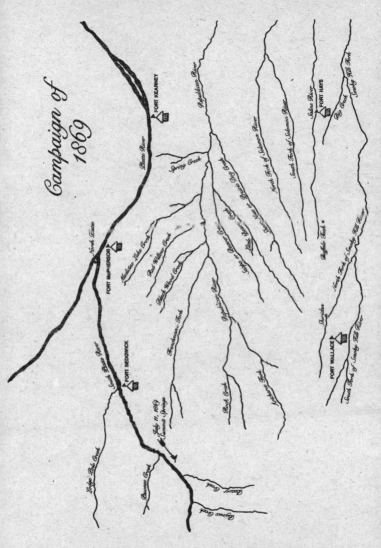

Map drawn by author from an official map provided
courtesy of the National Archives, Washington, D.C.
(graphics drawn by Victoria Murray)

Author's Foreword

Perhaps most of you read this sort of thing last. After you've given the story a chance—and only when you're willing to come back here and give these thoughts a moment of your time.

But not while there's a story to be told.

That's all right with me. Just as long as you remember while this story is still fresh in your mind that what you have read is the true stuff of history. Everyone here lived and walked the high plains of Kansas, Nebraska and Colorado in 1868–69. Everyone except two: Seamus Donegan, the reluctant Irish warrior, and the mulatto-turned-Cheyenne, Jack O'Neill. The rest of the characters in this account were breathing, living beings.

Through them you will not only learn of an obscure fight on the high plains in the summer of 1869, but you will ride along as a participant in the months leading up to that fated confrontation between the Fifth Cavalry and the feared Dog Soldier Society of Tall Bull's Cheyenne which occurred at an obscure place given the name of Summit Springs

—not far from present-day Sterling, Colorado—by the victorious leader of the blue-clad soldiers.

A time rich in momentum! Our grand republic speeding onward toward her centennial. At long last the nation had been joined by rail. In May of 1869 the Union Pacific and Central Pacific united in Utah by driving a symbolic golden spike to wed their rails. At the very least it was the hope for riches, if not gold itself, that would finally bring about the greatest of all Indian wars and effectively drive the nomadic tribes from the plains and back onto their reservations.

Furthermore, that year was a pivotal, fateful one for the frontier army. On March 3, just before the regiments took to the field for spring campaigns, Congress slashed both the appropriations and size of the army from 55,000 troops to almost 37,000. Those officers who remained after the Benzine Boards got done paring away the Civil War "fat" were once again left reeling under the cuts of manpower and matériel, complicated by a lack of national will to get the job done.

Yet within that core of the victorious Union army there remained some of the best fighting men this country has ever known. Besides Grant—who was to be inaugurated that spring of 'sixty-nine—there were his two closest subordinates, William Tecumseh Sherman and Philip H. Sheridan. While the former reorganized the army and railed against the forces in Washington City who would emasculate the frontier army, the latter set about taking the fight to plains Indians.

Instead of merely reacting each time the Sioux or Cheyenne attacked a settlement, Phil Sheridan devised a plan whereby the army would search out and destroy those peaceful villages to which the guilty warriors returned after they had their fill of blood, booty and white prisoners.

Major Eugene Asa Carr's role in Sheridan's first winter campaign of 1868–69 is not generally known even by those conversant with General George Armstrong Custer's more glamorous defeat of Black Kettle's Southern Cheyenne on the Washita River. Yet Custer's Seventh Cavalry would not have enjoyed success at the Washita in November of 1868, much less brought about the capture and eventual surrender of Satanta's Kiowa near Fort Cobb or Medicine Arrow's Cheyenne on the Sweetwater that following spring, had it not been for the fact that Carr's Fifth Cavalry had simply left the tribes no place to run.

Perhaps even fewer readers know of this dramatic Battle of Summit Springs and how it effectively brought to an end the Cheyenne depredations against the settlers and freight routes across the central plains. Truth is, historians agree the victory of the Fifth Cavalry was of more lasting consequence than was Custer's campaign against Cheyenne and Kiowa in Indian Territory. Carr broke the grip of terror and bloodshed at the hands of the Dog Soldiers along the upper Republican and Smoky Hill rivers. The Fifth Cavalry effectively ended all cohesiveness of the powerful warrior society. Never again would the Dog Soldiers be the force they were before that July day in 1869. The remnants of that once-great fighting fraternity split: while most wandered south under Bull Bear to surrender in small bands at Camp Supply in what is now Oklahoma,

only a few pledged allegiance to White Horse, who
hurried north with his faithful to continue the fight
alongside their northern cousins.

So successful was the Fifth Cavalry in this victory
that in the fall of 1869 both the Nebraska legisla-
ture and the Colorado territorial assembly presented Major Carr with their unanimous
resolutions of commendation and appreciation.
Nebraskans praised the Fifth Cavalry for "driving
the enemy from our borders and achieving a victory at Summit Springs, Colorado Territory, by
which the people of the State were freed from the
merciless Savages." Soon afterward, the Coloradans
praised both Carr and his soldiers for ending a
reign of terror by the Cheyenne during which "the
prosperity of the Territory has been greatly retarded during several years past . . . [and] de-
fenceless women and children of our pioneer
settlements have been murdered by Savages, or sub-
jected to a captivity worse than death."

As you read the story, realize there was a flesh
and blood Tom Alderdice, Kansas settler and former scout for Major George A. Forsyth at Beecher
Island.* There was as well a Mrs. Alderdice,
Susanna by name, kidnapped by Tall Bull's band in
raids along the Solomon. In that same camp was
the second white female captive, Mrs. Maria
Weichel, whose husband Gustaf was killed in a like
raid. In one of those interesting footnotes to history,
one can note that at Fort Sedgwick, where Mrs.
Weichel recuperated, she fell in love with one of her
attendants, a hospital steward. They were married

* See The Plainsmen Series, vol. 3, *The Stalkers*

soon after the Fifth Cavalry departed on the August campaign north to the Niobrara River country.

There is color beyond compare here during the fateful spring and summer of 1869 on the central plains—a story the reader can continue to study in many fine books he will find available in the library. If anything, this is a tale of the Fifth Cavalry at a crossroads in its own history. To enjoy the richness of that unit's activities on the plains, read *Across The Continent With The Fifth Cavalry*, compiled by George F. Price. From its pages I have drawn many firsthand reports and accounts of the winter and summer campaigns of 1868–69.

Herein you will come to learn of the stoic Eugene Asa Carr, senior major of the Fifth Cavalry. The story of his career fighting Comanches in the southwest following the Mexican War, all the way through the end of the Indian Wars on the Northern Plains, is splendidly told in *War Eagle—A Life of General Eugene A. Carr* by James T. King.

A second firsthand account of that summer campaign and Summit Springs fight is given by soldier J. E. Welch, which appears in Cyrus Townsend Brady's book, *Indian Fights and Fighters*.

My firsthand accounts from the Cheyenne side of the fight were gleaned from George Bird Grinnell's monumental work, *The Fighting Cheyennes*, which in detail explores the skirmishes that led up to the defeat for the Dog Soldiers at Summit Springs.

Should any reader want to gain more of an overview of this period of the Indian Wars, he should put his hands on any of the following, highly readable studies: *The Long Death—The Last Days of the Plains Indian* by Ralph K. Andrist; *The Indian Wars of the West* by Paul I. Wellman; *War Cries on Horse-back—The Story of the Indian Wars of the Great Plains* by Stephen Longstreet; *The Buffalo Soldiers —A Narrative of the Negro Cavalry in the West* by William H. Leckie; and most especially one should read and reread Robert M. Utley's *Frontier Regulars —The United States Army and the Indian, 1866–1891.*

But as much as this is a story of the Fifth Cavalry and its soldiers, it is even more so a tale of the Indian and civilian scouts who led the soldiers across the plains, tracking the nomadic and highly mobile warrior bands. Of invaluable help to this novel in this regard was the book *Man of the Plains—Recollections of Luther North, 1856–1882,* edited by Donald F. Danker. Time and again I referred to it for the rich story of the North brothers and their famous Pawnee Battalion of scouts.

Standing more boldly outlined against lesser or more finely-etched characters is no less than William F. Cody himself. Unlike what the public is served in television's popular version of the short-lived era of the Pony Express, the real character is all the more exciting. In the brief period encompassed by this novel, Bill Cody first rides for General Philip H. Sheridan and the army. It is his taking on a dangerous task for Sheridan that no one else will accept that leads the general to select Bill Cody as chief of scouts for Carr's Fifth Cavalry. The legend was well on its way.

In addition, the first use of the now-famous nickname "Buffalo Bill" was made that winter of 1868 as the young scout was hailed by some buffalo soldiers who earlier had witnessed his incredible marksmanship among a buffalo herd near Fort Hays, Kansas.

The first of many controversies that would mark Cody's life began with his association with the North brothers and their Pawnee scouts in the summer campaign in 'sixty-nine. All of this and more are there for the reading in the best and the worst of accounts: *Last Of The Great Scouts—The Life Story of Col. William F. Cody (as told by his sister, Helen Cody Wetmore); Buffalo Bill—The Noblest Whiteskin* by John Burke; *Buffalo Bill and The Wild West* by Henry Blackman Sell and Victor Weybright; and *Buffalo Bill—His Family, Friends, Fame, Failures, and Fortunes* by Nellie Snyder Yost.

Yet I can recommend no more highly any study of Cody's life than I do the marvelously written *The Life and Legends of Buffalo Bill* by Don Russell. The author brings to his story a wealth of knowledge and a lifelong study of the frontier period of the Indian Wars that provides a rich tapestry against which the exciting career of Cody is splendidly portrayed.

By citing the most heavily used of my sources, I've attempted here to establish some of my credentials for telling this story. After all, the writer of historical fiction assumes a perilous task: while he must remain true to history, there are the demands of fiction pressing in on the novelist at every turn. So with not only the battle of Summit Springs studied and restudied, but the winter campaign of 1868–69 for the Fifth Cavalry as well, it remained for me to visit the sites, walking over the ground as I do with every one of these stories in hopes of gaining a sense of place and time, if not to hear the nearby ghosts speak at my shoulder. The story of that dramatic summer in 1869 spread itself before me.

Bill Cody and Bill Hickok, Frank and Lute North, and Major Eugene Asa Carr were there to help me—I had only to let them, indeed all the actual participants of that marvelous time, tell their tales.

Into their midst ride my two fictional plainsmen: Seamus Donegan, who is growing old before his time; and the mulatto-turned-Cheyenne Jack O'Neill, who is sent after the Irishman with a deathbed vow to Roman Nose at the Battle of Beecher Island.

Yet unlike the three previous volumes in the Plainsmen series, *Black Sun* will portray for the reader some other elements of the life of the frontier scout that were new and interesting to me: the hijacking of the beer shipment by Cody and Hickok did occur as I have portrayed it; in addition, Cody's tracking down horse thieves to Denver City to regain Major Carr's animals is another actual incident. All in the life of that era and the hardy few who stood the test of all that was thrown against them.

As a historical novelist, I long ago assumed a task beyond the mere *retelling* of this history. For in picking up this volume, you demand of me to add something that history alone can't convey to most readers: a warm, throbbing pulse that truly allows you to *relive* the bloody, tragic, but always exciting history of the winning of the West.

So it is that this story of *Black Sun* tells something of the wide-ranging and often frustrating life of the frontier scout, besides the more dramatic tracking of the fierce Dog Soldiers, the battle, and the rescue of but one of two women captured by the Cheyenne.

The soldiers did gather around the grave they dug for Susanna Alderdice beside Summit Springs to sing their hymns. They did stand their crude, hand-lettered headboard beside her resting place. And they did turn over most of the money found in the village to the sole surviving white woman, Maria Weichel.

The dramatic story chronicling this clash of cultures across a quarter-century will take over the next half-dozen years to relate. We began the Plainsmen, our account of this epic struggle of the Indian Wars, with that story told in *Sioux Dawn* of a bitterly-cold December day in 1866 as Capt. William Judd Fetterman led eighty men beyond Lodge Trail Ridge and into history. The tale continued with *Red Cloud's Revenge* and *The Stalkers,* so that now with *Black Sun* we find ourselves more than two years into this captivating era, a time like no other, a time that would not come to an end until another bloody, cold December day in 1890 with another massacre along a little-known creek called Wounded Knee.

The fever of that quarter-century made the Indian Wars an era unequaled in the annals of time, when a vast frontier was forcibly wrenched from its inhabitants in a struggle as rich in drama and pathos as any in the history of man.

Into the heart of the red man's paradise of the central plains, both the government and daring entrepreneurs alike were thrusting the prongs of their railroad and freight roads. To protect both the settlers on the Kansas plains and travelers alike, the army erected its outposts: Forts Harker and Hays, Larned, Dodge and Lyon. And, far out on the Federal Road to Denver, Fort Wallace.

It is we who are left to wonder, as only a reader in the safety and comfort of his easy-chair can, if we too would have measured up. Here you have the chance to judge, for in these pages you are asked to *relive* the story of real people. Indeed, you are reading a story peopled with flesh and blood that walked and fought, cried and cheered on little-known but hallowed ground now swept clean beneath the relentless march of spring floods and prairie drought.

So it is that good historical fiction fuses the fortunes, adventures and destinies of numerous characters. Glory-seekers and murderers, settlers and cowards, army officers and soldiers. Remember as you read—these were actual, living souls striding across that crude stage erected on the high plains of western Kansas and Colorado Territory . . . all, save Donegan and the blackhearted renegade, Jack O'Neill.

With each new volume in this Plainsmen series, which will encompass the entire era of the Indian Wars, you will follow Seamus as he marches through some of history's bloodiest hours, marching as well among a changing cast of actual historical characters.

Donegan is the sort who is not capable of always doing the right thing, yet he tries nonetheless.

History has itself plenty of heroes—every one of them dead. Perhaps the thing I like best about Seamus Donegan is that he represents the rest of us. Ordinary in every way, except that at some point, we are each called upon by circumstances to do something *extra*ordinary . . . what most might call heroic.

That's the epic tale of the Indian Wars. If you will listen carefully now, you'll hear the grunts of the lathered horses and the balky mules straining to carry their riders into the midst of the Dog Soldier village after four grueling days of relentless pursuit. You'll hear the shrieking panic of the white women struggling to escape their captors and rushing for the blue-clad saviors on horseback. You can hear the war-cries of the warriors who will not retreat, but instead turn to fight, protecting the flight of families and old ones.

Sniff the air—you'll likely smell the burning fragrance of gunpowder or the aroma of boiled coffee (if you're lucky enough to have any left). Run your tongue around the inside of your cheek one last time now, trying to remember how good that mule haunch tasted last winter—especially when mule meat was all that stood between you and starvation in the snows of a winter wilderness.

The fight for survival that harsh winter happened every bit as did the gallant chase after the Dog Soldiers the following summer. Carr's Fifth Cavalry caught Tall Bull's camp at a little known spring near the South Platte River. As history, this story needs no false glamour, no shiny veneer of dash and daring. What has through the centuries been the story of man at war—of culture against culture, race against race—needs nothing special in its telling.

My hope is that you will enjoy this ride stirrup to stirrup with Seamus Donegan and Bill Cody.

Come on along—we've no time to waste. Tall Bull

and his band of deadly warriors are four days ahead of us now and gaining ground. If you're of a mind to, you'll sleep this night curled up in a blanket on the frozen ground and warm your hands over buffalo-chip fires.

Saddle up, my friend. We're riding out now and not looking back.

—Terry C. Johnston
Summit Springs Battleground
Colorado Territory
July 11, 1988

Characters

Seamus Donegan

Cheyenne

Tall Bull (Tatonka Haska)
Feathered Bear
Breaks The Arrow
Big Head
Yellow Nose
Plenty of Bull Meat
Pile of Bones
Red Cherries
Heavy Furred Wolf
Pretty Bear

Bullet Proof
Bobtailed Porcupine
White Man's Ladder
Wolf Friend
Two Crows
Lone Bear
Bad Heart
Standing Bear
Tall Sioux
White Horse

Sioux

The Whistler

Pawnee Killer

Army Scouts

William F. "Buffalo Bill"
  Cody
James Butler Hickok
James Curry
John Donovan

Bill Green
Jack Farley
Eli Ziegler
Thomas Ranahan

Pawnee Battalion

Major Frank J. North
Captain Luther ("Lute")
  North

Lt. Gustavus W. Becher
Mad Bear

Civilians

Louisa/Lulu Cody
Arta Cody (daughter)
Mrs. Gustaf (Maria) Weichel
Tom Alderdice
Mrs. Thomas (Susanna) Alderdice (and infant)
Nebraska Governor David Butler
J. E. Welch
I. P. Boyer (trader @ Fort McPherson)
William McDonald (contract sutler @ Fort McPherson)
William Reed (clerk for sutler McDonald @ Fort McPherson)

Dave Perry (owner/California Keg House Exchange–North Platte)
Walt Mason (innkeeper—Sheridan, Kansas)
Dave Cook (Denver City Marshal)
Robert Teat (son: Eugene Teat)—owners of Elephant Corral
Nate Williams—horse thief
Bill Bevins—horse thief
Reuben Wood (contract sutler at Fort Sedgwick)
John Wilson—wagon-master, winter campaign, Fifth Cavalry

Soldiers

Major General C. C. Augur—Commander, Dept. of the Platte
Colonel Henry C. Bankhead
Captain Samuel B. Lauffer—Fort Wallace Quartermaster
Captain Israel Ezekial
Captain George Wallace Graham
Captain William H. Penrose—Third Infantry
Reuben Waller—10th Negro Cavalry

FIELD AND
COMPANY OFFICERS
Fifth U.S. Cavalry

Colonel—William H. Emory
Lieutenant Colonel—Thomas Duncan
Major—Eugene A. Carr
Major—William B. Royall
Major—Eugene W. Crittenden
  Captain Sylvanus E. Cushing
  Adjutant—Robert H. Montgomery
  Quartermaster—Alfred B. Taylor (till 6/22/69)
              —Edward M. Hayes (after 6/22/69)
  Sergeant-Major—Joseph H. Maynard
  Quartermaster-Sergeant— John Young
  Chief Bugler—John Uhlman
  Saddler-Sergeant—Jacob Feathers
  Surgeon—Louis S. Tesson
  Veterinary Surgeon—Francis Regen

Company A
Captain—Robert P. Wilson
First Lieutenant—George F. Price

Company B
Captain—Robert Sweatman
First Lieutenant—Jules C.A. Schenofsky
Second Lieutenant—Charles H. Rockwell

Company C
Captain—Thomas E. Maley
First Lieutenant—Edward P. Doherty
Second Lieutenant—Frank C. Morehead

Company D
Captain—Samuel S. Sumner
First Lieutenant—Calbraith P. Rodgers
Second Lieutenant—Robert A. Edwards

Company E
Captain—Philip Dwyer
First Lieutenant—Robert P. Wilson (till 6/12/69)
　　　　　　　　—Robert H. Montgomery
　　　　　　　　　(after 6/12/69)
Second Lieutenant—Jacob A. Augur

Company F
Captain—William H. Brown
First Lieutenant—Edward W. Ward
Second Lieutenant—William C. Forbush

Company G
Captain—John H. Kane
First Lieutenant—Jacob Almy
Second Lieutenant—J. Edwin Leas

Company H
Captain—Leicester Walker
First Lieutenant—Peter V. Haskin

Company I
Captain—Gustavus Urban
First Lieutenant—George F. Mason
Second Lieutenant—Earl D. Thomas

Company K

Captain—Julius W. Mason
First Lieutenant—James Burns
Second Lieutenant—Bernard Reilly, Jr.

Company L

Captain—Alfred B. Taylor
First Lieutenant—Charles B. Brady

Company M

Captain—Edward H. Leib
First Lieutenant—John B. Babcock
Second Lieutenant—William J. Volkmar
Corporal—John M. Kyle

Prologue

October 1868

$\mathscr{A}$s bad as the whiskey was, it proved the cure.

By the time he had thrown the fourth splash of its liquid fire against the back of his throat, Seamus Donegan sensed the tension easing the long cords in his neck. Not to mention the tension seeping from those great muscles in his back which bore the scar carved there by Confederate steel. Slowly, ever slowly, his big frame strung with muscle was loosening like a worn-out buggy spring after a long haul of it over a washboard road.

It had been some ride for the Irishman. His great bulk now sat hulking like a predator over the small glass all but hidden within the big, roughened hands. Returned from the dead he was again, and working steadily to pickle himself even more than the last.

Back from the grave that had done its best to swallow the Civil War veteran at Beecher Island.

In the space of the past three weeks, Donegan had

returned with Major George A. Forsyth's band of civilian scouts to Fort Hays, where the survivors of the bloody, nine-day island siege were promptly reorganized under Lt. Silas Pepoon. Yet, without a look back, the Irishman decided he had had himself enough of the plains and Indians, enough of blood and sweat and death to last him for some time to come. Seamus pointed his nose north, aiming for Nebraska. He had started there once before—a year gone now.

Nebraska. There in the Platte River country near Osceola, the widow Wheatley had promised she would be waiting for him to fetch her.

But Donegan's quest for Uncle Liam O'Roarke had pulled him off that trail to Osceola and to Jenny. That quest, and the Cheyenne of Roman Nose.*

Seamus was too late getting out to the Wheatley place.

He angrily threw another splash against the back of his throat, remembering the old woman's eyes as she glared up at him in the late afternoon light from beneath her withered, bony hand.

"No, mister. Jenny took herself and the boys back east. Dead set on getting back to her own folk, she was," James Wheatley's mother confided.

"Ohio?" he had asked numbly.

She had nodded, her eyes softening, perhaps recognizing what crossed the tall Irishman's face. "Ohio."

He had thanked her, crawled into the saddle with-

* The Plainsmen Series, vol. 3, *The Stalkers*

out feeling much, and reined about toward the
south. Kansas and Fort Hays.

Nursing his grief and anger like a private badge
of passion he alone could wear.

For some time he had looked forward to this moment with the tall-necked bottle. Promising himself
all the way down that long trail from Osceola that
he would sit here and drink the night through if he
had to—until he decided where next to go and what
next to do. Feeling adrift and lost, having no clue
worth a tinker's damn where he could find his
second uncle, Liam's brother, Ian O'Roarke—was
Seamus cursed now to wander aimlessly, searching
the California Territory where Liam had hinted Ian
would be found?

Yet that was the only thing left for him now that
Jenny Wheatley had moved on after a year of waiting for a restless man.

"Maybe 'tis better, after all," he murmured, bringing the chipped glass to his lips beneath the shaggy
mustache once more. "Better a woman like that has
her a man who can work the land and stay in one
place. I could never give her kind of woman something like that."

Over and over in his mind on that long ride south
a scrap of Irish poetry had hung in his thoughts like
a piece of dirty linen. John Boyle O'Reilley's words
reminded him most of her.

> The red rose whispers of passion,
> And the white rose breathes of love;
> Oh, the red rose is a falcon,
> And the white rose is a dove.

But I send you a cream-white rosebud
With a flush on its petal tips;
For the love that is purest and sweetest
Has a kiss of desire on the lips.

Too much of an unquenched burning inside him yet. Unanswered yearnings. Better for everybody now that Jenny moved on without him. Seems she needed something more than he could give, and he sure as hell needed more right now than any one woman could find herself giving him in return.

Slowly the whiskey reddened his gray eyes, appearing to soften the harsh edges on things, especially the noise of this dimly lit Hays City watering hole. Soldiers and wagon-bosses, teamsters and speculators, all shouldered against one another at the rough bar beneath a growing cloud of blue smoke. The smoky oil lamps cast dancing shadows on the murky canvas walls and muddy plank floor each time the door swung open to admit some newcomer along with a cold gust of October wind.

He would need something to eat eventually . . . hell, it could wait until morning now.

Perhaps if he wasn't careful, he'd end up spending the night right here at this table near the corner where the stench of old vomit and dried urine could make a strong man lose his appetite for anything but whiskey. Perhaps if he punished the bottle until he passed out right here, Seamus would not need to fill the gnawing hole inside his soul with one of the pudgy chippies who worked the half-dozen cribs in the back of this place. Lilac-watered women all, come to ply their trade in the fleshpots that followed the army and the railroad west.

"Lookit this, will you? I wouldn't've gambled a warm piss that I'd find Liam O'Roarke's favorite nephew hugging up to a bottle of saddle varnish here in Hays City ever again!"

Through the late afternoon light sneaking through the few smudged, smoky windowpanes, Seamus immediately recognized the war-lined face of Sharp Grover. Major Forsyth's former chief of scouts strode across the crowded room, heading directly for Donegan's table. Abner Grover—comrade in arms from the private hell that had been Beecher Island.

"If it ain't Mother Grover's ugliest son!" Seamus cheered, momentarily eyeing the younger man who came up close on Sharp's heels. "Sit, gentlemen!"

"You're in a better humor than when I found you here in the Shady Rest end of last winter," Grover said, dragging a wobbly chair close.

"And you a goddamned scout, Abner. You're supposed to know where to find me." Seamus held up his cup of amber whiskey to them both, then tossed it back.

"You're drinking alone again?"

"Till the two of you sat down."

"You going to invite us to drink with you?"

He glanced at Grover's young blue-eyed companion who sported a long, blond bantam tuft below his lower lip. Then he answered. "I never enjoyed drinking alone, Sharp."

"Get us some glasses, will you, Bill?"

Grover's companion nodded and rose from the table without a word, shoving his way into the crowd milling at the bar.

"He's a big one," Donegan whispered.

Grover agreed. "Almost tall as you, Seamus."

"He a scout for you . . . riding with Pepoon now?"

"Not working for me. Bill tells me General Sheridan's wired him orders to sit right here till the Fifth Cavalry comes through."

Seamus went back to regarding his whiskey glass as Bill came back to the table with a pair of glasses and another bottle of whiskey. "Didn't figure none of you'd still be hanging 'round Hays, Abner."

"We're getting ready to hove away for Fort Dodge soon enough, Seamus," Grover replied. "And you could go too. It'll be good winter's wages—riding with Pepoon's scouts."

"Where you riding this time?" he asked, watching Grover's young companion pour two glasses of the whiskey from the new bottle.

"Word has it that most of us will be marching with Sheridan himself—down into The Territories."

"Right into the heart of Injin country, eh?"

"That's right, Irishman. Them young bucks been busy since late last summer."

"Don't we know it, Sharp? Penned up like we was on that island far out in the middle of hell itself."

"No," and Grover shook his head. "This is something different. The Cheyenne been raiding up on the Solomon and Saline rivers. Burning, raping, killing stock. Carrying off white women and children."

"Sheridan's going down into The Territories to get them women back, is it?"

"He's called Custer back to do it for him."

That struck Donegan like a chunk of winter river-ice thrust into the middle of his chest. Seamus leaned back in his chair, a fingertip playing at the chipped lip of his glass. "Custer, you say? I heard he was serving out his year away from the Seventh—for having them deserters shot."

Grover hunched over the table as he glanced about quickly. "Hays is Custer country, Seamus."

"I damned well know that."

"You're aiming to start a fight of it?" Grover asked.

"If one steps up, I won't back away."

"Best keep your voice down in this town when you're speaking your mind about Custer."

"I'm touched you care so much about me spilling me blood, Abner."

"I do, you thick-headed Irishman," he said, slapping Donegan on the shoulder to show all was forgiven. "Best you know—Custer's already back with his regiment."

His eyes narrowed and he felt his windpipe constrict. "Here?"

"The Seventh's marched on to Fort Dodge, where they're training for the coming campaign. Custer's there with 'em."

Donegan's teeth ground with disappointment.

"You were hoping to meet up with the boy general again, were you?" Bill asked, speaking for the first time.

Seamus looked at Grover's companion. Then smiled. "We—We just go back to the war, let's say."

"Never fought in the war myself," the young Bill admitted, speaking for the first time with some wistfulness in his voice. "Too young. But I have heard all about Custer's part in Hancock's campaign last year. Sure glad I wasn't no thirteen-dollar-a-month private . . . living on beans and dreams of whores —following that curly-headed bastard. For a time last month I worked 'round some of his soldiers. Out to Fort Larned."

"Larned is some way from here," Seamus muttered.

Grover nodded, saying in praise, "Bill here just come in from one hell of a ride, Seamus."

"First job I had for the army, Lieutenant Billy Cooke signed me on ninth of September to resack forage for their mounts. Week later on the fifteenth, Cooke finally hired me as a scout."

Seamus regarded the young man more carefully, recalling the youth of Jack Stillwell who had handled a man's job and more during Forsyth's chase after the Cheyenne. Donegan looked down into the amber of his glass. "The fifteenth, eh . . . Sharp and me was less than two days out from that godforsaken island in September."

"Bill here is the kind what could have held the muster for them nine days on Beecher Island."

Seamus studied the young man. "Sharp said you had quite a ride in from Larned."

"Over sixty miles," Bill accounted. "Bringing word that the Kiowas and Comanches finally broke out. They're joining the Cheyennes on the warpath."

"Bill gave Sheridan that report at Fort Hays—the sort of news that the general had to send out to other posts as well. Seems Sheridan asked around for a horseman to ride down to Dodge with his report." Grover wagged his head a moment. "But too many been killed on that route lately. No one wanted to carry Sheridan's dispatches, what with the Injuns rising up."

Seamus watched the young man's eyes hold the table. He figured Bill for being a bit self-conscious. "So you told Sheridan you'd go?"

Bill looked up. "I told the general I'd ride, nobody else having the balls to take the chance . . . what with the Kiowas and Cheyennes both jumping off their reservations."

"Out at Fort Hays Bill got himself a bunk and slept for five hours before saddling a fresh mount."

"On the way to Fort Dodge I stopped at a road ranch down at Coon Creek for another hour of shut-eye," Bill said, warming to the story of it. "Rode off on a new mount borrowed from a troop of cavalry bivouacked there . . . reached Fort Dodge without seeing nary a feather or war-paint."

"But that still wasn't the end of it for you," Sharp said, smiling as he poured more whiskey in their glasses. "Bill grabbed himself a few hours sleep then carried dispatches from the commander of Fort Dodge, bound for General Hazen at Fort Larned."

"How'd you end up back here at Hays?" Seamus asked before throwing his whiskey back. It had ceased to burn his tongue.

"Hazen wanted Sheridan to have the latest word in from his scouts—the Kiowa villages all running south of the Arkansas."

Grover nodded, smiling widely. "Ain't that just like Sheridan now? The general's a man who wants to know exactly where the Injuns are every minute."

"Damn funny it seems . . . especially after Sheridan and the rest of them didn't have an idea where

Roman Nose and his bunch was when we bumped into 'em last month on the Arikaree, eh?"

Grover swallowed hard on his whiskey, sputtering slightly as he watched the sour grin fade from the Irishman's face. "I figure the army learned a hard lesson there."

"Ever the army learns a lesson—it's for sure the poor sojur be the one to pay." Seamus poured more whiskey in his own glass, offering some to the blond-haired youth across from him. "And you, Bill —have you had your fill of riding for the army?"

"No. Pay's good. Seventy-five a month and found. Better that than scratching out hardscrabble for the coming winter."

"How 'bout you, Donegan?" Sharp Grover turned fully toward the Irishman. "You got shet of what's eating you and ready to ride again?"

"With you?"

"With Pepoon and me, Seamus. We're heading down into Indian Territory with George—by God— Custer."

His beetled eyebrows twitched. "That would be something, wouldn't it now? Me riding scout for the man what stole me stripes back in the Shenandoah?" He hung his head, brooding on it, staring into the dancing ripples of his amber whiskey. "No. I'd better not tempt the fates again with Custer."

"Then Seamus Donegan will ride with me, by damn!" the youngster said.

He looked up at the scout's hard, gray-blue eyes again, seeing there some strength he had not taken the time to notice before. "Ride with you? Just where in hell would we be riding?"

"With the Fifth Cavalry."

"And what the divil would you be having to say about me riding with the Fifth?"

He gazed back at the Irishman steady and long. "I suppose I'd have everything to say about it. Sheridan's commissioned me chief of scouts for the Fifth."

Seamus nodded approvingly, then raised his glass in toast. "To the chief of scouts." Seamus tossed it back, then licked his lips. "So . . . tell me just where this Fifth Cavalry of yours is heading."

The young man leaned close over the table, drawing the other men in as he whispered in husky tones. "We're going south and west . . . then turning east toward The Territories."

"You're going to Injun country same time as Custer?" Grover asked.

He nodded eagerly, the ready smile cutting his young face. "We're serving as beaters to drive the villages and war-parties toward the Seventh Cavalry."

"Sounds like a winter's work," Donegan said.

"You damned right," Bill answered. "We'll likely face a blizzard or two, and freeze your balls to deer droppings before we're done. If you're not up to riding into the jaws of winter itself, I'll understand, Irishman."

Seamus sat back, smiling as he sloshed some more amber into his glass. He held it up again in toast. "All right—you've got yourself a scout for the winter. Here's to riding with you, Bill . . . Bill— what's your last name?"

He grinned widely, thrusting his big hand across the table at the Irishman. They shook.

"Bill Cody, Seamus. My name's Bill Cody."

Chapter 1

October 1868

$\mathcal{M}$arching west, the Fifth Cavalry halted at Fort Hays only long enough to pick up its new chief of scouts along with orders from General Philip H. Sheridan, Department Commander. Cody and Donegan crawled into their saddles that mid-autumn morning as the sun blinked a bloody eyelid over the far rim of the earth. Both suffered a hangover of the worst variety: all liquor and no breakfast.

Staring at a mess-tin filled with fried salt-pork swimming in some greasy gravy and two slabs of hardtack was not the sort of thing to inspire a man's appetite after a hard night punishing the bottle.

William F. Cody was a hard-drinker of a youngster but, more than that, he was a hard-worker as well.

"I was born in Scott County, Iowa," Bill explained to the Irishman as they rode ahead of the cavalry column. "Not long afterward, my folks moved to Kansas Territory. I grew into a lanky, muscular youth who earned his pay not only as a wagon-master and a herder for freight outfits, but as a rider for the Pony Express, racing mail between Missouri and California."

"I've heard some about that time out here," Donegan replied. "Dangerous work, it was?"

Cody smiled the youthful smile that belied his early honing of survival skills. "Man watched himself on the circuit, he didn't have no truck with the Injuns. But some riders, it seemed, always had themselves trouble on certain parts of the trail."

"You?"

The smile faded somewhat as he rubbed at some gummy sleep in a red eye. "Yeah. Time or two I had some trouble myself. But the express was over before it really got fun, Seamus. The coming of the telegraph put us off that road."

"You're on a different trail now. Still be fun."

The smile was back. "Damn right, Irishman! Except this time—instead of trying to run away from the Indians—my job is to find 'em for the army."

"What'd you do when you quit riding for the express?"

"Not long after, news come to Kansas that some prospectors made strikes in the Colorado Rockies, so I made my way into the mountains."

"Two years back, was myself heading up the Montana Road to Alder Gulch."

"Didn't make it, Seamus?"

He wagged his head. "Maybe someday I'll quit this roaming and decide to go back to scratching at the ground for them yellow rocks make a man crazy."

"They will make you crazy. I lost my poke, and a

sutler's grubstake as well . . . digging at the goddamned ground, moving sand at the bottom of four
streams. None of it worked."

"You came on back to Kansas?"

He nodded. "It's all I knew—what with the war
going on back East."

"Good you didn't have no part in that madness,
Bill."

"While you were busy killing Johnnies and waving that big saber of yours around, I was living day
to day, running two trap lines."

"It feed you?"

"Enough. Sold my furs to buy coffee and flour,
some ammunition and an extra blanket when
needed. Whiskey when there was a little something
left over."

"You're the kind I figure made sure he had something left over for whiskey most of the time."

They laughed together, but briefly. It was too
painful for their throbbing heads.

"Man after my own heart, Seamus Donegan."

"Then why the divil you talk me into going along
with you on this campaign, Bill Cody? We sure as
hell aren't marching toward any whiskey taverns
with these sojurs. I figure it's that major's job back
there to keep us and his boys in blue as far away
from whiskey as he can for the next few weeks."

"It is. This first day's the worst for me, Seamus.
You know what it's like since you been in the saddle
on campaign before—with Sharp Grover and Forsyth's men."

"Sun pulls the whiskey right out of a man, it does.
Be some time before we get a chance to soak in it

again, though. So, tell me, how'd you get started with the army?"

"Come the spring of 1867, I'd grown tired of the hand-to-mouth of it, and figured there was better money to be made doing what I could do best for the railroad pushing rails through Kansas."

"What do you do best?"

"Kill buffalo."

"Good shot?"

"Good enough that I got me a contract with the K.P. to feed their workers in western Kansas."

"How much the Kansas Pacific pay you?"

"Five hundred."

"A month?" he asked, his voice rising in wonder.

"Yes," he answered, his head bobbing. "Good pay —'cause I was good at bringing in the meat."

"How old were you when you started?"

"Let's see . . ." he replied, tapping a fingertip against the blond bantam-tuft of hair hung from his lower lip. "Started just a year ago—when I was twenty-one."

"You're just a child, Bill Cody!"

"You're claiming to be an old man yourself, Seamus Donegan?"

"Aye," he sighed. "Time enough left for two lads like us to get into all kinds of trouble, don't you think?"

"Always time enough, Irishman."

The Department Commander's orders for the Fifth Cavalry were to proceed north from the Kansas Pacific tracks, to make their way in the direction of Prairie Dog Creek where, reports from Major George Forsyth's civilian scouts had it, the Cheyenne Dog Soldiers who'd been causing havoc among the settlements were to be found. The ground they crossed was tracked with the sign of several large encampments, all more than a month old. But recent buffalo sign lay anywhere a man cared to look, or take a step.

That first night out of Hays on the Saline River, the Virginia-born junior major for the regiment, William B. Royall, ordered Cody out to do what he did best.

"All right, Major. I'll get your men some buffalo. Why don't you send along a wagon or two with me to bring in the meat."

Royall, who had served in the Mexican War, snorted at the youth. "Surely you jest, son! I'm not in the habit of sending out my wagons until I know there is something to be hauled in, Cody." He waved his hand, dismissing the scout. "Go kill yourself some buffalo first—then I'll dispatch the wagons."

Cody turned away, head wagging as he fumed, yet he did as he was told. That afternoon he dropped six buffalo before he returned to request the wagons.

At the next day's camp, one march north to the South Fork of the Solomon River and very much in the midst of buffalo country, Major Royall again requested Cody bring in some meat for the soldiers.

"I learned my lesson last time, Major. I won't ask for use of your precious wagons," Cody replied, winking at Donegan as if he had something up his buckskin sleeve.

The pair of scouts loped over the hills, leaving the bustling encampment of soldiers to build their fires and boil their evening coffee.

"There," Seamus said minutes later, pointing ahead at a herd of black-humped beasts.

"Good," Cody replied with a grin. "Now we'll take a half-dozen back for the major."

Donegan began to drag the big Henry rifle from the saddle scabbard under his right leg when Cody's hand reached out and stopped him.

"Hold it right there, Seamus. We won't need the guns just yet."

"Won't? What the divil—"

"We're gonna run 'em back."

"Run 'em?"

"That major's so damned proud of his wagons," Cody snarled. "I figure I'll take these buffalo right to the sonuvabitch. We're gonna run 'em!"

Bursting from a stand of trees, Cody left Donegan at the base of the hill when he put heels to his horse. Whooping lustily, every bit as loud as Cody, the Irishman hammered his horse into a gallop. Side by side they raced into the midst of the small herd, scattering the buffalo until Cody pointed his Spencer carbine at a small bunch.

"There!" Cody shouted. "We got 'em headed in the right direction."

"Camp?"

"Right on their doorstep!"

With all the bluster of a prairie thunderstorm, the two scouts kept the seven buffalo lumbering before them, retracing their steps back to outskirts of the camp of the Fifth Cavalry. Only then did Cody bring his carbine up, drawing alongside a young bull. He dropped the animal on the edge of the wagon-yard as the teamsters and troopers began hollering, some laughing as those in the path dove for cover. Horses and mules snorted, tearing panic-filled at their picket-pins, wide-eyed and screeching.

Donegan dropped a cow at the picket-line where the civilian herders and teamsters had just started their fires.

Cody brought the next one down, near the first company camp. The huge beast tumbled hide over horns into the captain's wall-tent, tearing up its stakes and flattening the poles into kindling wood.

One by one the rest of the seven went down in quick succession, until the camp was a swirl of dust and cursing men, screaming horses and mad confusion. Cody and Donegan reined up, bringing their mounts around just as Major Royall appeared out of the haze of dust, the low sun slanting through it like a golden window curtain.

He was sputtering, gesturing wildly, standing there potbellied in his yellow striped britches held up by galluses over his sweat-stained gray pullover. "What's the meaning of this, Irishman?"

"It wasn't his idea, Major," Cody said, looking at Donegan. "Donegan just come along 'cause I needed another good shot."

"Your idea—making a mess of our camp like this?"

He looked around, both wrists crossed casually atop his horn. "Didn't mean to make a mess of things. Thought we'd just as well not cause you any problem with the wagons. Seems you don't like sending wagons with me when I go out to hunt. So, I figured it might be a good idea to have these buffalo provide their own transportation back to your camp, Major Royall."

"Why, you—I ought to put you in irons for this, Cody!"

"Major Royall, Cody and I only brought the buffalo to you," Donegan said, edging up to prevent things from going to blows. "This way there's no wear and tear on government property. And no use of government employees—them soldiers of yours —to provide meat for the camp."

The much-scarred Royall eyed them both, grinding his palms on the front of his britches as if he itched to be at them both, then thinking better of it. "You got the meat here. Now be at it, Cody."

"Can I get some of your boys to help me butcher our supper, Major?" Cody asked.

"Captain Sweatman!"

"Yessir," replied the young officer, loping up.

"Get a few squads of your men to help these two," Royall growled. A longtime veteran of the Indian country, serving from the days of the Dragoons, Royall commanded respect among his soldiers. On his forehead and cheek he wore scars of Confederate steel. Frustrated, he waved at the crowd gathered four and five deep. "Rest of you—get this damned camp picked up! You, there—get those animals quieted!"

Royall turned on his heel, forcing his way through the crowd. Renewed hurraws and laughter swallowed up the two hunters.

"The major won't forget this, Bill," Donegan whispered as they eased out of their saddles.

Cody stared after the man disappearing through the shove of bodies. "Hope he doesn't, Seamus. I suppose I've grown to hate pompous officers 'bout as bad as you do."

"I've heard barracks-talk about Royall. In 'sixty-two at the battle of Hanover Court House, he took six major saber wounds in hand-to-hand combat with the Johnnies. His unit was cut off, surrounded —but he and a few more cut their way out and made it back to their regiment."

Cody chewed on it a moment. "Maybe I was having too much fun with the man, eh?"

"Not that fun ain't good, Bill. Just . . . might not do to tempt the man this early in the campaign. He's the sort who's all spit and polish."

"Goes by the book?"

"Old Dragoon veteran like him—it's all he knows, Bill."

The autumn wind rattled the buffalo hides against the lodgepoles, reminding Tall Bull that it was the middle of the Moon of Scarlet Plums. Soon enough his people could expect the first snow. Their raiding would be over for another season.

Yet, many of the head men of this large band of Cheyenne Dog Soldiers had decided not to go the way of the other villages and bands who were presently going into winter camp. The warriors had come here tonight to discuss their many victories, fine plunder, scalps, and a handful of prisoners taken during their raids along the Saline and Solomon rivers. Even more, the blood among the Dog Soldiers beat hot and strong for continuing the pressure on the white man. Many voices were raised in favor of denying the soldiers any rest come the time of snow.

Tall Bull was their hero, no mistaking that. He had survived the attack of Colorado Volunteers on the Sand Creek camp of Black Kettle four winters before. Last summer he had seen again firsthand the treachery of General Hancock when soldiers surrounded a Cheyenne camp under a promise of peaceful negotiations, then attacked and destroyed the village after the Indians had sneaked away in the night.

Any soldiers looked the same to Tall Bull. They were his enemy.

He took great pride that he and his warriors did not follow the main leaders of the Cheyenne who had made peace with the white man and the army. To Tall Bull's camp had come some of the most hardened veterans of plains warfare. Not only Cheyenne Dog Soldiers who'd taken a vow to die with honor fighting the soldiers, but Arapahos and even some renegade Sioux under Pawnee Killer.

Theirs was a fighting band. Women and children readied at a moment's notice to tear down lodges and be on the march, to suffer the privations of the warpath as much as their men. Young, green warriors the Dog Soldiers were not.

These were the proven. The elite. And many times the most cruel. Among the Cheyenne, they were the *hotamintanio*, a select warrior society with its own magical rituals and omens, prayers, songs and taboos.

These were the Cheyenne who vowed to clear their land of the white man for all time.

These were the Dog Soldiers of Tall Bull.

Chapter 2

October 1868

The air at twilight already had a bite to it. Nothing at all like the sweltering heat he had suffered a month ago when Forsyth's fifty scouts rode baking beneath this same sun, tracking Cheyenne across this same piece of ground.

An hour before the Fifth Cavalry had reached Prairie Dog Creek, called the Short Nose by many of the plainsmen Cody knew. Major Royall immediately set Company L to establishing a base camp while he divided the rest of his command into two battalions, which would bivouac some distance away. Come morning, Captain William H. Brown with Companies B, F and M, would work their way downstream, scouting east for more recent sign. At the same time Captain Gustavus Urban, leading Companies A, H and I, would follow Cody upstream, south by west, in hopes of running across some newer campsites abandoned by the Cheyenne.

"Evidently the old man figures it's better that

we're split up for a time," Donegan muttered as he loosened his mare's cinch. He watched longingly as Cody tightened his, checked the loads in his pistols then swept into the saddle once again.

"I'll be back to raise hell with you before you know it, Irishman. Major can't keep us apart all that long. Watch your hair!"

With a whoop, Cody leaped away, heading for Urban's command, just then getting their order to go to saddle. Both battalions headed for campsites over the hills, and those left behind settled into the routine of fire-building, coffee-brewing and watering the horses while beans and salt-pork bubbled above the flames.

The feeling would not free him—this loneliness and dread. It was the fourteenth of the month. Little more than a month since Forsyth had led his civilian scouts into this country. Two more sunrises and he would be forced to remember that bloody first day on the island. Seamus had promised himself he'd keep his mind busy. That was the whole idea about coming along on this scout with Cody and the Fifth Cavalry—so he would not have to drink himself crazy at Hays City, just to keep from remembering. He hungered now for a drink in the worst way and ran his tongue inside his cheek. It didn't kill the deep hunger, but it took some of the edge from it.

All he had to do now was deal with the loneliness and the dread. Captain Taylor's L Company weren't bad sorts. They were mostly boy soldiers, and not a bit interested in the big civilian scout who had been keeping to himself ever since the command pulled out of Fort Hays.

"Quiet is good," Donegan whispered into the

mare's ear as he rubbed her down with a handful of dried grass. "Sometimes, quiet is real good."

Yet he longed for the company of soldiers with good talk and new ears for his old stories or perhaps new stories from others' lips. His loneliness would set in once the sky darkened and the stars came out in force, dusting the big canopy from horizon to horizon, with nothing to stop the view or clutter up the night but the full rising moon poking its big egg-yellow head up in the east at the edge of the endless prairie.

Sitting alone at his small fire and drinking his alkali coffee, it gave Donegan a little comfort to touch the medicine pouch hung at his neck. He pulled it from his shirt, thinking on the old mountain man who gave it to him a year gone now. Jim Bridger was of that breed who had spent a lifetime of nights separated from friends. Yet Seamus could not drive away the memories of one uncle dead on a sandy island— no more than he could resist the despair that he would never find Liam's brother, Ian.

Yet having Bridger's memory there at the fire tonight got Donegan's feelings all tangled up with his memories of Liam and the kind of man his uncle must have been. Seamus had few regrets in his life, yet one of the weightiest was not having known Liam better.

Ian—now he was a different matter altogether. The darker of his mother's two brothers from County Tyrone. Always brooding while younger brother Liam acted like a big leprechaun dancing through life the way sprites glided through the clover. Ian was the older of the two, always acting as if the world weighed on his shoulders. While Liam drew folks to him like magic, Ian took brutal pride in the fact that no man of Eire called him friend. He took no stock in people—telling his young nephew Seamus that friends only caused one heartache. Since Ian did not need people, he could not be hurt.

Donegan knelt at the fire, dragging the pot from the flames when the first shot rang out.

Cries erupted from the far side of camp, near the picket-line. A handful of shots rattled the dry night air beneath that rising moon that shed full, silver light on the tableland.

His coffee cup lay gurgling into the thirsty soil as his legs began churning, just as the first war-whoops sailed over the small encampment. Inside, his belly went cold, his mind working over the numbers and the odds if they were hit by something big. No small war-party this. That old saw that Sharp Grover and the other old-timers always told about Indians not coming at night—well, those old hands would just have to think that over now.

Seamus figured if the warriors were here after dark, they were here in numbers.

The growing intensity of their cries seemed to circle the camp as soldiers darted here and there, following orders of a few officers. Major Royall and Captain Taylor and Lieutenant Brady each shouted at once to form up, hold their fire, volley-fire, secure the horses, and get out of the firelight.

Didn't matter, the moonlight shone bright enough for a man to stand out plain as day and make himself a good target to boot. But what the moon did to the soldiers, it did every bit as well to the warriors sweeping along the perimeter of the camp, working in and out of the horse herd. There were screams from the horses, and shouts from the soldiers punctuating the war-cries of the horsemen flitting in off the prairie like bat-winged shadows flying beneath the silver light.

Seamus brought the Henry to his shoulder and set to work on the riders. Most of them stayed upright atop their ponies in the dark, not too concerned with dropping off to the side as they rode in close.

The first he hit spilled to the sand and skidded to a stop as two more rode close behind, sweeping low and lifting the wounded warrior from the ground as they raced over the body.

Seamus levered four more rounds at the rescuers while the horsemen disappeared over the hills. There were a few final shouts and cries of pain from both sides as the riflefire slowed to random shots, then stopped altogether. It grew strangely quiet for long moments, until Royall was standing there in the moonlight.

"Reload immediately and report casualties. Mr. Brady—take a squad and secure the horses. Report back to me how many head we lost to the buggers."

Royall turned on Donegan. "Irishman."

"Major?" he replied as the officer stopped close.

"Looks like you were the only one to draw blood with that run-through they made on us."

"Run-through?"

"Just like the Comanche I fought on the southern plains some twenty years ago," Royall sighed.

"Comanche, eh?"

"Mouth of Coon Creek, that's on the Arkansas River."

"You fought Injins before, Major. Well, a-well."

"You and I're not the only ones. There's a few.

But, I must say you were the coolest of the bunch just now."

"I'm afraid we won't get a chance to find out how many we wounded. They always drag their dead away as well."

"I'm a trained officer, Mr. Donegan. Rather than participate firsthand, I observe during the heat of battle. It's my duty to know how we stung the enemy—and you were the only one who stung these buggers tonight."

Brady loped up. "Major!"

"How bad is it, mister?"

"Twenty-five . . . maybe twenty-six horses."

"Damn!" Royall muttered. "God*damn* them!"

"How're your sojurs?"

Royall hollered into the night as the camp settled into an uneasy silence. One trooper wounded. Another dead. Both with arrow wounds. A few of the remaining stock had arrows stuck in them during the melee.

"I want a double watch, Captain Taylor," Royall ordered. "Put your men around the herd now."

"I'll go out yonder on the prairie, Major," Seamus offered.

Royall seemed to size the civilian up. "You figure to see them coming back and give us a bit of a warning—that it?"

"Something like that."

He pursed his lips and nodded once. "Good."

Donegan started to go, pulling cartridges for the Henry from his vest pocket.

"Irishman!"

He turned on Royall.

"Just wanted you to know, Irishman—it was good having your gun on my side of things tonight."

"You're welcome, Major."

"Before the sun rises to the middle of the sky tomorrow, the soldiers will regroup and be on our trail," Tall Bull warned his warriors when they finally came to a halt several miles from the soldier camp they had just raided.

"We will return to the village well before the sun rises," Pile of Bones replied. "There is plenty of time for the women to tear down our lodges and begin the trail north."

"Do not forget that some of our lodges have prisoners," Tall Bull added. "They must be watched closely as we break camp."

"I am for killing the white women!" growled Heavy Furred Wolf.

"No!" Tall Bull shouted. "These white women are ours to keep. Not to kill. They will prove of use to us yet. If nothing more, their wombs will nurture more Cheyenne warriors. We will make Dog Soldier squaws of them yet!"

"*Heya! Heya!*" exclaimed many of the other warriors gathered close.

"Come now. We must get these new horses among our herd quickly . . . so they grow accustomed to the smell of us and our animals. Tomorrow will be a long day riding south."

"South?"

"Yes. We should march south toward the white man's settlements one last time—making a run at the soldiers before we turn about and head north for the winter season."

"We will travel to the land of Red Cloud's Sioux?" asked Pile of Bones.

"Perhaps," Tall Bull answered. "I hear the great Oglalla chief has driven the soldiers from his country. He and the Northern Cheyenne have defeated the white man. Perhaps it would be wise for us to spend the winter closer to that land where no white man dares come."

"*Heya!* Let us go winter where the water is cold and sweet, and the buffalo grow fat for the coming cold!" Heavy Furred Wolf agreed.

"Soon enough there comes a time when we again make war on the soldiers," Tall Bull said. "I pray this coming winter will not last long—the sooner to return to spill the white man's blood on this ground. My heart yearns to watch this land of my birth drink on the blood of these soldiers who follow our trail. They always follow."

The next day saw the return of the two battalions about the time a grave detail finished burying the dead soldier. After hearing the brief reports of their fruitless reconnaissance, Major Royall gave the command to move out once more.

"Major, if I might make a suggestion." Donegan halted his mount beside Royall's.

"What's that, Irishman?" Royall eyed Cody suspiciously.

"As you come about with the columns, lead them over the soldier's grave."

"You want us to ride over the place we buried the man?"

Cody nodded. "It's a good idea. Critters won't be

so likely to come dig his body up when you trample over the ground."

"Major, if those warriors can't find that sojur's grave," Donegan explained, "they can't dig the man up, now can they?"

Royall grinned slightly, a look of bemused respect on his face. "All right, Irishman. It's a good idea. Sergeant Major Maynard!"

"Sir?"

"Carry the word back with my compliments to the commands. We're marching over the grave—in silence . . . with bare heads."

"Yes, sir!"

The Fifth Cavalry moved out, circling their encampment so they could pound hoofprints over the newly-turned ground. In absolute silence that cold fall morning, the horsemen pointed their noses south by west, pulling their kepis and slouch hats from their heads in paying this last respect before they marched up the Prairie Dog Creek, flankers out and scouts roaming far in advance to pick up the trail of the fleeing hostiles who had stolen twenty-six head of army horseflesh.

By evening Cody found the Cheyenne trail turning south from the creek, angling back toward the country of the Solomon. Yet across the next two days the trail grew more and more faint.

"They're splitting up, Seamus," Cody announced over a cup of evening coffee.

"Army chases a village, that's what they'll always do."

"In two more days I may not have but one lodge left to track."

"You tell the major?"

"He's damned disgusted with me."

"Ought'n be disgusted with the Injins we're tracking."

"Major's gotta be mad at someone, Seamus. He's run out of time. This was his big chance to be the one to catch these Cheyenne been burning and killing and kidnapping all summer long."

"His big chance?"

Cody nodded. "Right. Drawing close to the time his orders tell him to head down to Buffalo Tank."

"What's that?"

"Water stop on the Union Pacific line south of here."

"Why's Royall going there if the Injins are splitting up?"

"Sheridan has a Major Carr coming in to take command now for the winter campaign."

"Who's this Carr?"

"Don't know him. Just his reputation. Good man from what the word is."

Donegan nodded. "So now the junior major is ordered to ride behind the senior man—that it?"

"Way I see it."

On 22 October, Royall marched into Buffalo Tank with his battalions, turning over his command of the Fifth to Major Eugene Asa Carr, a thirty-nine-year-old veteran of plains warfare, who sat in camp awaiting the arrival of the regiment. Joining his cavalry at Buffalo Tank were about a third of the reorganized civilian scouts first assembled by Major George A. Forsyth, now commanded by Lieutenant Silas Pepoon of the Tenth Negro Cavalry.

Chapter 3

October 1868

$\mathcal{I}$t was a somber reunion for the most part, yet not without some joy when Seamus Donegan walked among those familiar faces at Buffalo Tank on the Union Pacific Line in central Kansas.

A month before, many of these same plainsmen had been pinned down by the Cheyenne like cornered badgers in their holes, on an island Forsyth named after Lieutenant Fred Beecher. After returning to Hays, most had elected to stay on scouting with Lieutenant Pepoon, although a handful had gone their way, having had enough of Indian fighting to last them. Besides Sergeant William McCall and veteran scout Sharp Grover, there were a few who sought out the tall Irishman, to shake a hand or slap a back and talk of nine days of siege on Beecher Island. Only one of the boy-faced men was still among those scouts to celebrate the grim reunion.

"Jack is the one who carried word from Beecher

Island to Fort Wallace," Donegan bragged on the youth after he had introduced young Stillwell to Bill Cody.

"Just one of four, don't forget that," Stillwell admitted.

"Where's Slinger? He riding with Pepoon and Custer?"

Stillwell shook his head. "Had a letter waiting for him at Hays when we got in there. His family back East thought it better for him to come home," Stillwell explained.

"Not like you—grown up out here."

"He might not be born in these parts, but I heard Slinger held his own on the island after I left."

"He did, Jack. Every bit as much as any man, and more."

"Who is this Slinger?" Cody asked.

"Name's Sigmund Schlesinger," Donegan said.

"Damn but I remember a fella of that name," Cody replied.

"He ain't the sort you'd forget," Seamus continued. "Him or the name."

"Met him earlier this year at Hays while I was hunting buffalo," Cody said. "So Slinger was on the island with you two?"

"Damn right. Major Forsyth was proud of the man." Donegan turned to Stillwell to ask, "How's this Pepoon?"

"Sharp don't like him worth squat," Jack admitted. "But, the man's all right at his job for a soldier. He's just dyed-in-the-wool army is all."

"Thing is, it sometimes takes more than soldiering to get the job done out here," Donegan replied. "Major Forsyth was the sort of man who didn't let his army-mouth overload his common-sense ass. Forsyth had sense."

"Him and McCall was the best I served with," Jack sighed as orders thundered up and down the line of picketed horses.

"Prepare to mount!" the sergeants were bawling at their men, soldiers and civilian scouts alike.

"Looks like it's come time we're gonna find out what this Major Carr is made of," Seamus said, slapping his big hand into Stillwell's. "See you come evening camp, Jack."

Retracing Major Royall's inbound steps, Carr marched his Fifth Cavalry and Pepoon's scouts north to Prairie Dog Creek in two days. There, on the morning of 25 October, Captain Jules Schenofsky's M Company and Seamus Donegan joined the civilian scouts to form the advance guard for the day's march north by west to Little Beaver Creek. With flankers out, the Irishman joined the point riders carefully picking their way along, searching the country for fresh sign as they ascended a hill.

"Little Beaver should be over this rise," Sharp Grover said, pointing.

"You got any idea what would be kicking up that much of a cloud off over there?" Donegan asked, the only one looking in that direction.

A dozen heads turned to the west, only then noticing the fine film of dust rising up the valley of the Little Beaver.

"Ain't no whirlwind, that's for sure," Grover said with a growl. He brought his horse about, hammering it with his heels. "Lieutenant!"

Schenofsky galloped to the top of the next rise to

join the point riders. The tree-lined Little Beaver meandered through the wide, grassy valley just below. And off to their left ambled the tail end of a Cheyenne village on the move.

"They know we're here?" Schenofsky asked.

"They do now," Grover replied, pointing at the rear of the procession.

Half a hundred warriors streamed past the rear of their march, bursting through the milling squaws and children, barking dogs and travois ponies.

"How many you figure in that village, boys?" Schenofsky inquired after he had dispatched a rider to dash back across the miles, carrying word to Major Carr.

"Four hundred," said scout Tom Alderdice.

"Closer to five hundred, I'd say," Grover replied.

"You're probably right," Alderdice agreed. "That makes at least a hundred warriors."

Schenofsky regarded the scouts a moment before speaking. "That makes us almost equal in manpower, gentlemen."

"Just what I was thinking," Grover agreed, a big smile crossing his tanned face. "We have one of two choices: stand here and take their charge, or we can take the fight to them."

"I'm all for taking it to 'em!" Alderdice shouted.

"Hit 'em hard and make 'em reel!" Donegan said.

"Let's fight 'em on the run!" Schenofsky hollered above the clamor. "Skirmish formation—flankers in!"

The columns quickly rattled into formation at the top of the hill, sending that old shiver of anticipation down Donegan's spine as the restless horses snorted and pranced, sensing the coming of battle through their riders.

"Right flank loaded!"

"Left flank report!"

"Left flank loaded and ready, sir!"

"Forward at a walk—to gallop on my command!" Schenofsky shouted above the squeak of dry leather and the rattle of bit-chain, the noisy thunk of bolt and the mumbled curse of a green rookie worried of soiling his pants.

"Forward!"

"Jesus God!" grumbled someone to Donegan's left as more warriors broke from the trees like maddened wasps, splashing across the shallow, late summer flow of the Little Beaver.

"Weapons ready!" bawled Schenofsky as the line of soldiers loped down the slope into the valley.

It was the last order Donegan heard clearly, for in the next heartbeat there arose a resounding clamor up and down the line as they began to take the first fire from the warriors. With a wild whoop the skirmish line broke into a ragged gallop.

At two hundred yards the warriors turned, racing down the line of soldiers. Dropping from the side of their ponies, they fired beneath the animals' straining necks as soldier bullets whined harmlessly over their heads.

"Aim for the ponies—their ponies, goddammit!"

Frustrated, many of Forsyth's veterans hollered at the green troopers, knowing from firsthand experience that a man must shoot the target presented him by the enemy.

"Drop the horses, by damn!"

A few of the ponies spilled, pitching their riders

into the grassy sand. Some held up a hand for rescue, others crouched, awaiting riders in the midst
of the powder smoke and swirling dust.

Two dozen warriors suddenly swept back on the
end of Schenofsky's column, effectively bringing
the charge to a halt as the horses wheeled back on
themselves. With the white men stopped in the
open, the warriors began to circle back and forth,
firing into the confused soldiers.

"They're gonna get chewed up down there!"
Grover shouted from the hilltop where the civilians
had watched the soldiers charge into the fray.

Stillwell nodded. "We've got to help."

"Look there, boys," Cody said, pointing west. "The
village is getting away."

"That's what this is all about," Grover replied.
"Them bastards are covering the escape."

"I'm for going after the village!" Alderdice
shouted. Several others hollered their agreement.
"Those soldiers can take care of themselves."

"Don't think so," Donegan said. "Those men will
be butter if we don't get down there now."

"The Irishman's right," Cody shouted. "Time
enough to chase squaws and travois!"

"Let's ride!" Grover bawled.

It was a mad dash made by the whooping civilians as they tore down on Schenofsky's command,
splitting at the last minute to race past the pinned-
down soldiers, racing among the ring of warriors.
The Cheyenne scattered, regrouped and tore off for
the west, where once more they would cover the
retreat of their village.

It took some time to regroup the commands.
Schenofsky had to get his soldiers back into the sad-

dle, and Grover had to regroup Pepoon's civilians before they were off again, trailing after the disappearing village. North by west, the fleeing Cheyenne hurried toward Shuter Creek, and crossed late that afternoon. Rarely did the warriors turn to fight the rest of the day, more often choosing to snipe at the outriders as the white men came on like troublesome gnats.

Only once, when the women and old ones were forced to slow their escape due to a narrowing of a canyon, did the warriors wheel and stand their ground, before breaking into a gallop with wild screeches climbing into the afternoon sky.

Shaking their rifles and bows, lances and warclubs, the hundred charged back on their pursuers, like swallows turning about and swooping down on the nighthawk.

"Halt!" the order thundered up and down the line.

Horses were reined up in a swirl of dust.

"Dismount! Horse holders to the rear!"

"By God, this is it!" Cody shouted.

"Let's hope it's nothing more than a good scrap!"

"Aye, Irishman! Nothing like a good scrap!"

At a hundred yards the order was given. *"Fire!"*

The warriors reined in, confusion electrifying their ranks. A few ponies cried out as the white man's bullets slapped among them. Only two went down, their riders swept up behind other warriors as the Cheyenne turned, parted, and two waves dashed up the parting slopes of two hills.

"Don't wait, Lieutenant!" Grover advised, dashing up to Schenofsky.

"By the devil, we won't!" Schenofsky whirled, arm waving. "Mount up! Hurry, boys—mount up!"

"Got 'em on the run now," Tom Alderdice cheered.

The soldiers and civilians both hollered as they sorted through the horse holders for their mounts and swung into the saddle.

"By fours!" Schenofsky ordered his men as they quickly formed. "Civilians—take the east trail. I'll follow the west. Cody, you and Donegan come with me!"

The two groups kept within sight of one another through the rest of the afternoon, chasing the dust cloud that always managed to stay just out of reach, over the next hill, in the next valley, until the light began to fail and Grover advised giving up the chase until sunrise.

"We'll wait here for Carr to come up," Schenofsky said.

"Good a place as any for a camp," Cody agreed.

Darkness descended on the command as the men gathered greasewood and started their fires. Royall led an advance into camp, dispatched by Carr at a gallop to bolster Schenofsky's skimpy command. Instead of a fight, Major Royall found beans, coffee and hardtack. The moon had come up by the time Carr brought in the rest of the regiment. Their fires twinkled along the Little Beaver.

"I'll be glad we get a chance to do some hunting," Cody grumped as he took his plate of beans and a steaming tin of coffee from the mess sergeant.

"That's just what's lacking in your education, Bill," said Donegan. "Had you fought in the war back East, you'd be one to appreciate the finer varieties of beans."

"Ain't nothing finer than these white beans," Grover hissed. "Make a man mighty gassy."

"White beans and corn dodgers. Mmm, mmm," Donegan replied. "Food for an army on the march."

"Time was, Cody—we'd both killed for white beans like these. Even some moldy hardtack like this here," Grover said, clanging his hard bread on the side of his tin plate.

"Your kind is always complaining, Abner," Seamus said, then chuckled as he shoved a spoonful of the beans in his mouth. "You want fresh game, when you had some of the finest horseflesh to dine on west of the Republican!"

"Horse or mule—I don't care. Just give me some meat!" Alderdice said.

The surrounding hills suddenly erupted with sporadic riflefire.

In panic, soldiers and civilians scattered back from the fires, bullets whizzing into camp, zinging tin plates and cups, exploding into the fires with firefly flares. The horses whinnied in the dark. Men shouted. A few crawled on their bellies toward the low bluff rising nearby. Above them the bright muzzle-flashes could be seen against the prairie night sky.

After half an hour of troublesome sniping, the bright orange flares of light tapered off and the night grew quiet once more.

"You think they're done with us for the night?" someone asked.

"No way of telling," Grover answered the voice from the dark. "They could be back."

"I'll gladly give 'em my beans!" Cody hollered.

The camp erupted in laughter.

"Call 'em in, Cody!" suggested someone.

"Yeah, tell 'em we got good food here we'll trade for some of their dried buffler meat!"

"Ah, that's the right of it," Donegan said. "Trade these white beans for some good belly food—buffalo. And while we're at it—we'll throw in some hardtack to boot."

"Just don't throw it my way!" yelled a soldier.

"That's right—I don't want to get hit with those damned hard crackers!" cried another.

"You'll all be wishing you had those beans to eat come morning, when you'll be in the saddle before breakfast," Schenofsky said, crawling up, staying out of the firelight.

"Why no breakfast, Lieutenant?" Grover asked.

"Carr wants us out early."

"To find the village?" asked Cody.

"Right."

"Way I've got it figured," Cody said, "that bunch will keep moving most of the night. Might stop for a few hours for the old ones and the children. But them bucks and squaws—they can keep on running for days, they have to."

"Cody's right," Grover agreed. "We have our work cut out for us catching that village once they've got the jump on us."

"Well, boys," Cody said, slapping a thigh as he got to his feet in the darkness, punching a black hole out of the starry sky. "Let's just do everything we can, come false-dawn, to eat up some of that ground they've put between them and us."

Chapter 4

October 1868

Only one of Carr's cavalrymen was wounded in the daylong fight. And from what his officers reported after the confusion of the battle, the major dispassionately listed thirty warriors killed in his official report.

Beginning early that next morning, 26 October, the advance guard had several brief skirmishes with the warriors protecting the flight of their village. They lasted until dark, when the soldiers finally gave up the chase and went into camp on the North Fork of the Solomon. Throughout the following day the closest Cody's scouts got to the warriors was to follow the distant dust cloud raised by the many horses and travois.

During that late morning and into the afternoon, Donegan noticed not only that the cloud was becoming thinner, but that the dust billowing over the fleeing Indians appeared to be widening. That could mean but one thing.

"They're scattering, Bill," Seamus said, offering his canteen to Cody as they sat atop a low rise in the endless swell and fall of land, allowing their horses to blow.

"No doubt of it now."

Behind them in the distance plodded Carr's cavalry, with Pepoon's civilians out as flankers to protect the unit from any surprise hit-and-run attacks by the warriors who might double back on the soldier column.

"You take one trail, I take another?"

"Not yet, we don't," Cody replied. "They're bound to be heading same place we need to be." He gave the canteen back. "Water."

"Where they going?"

"My guess is the headwaters of the Beaver."

"Been across it meself."

"With Forsyth?"

He nodded. "You want me go back and tell Carr what's on your mind?"

Cody shook his head. "No, not just yet. We've got two jobs now, Irishman. Staying with the Indian trail—and being sure these soldiers have water."

"You ask me, I'll tell you how important water is to a sojur!"

They laughed easily as the canteen strap went back over the saddlehorn and Cody led off. Both kept their eyes on the shimmering distance where the dust cloud dispersed across the hazy, shimmering horizon.

Three hours later the pair stopped on another low rise, where they dismounted, loosening the cinches for a few minutes while they waited until the rear column came in sight once more. Four riders loped into sight. Two of the group waved their hats when it appeared the two scouts had spotted them. Cody took his floppy slouch hat and signaled with it.

"Carr and Royall?" Cody asked as they waited for the four riders.

"I doubt Royall's with him. The old man probably left Royall in charge of the column while he rode up here to have a chat with us, Bill."

They waited, Cody more irritated than impatient for the delay caused by the soldiers.

"Glad to see you boys held up," Carr said as he reined up with three junior officers, each of them sweating in their wool tunics although it was a cool autumn day on the high plains.

"We figure we'll have to split up soon, Major," Cody announced.

"The village breaking up?" Carr asked, his face showing that he already knew the answer. "Stay with the biggest trail, Cody."

"We'll do the best we can."

Carr inched closer, his voice softer. "Cody, one of Pepoon's scouts says he figures today's march to water is a lot longer than the twenty-five miles you told me it would be when we broke camp this morning."

Cody glared at the major. "One of Pepoon's boys want to be your chief of scouts, eh?"

"Don't go getting testy on me, Cody."

"You're right, Major. No right of me doing that—"

"What Bill's trying to say is—we got a choice of trails right now," Donegan interrupted. "But the Injins are going to water just like us."

"That's another thing Pepoon's men tell me. They say we won't find any water where you're leading us, Cody."

The young scout squinted his eyes and shifted the hat on his head, grinding his teeth angrily. "Who the hell you want guiding you, Major? Me? Or this other fella?"

"Which one is it, Major?" Donegan asked.

"You know them, don't you?" Carr inquired, studying the Irishman.

"Most. Which one tell you Cody's steering you wrong?"

"Name's Alderdice."

"Tom Alderdice," Seamus repeated. "He's a Kansas boy all right. But I'll still put my money on Bill here."

Carr appeared to reckon with that a few moments, then measured Cody once more. "Will we find water by nightfall?"

The scout peered into the northwest. "Before slapdark, Major."

"How far, Cody?"

"Eight . . . maybe nine miles."

"What's there—a spring?"

"Beaver dams, on a small creek."

Carr sighed, glancing at his junior officers, then swiped a kerchief over his face. "All right, Cody. I'm going back to hurry the column along. Take us to this water of yours."

Cody spoke before Carr could rein about. "You believe me, don't you, Major?"

He finally nodded. "Looks like I've got one of two choices, and you're the best game in town right now, Cody. You lead the way."

Some three hours later Cody and Donegan ascended a low rise of land to look down on the valley of a small stream that would feed Beaver Creek several miles farther north.

"It's there—just like you said, Cody," Seamus cheered.

"Sounds like you doubted it yourself."

He smiled. "I'll admit there was a time or two the last few hours I had me doubts." He reached over as Cody reined up alongside him, slapping the young scout on the back.

"I'll teach that Major Carr to believe in me yet."

Both waited atop the rise for the flankers to come in, including Alderdice, about the time the advance guard hoved into view. Cody and Donegan waved them on.

"I've got to hand it to you," Carr said, beaming. "The water's where to said it would be, and what you said we'd find." His eyes ran up and down the narrow, green valley, its entire length dotted with small beaver dams that pooled the trickle of water at this late season of the year.

"This settle things for you, Major?"

Carr nodded. "Yes. I won't doubt you again. Only, tell me what the devil this creek is named."

Cody shrugged. "Far as I know, doesn't have a name. But—you might go check with them scouts of Pepoon's. One of them might know."

"No need of that," Carr replied, grinning in his dark beard. "We'll name it ourselves, here and now —for the record. The military record, that is. Adjutant, note that this creek where we spent the night of twenty-seven October is to be called *Cody's* Creek."

Donegan laughed, then gave the young scout a

hearty slap on the back. "That's the kiss of fame, me boy! A creek named for Bill Cody!"

That next morning the sun was barely awaking over the eastern rim of the prairie when the column was put on the march, moving north by west toward a creek known as the Beaver to some, the Sappa to others.

Cody enjoyed riding out ahead of the scouts at times, and this morning it suited him just fine. The crisp air of late autumn, with no sound to clutter the morning save for the wind soughing through the dried buffalo-grass, the rhythmic crunch of hooves as his horse picked its way, added to the occasional, faint call of the great long-necks sweeping overhead in great vees against the blue canopy, moving south once more.

He twisted in the saddle, assuring himself that Donegan and some of the others on point could see him far to the rear across the softly undulating land, then urged his mount down into the valley of the Beaver. Before the column came up, Cody had to find a suitable ford for crossing the men, animals and bulky wagons.

Dropping to his belly, his hands supporting his weight as he extended himself out over the water, he drank of its cool refreshment alongside his noisy mount. Cody soaked his bandanna in the creek, wrung it out then retied it around his neck before crawling back into the saddle. He nudged the horse downstream, his eyes on the creek all the time as he worked in and out of the trees, searching for a suitable ford.

As the gurgling creek slowly swept around a gentle bend, a loud crack rang out.

The horse stumbled backward a few halting steps, then keeled to its knees sideways as Cody leaped out of the saddle, his heart racing. A rapid spread of crimson just behind the animal's foreleg bubbled with froth.

Cody wasn't quick enough getting out of the way.

The animal tried rising for an instant, heaving against the scout, throwing him off balance. Cody was pitched straight down into the grass on the creekbank while the horse settled with a loud, humanlike scream on one of Cody's legs. A second, then a third shot whistled overhead as he struggled to heft the dying animal from his trapped foot. It flashed vividly in his mind—those days he had made a living running trap-lines along creeks just like this one. His prey being caught, a foot held in the jaws of an iron trap.

Every bit as unrelenting as this.

Peering over the heaving ribs of the animal, he watched puffs of white smoke dot the dry leaves of the cottonwood and willow just yards across the creek. Still struggling to free the foot from his boot, he fired a few shots at the powder smoke that marked his targets. A bullet whistled past his cheek, causing him to jerk about in surprise.

Upstream, to his left—another rifleman. And this new warrior had him dead to rights in the open.

Cody stretched out on his back, not only to make himself as small a target as possible, but to push against the rear flank of the great animal with his free leg. His trapped foot popped free, without his boot.

Rolling onto his belly, Cody fired two shots across the creek, then crawled up beside the dead animal. He pulled and yanked, finally freeing his boot from its sandy prison. His toes wriggled in the sand, peeking from the holes worn in his stiffened stockings as he yanked the long boot on—just as a bullet nicked a large splinter from the butt of his Spencer carbine still in its scabbard on the saddle.

He dragged it and the canteen free from the horn once he had clambered over the horse. Its carcass was not the best protection a man could hope for—still, the big neck and legs gave him some cover from one direction, the rear flanks cover from the second sniper as he began to put the Spencer into use.

"Damn," he muttered, looking beyond the fringe of trees lining the opposite creekbank. "Looks like you flushed 'em from their roost."

A small band of squaws and children, with ponies pulling travois, hurried away from the scene, protected by the two warriors who had dismounted the white scout. They disappeared in the distance between two flat hills.

"By God, we do have the bunch of 'em split up and running from us."

For long minutes as the sun continued its climb into the sky, Cody fired back only when he saw gun smoke on the far creekbank. He kept the pistol beneath him, come the time for the close work.

The bloody cry shocked him, erupting so close, driving his heart right into his throat. A few yards downstream one of the warriors had mounted and burst from the timber, screeching out his war-cry as his pony splashed into the shallow creek, droplets raining in a cascade like a thousand tiny jewels in the golden autumn sunlight.

Leaping up on Cody's bank with a spray of water, the warrior slipped behind his pony, firing beneath his neck with a repeater. Coming on in a wide circle around the dead horse so that in a matter of seconds the white man would have no shelter. It was time for a decision.

Cody bellied the ground as flat as he could, stuffing his head between the dead horse's rear legs. In that cramped and odorous spot, the young scout pressed the Spencer to his cheek and fired.

"Damn!" he muttered. He had missed, and cursed himself for it.

More shots rattled through the still air. He jerked backward from his hiding place, peering over the brown flanks of the horse to find Donegan and a handful of soldiers breaking the skyline directly above him.

The lone warrior immediately righted himself and tore back into the stream, looking over his shoulder at the advancing rescuers as he splashed across the Beaver. In the next moment his companion had joined him in a mad dash after the fleeing women and children.

"You hurt?" Donegan asked as he reined his horse up beside Cody, casting a big shadow over the young scout.

He looked up and smiled crookedly. "Nothing but my pride. I missed a damned good shot at one of 'em."

A sergeant was shouting at his soldiers to return, denying them the chase just when they had the scent good and strong in their nostrils. He rode over to the two civilians.

"We'll wait here for Carr to come up," explained the sergeant.

"Best you keep them from running on, Sergeant," Cody said, standing at last. "Them two we saw—and more we didn't—might have a mind to double back and ambush your boys."

"They'll gripe, not getting blooded today."

"Their time will come, Sergeant," Donegan assured. "Your sojurs will see plenty of blood soon enough."

He could almost ignore the wailing of the squaws, keening in their grief. Days ago the running fight with the soldiers had cost Tall Bull some good warriors. But this day near the beginning of the Moon of Leaves Falling had cost him no more than a half-dozen ponies and sixteen lodges some of his people were forced to abandon in their hasty flight.

After sundown a few of the small bands had come in. Two of them reported skirmishing with the soldiers throughout the day, being chased until darkness forced the white men to give up their hunt. Between them, both groups had lost some of their animals and many of their homes tied to travois, along with cooking utensils and clothing.

With his entire village of fighting men licking its wounds, the tall chief seethed, wanting so badly to gather his warriors and strike the soldiers beneath the starry night sky. But he again listened to his medicine man, who advised the Dog Soldier camp to turn about and point their noses north for the winter. The white man would eventually give up his chase and snow would blanket the land.

There were many who would sleep in borrowed blankets this night. Worse yet were the women and children, keening pitifully at the loss of home and husband and father.

There in the silvery autumn light of a quarter-moon spilling its faint brilliance on the far prairie, Tall Bull vowed he would return. When the short grass time came next spring, he and his Dog Soldiers would come to burn and steal, to kill and carry off many white women and children.

Come the short grass time, Tall Bull pledged to renew a war so bloody, exact a revenge so terrible, that the white man's heart would turn to water.

Chapter 5

November 5, 1868

The pink limestone walls of Fort Wallace lit up with a rosy light this autumn sunrise. The sky came up red in the east, then softened to an orange glow on the squat buildings that cast long shadows across the cold parade.

Seamus Donegan watched his breath rise gauzy before his face as he saddled the big mare at the hitching post outside the stables. Cody and ten of Pepoon's scouts strapped on bits and tightened cinches. Nothing more than a morning hunt, with hopes of feeding Carr's Fifth Cavalry, troops who had put an unexpected strain on the post larder.

"We'll be all right," Seamus said, seeing Cody turn in the saddle with a look of apprehension on his face, sizing up the soldiers who followed the pair out the gates.

Cody settled, pulling his heavy collar up against the dawn wind. "Had my way—we'd have more along."

"Too many still hung over, Bill."

The young scout finally cracked a smile, his gray-blue eyes merry as he looked back at Donegan. "Not many like you and me, eh? We drank our share."

"And then some, Mr. Cody!"

"Aye, you goddamned Irish bastard!"

They were of a kind, the sort who worked over a bottle until it hurt, yet still young enough that they rarely felt their liquor the next day, that head-pounding and queasy belly. All of that would come soon enough, Sharp Grover warned them like an austere uncle last night . . . in the end, the aging scout added, a man had to admit he was getting on in his years when he finally felt his cups.

"Life's short enough not to celebrate what little we got to celebrate," Seamus repeated the sentiment.

"Out here, life can just be too damned short."

"All the more reason for a man to celebrate with his friends."

"You know, Irishman—every day I get reminded why I liked you from the start."

"You needed someone to drink with, Cody."

"No," and his eyes got that serious, cloudy look to their blue, like clouds suddenly soiling the sun-bright sky. "I just needed someone who understood that a man could have his fun and still be good at what he did. I needed a friend."

"I'm glad to know you, Bill Cody."

He held out his hand, and they shook awkwardly in the saddle. "Let's make meat, Irishman."

For better than three hours the twelve hunted the draws and coulees of the rolling country north of Fort Wallace, dividing into three groups which stayed in sight of one another. Each band of hunters took with it a pair of the pack animals—big, black army mules, ugly as sin and twice that mean to the unwary. Yet it was one of those yellow-eyed brutes who brought the first warning to the hunters.

Cody and Donegan had stopped atop a low hill, enjoying the shade beneath a small stand of trees to allow their horses to blow. Tom Alderdice and another scout, Eli Ziegler, squatted on the ground, smoking their pipes as Seamus cut a slice of chaw from his plug with the folding knife he carried in his boot.

"You still see 'em, Seamus?" Cody asked beneath his hat brim.

He nodded, his eyes locating the other two groups inching over the rolling oceanlike landscape far to the left, working up and down through the broken countryside. Donegan turned when the big mule snorted and stamped the ground, pulling cautiously at the tree where Alderdice had tied it.

The civilian got to his feet and ambled over to calm the animal. "What the devil got into you now?"

"He's just a strange one, Tom," Bill Cody said.

"Don't like the smell of civilians like us, I'll bet," Seamus joked.

The mule's eyes widened, its nostrils flaring as it pranced back from Alderdice when he again attempted to calm it. Then of a sudden, its ears twitched and laid back.

Several gunshots drifted to them from the direction of the other groups, off more than a mile across the broken country now.

"Maybe they've had some luck," Seamus said.

" 'Bout time," Cody agreed.

"What the hell?" Alderdice muttered as he stepped around the nervous mule, shading his eyes with a hand, gazing across the far prairie.

"They chasing something?" asked Donegan, watching the faraway dark specks. "Antelope?"

"Only one thing mules hate worse than civilians," Cody grumbled, scrambling to his feet quickly. "Injuns."

"By the Mither of Saints!"

Donegan was on his feet in an instant, joining the rest as they peered across the landscape, watching the two other groups riding hell-bent up and down over the gentle swales of the tableland.

A war-cry broke the cold air below that hilltop, announcing the arrival of more of the war-party as it burst from the trees down along the dry creekbed below.

"Appears we're not the only ones in trouble!" Donegan shouted, whirling to his mount, tightening the cinch with a frantic yank before he swung into the saddle.

"There's more'n twenty of 'em!" Alderdice yelled.

"Twice that now." Cody reined up, snagging the mule's lead from the brush where it had been tied. "Best we join up with the others—and now."

"Let's go, Irishman!"

The four hammered their heels into the army mounts, clattering downhill toward the two other groups racing back across the rolling land with the same intention of rejoining for strength. Behind Donegan's group more than a dozen warriors topped the hill just abandoned by the four white men and their mule.

Over his shoulder Seamus watched one of the

Cheyenne send half a dozen Dog Soldiers in one direction down the slope, waving the rest on with him in another.

The war whoops crackled on the air behind them, and in front as well, as the first group of hunters reined in among Cody's band, spraying dust that lit up like fine gold.

"Where, goddammit?" one of the scouts shouted.

"Jezuz—we gotta find a place to make a stand of it!" cried Beecher Island survivor Thomas Ranahan.

"Everyone shut up and we'll make it out with all our hide!" Cody growled.

"Down there!" James Curry said, pointing. "In them trees."

He and Ranahan were turning their mounts, ready to lead some of the others as the second group of hunters reined in.

"You boys go down there—ain't none of you coming out!" Seamus said. "It'll be your grave."

"Them trees is enough for me!" shouted Ziegler.

"Those Cheyenne can pick you off from the hillsides, easy as you please," Cody said. "You care to make a ride of it, we've gotta take some high ground. Right, Irishman?"

Seamus liked the way that cocky smile blossomed on the young scout's face whenever trouble drew near.

"Time for this cavalry to make a stand—up there."

Seamus pointed, then heeled his horse around savagely, yanking on the lead to one of the mules.

Curry shouted in protest. "You're heading back through them bastards—"

"Back to the hilltop—all twelve of us!" Donegan ordered, leading the rest into a ragged hand gallop.

"Don't shoot at the red bastards," Cody suggested. "Just worry about riding through 'em for now."

"We can't just ride—"

"Shuddup, Curry!"

Cody spurred the rest into a hard gallop as they neared the half-dozen Cheyenne. For a moment the odds were in their favor. Behind them, more than forty painted, feathered warriors came on at a full gallop. Another half-dozen Cheyenne burst 'round the brow of the hill in a splash of color and sound.

A few of the warriors drew back bows, others brandished rifles overhead, threatening. As arrows sailed in among the white men, Seamus freed his pistol and fired.

The smell of burnt powder raked his nostrils. He fired a second time. And missed again.

A third shot sent a warrior tumbling from the back of his pony. The rest broke off as the dozen white men clattered to the top of the hill.

"Get the stock tied off in them trees!" Cody ordered. "Donegan—you, over there."

"There's more'n fifty of 'em, Cody," Ranahan hollered.

"Don't matter. They can't get close enough to do us damage—we don't let 'em. Now get down and put your carbine to work!"

The twelve sprawled in the tall grass, fanning out in a crude half circle about the time the warriors made their first serious charge past the defenders clustered at the crest of the hill. For the better part of an hour the Cheyenne kept at it, racing back and forth, sweeping the hillside in a giant arc before they would rein about to sweep in the opposite direction.

While bullets for the most part sang harmlessly overhead, it was the iron-tipped arrows falling among the defenders that created the greatest danger. A bowman could fire uphill without showing his position with a puff of rifle smoke. And, perhaps even more telling, a warrior using a rifle had to expose himself to his enemy, rising from the grass long enough to fire his bullet in a straight line.

The Cheyenne archers, on the other hand, had only to fire their arrows into the air, where they would gently arc, falling from the autumn sky onto the hilltop.

From time to time the whistling shafts fell among the white men, but for the most part did little damage. One scout's leg was pinned to the ground. Another had his coat sleeve pierced. Even Curry shrieked in panic when a shaft punctured the wide brim of his slouch hat. Yet the greatest number of arrows fell among the frost-dried leaves of the trees where the horses stood hobbled and tied. Each time the shafts came down in waves, clattering like dry beans falling through the limbs and branches, the animals pranced nervously, snorting and pulling at their halters.

Three warriors lay dead down the slope, close enough to the white men that none of the rest dared rescue the bodies. Back and forth the Cheyenne milled for a few minutes, as if debating among themselves.

"What you make of it, Cody?"

"They're trying to figure why their medicine went bad, I suppose."

"One of them bucks is brave enough to try," said Ziegler.

"Yep, here he comes," Donegan said.

A single warrior had removed his war-shirt, handing it to a companion before he kicked heels against his pony's ribs. He carried only a military carbine as he charged up the hillside, from the muzzle of which dangled a single war-eagle feather.

"You want him, Irishman?"

"Tell you what, Cody—I don't get him, he's yours."

"I like the cut of your cloth, Donegan," Cody said, smiling as he pushed another cartridge into the Blakeslee loading tube for his Spencer. "Let's see how good you are."

"Like running buffalo?"

"You might say that."

Over the front blade of his Henry, Seamus worked at keeping the warrior down the blued barrel, between the notches of his rear sight. Swaying side to side, then dropping off the far side of his pony, the Cheyenne was not about to give the Irishman a good target.

"Bleeming bastird," he muttered, at last moving the front blade to the pony's head as it strained upslope. Donegan squeezed the trigger.

The war-pony pitched forward, spilling its rider into the tall grass, both bodies kicking up thin clouds of dust as they settled.

"You still want the rider?" Cody shouted as a few of the scouts hurrawed behind Donegan.

"Damn bloody right I do!"

"Then knock 'im down, by God!"

The hot brass spat from the chamber as he levered another round into the breech, the smell of hot oil and burnt powder like nothing else on the dry, autumn wind with a bite of winter to it.

Standing to face the knot of white men above him, the warrior brought up his rifle, firing it without fear when Donegan squeezed off his own shot.

The blast knocked the Cheyenne backward two steps. He stopped, staring down at his chest, which began to seep red.

Donegan chambered another round and let out his breath, held high again, then squeezed.

Disbelieving, the warrior stumbled three more steps downhill, clawing at his chest still, then fell backward, still-legged. And moved no more.

Down the slope arose cries of frustration as the warriors milled about for a moment then slowly, one by one, headed off to the northeast.

"You boys wanna follow 'em?" Cody asked, that big smile on his face.

"You and your ruddy notions!" Donegan replied, crawling to his feet. "Do we wanna follow 'em? he says."

"I'm for getting us them four scalps," Curry cheered. "C'mon, boys!"

Curry led the others down the slope where the white men yanked and pulled at the Cheyenne bodies, searching for plunder or at the least a souvenir to show the soldiers back at Wallace.

"I've taken a liking to that belt pouch, Ranahan," Donegan said as he strode up on the frantic activity over the dead warriors.

"This?" Ranahan held the pouch up, admiring the colorful porcupine quillwork. "Thought it was pretty myself."

"The plunder is mine, Ranahan."

"We all got call to it, Irishman."

"You watched me, like the others. I killed this one."

"Get something off one of them others, Donegan. I like this pouch—"

"No," and he said it quietly. "I want that pouch."

"Best give the Irishman the pouch, Ranahan."

He eyed Cody like a frightened animal. Then the small, feral eyes went back to Donegan. "All right, Irishman." He slapped the pouch into the big man's hands. "It's yours. Take it. I . . . I didn't want it anyway. Just leave me his scalp."

"You know how I feel about scalps—don't you, Ranahan? Remember Slinger—how you and Lane chaffed on him?"

The black eyes hardened with a glint of fire to them.

"Don't push the Irishman, Ranahan," said Tom Alderdice. "Just leave it alone."

Scamus watched as Ranahan suddenly turned on his heel, grumbling, moving off down the slope to join some of the rest combing over the other dead.

"That one doesn't like you much, Seamus."

He looked at Cody a moment, then grinned. "Don't like him much either." Seamus stuffed the pouch under his belt, letting the decorated flap hang free. "I'll damn sure be glad when he goes south to rejoin Pepoon fighting with Custer."

"Soon enough."

"Never soon enough for me," Seamus whispered so that no other man heard. "Cowards and back-shooters only men I'm afraid of. I'll be happy when that one's gone south with Custer. Cowards and back-shooters . . ."

Chapter 6

December 1868

Reuben Waller didn't know if he liked the cold of December any better than the damned heat of September on the high plains.

And once again he wasn't all that sure what the hell he was doing in a place like this. Yet, one thing was certain—he had to keep moving or his toes might damned well freeze off.

Weeks ago, when the white soldiers of Carr's Fifth Cavalry had arrived at Fort Wallace, four companies of the Tenth Negro Cavalry received their marching orders. These buffalo soldiers, as they were called on the plains, were sent to Fort Lyon, some hundred miles southwest of Wallace. There they were to join Captain William H. Penrose of the Third Infantry, and one company of Custer's Seventh Cavalry, for a winter campaign. The combined force would drive the hostiles east toward the bulk of Custer's regiment, which at that moment was marching south into Indian Territory to punish the

Cheyenne, Kiowa and Arapaho for their bloody raids on the Kansas settlements.

After loading a small pack train with what supplies Fort Lyon could spare for the coming campaign, Reuben Waller's unit under Penrose struck out south by east, with plans of establishing a depot in advance of the arrival of Carr's Fifth Cavalry, a much larger force. The commander of the department of the Missouri, General Philip H. Sheridan, feeling time was critical, ordered that a unit be sent into the field at the earliest moment. Therefore, Penrose's command was instructed to leave the lion's share of forage and rations for Carr.

Captain Penrose, breveted a brigadier general in the recent war with the South, did not lack for courage. He was determined to travel fast and lean, counting on Carr's main column to come up in time to resupply his small battalion. In that way he clearly intended to make a mark for himself and his men on the coming winter campaign, even if he had to do it the hard way.

Which is just what happened.

On the fifteenth of November, five days out of Fort Lyon, the Penrose wing reached the arid country north of the Cimarron River. There the troops were hammered by a heavy, wet snowstorm that sustained itself long enough to force his command to bivouac on a barren piece of ground that offered not only no wood, but no buffalo chips for burning as well.

Reuben Waller's advance guard ran relays to keep the rest of the troops moving through the driving snow until they reached the cheerless camp Penrose had selected. More than twenty-five horses in the rear-guard floundered as the temperature dropped brutally and the snow grew deeper. The animals gave out, refusing to go on. Waller ordered his squad to kill the horses where they had collapsed.

"It don't make no sense leaving a good animal behind for the Injuns," Waller had explained to them that day as they fought to keep their bearings in the swirling buckshot of snow. "Likewise, it don't make no sense seeing a animal suffer what's gonna die anyway."

For the next three weeks Penrose pushed his men forward a little more each day, crossing the Cimarron, eventually moving down to the barren water-scrape country north of the North Canadian. In the old days, Penrose informed them, this country had been part of the old Santa Fe Trail, a section called the "Journada del Muerte"—the Journey of Death. Wasn't a man in Reuben Waller's squad who failed to understand why the Spanish had give that name to this barren sheet of trackless landscape.

Death seemed to haunt every step of Penrose's command now.

For days the temperature refused to climb above zero while the troops hacked away at snowdrifts and cut away creekbanks for the wagons, working in relays, as no man could stand such exertion in the brutal cold for longer than fifteen minutes at a time. Still, Penrose pressed his men to make some progress every day, telling them Custer and Sheridan were counting on them. Somehow he convinced his troops the cold weather could not hold a grip on them much longer. Sooner or later a break would come.

By the time the Penrose command had slogged

into the valley of San Francisco Creek, a tributary of the North Canadian, the Tenth Cavalry had marked their passing with a trail of horse carcasses.

It was 6 December. No Indians nor sign had been found since leaving Fort Lyon, nor had there been any reason to believe the troops had been seen by hostiles. With Waller's assistance, Penrose attempted to boost the morale of his men by keeping them busy on short scouts in the area. The forays accomplished nothing more than an explosion in the number of frostbite cases. Eventually the troops were forced onto half-rations, while they struggled to find forage in the barren valley for their starving animals.

"Care for a drink of something warm, Cap'n?" Waller asked, beating together the makeshift boots he had fashioned from horsehides when his own boots had cold-cracked and split wide open.

Penrose strode up, working his mittened hands and stomping his feet. His boots were lashed together with wangs made from strips of green horsehide. "You made coffee, Corporal?"

He looked sheepish. "No, sir. I don't got no coffee left. Just been heating water."

"Drinking hot water?"

"That's right," and Waller smiled. "Makes me warmer on the inside. Don't taste all that good, but it does warm me on the inside. Makes me think on last summer."

"Well . . . now—yes," Penrose finally stammered. He collapsed to a pile of saddles where he made himself comfortable. "Suppose you do get me a cup . . . a cup of that summer warmth you're drinking there, Corporal."

After languishing nearly three weeks in bivouac at Fort Wallace, Major Eugene Carr received marching orders for his Fifth Cavalry on 20 November.

By the twenty-ninth the regiment reached Fort Lyon on the Arkansas River, now aware that Captain Penrose was already attempting to forge a trail into Indian Territory for Carr's command to follow. In two days his seventy-five, six-mule wagons were loaded. In addition to a government sutler who Major Carr was allowing to come along, the Fifth Cavalry would bring a half-dozen ambulances, as well as a remuda of mules, and a good-sized herd of cattle to feed the troops.

With Penrose already three full weeks ahead of him, Carr and three hundred men pulled away from Fort Lyon as the sun rose on 2 December.

Three days out a blizzard struck the command in almost the same place a howling storm had battered Penrose's column. Nonetheless, the soldiers struggled onward for three days against the mounting snow and dropping temperatures.

"Cody, what shall we name this barren piece of ground?" Carr asked that third evening beneath a canvas tarp where the major sat, penning his daily report.

"Freeze-Out Canyon."

Carr and most of his staff chuckled.

"Agreed. On all future maps of this part of the country, Freeze-Out Canyon will be its name."

"Wish you had a map to tell me where I could find Penrose's trail, Major."

Carr set his pencil down on the tablet, staring at the dancing flames a moment. "I'll send you out to-

morrow to do just that—do anything and everything
to find the track of their passing."

"Sounds as if you fear for them," Donegan said.

"I do," Carr said, looking up at the Irishman. The
major was the sort of career officer who often found
himself passed over because of his complaints to
command about the welfare of his men in the field.
"Likely by now Penrose has run out of forage for
his animals, and what rations they have along can't
last them much longer."

"I'll take Donegan with me," Cody said.

"And two more," Carr advised, again brooding on
the fire. He was evidently thinking of his dimin-
ished force of civilian scouts ever since Pepoon's
men were ordered south from Fort Wallace to join
up with Custer. "Take enough in case you get into
trouble."

"Only trouble we'll bump up against is winter do-
ings out there. But Seamus and I will take two more
along."

"Take Ziegler and Donovan," Seamus suggested.
"They've got bottom enough."

"On the Arikaree with you?" Cody asked.

"They'll do to cover my backside any day."

"Donovan and Ziegler, General Carr," Cody replied, using the major's brevet rank won during the
war. "The four of us—we'll find that trail for you."

The next morning the civilians pushed their
weary mounts into the frozen wilderness, staying
close enough together for safety, yet far enough
apart to scour a wide chunk of territory. By the second day their search paid off.

"Sure this was Penrose's camp?" asked Eli Ziegler.

Cody stood, dusting his hand after feeling the ashes of several fires. "It's his."

"How you so sure?" inquired John Donovan.

"It's a white man's fire," Seamus Donegan replied. "Indian won't build anything that big." He kicked more of the snow aside to expose the blackened fire-ring.

"Bridger smartened you up right nicely, Irishman," Cody said, grinning. Then the smile was gone. "I suppose we need to get word back to the major."

"I'll ride back with you, Bill."

"No, Irishman. You three stay put."

"How you—"

"I can damn well follow my own trail coming here."

"And get those soldiers back here to us? How far you make it we've come?"

"Twenty-five . . . no more'n thirty miles," Cody answered, swinging into the saddle. "Best get a fire started, boys. Sky looks bad and we might get snow."

Seamus grabbed Cody's rein. "You'll be all right on your own?"

"Listen to this, will you, boys? The Irishman worried about me!" Cody laughed easily, throwing his head back in that way that made his blond goatee jut proudly from his chin. "Maybe while I'm gone, you two have Donegan here tell you about his little walk in the snow two winters gone now."

A curious look crossed the Irishman's face. "That trail I took to Fort Smith?"

He nodded, pulling gently on the reins. "Tell 'em how you done it on foot."

Seamus watched until Cody disappeared into the scant timber upstream. He turned about to find the two scouts staring at him, expectation clear on their faces.

"What say we get us some firewood first—then I'll tell you the story of my winter's walk along the Bozeman Trail."

Cody reached Carr's camp long after moonrise that night by picking his way carefully through those cold hours, across those twenty-four miles of frozen wilderness.

"It's eleven o'clock, Cody," Carr grumbled, rubbing sleep from his eyes as he joined the scout at the fire where a pot of coffee had been simmering all evening.

"Sounds like you didn't expect me."

"Didn't," Carr replied. "Figured you'd have enough horse sense to come back in the morning."

"What? And miss this coffee you've had burning for me?"

"Don't drink enough of that axle grease to keep you up," Carr said. "I've already sent word to the company commanders that we're pulling out early in the morning. We'll have to push hard—my wagons can't roll through these snow drifts as fast as your scouts moved in the last couple days."

Cody stood, tossing the rest of the sour coffee into the fire. "May take a couple days, but—I'll get you there, General."

"With every day, I grow more worried about those men with Penrose."

"You afraid we won't find 'em in time?"

Carr nodded. "Unless they're eating their boot-soles for rations—I figure they've run out of the rations they packed with them from Fort Lyon. And, in this snow, with this godawful weather—I don't feel all that good about us being able to find those soldiers before they starve, or freeze to death."

"You get your sleep, General," Cody said, handing his cup to a picket near Carr's fire. "We'll find Penrose before his brunettes are done in."

"I'm counting on you, Cody."

He was up with the first to kick their way out of warm blankets the next morning, pushing and prodding his own civilian scouts. The new snow that began falling sometime after midnight did nothing to raise spirits in Carr's camp.

For hours the soldiers shoveled their way through snowdrifts, cutting passage for the cumbersome supply wagons. Just past noon Cody rode back to the advance guard, his horse heaving through the deep snow.

"Major, this is where me and the others crossed to the west side of the Cimarron," he explained, pointing across the river.

"Looks like some rough country over there."

"It is," Cody replied. "That's why I'm recommending we keep your wagons and men on this side of the river—the going's a little easier up ahead."

"You're leading the way, Cody." Carr waved his command into motion once again.

As sundown approached, throwing its gloomy light on the winter countryside, Cody had led Carr's cavalry to a high plateau among the Raton foothills. He waited for the major to come up with the advance guard.

"There's water and grazing aplenty down there, General Carr."

The major studied the steep slope dropping into the valley of a creek feeding the Cimarron. "Not too big a problem for the horsemen, Cody. But I don't think the wagons can make down. Where can Wilson and his teamsters find a decent grade?"

Cody shook his head. "There isn't one, General. At least, not something fit for wagons for a good thirty miles in either direction. Thirty miles off . . . then another thirty getting down to the creek below where we found Penrose's camp—that means close to a week you'll lose to lollygagging with these wagons."

"Lollygagging?" protested wagonmaster John Wilson as he stomped up, curious at the delay. "These are my wagons, by God—and I'll say what's done with 'em, General Carr."

Carr studied the slope a few moments, then looked at Cody. "We'll gain a week if we drop down to the creek here?"

"Three days off . . . three days back—six days minimum."

"You're taking the word of this boy here, General? I'm not asking my drivers to take a chance on that icy slope!" Wilson complained.

"You don't have to, Mr. Wilson," Carr replied. "I'll have soldiers drive the wagons down if your men won't tackle that ride."

Wilson drew back, puffing out his chest. "You're forgetting, General—these are my wagons."

Carr stepped right up to the civilian, his feathers ruffled now. "And you're forgetting, Mr. Wilson— this is an army campaign you're contracted for. Not some ride in the park. You don't want to drive your wagons down there, I'll find someone who will. And, if any are damaged in the process—the army will gladly reimburse you for the cost."

Wilson sucked on a tooth a moment, thinking on that. "You'll replace any—"

"He said he would," Cody interrupted and in a hurry. "Now, you want to take the first ride down that slope—run down, slide down or fall down . . . it's your job to get your equipment down, any way you can."

"I'm not going down that slope with my ass nailed on a wagon seat —any less taking orders from some wet-eared young rake like you, Cody!"

"Then step out of the way, Wilson—'cause I'll sure as hell take the first seat down that slope, and cut the way for the rest of you."

Carr turned on his chief of scouts. "You know anything about handling a wagon and team?"

Cody laughed engagingly. "General, for years I ran freight for the top outfit here on the plains."

"Who was that?" Wilson demanded.

"Russell, Majors and Waddell," he answered, shutting the wagonmaster up.

Carr waved an arm at the wagonmaster. "Bring up a wagon, Mr. Wilson. We're going to see how Cody gets this done."

The wagonmaster brought up the mess wagon which rode at the head of the train, halting it at the lip of the steep slope where the mules wide-eyed the drop below their traces.

Following Cody's directions, a group of the teamsters brought out their chains and locked the wheels together on one side, then did the same with the second pair. That completed, the young scout leaped onto the seat, heaved forward on the brake and coaxed his reluctant mules down the slope.

Most of the way down the animals kept the wagon in control, working with Cody as he struggled against the icy slope beneath the locked wheels. But nearing the bottom the mess-wagon gradually worked up on the mules so hard that the animals broke into a run, galloping into the snowy valley in a wild ride that caused Cody to yahoo all the way into the bottom. He brought the mess-wagon to a halt beside the creek, leaped off the seat and waved his hat at the top of the hillside.

Soldiers and teamsters alike cheered and stomped and whistled their admiration.

One by one, each wagon was rough-locked and eased down the slope so that within a half hour, Major Carr and wagonmaster Wilson had the entire column in camp, including the two hundred head of cattle.

"Cody, by Jupiter you've earned yourself a fresh cup of coffee!" Carr hailed, waving the scout to his fire.

He rubbed his hands over the flames. "Hoping you'd offer me something a bit stronger, General. After that ass-puckering ride, I could sure use something of a bracer."

Carr finally laughed. "Well, now—I suppose we both can at that, Mr. Cody. And I have something along that just might be strong enough to warm the man within."

Chapter 7

December 21, 1868

*F*our days until Christmas.

A damned lot he had to be celebrating. He or any of them out in the middle of this wilderness after another cold, wet snow had battered the land before blowing on east into Indian Territory.

Yet Seamus could not help remembering Christmases past, celebrated in that favorite pub of his back in Boston Towne. The memory of the special smells and the tastes, surrounded by fragrant greenery bound up in bright red ribbons, and the air itself rich with simmering spices and pine tar—just the recollection itself made Donegan as warm inside as if he were sipping at the hot buttered rum that was the pub's specialty at this merry season.

How he longed now for something thick and potent and bubbling hot.

Instead, he shivered, not knowing if he would ever be warm again.

Slowly moving across the winter countryside, letting his horse pick its own way through the snow and bramble, willow and bunch-grass. Each day like this he joined Bill Cody riding far ahead of Carr's column. Leaving in the gray of dawn, not riding back until the dark of twilight to the merry fires over which the Fifth Cavalry cooked their supper fare. Without asking, Seamus still knew Cody was feeling his way along more than planning out his route. Sensing through intuition where Penrose's scouts had taken the buffalo soldiers.

It was a gamble any way a man might choose—especially after the countryside had been battered by storms.

This cold in the saddle—he wondered if it were any worse than the winters in his green homeland back across the ocean. It made him smile wryly, that he still thought of Ireland as his home, when a growing part of him had come to believe he would never make it back to Ireland and County Kilkenny before his mother died. If ever.

It had been a year and a half since he had received that letter from her. Could a woman like her last that long or more? Sure it was that she came from strong stock—just look at those two brothers of hers: Liam and Ian. But still she could be the sort worn down with the woes of life, and the loss of a husband was not the least of these. Could she? Was she . . .

He squeezed the specter out of his mind, pushing a cold pain from his chest as he struggled to latch his mind to something else.

There's been no letters since, Seamus. But, then after leaving the Bozeman Road—you've not been an easy one for a letter to track down . . .

"What the hell are you doing out here anyway, you bleeming bastird?" he asked himself out loud, startling himself with his own voice amid all the aching silence of the wilderness that made him yearn all the more for the woman he left behind up the Bozeman Road.* "You ought to be finding Jenny and making it right with her."

"What'd you say?"

Of a sudden he snapped to, finding Cody stopped ahead of him, turned in his saddle to peer back at Donegan with a truly quizzical look on his frozen face.

"Nothing, Bill," he muttered. "Just . . . talking to meself."

"Like it better if you talk to me—especially you've got to talk of women."

"What's the use of talking of women out here, where we have none to look at?"

"Ah, Irishman—that's just it, don't you see? We don't have them to look at . . . but, what do you remember most about the woman who weighs most heavy on your mind?"

He clamped down hard, not sure if he wanted her to have a grip on so big a piece of him right now. Any time. Yet he could not help himself—for if nothing else, it was truly the smell of her, the feel of her, that haunted him now after all this time.

"The smell of her, maybe."

"Good!" Cody cheered as together they worked their way down a short slope. "Ah, how I remember Lulu's smell." He drank deep of the dry, cold air.

It reminded Seamus of a man drinking in a wom-

* The Plainsmen Series, vol. 2, *Red Cloud's Revenge*

an's perfume. He tried it himself, drawing a breath, deep, to the full extent of his chest. There was a perfume to it at that. And one that reminded him of Jenny. Was it that she smelled so much like this great land? Or, was it simply that he had no other sweet fragrance to prick his thoughts with remembering?

"God, how I miss Lulu," Cody said, his voice a little softer now, even plaintive. Then he suddenly straightened in the saddle, as if steeling himself against the hurt.

"Where is she now?"

"St. Louis, Seamus. She and my daughter, Arta."

Donegan remembered the boys. "It's good to know where your woman is, Bill."

"You don't?"

He wagged his head. "Doubt I ever will now. She gave up on waiting for me. Went back to her folks and the life she lived before coming west."

Bill shrugged. "What do you expect a woman to do?"

Seamus nodded. "Can't blame her."

"She gets scared, Seamus—she runs back to those she remembers protecting her."

"Like your Lulu."

"Yes," he sighed. "She doesn't belong out here— not yet. Not till I can build a decent home for her and the girl."

"Where you want that to be?"

"Don't know. So for now, I ride across these plains, doing what a man has to do to make a living. And she lives with her family back East—where we both know it's safe."

"Yet I wonder, Bill—is there truly any place safe?"

Cody thought on it, the way a bear would cock its head over the burrow of some animal it was hunting. Listening. Hoping for some sign to continue its pursuit.

"No place truly safe, Irishman. I only hope to find a place for those I love where they can be safer than the way of things out here."

"Injins?"

"Them, and . . . others."

"You don't fear for them as much from Injins as you do other white men, do you?"

"I know what to count on with an Indian, Seamus. It's the white man that keeps me wondering some—"

When Cody stopped talking mid-sentence, it snagged Donegan's attention as if it had been yanked hard with a rope knotted around his middle. The young scout ahead threw up an arm as he reined back. He pointed.

Both strained their eyes ahead, across San Francisco Creek. Finally seeing something to go with the faint noise that had been brought to their ears. The sound of hooves on old, icy snow. And the low, mumbling voices of man.

"Look at them, will you?" Cody said in a whisper, certain at last the two white men had not been spotted.

"Who are they? And what they doing out here?"

Bill snorted. "Don't you figure it, Irishman?"

He shook his head. "I see two men bundled on horses."

"But them ain't Indian ponies, are they?"

"No, they aren't." Then it struck him, with the way the two riders were bundled against the cold and hunkered down in the saddle, allowing their big horses to pick their way along the creekbank and snowdrifts. "Are they scouts from Penrose's column?"

He nodded, grinning. "I don't doubt it, Irishman! Damn, but won't the general be happy now?"

Cody turned back in the saddle, looking down the slope at the two riders as they drew nearer, unaware they were watched. Until the young scouts called out.

"Halloo!"

Both riders suddenly jerked back on their reins as they sat up straight in their saddles, heads turning like wind-up toys on a string, this way then that while Cody's greeting echoed off the hills. They were pulling up the rifles suspended from slings strapped over their shoulders.

"Don't shoot, boys!" Donegan hollered out this time.

"Over here!" Cody said, waving his big hat.

"Let's go talk," Seamus suggested, nudging his horse past Cody's.

The creek gurgled under their horses' bellies in an icy flow as the animals carefully stepped across the rocky bottom. By the time they reached the other side, the two buffalo soldiers were coming down to the crossing.

"Buffalo Bill! I'll be damned, if this don't beat all!" exclaimed one of the black soldiers. "You riding with Ginnel Carr?"

"That's right!" Cody replied. "We're out looking for—"

"You got a nickname, Cody?" Donegan whispered, looking with wonder at his white companion.

"Seems I got one now. And, if you ask me—I take a fancy to it."

"That's right, Buffalo Bill," the first soldier said. "I see'd you shoot a bunch of buffalo up to Fort Hays last year. You was working for the railroad."

"Damn if I wasn't. *Buffalo Bill*—got a nice ring to it, don't it, Seamus?"

The first buffalo soldier got wide-eyed of an instant, cranking his head to look at the Irishman. "Seamus—that what he called you?"

"Yeah," Cody replied.

Donegan's eyes narrowed, studying the black soldier's face as he pulled down the wool muffler he had wrapped around his own. "By the saints! If it ain't Reuben Waller himself!"

"Gloreee!" Waller screeched, kicking a right leg over to leap from his saddle.

Donegan dropped to the ground in the next heartbeat, lunging for the buffalo soldier. They met with a thud, pounding each other and dancing about in a cascade of snow, heads reared back and laughing with a sound that spooked some robber jays from the branches overhead.

"I take it you boys know each other?"

Seamus stopped, one arm still clutched around Waller. "Bill, this man probably saw you shoot buffalo last year, before I ever ran onto him at Fort Wallace last fall. I kept some white sojurs from jobbing on him."

Waller grinned, the teeth bright in his dark face. "He kept them white soldiers from kicking the shit outta ol' Reuben. Likely they would'a done more'n pound sand up my ass—this tall, ugly Irishman didn't come along to help me."

Cody sat hunched over the saddlehorn, watching the reunion. "Don't that beat all? Out here in the middle of all this, and you bump into a old friend. I'm Bill Cody." He pulled off a mitten and held down a hand.

Waller shook it enthusiastically. "Proud to make your 'quaintance, Buffalo Bill. This other'n's Silas. Private Rutt."

The second soldier nodded and saluted the white men.

Seamus pounded Waller on the back again. "Reuben was in the bunch rescued Forsyth's scouts, Bill."

"Captain Carpenter's orderly, I was."

"Was?"

"T've been assigned to Ginnel Penrose for this winter campaign."

"I knew it!" Cody cried. "Where's Penrose?"

Waller waved down San Francisco Creek.

"How far?"

"We been out since yesterday morning," Waller answered.

"Penrose is staying in camp—not moving?"

"Just squatting," Waller replied. "He's sent out patrols to comb the country every day, looking for Carr."

Donegan turned to the buffalo soldier. "How you fared with Penrose, Reuben?"

"Two hundred head of horses froze on us. No, none of us done good at all."

"Down to quarter rations," added Silas Rutt.

"Mither of God!" Seamus exclaimed, twisting 'round and tearing at his saddlebags. "Get these sojurs some food."

As Waller and Rutt lunged close, the two white

scouts pulled hardtack and salt-pork from their own supplies.

"I suppose we can go without till we get back to Carr," Cody added cheerfully.

Donegan grinned, watching the two hungry soldiers wolf down everything laid in their hands. "Damn right if we can, Buffalo Bill!"

After retracing their trail back to Carr's column, carrying word of Penrose's condition, Cody, Donegan, and the two buffalo soldiers prepared to move back down San Francisco Creek once more.

Carr dispatched Captain William H. Brown and two companies of the Fifth to push ahead, accompanied by fifty pack-mules swaybacked with provisions. The senior major would hurry the rest of the command and his wagons as fast as the snowbound countryside would allow.

But for the meantime, Cody would lead the relief column hurrying to lift the specter of starvation from Penrose's buffalo soldiers.

Two days after running across Waller and Rutt, Bill Cody located the bleak, cheerless camp on Paloduro Creek. Despair-filled, watery-eyed buffalo soldiers loped out to greet their saviors. They hollered with weak, hoarse voices at their deliverance.

"Makes me proud to return the favor I owed you," Seamus whispered to Waller, who rode at the Irishman's side into camp. "After you and Carpenter's boys rescued those of us on that island with Forsyth.* Time I repaid—"

"Hell, you don't owe me a damned thing," Waller

---

* The Plainsmen Series, vol. 3, *The Stalkers*

replied. "I was never more proud to do anything in my life than I was riding with Cap'n Carpenter's company that day—fixin' to fight our way into some Cheyennes—then finding what bad shape you fellas was in on Beecher's Island."

"We held out. Looks like your sojurs did the same here, Reuben."

It was the best a man could say about Penrose's soldiers—that they held out. Skinny and growing more emaciated by the day, they had been on quarter rations for over two weeks, supplementing it with some stringy mule or horse from the few carcasses left in camp. It was plain to see the buffalo soldiers were hungry most for grease—the salt-pork and bacon would do nicely they said as they lunged at the crates of rations like packs of wolves. Mess sergeants stood on the backs of their wagons, tossing out the hard bread to tide both Negro soldiers and the hard-bitten Mexican trackers over until beans and bacon had been cooked.

And coffee. One of the soldiers hollered out in his weakened, husky voice for some hot coffee.

"I could go for a cup myself," Cody said, sliding from his saddle at the fire Waller chose for their mess.

"You drink about as much coffee as I do, Cody."

At a nearby fire a gaunt figure turned around to stare back at them, his wide-eyed, skinny face filled with wonder. His mouth yawed a moment before any words came out.

"Cody? That you?"

Bill Cody stopped punching up the coals at his own fire and stared back at the wolfish figure standing not twenty feet away. A white man he was—

dressed in a long buffalo coat that nearly reached the ground, atop it all a cap fashioned from the hide of a wolf snugged clear down to his eyebrows. From the bottom of the cap poured the man's long, dark hair, spilling over his shoulders.

"Bill?"

"Yeah—it's me, Cody."

They rushed each other, hugging and pounding on one another as much as the weakened white man could take before he drew himself back.

"Let me take a good look at you, Cody."

"Ain't been all that long, Bill."

He wagged his head. "Didn't know . . . if we'd make it."

"How you get mixed up with these brunettes?"

The dark-haired man smiled, his teeth big in his shrunken face. "I'm scouting again. Like I done for Hancock and Custer last summer. Sheridan put me to work for Penrose, working out of Fort Lyon. And you're scouting for Carr."

"Damn, if this ain't good news. Say, I've got an Irishman you've got to meet. C'mon over here, Seamus."

Donegan strode over, holding out his big paw.

"Seamus—want you to meet a fella smells almost as bad as you. Seamus Donegan, recent of Beecher Island, like you to meet an old friend of mine— James Butler Hickok."

"Cody called you Bill?"

"That's what folks call me mostly: Bill Hickok."

Cody smiled, inching between them to slap both men on the shoulder.

Chapter 8

January 1869

"Keep your eyes open for any sign of Evans," said Major Eugene Carr to his chief of scouts when Cody settled to his saddle. "He's bound to be operating anywhere here on the Canadian."

Back on 30 December, when Carr reached Penrose's camp on the Paloduro, he had immediately unloaded his wagons to establish a supply base. The following day the major turned Wilson's civilians and their wagons back to Fort Lyon for more supplies. Through the next week, Carr and Penrose recuperated their outfits, readying them to continue the winter campaign. From both wings they chose five hundred of the strongest men, in addition to selecting the best of the surviving horses. Without the wagons, the soldiers outfitted a train of pack-mules to accompany the expedition. Those soldiers remaining behind would garrison the supply camp on Paloduro Creek.

On the seventh of January a dispatch rider came

in with news from Fort Lyon that the main column under George Armstrong Custer had struck the Cheyenne of Black Kettle in their Washita River camp back at the end of November. Other dispatches from Kansas stated that Custer's regiment was at that point driving the Kiowa, along with more bands of hostile Cheyenne, back to their reservation at Fort Cobb.

The day after those dispatches arrived, Carr led his handpicked five hundred away from Camp Carr, heading south toward the Canadian River in Texas, only forty miles away, hoping to find some sign of Major Andrew W. Evans, who was reportedly working his way east out of Fort Bascomb in New Mexico as the second arm of Sheridan's pincer movement to aid Custer's attack on the Cheyenne. Rumor out of Kansas had it that back on Christmas Day the Evans column had struck a large band of Comanches camped at Soldier Springs on the North Fork of the Red River.

The Fifth Cavalry was drawing close to the center of the action.

For three days now Carr had relentlessly pushed his men south under clear, cold skies of the new year. Nearing their goal, Cody and his advance scout reined up, awaiting Major Carr.

"To a Mexican, that's the Rio Colorado down there, General," the scout explained.

"The Canadian to us, Cody?"

"Right. Not far downstream, you'll find a place called Adobe Walls."

"A town? Out here?" Donegan asked.

Cody laughed lightly. "Hell no. Nothing more than a group of low-roofed, mud buildings that leak when it rains or snows. Sometimes used by buffalo hunters."

"I take it you've been there, Cody?" Carr inquired.

"I hunt buffalo, General."

"Right now, how about hunting us a campsite. Sun's fixing to go down."

"Have your advance follow my trail down into the valley. C'mon, Irishman."

Donegan nudged the big mare into an easy lope behind Cody as they broke off the top of that hill. Down into the cottonwood and scrub timber they pushed, searching for suitable grazing for the many animals, enough open ground for so many men.

"Look up there, Bill," Donegan whispered, his eyes catching some movement just below the skyline of the ridge on the far side of the river.

"They look like scouts, don't they?"

"Ain't dressed like sojurs. You figure those three for Evans's scouts?"

"Yep. Let's go pay our respects."

Cody took the lead, fording the icy river. From midstream they watched the trio halt as if they had spotted the two horsemen below in the valley. Donegan took the big hat from his head and waved it back and forth at the end of his arm. One of the three on the hill did the same before pushing their horses on down the slope.

"You boys with Evans?" Cody hollered out as they closed on fifty yards.

"That's right," answered one of the three. "Sure hope you fellas are from Fort Union."

Cody and Donegan glanced at one another, reining up as the trio halted before them.

"No," the Irishman answered.

"We're from Major Carr's outfit—Fifth Cavalry," Cody replied. "You expecting a supply train from Fort Union?"

The scout laughed lustily, glancing at the two on either side of him. "Hell, more'n supplies. Major Evans is expecting a bull-train loaded down with Mexican beer. Something he's been promising us ever since Christmas Day when we routed them Comanch' at Soldier Springs."

Donegan glanced at Cody, finding in the young scout's eyes the first flickers of some mischief. "You said beer?"

"Yeah—Mexican beer."

"Never had any meself. Have you, Cody?"

"A time or two," and he licked his lips as a dry wind tousled his blond curls. "You say your supply train's coming in from Fort Union?"

"We figured we would find 'em coming in along the Canadian," the scout answered. "Major's gonna be disappointed to hear you ain't scouts leading that beer to his outfit."

Cody winked at Donegan. "I can understand the man's disappointment—what with you fellas stuck way out here, waiting for that beer all this time. Sure sorry I had to be the one to disappoint you."

"Where's Carr?"

Cody pointed. "Coming over the hill now."

"We'll ride back and tell Evans about your column. You're making camp?"

"Downstream a bit. How far is your camp?"

The scout pointed. "No more'n twelve miles on down the river. Place already named Fort Evans."

"Twelve miles, you say?" Cody replied, thoughtfully gazing upstream. "Ain't far a'tall." He turned back to the scout, nodded and tipped his hat. "We'll sure keep a lookout for that beer train of yours."

" 'Preciate that, fellas. Evans got a lot of thirsty soldiers."

"I'll bet you boys are just as thirsty as them sojurs!" Donegan said.

The three reined about to head back to the Evans camp as the leader said, "Shit, I was born thirsty!"

Seamus watched the trio disappear into the timber before he turned to Cody. "Are you thinking what I think you're thinking?"

Cody smiled, wiping his glove across his mouth, then licking his lips. "You're sure the confusing one, Irishman. All I'm thinking about is you, me and Hickok having us a draft or two of that Mexican beer. I figure Carr's soldiers deserve that shipment more'n those quartermasters running high-roll downstream at Fort Evans."

"By the saints! I was sure hoping you was thinking hard on that beer."

"Well, then—what are we waiting for? Let's find us a camp for the general . . . so the three of us can get down to the business."

"Business?"

"Planning how we're gonna get our hands on that Mexican beer bound for Evans's boys!"

"What the hell good are those greasers with Penrose anyway?" Bill Cody asked of Hickok.

Along with Seamus Donegan, the two of them were crouched in the willows thick along the bank of the Rio Colorado, watching upstream for the approach of the bull train from Fort Union. The beer it hauled would be a welcome diversion for the disappointed winter campaigners. While both Evans and Custer had gone into action and put victories under their belts, the Carr-Penrose command had yet to see a red hide or hint of a feather.

Hickok wagged his head, then gave his grudging compliment. "About all the good they were is knowing some of this country. Still, I ain't got no stomach for the sons of bitches."

"No better'n you know it," Cody sneered. "Mark my words, Bill—them greasers gonna be trouble for you."

"They already are," Hickok grumped. "They been wanting to crawl my hump ever since leaving Fort Lyon. I just stay away from 'em. Let 'em alone."

"That works as long as they leave you be," Cody said.

"But they ain't."

"You need to kick the sun out of 'em, sounds like," Donegan finally whispered.

"It's coming to that, Irishman. They keep pushing —one of these days, I'll push back."

Seamus patted the dark-haired scout on the shoulder. "Call me if you want my help, Hickok."

Hickok looked at Cody, smiling. "You imagine anybody getting in a fight and turning down the help of this big ox of an Irishman?"

"Sure as hell glad he's on our side, Hickok," Cody cheered, jabbing a glove at Seamus.

"In fighting . . . or fun," Hickok whispered. "Ho —here they come."

From upstream came the sounds of teamsters and bull-whackers, urging their animals and wagons down the Canadian. Without a word the three scouts rose, went to saddle, and pushed their horses from the timber.

"Halloo!" Hickok called out, throwing up an arm as soon as the scouts could be seen by the teamsters.

"Howdy!" yelled a horseman riding alongside the first team. He threw up his arm as well, putting the teamsters to their brakes. He loped his mount on up to the trio.

"You got the beer from Union?" Cody asked.

He smiled. "We do, by golly. You three must be from Evans's outfit."

"Been waiting on that beer for some time, we have," Cody replied, without lying.

"Bet you have," the outrider answered. "Only thing good about this trip is getting my money and getting back to Union to spend it."

"Sure as hell can't spend it out here, can you?" Hickok asked, grinning.

He wagged his head. "That's for damned sure, son. Way out here."

"Army paying for the beer you're hauling?"

The rider looked at the three, sort of curious a moment. "Now, that's a funny question to be asking. Don't Evans know?"

"He does," Donegan answered. "But we don't."

"You boys here to guide me into your camp, aren't you?"

"We're here for the beer, mister. You been paid for your trip?"

The man studied Hickok real carefully. "I will be, soon as I get back to Union. Now, why don't you boys lead us on in to Evans's supply camp."

"We was just hoping to save you some miles, mister," Cody said, smiling engagingly.

"Save me miles?"

"Let you drop off the beer just a couple miles up the road."

"That Evans's camp?"

"No, his camp—the main camp—is still some fourteen miles on downstream."

"Why you want me to drop the beer off closer?"

"Let's say you'll make one bunch of soldiers real happy you did."

The wagonmaster shook his head, then looked back at his bull-teams as he chewed on a lip. "Long as it's a soldier camp—I done my job, I suppose," he finally muttered. "Whyn't you fellas lead on. I could use a drink myself."

"I'll bet coffee would be the best thing for you right now," Cody replied as the wagons were set in motion again.

"Coffee, hell! The weather may be cold, son—but I'm wanting to wash my gullet with some of that Mexican beer. Strongest mule piss this side of the Rio Grande, I'll tell you!"

"That's what I like to hear," Hickok replied.

"Been doing any good chasing them damned In-juns, fellas?" the wagonmaster asked.

"Not a dried tit's worth of good, mister," Cody answered. "This beer is bound to cheer the place up."

Which is exactly what it did.

After unloading the beer kegs near the mess wag-ons, Carr's men began lining up, ready to buy the beer from Cody a pint at a time with their huge tin cups in hand. But, as luck would have it, the beer was too cold for a man to drink that frosty winter's afternoon. Cody and Hickok quickly put some picket-pins in the mess fires and heated them till they glowed. When these were dashed into the huge pint cups, the beer was warmed enough to give every happy soldier a toasty glow in his belly.

"Been a pleasure doing business with you," said the wagonmaster as he strode up later that afternoon, his hand extended.

"This has turned into one helluva jollification," Cody said, smiling, hoisting his cup as he patted his pocket, newly filled with army scrip from this windfall.

"We'll stay the night, boys—and start back in the morning."

"You're welcome to stay as long as you want, mister," Hickok replied. "I'm never inhospitable when it comes to a man freighting the beer!"

"I'd like to shake hands with Major Evans," said the wagonmaster quietly. "You point him out."

"He ain't here," Cody answered, trying hard to keep from laughing.

"Out on patrol?"

"No," Donegan answered, more able than the other two thieves to keep a straight face. "I suppose Major Evans is back in his camp."

"His . . . his camp?"

Seamus threw a thumb over his shoulder. "About twelve miles, downstream."

"This . . . you mean to tell me . . . you're not Evans's men?"

"No, mister—we ain't!" Cody sputtered.

"But," Hickok grabbed the wagonmaster's arm, pulling him away from the kegs, "we would like to introduce you to Major Eugene Carr—of the Fifth Cavalry."

"Is he the one put you up to this—this hijacking my cargo?" fumed the wagonmaster.

Cody shook his head. "No, General Carr had no part in this. But you'll be paid by the army when you get back, won't you?"

He squared his shoulders and shrugged Hickok loose. "I will—you can bet on that."

"And the beer went to soldiers, didn't it?" Cody asked, pointing out the happy troopers gathered at their fires, singing and laughing.

The teamster nodded his head reluctantly. "I suppose it did at that."

"Then what's all the fuss?" Hickok asked.

The man finally smiled, then swung a big hand and clapped Cody on the back. "Not a goddamned thing, boys! Not everyday three young whelps like you hijack an army quartermaster shipment—and get away with it! What's for dinner!"

Chapter 9

Late January 1869

"*You* greasers are women!" Hickok shouted out the worst, profane Indian curse he could think of, his voice ringing off the rafters of the campaign sutler's high-walled tent. "Your bowels will run cold as winter rain afore I get through with you."

"We'll cut you, Hickok! Then you run with blood," shouted the biggest of the fifteen Mexicans arrayed against the three white scouts. "The same will do for your friends."

Bill Cody had been waiting for this to happen for some time. At long last the Mexican trackers had tired of Hickok's slurs—being treated with laughter and derision. For the past three weeks Hickok had been watching his back. It seemed both sides had known that one day would come the reckoning that was now at hand.

"You are water-hearted women!" Cody swore. "The spirits scowled on the day your bunch was born. And it'll be your blood we'll spill on this dust today."

The big Mexican grinned, glancing over his companions. "Eh, there are five of us to every one of you gringos."

Cody bared his teeth. "Then it looks like we're even on the odds, you yellow-hearted bastard."

The Mexican's big knife flashed into the play of sunlight and muted shadow that was the high-walled tent erected by the sutler here at Camp Carr. It had been an unproductive winter. Freezing weather, swallowing snowdrifts, and no Indian fighting to relieve the boredom of bad food and rampant scurvy among the soldiers. For weeks the bad blood had festered simply because the antagonists brooded on nothing else.

Licking wounds over imagined insults, planning revenge and ambush and assault, until the kettle finally boiled over and the sauce hit the fire.

"Knives, is it?" Hickok dragged a big blade from his belt scabbard.

"A man dies slow from a hundred knife wounds, Hickok," replied a second Mexican scout.

"I say we clean out this nest of vipers with hand-guns," Cody whispered to his partners.

"No time for cheap poker, Bill," Hickok replied, "we've got to throw ourselves a decent hand this time out."

"Playing blades with this bunch will get us all killed," Cody hissed.

"Stop the talk!" ordered the Mexican leader. "Time to bleed, gringos."

"You boys must be afraid," Donegan said, suddenly stepping ahead of Cody and Hickok, glaring back at the pack of Mexicans. "To have fifteen to three odds . . . and still you pull them knives. What's the matter with you? Are you not men? Are you afraid to fight us with your fists?" He brought a clenched one up right beneath the Mexican's nose.

The man's dark, marblelike eyes narrowed, the thick black eyebrows beetling together as they bore into the Irishman. It seemed as if he were weighing things a moment.

"All right, gringo. You are right. We do not need knives. We will tear you apart with our bare hands —slowly."

Cody felt something sigh with relief inside him at that, and then watched the big Irishman's shoulders tense as his right arm moved in a flash, like light in a mirror. Pop, crack, thud—three blows so fast that the biggest of the Mexicans fell back against his companions, his nose spurting blood, an eyelid instantly puffing. He was out as cold as a beaver dam in winter.

Some of the others caught their leader while a handful poured around his crumbling body, swallowing the Irishman whole.

"Seamus has gone and pulled the cork out of the jug for us!" Hickok howled. "Let's help!"

Cody and Hickok leaped into the fray, pulling aside a few of the Mexicans, flaying away with their practiced fists, quickly working their way into the midst of them all to reach the Irishman. Donegan was almost flattened by the weight of bodies bearing down atop him. With a heave here and a shove there, the two freed Seamus momentarily from the mob. Donegan's face was slicked with blood, red as boiled jam. Cuts above his eyes and one on each cheek. His nose puffy and seeping.

"Back to back!" Hickok shouted amid the cursing and grunting, the cries of pain and howls of frustration.

The three of them backed against one another, continuing to lash out: jabbing with the lefts and swinging wide and powerfully with the rights. Giving the Mexicans an honest thrubbing. Twelve, then eleven stood against them. Eight then seven. And finally the remaining four decided they had all had enough and dragged their wounded away. Cursing, jabbering, swearing that there would come a new day of reckoning yet as they left the tent.

Cody stood there, weak, his legs going out like wet burlap rags. He stumbled forward two steps then reclaimed his balance.

"You all right, Bill?" Donegan asked, catching the young scout.

Cody looked into the Irishman's face. "You're a sight, you are now." He glanced at Hickok's. Both had split, puffy lips, bloodied eyes, and were frothing blood from the corners of their mouths. Cuts oozed along the hairline. "You too, Hickok."

"Can't be nowhere as beat as you, Cody," Hickok replied.

"I think this calls for a drink," Donegan suggested quietly, volving a shoulder that made him wince with pain.

"I damn well don't believe it," muttered the sutler himself as he came up from hiding. He stood behind the makeshift keg and plank bar, slapping a hewn timber across a palm.

"You damn well saw it with your own eyes, didn't

you?" Donegan said as he collapsed against the bar, raking a dirty cup into his hand and presenting it to the sutler.

"I know I saw it with my own damned eyes, Irishman—but I still can't believe it. Fifteen of them blood-eyed greasers again' the three of you. Jeezuz Keerist, that was some pounding you boys took before you run them off."

Cody felt the pain burn through his shoulder and into his neck, only now going numb at last. As if one of the Mexicans had used a club to work over his back in the middle of the melee. He looked down at Donegan's leg, finding the faded blue cavalry britches slick with blood.

"All of that ain't the Mexicans'."

Donegan looked down a minute, prancing gingerly, afraid to put a lot of weight on the leg.

"Damn, but you're bleeding still, Irishman," Hickok said, ripping the greasy bandanna from his neck and offering it to Seamus.

"One of the bastirds must've stuck me right in the beginning—when I was a bit too busy to notice."

"Best we get someone to have a look at that."

"They just got the meat of me. If the Sioux and Cheyenne can't put me under—it's for sure that bunch can't."

"C'mon—let's round up the surgeon . . . let him have a look at that leg."

"I won't let anyone sew on me."

"What'd they do on your back in the war when you were carved up so fierce?" Hickok asked.

Donegan smiled, threw back his whiskey and then looped an arm each around the two men as they helped him away from the bar. "Let's not talk about them plucky army surgeons who loved to wager which of them would make the biggest pile of arms and legs and mortified limbs even before the battle's half done."

"That'd be something, wouldn't it, Bill?" Cody asked Hickok as they pushed their way out through the tent flaps. "Piles of amputated limbs."

"Just where the hell are you three reprobates headed?" bellowed Eugene Carr as he hurried up, surrounded by some of his staff and the officer of the guard.

"Funny thing, but I got an idea you already know what's going on, General," Cody replied.

The major stopped right in their path, looked down at Donegan's leg and wagged his head. "The three of you going to get yourselves gutted yet—if not hung."

"Not if we have any say about it, sir," Donegan said in his most contrite of tones.

"Been anyone else, Major Andrew Evans had you hung from a tree for pilfering his shipment of beer. And now they come running to me—saying the three of you've gone and picked a fight with Penrose's Mexicans."

"I'm right behind you, General," growled Captain Penrose as he came up on the gathering. "Hickok, I suppose you and these two with you can explain why I've got over a dozen bloodied, cursing Mexicans in my camp, swearing they won't work another day for me?"

"A dozen?" Carr asked of Penrose.

"Yes, Major."

"More like fifteen of 'em," Cody replied.

Carr wagged his head, his grin growing bigger despite himself.

Finally Penrose threw up his hands, exasperated. "You best stay out of our camp for a while, Hickok." He turned to Carr. "Whatever you decide for punishment, General. They're in your hands now."

Penrose turned on his heel and hurried off, muttering to himself.

"For some time, seems to me the three of you haven't had enough to do," Carr began.

"You've had us sitting on our hands here in camp —no scouting to be—"

"And the three of you are always partaking too freely in the tanglefoot," the major pressed ahead. "So, instead of scouting for the army —you three are going to turn over a new leaf starting at sunrise tomorrow. As for you, Hickok . . . you'll be kept busy carrying dispatches between here and Fort Lyon.

"Major—"

Carr waved off his objection, immediately turning on Cody. "I'm making hunters out of you two—putting you both in charge of keeping my command supplied with game."

"But, General—"

"Cody, you three listen and listen to me good: there's plenty of antelope in this country, and you two will damn well do some hunting every day while we're still sitting in this camp and Hickok's away. The men of my command are suffering from scurvy—and the fresh meat will help. Now do it—or you can forget about ever riding back to Fort Lyon with me to collect your pay for this campaign."

Cody gazed at Hickok, then Donegan, and finally

shrugged. "General, we was on the way to wrap up
the Irishman's leg. He'll be needing it . . . especially come morning when Hickok leaves for Lyon,
and the two of us go out hunting."

The coffee-skinned mulatto brooded over his pep-
pered whiskey, eyeing the motley gathering of dirty
soldiers, buffalo hunters, teamsters and assorted
prairie riffraff that had gathered in the low-roofed
sutler's hut here at Fort Lyon to weather out the late
winter blizzard ravaging the central plains. He eyed
them carefully just to be certain he hadn't missed
the man he was looking for.

Jack O'Neill kept the wolf-hide cap pulled down
to the bridge of his nose. Time would come his eyebrows would grow back. Right now they were more
like stubby whiskers. Eyebrows plucked, every fa-
cial hair pulled from his skin with bone tweezers
during those moons he spent with the Cheyenne of
Two Crows and Roman Nose. But now he was back
among the white man.

From what he remembered the sutler telling him
when he rolled in here two days ago, it was early
February. O'Neill would have to get used to that
once more—thinking like a white man. A few times
he had caught himself slipping into the singsong
guttural talk of the Cheyenne tongue. Even asking
what moon it was instead of month. He didn't want
to give anything away.

From Fort Hays to Wallace, and now down to this
mud-walled post on the Arkansas River. Tracking
the killer of Roman Nose as he vowed he would that
summer evening when the mighty Cheyenne chief
died, with a shattered spine, legs useless forever

more. Now O'Neill followed the faint trail of an unknown Irishman. The powerful vision that had visited Nibsi, the black Cheyenne warrior, clearly showed O'Neill that he would find reckoning with the gray-eyed one by still water. Yet as time passed, O'Neill found he would not be able to kill the tall, gray-eyed one at Hays beside Big Creek, at Wallace on the Smoky Hill River, or at Lyon on the Arkansas.

Still water.

Jack had followed the bits of news to Fort Wallace, asking the whereabouts of the scouts who had fought against the Cheyenne in September. But there at Wallace the trail went cold again. The sutler heard that a soldier named Pepoon had command of the outfit now, and they had been ordered last fall into The Territories with Custer's regiment. Word had it the whole bunch of them were working out of a place called Camp Supply, due south from Fort Dodge.

Jack O'Neill knew where Fort Dodge was. And he could wait there if he had to, until the white scouts under Lieutenant Pepoon returned from waging war on the Kiowa and Southern Cheyenne. But the unexpected blizzard roared in about the time he was fixing to light out.

Which put him in a very sour humor. Another delay, having to suffer the curious, sharp-edged glares of the reeking white men who peopled this mud hovel, rubbing up against him and laughing at his expense. He would always be nothing more than a high yellow no matter where he went—except among his adopted people, the Shahiyena.

Soon enough, he would find the scouts. And get

his hands on the gray-eyed one. The Irishman, he was called. Jack didn't know what an Irishman was just yet.

But he figured he would come to know in time. And when he had returned to his adopted village of Dog Soldiers, now commanded by Tall Bull, Nibsi would be there, would revel in telling the copper-skinned women he laid with of how that gray-eyed Irishman died.

Carr led his Fifth Cavalry back to Fort Lyon on 19 February, the entire unit heroically surviving a seventy-five-mile march in twenty-six hours during a blinding snowstorm to do it. They had accomplished just what Phil Sheridan had wanted them to: prevented the hostiles from fleeing when the general's favorite, George Armstrong Custer, came marching after them with his glory-shrouded Seventh Cavalry.

With Hickok gone cross-country to Fort Lyon carrying dispatches, and Donegan forbidden by the surgeon to put weight on the bad leg, much less ride in an exhausting hunt, Cody had taken up the lonely task with relish. He was given command of twenty of Wilson's wagons and teamsters, along with twenty of Penrose's infantry to serve as butchers. For the first four days not so much as the white fluff of an antelope was sighted, and spirits in Cody's small command grew dim.

But on the fifth day, Cody struck the mother lode —a buffalo herd. Best thing about hunting at that time of year, the animals were not pursued much, so it proved easy to stampede them for a few miles until a portion of the herd spilled into a deep coulee

filled with old snow. While the buffalo floundered
and snorted, pawed and bellowed, Cody went to
work with his powerful infantry "Long Tom"
Springfield. Fifty-five were killed that day. The next
morning he went out again to track down the herd
and killed another forty-one buffalo, running two
horses out from under him in the process.

For the next two days the infantry soldiers labored skinning and butchering, sending wagons
heaped with the rich meat back to Camp Carr. It
was fortunate that they had trouble keeping up with
Cody's amazing marksmanship, for the young
scout's right shoulder and arm had become so
bruised from the beating the rifle had given it that
he needed help each morning to pull on his coat,
each evening to pull it off him.

Yet he managed to keep Carr's cavalry fed on that
long march back to Fort Lyon, while Donegan
slowly healed. At the Arkansas River post they
watched Hickok depart east with Penrose. Awarded
leave by Major Carr two days later, Cody and the
Irishman moved on north to Fort Wallace without
the Fifth Cavalry.

"I suppose this is farewell, Bill," Seamus said,
holding out his hand.

The pair of them stood on the plank walk outside
Walt Mason's hotel and saloon establishment in
Sheridan, Kansas, thirteen miles northeast from
Fort Wallace. In giving the civilian scouts some
leave back at Fort Lyon, Carr had warned them to
keep their noses clean until spring. Cody promised
he would, since he had no other choice, he joked.
He was journeying east to visit his wife Lulu and
young daughter Arta.

"For but a short time, Irishman. I figure we'll have our hands full spring green-up."

"When the Injin ponies grow full of sass and vinegar, eh?"

Cody nodded, climbing the steps into the lone passenger railcar. "My mules I left with Mason. He'll keep 'em here till I can get 'em back to Carr's outfit."

The young scout stood there at the end of the car, tugging his hat down against a cruel wind. "You'll be here to ride with me come green-up, Irishman?"

Donegan grinned, smoothing his Vandyke beard as he stepped back from the edge of the depot landing. "I'll be here. Chances are we'll find us some more trouble to get ourselves into—Injins or whiskey one."

Cody waved as he turned through the open car doorway. "Like I said when we first met: I knew I'd like you, Seamus Donegan. Knew I'd like you a lot."

Chapter 10

Late March 1869

*B*efore Bill Cody had departed Fort Lyon on 26 February, traveling back east by way of Fort Wallace and Sheridan, Kansas, Major Eugene Carr gave written orders to his quartermaster, Lieutenant Alfred B. Taylor, to employ William F. Cody as scout at the rate of $125 per month, dating back to 5 October 1868. The effect of this order was plain. Not only was Carr allowing his scout some leave from service at a time when the general army practice was to dismiss scouts at the termination of a campaign, but the major was giving young Cody a fifty dollar per month raise as well.

Carr plainly wanted Cody back.

Problem was, Cody's return to the plains would not be without its knotty problems.

His curly blond hair had grown so long by the time he arrived in St. Louis that his young wife, Lulu, did not recognize him at first. Eager for the homecoming, he had bolted through the door of her parents' home. Upstairs, she had recognized the commanding stomp of his gait on the entry floor. But when she swept into the parlor where he awaited her, she found a tall, deeply tanned young plainsman she could not at first claim to know. The hair falling past his shoulders, the blond Vandyke beard, those leather britches and fringed coat—it all took some getting used to for Lulu.

But now, weeks later, as Bill Cody stepped off the Kansas-Pacific Railroad at its terminus in Sheridan, the young scout remembered how little daughter Arta had instantly recognized her papa. During his brief return from the plains, she bounced each day on his knee as he sang bawdy cavalry songs. Or, she giggled gaily as he lumbered about the house on all fours, carrying her on his back pony-fashion, bucking and snorting. Dear little Arta, the pride of Bill Cody's heart.

"Ho, Mason!" he called out, shoving through the door to Walt Mason's saloon in Sheridan. Much as he missed his wife and child, it was good to be back in the places he knew best.

"Cody? That really you?"

He threw down the carpet valise and held out his hand. "First a shake—then fill my hand with some whiskey. I've been dry a month!"

"You don't drink in front of your wife?"

He shook his head as he took the glass from Mason. "Never have. Doubt I ever will." Cody tossed it back, then brought the glass down. "Another—I'm dry as a prairie wind."

"That first one is on me, Cody." Mason sighed, his face screwing up. "You'll need it—with what I've got to tell you."

His eyes narrowed. "Dust it off, Mason."

"You know the quartermaster at Fort Wallace keeps a civilian agent on employ here in town—to watch over shipments coming in at the railhead, supplies and larder and such."

"I know, I know," he said impatiently, pushing his glass forward for a third tall shot. "What's this got to do with me, Walt?"

"Not long after you left town for St. Louis, the quartermaster's agent came snooping around my yard and found that army horse and mule you left with me—to care for while you were gone."

"What of it?"

"The son of a bitch claimed you was supposed to leave them animals with him at the quartermaster's corral down at the end of town."

Cody scratched at his beard. "Was I supposed to do that?"

Mason straightened, growing red from the neck up. "You messed this up something good, Cody— and got that agent stirred up enough to go running off to Wallace, telling the army that you sold me them animals!"

"Sold 'em to you?"

"That's right. I told the agent he was all wrong, but he didn't want to listen, so he run off down there and told the quartermaster—fella named Lauffer—and Colonel Bankhead too—that you gone off to St. Louis after stealing army property and selling it for a profit."

"Goddamn, that bastard!" Cody roared, wiping droplets from his mustache with a sleeve. "So what happened—the animals still here?"

"No, dammit! Bankhead sent some of his boys up

here to seize the horse and mule from me—they come in here all full of bluster."

"This all on account of that weasel-eyed agent squatting down the street in his army office, right?"

Mason nodded. "You got the picture."

"Pour me 'nother, Walt. And don't be shy on keeping the bottle handy." He picked up his valise and slung it to the top of the bar. He reached inside his vest and slapped down a single-eagle. "Here, while you're at it—go store my things in one of your best rooms. I'll be back shortly, and I'll want a bed with clean sheets on it for the night. Maybe longer."

By the time he had stepped out into the cold, bitter wind scuttling between the blank-faced buildings, and had crossed the muddy, rutted street, Bill Cody was feeling mighty warm inside. A generous but potent mix of whiskey and anger, and not a little singed pride as well.

He nearly threw the door off its hinges as he stormed into the small office warmed by a glowing sheet-iron stove in the corner. Near it, behind a small table littered with paper and ledgers, a wiry man sat hunched over his books. The bald spot at the back of the civilian's head was the most remarkable thing about the man, since that spot was the first thing Cody saw, until the clerk tore his eyes from his accounts and focused on the tall, blond plainsman.

"You the goddamned quartermaster agent for Wallace?"

"Who would be asking?"

"William F. Cody—that's who, by damned!"

"C-Cody?" stammered the agent, pushing slowly

back from his table, his eyes glancing here and there as the tall youth advanced on him. ·

"I'll show you what I think of sonsabitches lie about me!"

"I did no such thing!" he shrieked as Cody picked him up by the lapels of his wool vest, knocking over the chair.

Cody threw the agent backward into the coal scuttle, scattering kindling and wood. Like an enraged animal, he was on top of the agent before the man realized what happened. Cody never used his fists, choosing instead to cuff the agent with an open hand, swinging it back and forth over both sides of the clerk's face, swearing, shoving, throwing the man backward against the walls, picking him up and tossing him again, then holding him with one hand while the other continued thrashing the agent, who vainly tried to keep both arms clutched over his face through it all.

Finally the man crumpled into a sobbing heap. The anger seemed to drain from Cody, right into that muddy floor where the agent lay curled in a ball, whimpering, begging not to be hit again, in the next breath swearing that Cody would pay for assaulting an army employee.

"Army employee? Shit! I'm an army employee, mister. Ain't nothing special about kicking hell out of you—you go lying about me. Spreading word that I'm a thief."

"You stole army property," he said in muffled tones beneath his folded arms. "Sold it to innkeeper Mason."

"I can see my beating didn't teach you a thing!"

"Stay away from me, Cody!" he cried like a wounded calf.

For a moment Cody stood over the agent, fists flexing and relaxing. As much as he wanted to lash out until he got an apology from the man, he couldn't. The anger had seeped from him like milk from a cracked bowl.

"Get out of here!"

The agent peeked out beneath an arm, one puffy, red eye glaring in challenge.

"You're a damned joke, mister," Cody muttered, swinging a boot at the agent just to watch the man flinch. "I'm going, all right. But you can count on me coming back."

"I'm pressing army charges—"

"No you won't."

Cody was out the door, without closing it, across the street and back to Mason's place to borrow a horse.

"What'd you do to him?" Walt Mason asked in the wagon-yard out back as Cody swung into the saddle and adjusted the reins.

"Gave him the thrashing his contemptible lies deserved."

His heels hammered the horse's ribs as he shot out of the yard, into the street, past track's end, galloping southwest, down the Wallace Road.

By the time he had dashed the thirteen miles to Fort Wallace, Cody had himself worked into another blue lather. Enough of a fume that Quartermaster Samuel B. Lauffer ordered one of his men to bring Colonel Bankhead and the sergeant of the guard immediately the moment Cody darkened his door.

"You're fortunate we don't string you up, Cody," Captain Lauffer warned. "Horse thieves aren't taken to very kindly—especially in the army."

He lunged two steps toward Lauffer and watched the captain back away and unsnap the mule-ear on his holster. "I'm not a thief. Those are army horses —but I didn't sell 'em to nobody."

"My agent tells me otherwise. Comes down to it, your word against his. And frankly—you're not the sort of man whose word I'll take over my agent's."

"I just gave that lying son of a bitch a thrashing that he'll not soon forget . . . and I'm fixing to do the same to you—you don't change your tune!"

Lauffer's face blanched. "You assaulted my employee?"

"Hammered him like a nail through white pine, I did!" Cody yowled, shaking a fist at the quartermaster.

"That's enough out of you!" roared a voice from behind them both.

Cody wheeled, shoulders hunched, finding Colonel Henry C. Bankhead, commander of Fort Wallace.

"General," Cody said with some relief, addressing the officer by his brevet rank awarded during the Civil War.

"What's this all about, Captain?" Bankhead demanded.

Cody watched the half dozen soldiers pour through the door behind Bankhead. Every one of them had their pistols drawn, although they were quickly ordered to point the muzzles at the floor.

"Colonel, I didn't steal no—"

Bankhead waved him off. "I asked my quartermaster a question. You'll keep your mouth shut until I ask you to speak."

Lauffer explained the situation with the agent finding the animals at Mason's, how the agent had seized the animals and returned them to Fort Wallace since they were army property—and then proceeded to tell Bankhead how Cody had just admitted beating up his civilian agent in Sheridan only moments before the colonel had come through the door.

"What have you got to say for yourself, Cody?"

"I did thrash that lying dog who works for Lauffer—but I'm no thief. I demand those animals back, General. They were loaned to me by Assistant Quartermaster Hayes of the Fifth Cavalry, stationed down at Fort Lyon."

"Appears you're in a jam now, Cody," Bankhead replied.

"I'm responsible for them," said the scout.

"Should have thought of that before you left the property with Mason," Lauffer said. "Regulations and your orders both state that you were to leave the animals with Lauffer's agent in Sheridan. From all appearances—looks like the agent might have a case against you for assault."

Cody trembled, his fists clenching again, fuming for a chance at Lauffer.

"I'll be back, Captain. Promise you. And when I do—it won't just be a thrashing I'll give you."

"That's it, goddammit! I order you off this military reservation, Cody!" growled Colonel Bankhead. "I ever catch you near Wallace again without permission—I'll see to it myself you're a guest in my guardhouse."

"Don't you worry, Lauffer," Cody hissed, edged toward the door by the soldiers. "I'll be back. And as for you, Colonel—I'll tell you what you can do with all your army regulations—"

"Gentlemen, see that Mr. Cody is put aboard his horse and escorted off the Wallace reservation," Bankhead ordered of his guards.

"That won't be necessary, General," Cody said, shrugging the guards off. Bankhead nodded and the soldiers backed off. "I know my way back to Sheridan just fine."

"What the divil is this all about, Cody?" asked Seamus Donegan as Cody burst into Mason's saloon.

The young plainsman told them both the story, including the second thrashing he had just given the agent after working up another blue funk on the ride back to Sheridan.

"You beat hell out of the man a second time in one day?"

"I did," he answered, rubbing his knuckles, then washing down his tonsils with more whiskey. Cody was no longer drinking by the glass, he held his second bottle in his hand, swilling the amber liquid like it was creek water.

"You better take it easy on that saddle varnish, Bill," Seamus coaxed, seeing Cody begin to sag moments later.

"I'm going to sleep now, Irishman," he murmured, gently shoving the bottles out of his way as he slumped over the table.

"No you don't," Seamus said, attempting to keep Cody from passing out. "Too late, dammit."

Donegan struggled to drag the half-conscious

man to his feet, beneath his big arm. He shuffled Cody in front of him, then hoisted him over his shoulder. The Irishman stood like an oak.

"Ho, Mason! You got a spare room for this drunk?"

"He's already paid for it, Donegan. Number six." He snagged a key from under the rough counter, tossed it to Seamus. "Put 'im to bed before he gets himself in any more trouble."

Hours later the hammering of many boot-heels on the wobbly, creaking stairs leading up from the saloon below, along with the muffled voices in the hallway overlooking the gaming room, awakened Donegan from a fitful sleep.

He turned in his blanket on the floor, watching the spill of yellow seeping in under the door. Shadows of several legs polluted that whisper of light. He rolled over, grabbing for the two army pistols he kept rolled beneath his coat, which he used for a pillow.

A voice pierced the thin door. "Cody? Bill Cody?" The speaker hammered with a fist.

"Bill!" Donegan whispered at the younger man sprawled across the bed. "Wake up, goddammit!"

"You in there, Cody!" The fist hammered again.

"Who the hell is it?" Donegan hollered as Cody rolled his foggy head off the blanket and mumbled incoherently.

"Captain Ezekiel, Bill. Israel Ezekiel—you know me."

"What's he want at this hour?" Cody whispered, holding his head in both hands as he rose to the side of the bed.

"What you want, Captain?" Donegan called out.

"I want to talk to Bill Cody."

"Can it wait, Israel?" Cody said.

"Afraid not."

"Let 'im in." Cody took one arm from his aching head, waving it at the door.

Donegan stuffed one pistol in his belt, then slid back the bolt. He opened the door and stepped back as the light and noise from the gaming room downstairs spilled into the tiny room. Shadows from three of the soldiers muddied the yellow light.

"Bill, you gotta come with me," Ezekiel said quietly over the rattle of chips, the scraping of chairs and the banging of the out-of-tune piano.

"What's he gotta come with you for?" Donegan demanded, closing on the doorway. He watched two of the brunettes behind Ezekiel bring up their pistols.

The captain pushed the weapons down. "We won't need any gun-play here, mister. I merely came to ask Bill to come along with me."

"What for, Israel?" Cody asked, standing but wobbly still, anchored against the bed's crude foot-rail for support.

"Assault on the quartermaster's agent."

"Shit," Cody grumbled. "He had it coming . . . lying 'bout me the way—"

"I'm sorry, Bill. Sorry I had to be the one to come for you."

Cody staggered closer to the doorway, then of a sudden his eyes blinked clear as he straightened. Then wagged his head, angry, filled with disappointment. "You didn't have to bring these . . . bring your brunettes, Israel."

Ezekiel stared at his boots a moment, sheepish.

"Figured I had to, Bill. What with the way I heard you was acting. Beating on the agent, then coming out to Wallace to threaten Lauffer the way you did."

"A pompous duck, that one is," Cody snarled. He shook his head. "Why'd you bring your . . . brunettes. I thought we was friends."

"You haven't been in too good a humor last few hours. Didn't know how you'd act. You'll go with me now, as a friend?"

"I'll go with you—if you're gonna take me in by yourself."

"I got your word on it, Bill?"

Cody stepped right up to Ezekiel. "My word's been good enough for you until now. Anything changed that between us, Israel?"

The captain thought on it a moment, then shook his head. He turned, whispering to his squad of Negro soldiers. They quietly retreated down the steps to the gaming room as the saloon grew quiet, watching the brunettes march into the street, go to saddle then ride slowly away from Mason's place.

"All right, Bill. It's just you and me now. You ready to go?"

"Gimme a minute. Splash some water on my face."

"I wanna go along, Bill." Seamus whirled on the captain. "Can I go with him?"

"Afraid not, mister. It's just him and me going back."

"Where you taking him?" Donegan asked as Cody stepped to the bed table, dipped his hands and brought the water to his face.

"Wallace. Who are you? Do I know you?"

"Donegan."

"You're one of Forsyth's men, weren't you?"

He nodded. "What happens when he gets to Wallace?"

"I've got orders to lock him up, awaiting the pressing of charges."

"For beating that civilian?"

"Stealing army property."

Donegan chuckled as Cody came up, struggling with his coat. Seamus helped him get his arms through it. "Cody and me stole lots of things this past winter. Sometimes it was sleep, sometimes it was Mexican beer. But Bill Cody will never steal army property."

Cody leaned over and gave the Irishman a one-armed hug. "Thanks, my friend." He looked at Ezekiel as they scuffed from the room. "Donegan's right. I'd never steal army property, Israel. Shit, I never found anything the army owned that was worth the stealing."

Chapter 11

Late March 1869

"No place like home, Seamus," Bill Cody grumbled as they climbed down from their saddles in front of the guardhouse. The whiskey had given him a head the size of Kansas Territory.

By the time Captain Ezekiel and his prisoner had reached the hitching post outside Walt Mason's saloon, the Irishman had convinced the soldier that he should be allowed to come along to Wallace.

"I know Colonel Bankhead."

"Know him well?"

Seamus pursed his lips, then finally shook his head. "Not really. He brought out some troops from Wallace after Carpenter rescued those of us with Forsyth."

Israel Ezekiel studied the tall Irishman a moment. "Only place you can sleep is with Cody in the guardhouse."

Seamus smiled, winking at Cody. "You haven't scared me off yet, Captain."

"You want to ride with Cody and spend a night on a poor soldier's hay-tick mattress—that's your business. C'mon."

Now well into the wee hours of the morning, Fort Wallace was as quiet as the inside of a church on Saturday night. Some greasy-yellow light spilled from the window across the muddy parade to show that the Officer of the Day was on duty. Over by the quartermaster's billet the only other light coming from the window reflected from the muddy puddles of rain water slowly freezing as the temperature continued to drop. The guardhouse door opened when the three horsemen reined up out front.

"Take these horses to a stall and wipe them down," Ezekiel ordered a young soldier who took the civilian horses away. A second guard stood holding the reins to the captain's animal.

"C'mon in, boys," said a rotund officer who suddenly filled the yellow-lit doorway.

"I'll be damned—is that you, Graham?" Cody sang out.

"Nobody else gonna haul his ass out of bed for you in the middle of the night, Cody."

Cody dragged Donegan up to the door. "Like I told you, everything's gonna be all right. Seamus, here's another old friend: Captain George Wallace Graham."

After they shook hands, Graham led the pair into the main room of the guardhouse, followed by two young soldiers. "Why don't you go get yourself some sleep, Israel," Graham suggested.

Ezekiel nodded, looking at Cody. "You get some sleep too, Bill. I fear tomorrow's gonna be a long one."

He glanced at Donegan and was gone, closing the door behind him.

"Well, boys. I haven't got much in the way of anything to offer you—but I'll give you my best," Graham said, waving an arm toward the ring of cells surrounding the center room on three sides.

"Damn, this is a stroke of providence—having you here tonight, Graham . . . when they bring me in on these charges."

Graham's face went sour, as if he didn't like the situation any better than Cody. "My company's on guard duty tonight. That soldier took your horses away will see to them proper. So we'll do what we can to get through the night."

"Where's my bunk?" Donegan asked.

"Take your pick, Irishman," Graham replied.

"I'm not gonna sleep in a cell, Captain," Cody protested.

Graham wrinkled up his nose a moment, thinking. "I can sleep in this chair over here just fine. Why don't you sleep in the sergeant's bunk, back there." He flung a thumb at a bed against the far wall, one with a thicker, wider mattress than those bunks crowded in each tiny cell.

"Believe I will, George. G'night, Seamus."

"Got a extra blanket?" Donegan asked, heading back through an open cell door.

"We can rustle one up for you. Cold out tonight, ain't it?" Graham said. "Sorry about you being a guest and all."

"No need for apology, Cap'n. Slept some of me best nights in a prison cell. From Boston's constabulary to Fort Phil Kearny. Locked in some of the best and some of the worst in me time! Doubt this will be the last night for me behind bars."

By the time Cody got his boots off and his feet stuffed beneath the blanket, Donegan's snores already rumbled against the guardhouse walls.

After breakfast the next morning Cody asked Graham to have the post's telegraph operator come to the guardhouse.

"You want to send word to your wife, Mr. Cody?" the old soldier asked as he took back the sheet of paper on which the young scout had scrawled his message. He glanced over it once, then looked up at Cody a moment, before reading the note a second time. "You want me to send this, do you?"

Cody nodded. "To General Sheridan. He's the one hired me as a scout for the army. I figure Sheridan himself ought to know what a jam Bankhead and you boys got me in out here."

The old soldier glanced at Graham for guidance. The captain shrugged his shoulders.

"He's got a right to send the wire, Sergeant," Graham replied.

"All right," the operator responded, a strange, tight look come over his face. "You want to send this to General Sheridan—I'll see what I can do to reach him."

"Try Fort Hays first," Cody suggested, stepping back over to the guardhouse stove, where he poured himself another cup of coffee. He turned on the operator. "If not there, try Leavenworth. While I was visiting St. Louis a few weeks back, I heard Sheridan was called back East to attend Grant's inauguration."

The operator nodded. "You know the general pretty good, do you?"

Cody smiled, sipping at the hot coffee, enjoying every bit of it. "Sheridan hired me to carry dispatches between some posts when no other man jack of you would do it. And because I carried them dispatches, the general made me chief of scouts for the Fifth Cavalry. Can't say I know him like a brother—but good enough he oughta know what's happening to me out here."

"I'll see what goes—who's up and listening." The operator closed the door behind him as he left, a gust of wind blowing some orphan flakes of snow into the guardhouse.

Early that afternoon, Cody sat across the table from one of his guards, moving faded checker pieces back and forth across a scratched board when Seamus Donegan burst into the guardhouse.

"Cody—thought you ought to know: that rat-eyed telegraph operator never sent your message to Sheridan this morning."

Bill turned, the gust of wind from the door hitting him full in the face like the news. "How you so sure of that?"

"Heard it meself." Donegan plopped onto a stool. "He went right over to the colonel's office with your telegram. Bankhead tore it up—didn't want it sent."

"You know that for certain?" asked Captain Graham, coming back from the stove and coffeepot.

Donegan nodded, then looked at the young scout. "You're stirring trouble here that Bankhead don't want, Bill Cody. He'll do everything he can to keep a lid on you. If Sheridan finds out—"

"Damn him!" exploded the young scout, rising so

quickly the table tipped, sending coffee cups, checkerboard and pieces flying.

"Wait, Bill!" Graham shouted, waving two guards toward the civilian tearing for the door.

Cody felt them clamp his arms and wheeled on Graham. "You got no right!"

"I'm trying to help you, Cody," the soldier explained, warily eyeing the tall Irishman. "You go raring over there in the funk you are, there'll be big trouble—more than I can help with."

"He's right, Bill," the Irishman agreed, but he turned on the captain. "Still, he's got every right to send that wire. Sheridan is the one who hired him."

Graham hung his head, wagging it. "I know, I know."

"Damn you, George Wallace Graham—you and your boys rode with me before . . . you know me, George," Cody pleaded.

"That's so, Captain," said one of the guards.

"You're making things hard." Graham straightened, breathed deep. "All right. I'll go to Bankhead myself—tell him you want to go to the telegraph office—under guard—to send your message."

Donegan waited while Cody fumed. Finally the young scout nodded.

"All right. Go tell that pompous popinjay that I'm not gonna play soldier with him no more . . . that he better let me go or send my message to Sheridan. It's one or the other, George."

Graham nodded as he turned to go. "Understood."

Thirty minutes later both civilians stood outside the guardhouse, watching the pair of horses being brought to them by soldiers. Striding across the parade were Bankhead and some of his staff. The colonel came to a stiff halt about the time the horses arrived.

"Well, Cody," he blustered, "I'd just as soon put this whole thing to rest right here and now. Have you on your way."

Cody did not reply at first. Instead he took the reins to his mount before turning to Bankhead. "Colonel—I figure you for the sort who just doesn't like stirring muddy water."

Bankhead hard-eyed them both as the two civilians went to saddle. "I want you to remember your promise to leave the quartermaster's agent alone when you step foot in Wallace."

"Not going that way—not now, Colonel," Bill replied. "Heading for Lyon. Fifth Cavalry has work soon enough for us."

"Remember you're not welcome back on this military reservation, Cody," Bankhead repeated, stepping back as the scout brought his horse around. He looked up at the Irishman. "Seems I recall you with Forsyth's bunch."

Donegan nodded. "Right, Colonel."

"Maybe you should think twice about getting yourself into trouble—Indian or army—again, Irishman."

Seamus smiled at Cody, then gazed down at Bankhead. "Colonel, way I see it—you're the one ought to be skittish about things. See, the way you overstepped your legal bounds by arresting a civilian off this military reservation—holding him in a military guardhouse, not allowing Cody the rights of every civilian . . . why, I think General Sheridan would love to hear about what you've done to the chief of scouts for the Fifth Cavalry."

Bankhead's lips went into a white, straight line of seething hate beneath his flaring eyes. Finally, his lips trembled as the words came out. "See these two men away from the fort immediately!"

"Good day, Colonel," replied Donegan.

"Best o' luck to you," Cody said, saluting as they turned toward the gate.

"Made 'im mad, didn't I, Bill?" Seamus whispered.

"Yeah, damn you," Cody answered. "Didn't give me the chance to."

"Looks like you made your trip here from Fort Dodge for nothing, boy!"

Jack O'Neill stared at the black hole of a mouth in the man's face when the sutler plopped his head back to laugh with all the rest of the customers stuffed in the dingy, mud-roofed watering hole that smelled of urine and vomit and unwashed anuses claimed by soldier and buffalo hunter alike. He did not like the rancid smell coming from that brown-toothed mouth.

Jack stuffed his right hand under the flap of his wool coat at the same time his left snagged a handful of the sutler's dirty shirt.

"Suppose you say it a little nicer," O'Neill hissed, yanking the Fort Lyon sutler along to the corner of the crude bar so he could eye the rest of the dimly-lit place. Not wanting his back on a single one of the grumbling patrons shifting now away from their tables and the short bar.

"No nigger's gonna tell me—"

He hoisted the little man up to his toes. Off to his right a table and chair clattered across the packed dirt floor. O'Neill turned, yanking his gun hand from the coat, filled with the freshly-oiled Walker Colt. The big hammer clicked back at the same instant the stranger's hand moved for the pistol in his waistband. The white man's hand froze, suspended over the pistol butt, trembling.

"I want no trouble," O'Neill growled, as every set of eyes in the mud hovel widened, realizing he had spoken in Cheyenne. "I don't want trouble." He released the sutler. From the corner of his eye, he watched the man cautiously rub his throat.

"Like I said, suppose you speak a little nicer to me," O'Neill whispered, husky and mean across the low-roofed room. "Why you say I made the trip here for nothing?"

The sutler had poured a quick shot and thrown it back. He wiped his lips with the back of his hand, his eyes gone feral and fear-filled. "Man you're looking for already gone."

"Gone where?"

"I hear it was Denver City," answered the sutler, his shaking hand still wrapped around the bottle of red whiskey.

"Denver City?" O'Neill asked, his mind working on it.

"Don't you know where that is, nigger? Shit, no black-assed bastard like you gonna need directions where you're going!"

O'Neill turned toward the new voice, the right hand and its pistol coming around before him. He had seen the flash of movement as the skinny white man spoke, mocking him. Something like a ray of sunlight bouncing off a prairie pond when the clouds finally break up after a spring thunderstorm.

Standing from his table . . . going for the big

hog-leg pistol strapped against his left leg . . . the buffalo hunter's muzzle-flash blinded Jack for an instant—just before he pulled the trigger on his Walker Colt. And felt the hot tearing of flesh along his right side, in the ribs, right under his gun arm.

The smoke snaked up from the muzzle of the big Walker as the skinny stranger with the pockmarked face stumbled backward against the wall, bounced against it twice, his face gone white. Then he slowly sank, leaving a sticky, shiny track on the peeled cottonwood logs as he collapsed to the dirt floor, legs akimbo.

"Any more of you want trouble?"

They all shook their heads, showing their hands, eyes darting from the dead man with the hole blown in his chest to the big black man with his unkempt kinky hair spilling from his hat like charcoal-colored fringe tickling his shoulders.

"Who do I look for?" O'Neill demanded, his voice filling the place.

"Scouts is all the same," came the immediate answer from the sutler as he inched backward from the mulatto.

"Get over here." The sutler obeyed. Jack grabbed him again. "What is the name of the scouts."

"Name?"

He jerked the man off his feet again, jamming the Walker's front sight under his chin. "The scouts with this group at the fort."

"He means the unit," whispered one of the patrons.

The sutler's head bobbed. "Yeah—you mean the Fifth Cavalry."

O'Neill smiled. "That's right. The Fifth Cavalry.

You told me the scouts went to Denver City." He waited while the man nodded again. "So, you remember a tall white man riding with these scouts? Real tall. And if you get up close enough, he has gray eyes. Know him?"

He nodded, and swallowed, eager to please. "He's been in before—when Carr had his men out at the fort . . . coming and going. Maybe the one you're looking for . . . gone with that bunch just went to Denver City."

O'Neill smiled wider, the teeth gleaming in the oily light. "You—come with me."

"What for?" squeaked the sutler as O'Neill pushed him along toward the door, the gun barrel still under the man's chin like a fence-post.

"I don't want no back-shooting . . . unless these others figure I can't twitch my finger and blow out the top of your head, Mister Barman."

"D-Don't nobody move!" squealed the sutler as he shuffled along, his toes barely touching the dirt floor, clamped close to the big black man who towered over him.

Jack kept his eyes moving as he inched backward to the door, felt it against his left shoulder. He opened it, pulled the sutler out with him.

"Free all them horses."

He inched along the hitching rail as the sutler released the horses one at a time.

"Not that one. He's mine. Hand me the reins to the last one—there. I'll take him with me."

Behind the smoky glass windowpane O'Neill made out at least four white faces watching him climb to the saddle, adjust his long coat, then shove the sutler backward with the sole of his moccasin before he whirled away. He could hear them yelling as he galloped down the single muddy, rutted street the place boasted.

Jack turned in the saddle, leveled the Walker at the crowd that milled over the sutler plopped in the mud puddle filled with rainwater and horse dung. He pulled the trigger only when puffs of greasy, gray smoke appeared from the group.

Whirling back around in the saddle as the crowd scattered, leaving one man sinking to his knees, O'Neill laid low along the horse's neck, figuring no more bullets would come his way from that pack of yellow-spined white men.

If the mulatto was right, few men had the backbone of the tall, gray-eyed killer who had murdered Roman Nose at the island in the river.

O'Neill had just killed two. And that suddenly felt very, very good to him. He was warming up to the chase and the blood.

Chapter 12

Mid-April 1869

Overhead the ducks swept the sky, their great formations pointing north to the feeding grounds in the land of the Grandmother. They did not make as much noise as the great long-necks honking across the blue sky dotted with fluffy clouds left behind with the passing storm.

Tall Bull looked down at the puddle of rain collected in the depression. Like a plate mirror, the unruffled surface of the tiny pond reflected the unhurried passing of the white fleece above. The wrens and sparrows were busy as well. Gathering food for their young. Repairing their nests after the onslaught of the thunderstorm. Industrious animals, these with wings. So perpetually in motion.

Every bit like the buffalo his people followed season after season across the plains. And like the buffalo, the Cheyenne ponies were growing sleek and fat once more on the new grass poking its head through the hardened winter crust of the great prai-

rie that was the home of Tatonka Haska. The Tall
Bull had taken control of this collection of wild outlaws and renegades and outcasts from other bands.
He became their leader when the chiefs abandoned
the fight against the half-a-hundred white men who
had huddled together on the tiny island in the middle of the dry riverbed long before the snows of last
winter.

Around Tall Bull the young and the daring had
rallied. Perhaps because he would not give up the
fight. More so because Tall Bull was a war leader
who took the war right to the white man's doorstep.
While other chiefs were content to merely defend
themselves, Tall Bull led those who still boiled in
gall whenever they remembered the Little Dried
River. Black Kettle was an old woman who begged
peace from the white man. But again last winter the
soldiers had attacked the old chief's camp.

On the Washita.

It would not happen to his people, Tall Bull
swore.

He looked south, toward the land of his birth.
Where he learned to fire a bow and ride a pony.
Where season after season he had hung himself
from the sun-prayer pole to give thanks.

It was no longer the land he could call home. The
white man had come in with his black wagons that
belched oily smoke and ran on a iron trail. Behind
them came more white men who pulled huge
knives behind mules and oxen, cutting a swath into
the breast of the earth. Their kind drove the game
away and polluted the streams they camped beside.

At least his people had been safe up here close to
the Niobrara River for the winter. But now Tall

Bull yearned for the southland once more. If the Cheyenne could not stop the white man in the south, there would be no rest for his people in the north. For, one day, the white man would come north, wanting that land too.

Red Cloud had waged a relentless war on the soldiers and the civilians traveling the Prayer Road north through his coveted hunting ground. In doing so, Red Cloud had defeated the white man. Sent the soldiers scurrying from his land.

Tall Bull rose from the edge of the rain puddle, for the first time sensing the insistent breeze along his cheek, the same breeze ruffling the smooth surface of the blue sky-water.

"It is time," said one of the four who stopped nearby.

He nodded. "The others are gathered?"

"They wait for you."

Tall Bull smiled at the four, his lieutenants ever since the battle with the white men on the river. Without another word he led them into the village, to his lodge.

Around the fire his warriors had gathered, eaten and smoked before they began talk of the coming season, and with its approach, the raids they knew Tall Bull would lead.

"I have grown weary of chasing the white man's wagons up and down his roads. Stealing his horses and his mules. Killing and scalping the white man and his soldiers," Tall Bull explained when the group asked what plans the chief had for the short-grass time. "Still, the white man comes. There is no end to his numbers. We kill and steal—and there are always more."

"What is this talk?" demanded Feathered Bear. "You sound like an old woman ready to give up our fight."

Tall Bull turned on him. "I am not. It would be a very stupid man who thinks that I would deny my people this fight."

"Tatonka Haska is no old woman," agreed Bullet Proof, himself wounded in the battle against the half-a-hundred white men on the river island. "There are plenty enough here who remember how Tall Bull stood proud when Two Crows and Turkey Legs ran from the white men."

The chief held up his hand to silence the clamor. "If there are those among you who believe I should not lead our warriors into battle this season—let him speak it clearly . . . now."

Most of the eyes in the smoky lodge turned toward Feathered Bear. Many moments passed until the warrior dropped his gaze and spoke.

"Tall Bull will lead us in war against the white man."

"*Hau! Hau!*" roared the warriors with approval.

"All of us, Feathered Bear?" asked the chief.

"Yes—every warrior."

He nodded. Once more he had them in his hand. Now to excite them, make their blood hot for the hunt and the kill. To make their hearts pound and their temples throb with the promise of the chase.

"This summer we will not send out scouts to hunt for small bands of soldiers. Nor will we look for the white man's white-topped wagons to attack. Instead —we will concentrate all our warriors on one objective."

"If we do not attack the soldiers and the white

men who travel along the trails—who are we to attack?" asked Pile of Bones, a young and eager warrior.

"We kill soldiers . . . and still more come," Tall Bull explained, stroking the otter-skin pipe-bag he held on his lap. "We kill the white wagon men . . . and still more of them come the next time."

A veteran warrior spoke, "We steal horses and coffee and sugar. Our women like the cloth we bring them, and the kettles too."

Tall Bull looked at Pretty Bear for a moment before answering. "All these things are good—but in taking them we still do not have our land back. We have not driven the white man from our country."

"You have a plan to do this?" Bad Heart asked, speaking for the first time.

He nodded, watching the anxious silence come over the council. "The white man is many. He will always be many here in our land. But, you must remember there is one thing the white man values more highly than his soldiers, more highly than his coffee and kettles."

Pile of Bones's eyes narrowed. "What does he value more than all these?"

"We will attack the white man's homes . . . where he scratches at the ground and builds his mud-earth lodges."

"Is this what you call your great plan to drive the white man from our land?" demanded Feathered Bear.

"Yes," he answered quietly, turning to his rival.

"We have done this before—"

He held up his strong, powerful hand, silencing all. "This time will be different, my brothers. This time we will go to take what is most valuable to the white man . . . what he cannot replace. He can replace soldiers and kettles and blankets. But we will take something he will never replace."

"What is so valuable, Tall Bull?"

"Soon, we will be riding south and east toward the white man's settlements."

"To steal horses again," sneered Feathered Bear.

"No," and Tall Bull smiled, a wolfish slash across his face. "This time we steal the white man's women."

"Damn them, Cody!" growled Major Eugene Asa Carr when he had burst into the scouts' camp circle, accompanied by scout Bill Green. "They got away with a horse of mine."

"Hold up, Major," Cody had replied. "Who got away with this horse?"

Carr had gone ahead to tell the civilian scouts the story: Fifth Cavalry stock stolen right under the noses of the herders. Including a mule owned by Lieutenant W. C. Forbush and a horse very much prized by the major himself.

That recollection now rolled before Seamus Donegan's eyes as clear as the day Carr had sent them after the horse thieves.

He gazed from a foggy hotel window he had thrown open just after dawn. Beside it he sat in a crooked wooden chair, watching the huge Denver City corral below for signs of activity that would indicate the auction was about to begin. In the room's single bed lay Cody and the scout named Bill Green, back to back. Another civilian scout, Jack Farley, lay sprawled on his bedroll on the floor, snoring gently, his mouth hung open, tongue lolling like a hunting dog's.

Carr had continued his explanation, wringing his hands angrily. "Don't have an idea or a clue to give you, except that Green here followed the trail back downriver to the old fort site."

Bill Green had shrugged when the others looked at him. "The trail split up . . . mixed up and all. I couldn't make sense of it."

Cody looked at Carr. "You want me to get your stock back, General?"

Carr had nodded eagerly. "We don't have long, Cody. I'm expecting orders any day now."

Donegan remembered the young scout stretching before he replied. "Been looking for a chance to get out of camp, General. Figure I'll take another man with me."

Carr had shaken his head that morning. "Make it a foursome, Cody."

"General's right, Bill," agreed Green. "Sign shows there's at least two polecats involved. I'll go along—you want me."

"All right," Cody had replied. Then he nodded at Jack Farley. "You're good at reading trail sign, Jack. Wanna come?"

"I do," he answered readily. "Ever since my brother got his arm shot off at Beecher Island—and died from the blood poisoning—I been itching to see some action. If white men are the only thieves we can trail for now, so be it."

Cody had turned to Donegan. "I got one more saddle to fill, Irishman."

Donegan recalled how he had grinned, turning

away from that morning fire to scoop up both rifles and pistol belt. "Let's ride."

Later that morning the four had reached the site of old Fort Lyon. At one time the place had been known on the plains as Bents' Fort, purchased years before from the fur and Indian traders, George and William Bent. Later, when the annual spring floods on the Arkansas ate away at the riverbank below the fort, the army had raised a new post upstream.

Below in dawn's rose light spreading over Denver City, Seamus watched a high-walled freight wagon pull away from the corral and rattle up the ruts of Blake Street. Its taut white canvas top disappeared from view as he went back to remembering what had brought them all to this tiny hotel room overlooking the Elephant Corral.

"I marked the spot where I lost the trail, fellas," Bill Green had explained when he dropped from the saddle and handed his reins up to Farley.

As well, Donegan and Cody had dropped to the ground at the site of old Fort Lyon.

"Trail just up and disappears," Green apologized.

"Got to be something here," Donegan had muttered, his gray eyes scanning the tall grass. Something about it tugged at him, the way it stood and bent with the morning breeze, leading all the way to a large stand of cottonwood near the riverbank.

"Let's put your noses to work," Cody said, leading them from the spot Green had marked.

They fanned out, Farley bringing up the rear with the horses. Slowly working back and forth, studying the ground, the grass, the sage and willow for tracks, threads of clothing, horsehair, even a rock rolled out of the soil where it had been half buried by spring flood of years past.

"Looka here," Cody had said, motioning the other three close. From the broken grass he pointed.

"I bet we find something in those trees," Donegan had replied when they all stood staring at the stand of cottonwood.

They had not been disappointed.

"Must be about a dozen," Farley declared when he had gone over the ground in the cottonwood grove.

"Can't figure how I missed it, Bill," Green said.

"Don't matter," Cody had replied. "We got the smell of 'em now. Look fellas, how they led the horses out of here, one at a time—just to confuse any trackers coming along after 'em. You listening, Irishman?"

Watching the Denver street below him, Donegan remembered how he rose from the ground where he had been inspecting footprints. While Farley had studied the hoofprints, Seamus studied the clues of man's passing.

"Two of 'em come in," Donegan had told them. "Two of 'em rode out each time. I figure they rode a pair of animals off a distance each time. Come back on foot for another two. Rode them off in a different direction . . . just to confuse trackers."

"You read it that way, Farley?"

He had nodded at Cody. "Yep. I see it the same way."

"Let's do an Injun circle," Cody had suggested. "Till we cut some trail."

The four had ridden out a mile from the grove, making a large arc around the old fort site. When they hadn't cut any sign, Cody led them out another mile. Then three. And four. Finally, at a five-mile circle out from the cottonwood grove, Farley had come upon the joining of the tracks.

"I make it some eight horses and at least four mules," the tracker had said, beaming up at the three horsemen.

"By damned, we'll get Carr's horse back yet," Cody had said. "They got a lead on us, so let's buck."

The trail they had followed led them farther east down the north bank of the Arkansas River until it reached the mouth of Sand Creek. From there the trail led north, upstream from the Arkansas.

"Cheyenne call this the Little Dried River," Cody had told them. "Not far upstream is the place where Chivington destroyed Black Kettle's camp back to 'sixty-four."

"You was a young whip back then, wasn't you?" the older Farley had joked with Cody.

"Old enough, Jack—to know Sand Creek's nothing to be proud of."

After following the tracks a few miles upstream, the trail stopped in a copse of swamp willow where the prints became confused and split up once more.

"They're pulling the same stunt again," Farley had said, wagging his head.

"Don't matter," Cody had replied, staring off into the distance. He had turned to the rest of them as they loosened cinches and adjusted their saddles. "Tell me fellas—what are these thieves gonna do with a dozen horses and mules in this part of the country?"

"I suppose they're gonna sell 'em," Green had answered.

"Right. And where do you boys think these horse thieves gonna sell their booty?"

Farley had shrugged his shoulders. "Closest place . . . be Denver City."

"Exactly," Cody had said. He pointed to the confusion of tracks. "That may be a mess and won't tell us a thing . . . but my money says we can find the general's animals and those horse thieves in Denver."

"How far?"

"Does it matter, Irishman?"

Donegan recalled shaking his head. "Got nothing better to do, I suppose."

"Let's go to Denver City, boys," Cody cheered, climbing to the saddle and pointing them north.

Seamus stretched his back and shoulders now, stiffening with the sitting he was doing at the window. Over time he had become as certain as Cody had been they would find the thieves today.

It was Saturday. And every Saturday some of the finest stock in these parts came to Denver City, to be auctioned off at the Elephant Corral.

Below him inside the corral itself stirred the first sign of life for the day. It was Robert Teats's boy, Eugene, dragging a bucket of oats at the end of each arm.

The sun would come up soon to chase the gray from the day.

Seamus figured their chase was just about over.

Chapter 13

Mid-April 1869

Settlers and entrepreneurs had arrived in Colorado Territory close on the heels of miners in the summer of 1858 when gold was discovered in Cherry Creek, near where the stream dumped into the South Platte River along the front range of the Rocky Mountains. Those early arrivals had given the name of St. Charles to their first gold camp on the east bank of the creek. Scarcely a month later another group under the leadership of Dr. L. F. Russell established its camp on the west bank. They named their community Auraria, after Russell's hometown in Georgia.

The gold in Cherry Creek ran out all too quickly, and by autumn the weather began to conspire against the settlers who'd planned to spend their first winter in the shadow of the Rockies. Most of the sunshine residents promptly fled back East. Yet the teetotaling entrepreneur William Larimer cast his lot with the sole resident who remained behind in St. Charles when all others had abandoned the infant community. They renamed their town Denver City, after James W. Denver, governor of Kansas Territory, to which the area then belonged.

By 1859 news of another gold strike in the nearby Clear Creek, some thirty miles west of the infant towns, brought west another flood of miners and assorted hangers-on. That same year the town's first newspaper, the *Rocky Mountain News*, printed its inaugural issue.

Along both banks of Cherry Creek sprang neatly platted rows of log structures and clapboard buildings, with a scattering of newer brick homes. As early as 1860, when the two towns voted to combine and call themselves Denver City, the settlement boasted some twenty-nine stores, fifteen hotels, such as the Planters, the Broadwell, and the American House, along with various boardinghouses, twenty-three saloons serving a varying clientele, a pair of schools and two theaters, besides an assortment of sawbones and barristers, shoemakers and tailors, barbers and druggists, each kept busy in the boom of those early days.

From sunup to sundown the streets of Denver City were clogged with freight wagons bound for all directions of the compass. Freight came in at the rate of twenty cents the pound from St. Joseph on the Missouri River, a trip taking some three weeks. Here on these streets silk rubbed shoulders with buckskin. Wagonmasters and teamsters, Indians, prospectors and fur trappers mingled with the rich and soon-to-be wealthy in the muddy, rutted byways of the new town. Miners packed the boardwalk outside the office of the town recorder, waiting to record their claims. Businessmen of all sorts made it a practice to carry their own small scales, on which they measured a customer's purchase at two-bits a pinch.

Here so close to the newest source of gold, E. H. Gruber and the Clark brothers erected a solid two-story brick building to enclose their minting equipment. There they struck their first ten-dollar single-eagle coin in July of 1860.

Money moved fast and easy through the growing community. Luther and Charles Kountze founded the Colorado National Bank. Emigrating from Omaha, David Moffatt opened the first book and stationery shop in Denver City, staying on to found the First National Bank.

By the spring of 1869, which found Bill Cody and his fellow scouts on the trail of horse thieves, Denver boasted a population of more than 7,000 souls.

"Why don't you get you some sleep, Seamus," whispered Cody as he came to the window overlooking the Elephant Corral.

The Irishman gazed up at his young friend. "No use sleeping. Can't with the music Green's making over there on the floor."

"Then make yourself useful," Cody cheered, slapping him on the back. "Go buy us a pot of coffee."

"Aye, and a good idea that is."

Donegan rose from his chair, stretching the kinks from his muscles and working his joints. "Nothing much yet. Just Teats's boy—taking some of the stock out to pasture."

"Spot anything marked with army brands?"

"Nothing I could tell from here."

Cody settled in the chair. "Coffee do us both good."

Donegan nodded and left, pulling the door quietly into the jamb.

Hunched forward in the chair kept warm by the Irishman since the early morning hours, Cody watched the traffic begin to throb as the city came to life below his window overlooking the Elephant Corral.

In the autumn of 1858 businessmen Charles H. Blake and Andrew J. Williams had reached the Cherry Creek settlement from Iowa. Their stock of goods for miners and frontier customers had been packed into four prairie wagons, each drawn by a four-yoke of oxen. The two immediately erected their first double cabin on what was called "Indian Row" in Auraria, but in January of 1859 Blake and Williams moved their business across the creek and established themselves in the growing community of Denver City sprawling in the shadow of the front range.

On the north side of the street they named for Blake, they raised their building of cottonwood logs, thirty feet wide by one hundred feet long. The pitched roof that was first covered with canvas was shingled by 1869. The front part of the place was occupied by a bar with a dozen gambling tables. Beyond that the rest of the interior had been divided by frame partitions to which were nailed canvas to a height of seven feet to set off rooms for various purposes. The first section was a dining hall where meals were served. Behind it were six apartments set off on each side of a narrow passage, all divided by the canvas walls. First called Blake &

Williams Hall, then Denver Hall, and finally Denver House, the inn grew through that next decade, becoming Denver's finest, as well as its first, by that spring of 1869.

In the early days the inn's patrons fetched water for their tin washbasins from a common water barrel standing in the hallway. Those patrons emptied their basins on the dirt floor to hold down the dust.

Surrounding the hotel stood an eight foot wall, two feet thick, constructed of logs covered with groat, a mud and pebble mixture—something capable of withstanding the capricious climate of the high plains. Loopholes for riflemen were cut through the wall during construction, in the event of Indian attack. Enclosing the hotel itself, this corral spread 125 feet by 150 feet.

Near the end of the Civil War, Blake and Williams sold the corral and gaming house. Ed Jumps managed the famous gambling room of the Denver House, while Robert Teats and his son Eugene ran the former, which they renamed the Elephant Corral. It was to Denver City that stockmen from all across the central plains brought their horses and mules to auction. And there was no finer place in Denver City than the Elephant Corral for a man expecting top dollar.

Bill Cody watched as the first of the day's patrons entered the corral, passing through the huge iron gate that fronted on Wazee Street. From his tiny room on the second story of the Chase Hotel that faced Fifteenth Street, Cody could look directly down on the corral and watch the activity in each of the stalls that bordered the corral's three sides.

Over the next hour a curious mixture of customers entered the corral, eager to peruse the day's selection of animals for auction. Some wore the coarsest frontier clothing, or were dressed in fine Indian-made buckskins, while a minority sported styles freshly imported from the East—garments made of the finest velvets, silks and satins were in evidence. The few women who accompanied their gentleman friends carried parasols; flashing diamonds and sparkling jewelry accented their décolleté gowns.

Most of the early activity centered on the long row of tables near the east end of the corral, where owner Teats had spread a sumptuous repast for his guests that would easily rival even the famous Delmonico's of New York City. Here the contract teamster in muddy boots rubbed shoulders with the wealthy barons of this new city, every man with an eye kept on the auction ring.

"We're going to have to do something about dinner soon," Seamus Donegan groaned, watching the feeding frenzy below. He poured the last of the coffee into his tin cup, grounds and all. "Having to sit here and watch them starch-shirts eating canned oysters and goose livers."

"You're not the only one whose belly is hollering for fodder, Irishman," joked Cody. "We'll get Green to get us something—"

Donegan pushed the tin cup of cold coffee across the washstand, watching Cody go tense. "You see something down there?"

"Could be," then he pointed out the window. "See that mule they're leading 'round the crowd. Next up for auction. I'd lay my mother's watch that's Forbush's mule."

"The lieutenant's animal?" asked Farley.

"Damn if it ain't!" Cody cheered, standing of a sudden, flinging the chair out of his way. He yanked the pistol from his belt, slowly spinning the cylinder.

"How you want to play this?"

Cody smiled at the three of them. "Green will come inside the corral with us. Farley, you best hang back at the gate—in case the bastards make a run to light out."

"How many guns you figure on us coming up against?"

He wagged his head. "Don't know, Seamus. Farley counted two sets of tracks down there on Sand Creek. Chances are they've got someone up here in on things—help 'em get these animals sold off."

"Could be three, eh?" Green replied.

"That's why there's three of us going in—and Farley closing the door behind us, boys," Donegan said.

Entering the Elephant Corral, Cody sent Green up the north wall of stables. "Hang 'round the auction ring to see what comes up when the mule goes for sale."

He nodded for Donegan to follow him into the milling crowd. "Let's have us a look at the mule, Irishman."

The vivid perfumes of lilac water mingled with the earthy fragrance of horse dung and old sweat as the two strode slowly through the crowd, on a direct course for the black mule being led toward the auction ring.

Closer and closer they drew to the animal and its handler until the handler nervously looked back over his shoulder at the same moment the crowd parted.

"I know him!" Cody hissed.

The handler broke for it, pushing his way through the spectators and bidders, the mule rearing and scree-hawing, frightening the ladies with its gyrations.

"Damn well seems he knows you too!" Donegan shouted as they both darted into the pandemonium.

"He's going for the gate—cover me!"

Lunging heedless into a small knot of monied stockmen dressed in silk and fine skin boots, the thief stumbled, fell to a mud puddle and picked himself back up as the young scout reached out, snagging the thief. Cody wrenched him about by the shoulder.

"Williams! By damn—it is you!"

He tore at the grip Cody had on him, freeing himself long enough to go for the two long-barreled pistols stuffed in his waistband.

"Don't think about it, me friend."

Williams froze as the voice whispered harsh in his ears, the thief's hands hanging motionless over his pistols. His eyes grew wider as the big muzzle nudged his backbone a trifle impatiently.

"Good to see you could make it, Seamus."

"Just trying to help, Cody." He glanced around at the crowd, finding everything had stopped, everyone staring at the three gunmen. "Suppose you take this man's guns and we'll walk ourselves out of here, Bill."

"Why you steal army property?" Cody asked the thief once they were outside the corral.

"Didn't steal nothing."

"That mule you were dancing with belongs to Lieutenant Forbush," Farley snarled in the man's face.

"You know him too?" Cody asked of Farley.

He nodded. "Nate Williams. Small-time horse thief and road agent. Plays second fiddle to some bigger fish, Bill."

"Who's that, Williams?" Cody prodded, jabbing the muzzle of his pistol into the thief's ribs as Donegan tied Williams's hands.

"Don't know what you're talking about," he replied.

"I'm not gonna mess with him," Cody said, walking behind Williams so he could wink at Green and Farley. "Why don't you both take this lying bastard out of town—get him out of my sight. Hang him so we can get back to Fort Lyon with the major's horses."

"H-Hang me?"

"That's what's done with horse thieves out here," Farley hissed. "Didn't you know that when you started keeping company with Bevins?"

The thief licked his lips, his eyes darting anxiously. He swallowed hard, as if sensing a tightness ringing his neck.

"Bevins?" Cody asked.

"Bill Bevins," Farley replied. "He's the big fish in this bad act."

Cody stepped up to glare into Williams's face. "Tell you what, mister—I'll see what I can do so you don't hang, if you see that I get my hands on Bevins."

"He . . . he'd kill me—he found out I told you—"

"He won't know," Cody said.

"Here's the rope," Donegan said, striding up with a length of hemp he had taken from Farley's mount.

"We can't do it in town," Green said. "I know a tree south of here that's high enough to stretch his neck good."

"Help me get the bastard on a horse," Farley said.

Williams was actually shaking by that time, wagging his head frantically. "You ain't . . . no—you can't! That's murder . . . I just—"

"Just what?"

"All right—I'll tell you," he spit out in a gusher. "Bevins is out of town. Place we found. Where we got the rest of the goddamned animals."

"Where?"

"North. Down the Platte a ways."

"How far?"

Three miles farther down the Platte River, a frightened Nate Williams nodded to show that the rough cabin up ahead through the trees was the one where they would find Bill Bevins.

Seamus glanced at the sky, finding the sun was falling from its zenith, dipping behind some clouds. "Be a good time to go in now."

"What we gonna do with him?" Green asked, indicating Williams.

"Tie him up here," Cody directed. "We'll come back after we're done with Bevins."

Williams was left behind, seated, gagged and tied to a cottonwood while the three advanced on foot toward the cabin.

"Awful quiet in there," Green said as they huddled in the willows, watching for some sign from the cabin.

"Suppose he's spotted us?"

Donegan shook his head. "I'll wager the bastard's taking himself a nap—so he can gamble and play with the ladies all night."

Cody smiled back at him. "Sounds like he's a man after your own heart, Irishman."

Donegan nodded. "He does at that. C'mon, Cody —this is your show. Let's be about it."

The young scout led them out of the willows, sending Farley to the left and Green to the right. Donegan backed him up from a cottonwood as Cody ran in a crouch to the cabin door. He stood beside it a moment, as if listening. Then inched closer to the entrance, ears cocked.

Suddenly he whirled about, kicked at the door and burst into the cabin. Donegan sprang from the tree, sprinting toward the cabin as the voices erupted from the doorway.

"Drop it, Bevins!"

"Goddamn you! I'll see you in hell!"

"Drop the gun, damn you!"

"You all right in there, Cody?" Seamus asked.

It was another half-dozen heartbeats before he saw a tall, thin rail of a man duck out the cabin door, his hands on his head. Behind him came Bill Cody, holding the muzzle of his rifle against Bevins's backbone. The pair stopped halfway to the Irishman as Green and Farley walked up.

"By the saints, Cody. You gave me a start there."

Cody laughed, easy and full-hearted. "By the saints, indeed, Irishman! It was just like you said, goddammit—he was taking himself a bloody nap!"

Chapter 14

Mid-April 1869

*A*s the sky turned dark and the wind leed about out of the north with the smell of winter to it, Cody found the rest of the stolen animals roped off in a narrow, tree-lined draw not far from the cabin. They were all there: seven horses and three mules, in addition to Major Carr's prize thoroughbred and Forbush's animal captured that morning at the corral. All twelve were left with Robert Teats at the Elephant Corral just about the time the sky turned belly-up over Denver City, whirling over the scouts and their prisoners with a typical spring snowstorm: heavy and wet and wind-whipped to a white froth.

The animals protested the storm, coming rumps around as the horsemen dropped to the soggy street and attempted tying the horses off in front of the marshal's office. Narrow ribbons of yellow light spilled from the two windows on either side of a door that opened only a crack against the howling wind.

"You boys get on in here!" a voice shouted from the doorway.

A wild gust of snow snaked its way through the opening as the four scouts dragged their prisoners from the saddles and shoved them toward the narrow slit opened by the marshal.

"Is that you, Bill Cody?" the voice called out as the young scout stomped into the room, knocking wet snow from his tall boots.

"Dave Cook—I'll be go to hell in a hand-basket!"

They shook, pounding each other good.

"You fellas meet a friend of mine, Dave Cook. Met him hauling freight years ago. You're town marshal here?"

Cook nodded. "Just been nominated to run for sheriff, Bill."

He grinned and clucked. "You sure coming up in the world, Sheriff Cook."

"And you?"

"Scouting for the Fifth Cavalry."

"How's that bring you to Denver City?" Cook asked, eyeing the two prisoners with their wrists bound in rope.

"Horse thieves," Cody replied. "Army property. Gonna take 'em back to Fort Lyon come morning. You got a dry place for 'em to spend the night, Dave?"

"Sure as hell. The rest of you too, if you care."

"I've no mind," Seamus replied. "Soon as spend a night here. Just as dry as Chase's inn—and cheaper too." He presented his hand to Cook. "Name's Seamus Donegan."

"You're scouting with Cody?"

"Aye—but we've not found many Injins yet," he answered, winking at Cody. "Only hijacked a load of Mexican beer and waylaid a bathtub full of some Old Tom-Cat gin!"

The four scouts laughed as Cook closed the prisoners in separate cells.

"You'll have to tell me about that campaign," the marshal said.

"Tonight's as good as any, Dave," Cody replied. "Put some coffee on to boil."

Cook moved to the wall pegs where his heavy mackinaw hung. "Put it on yourself. I'll go on over to Singlaw's place and get us all something to eat."

"On you?"

He grinned. "That's right, Cody. I'm buying. Least I can do is to feed you boys—to repay you for feeding me your wild stories of the Indian campaigns."

Seamus Donegan poked the fire, sending a bevy of sparks into the cloudy, night sky. He looked longingly at the pile of firewood they had gathered to last them until morning, hoping it would stretch past breakfast. He truly wanted to put more on the flames, make himself and the others a bit warmer. But if the wood was to last . . .

Driving the recaptured animals before them, they had slogged through the drifted, wet snow since sunup, when Marshal Cook awakened them all with coffee and fried salt-beef. Not much to excite the palate, but it was a change from the pork and bacon the army offered its scouts. Williams and Bevins devoured their breakfast using only their hands, saying it was the first time they had eaten in three days.

Outside the marshal's office the horses stood saddled and readied to begin the trip south to Fort Lyon. First Bevins, then Williams—both were re-tied, wrists bound together, then lashed to the saddlehorn. Their ankles were roped together beneath the belly of their mounts.

It had been a long and exhausting day, keeping the small remuda of army animals plowing trail in front of them as they put Denver City behind them.

"I'll take first watch," Seamus had volunteered, arriving at their camping spot.

"You just want to do that because it's easier for a man to stay up than to wake up," Cody grumped.

"All right, you take first watch," Donegan replied. "Did I hurt your feelings, Irishman?"

"Not near as much as your nose is going to hurt when I get through knocking it sideways across your face, Cody."

"All right," the young scout said and chuckled, standing from his supper dishes as the moon rose in the east beneath a thick layer of heavy clouds soiling in the night sky, "Donegan will stand first watch. Farley, you're next. Then Green and me."

They nodded, setting down their tin plates and cups of boiled coffee.

"I suppose first watch means I clean mess?" Donegan asked.

"And I make breakfast on mine," Cody answered. "We'll stand three hours each. Here's my watch." He tossed the timepiece to Donegan. "Good night, Irishman."

As his three fellow scouts rolled into their blankets and canvas shelter-halves, Seamus was left to see that the prisoners were bedded down warmly.

"Take your boots off, Bevins."

"Go to hell, mick."

"I'll pretend I didn't hear you say that. Now, take off your boots."

"Like hell, I'm gonna do anything for you—"

"Best you do as he says, Bevins," Cody's muffled voice rose from his bedroll. "You'll be his meat if you don't."

Donegan watched the horse thief eye him critically. "Don't make no difference to me, Mr. Bevins. I can take you back to the authorities . . . or I can leave you staked out here in the snow as wolf bait. Now, suppose you tell me what's gonna be easier."

"Don't give no goddamned—"

Seamus pulled his pistol, pressing the muzzle of the .44 under the thief's nose. "I agree, Mr. Bevins. It's just as I thought as well—far easier to blow your brains out and be done with it here."

"N-No, goddammit! Don't shoot!"

"The boots, Mr. Bevins," Seamus reminded. He glanced at the man's wide-eyed companion. "Yours as well, Mr. Williams."

Nate Williams nodded anxiously, struggling with the broughams that had been soaked throughout the day, in and out of the wet, deep drifts.

"Proud of you, me boys. Now, make yourselves comfortable for a winter's nap. We'll be waking you come breakfast time."

With his toe, Donegan nudged Bevins's ankle-high boots aside in one direction, Williams's broughams in the other, before he stepped around the fire and resettled himself by the coffeepot.

Just past ten o'clock, Seamus shook a reluctant

Jack Farley awake. "You want some coffee poured down you before I crawl in me blankets?"

Farley ground some knuckles into his eyes and mumbled, "No, I'll be all right. G'won to bed."

"They're both sleeping like babies, Jack," Seamus whispered, nodding toward the prisoners.

"Like I wanna be."

"Get some coffee down," Donegan reminded as he pulled the heavy wool horse blanket up to his chin.

Overhead some stars were beginning to break through the thinning clouds. Those sky lights spelled nothing but a deepening cold across the rest of the night as he closed his eyes, feeling his breath freezing the skin on his face. Then all was delicious sleep.

"Goddammit!"

Seamus sat upright with Farley's shrill call. He found the army scout sailing into the firepit with an explosion of burning branches and red coals, sending a spray of bright fireflies into the dark of midnight. Williams was up on his feet after colliding with Farley, crouching only long enough to scoop up his broughams. As if on a mainspring, Bevins was leaping in the opposite direction, out of the firelight, dragging both boots out of the snow.

"Cody!"

"Stop—you two!" Cody shouted.

"What the hell!" Green hollered as Farley tripped over his feet.

Jack Farley was dancing around the firepit, kicking coals and burning limbs onto their blankets, wildly slapping his wool coat and britches free of smoldering sparks, cursing his luck.

"Son of a bitch! I didn't see it coming!"

"Shuddup!" Cody ordered, sprinting after Williams, disappearing into the dark. "Just get after Bevins, Farley!"

"What about me?" Green asked.

Donegan flung his voice over his shoulder. "Stay at the fire. Someone'll be back here soon enough."

"I don't like the sounds of that," Green muttered as Donegan disappeared into the darkness.

Within minutes the Irishman and Farley were back at the fire, finding a much relieved Green and Cody on either side of one of the horse thieves.

"You all right, Mr. Williams?" Seamus asked, kneeling in front of the thief who had his head slung in his hands.

"He's a might under the weather," Cody explained.

"Something you gave him?"

Cody nodded, showing the scouts the barrel of his pistol. "He didn't want to stop running at first—and I seriously considered shooting him. Instead, I gave him a .44 headache."

Green glanced at what Donegan took from under his coat. "What you got there, Irishman?"

Seamus held it up in the firelight. "A shoe."

"Bevins?"

He nodded at Cody. "Looks like his. Whoever's running out there, he's hobbled with only one good hoof now. All we got to track."

Cody turned to Farley. "You lost him, Jack. It's up to you to see we track him and get him back."

"You want me stay with Williams?" asked Green.

Cody was bending over his gear, yanking up the blanket and saddle, heading for his horse. "I'll take

Donegan with Farley and me." He glared at Green. "Don't lose this one."

Donegan stopped in front of Williams with his saddle and blanket hung over his arms. "That's right, Bill. We want at least one of these bastards alive for General Carr to skin."

Across the horizon to the east it looked like the white expanse of the earth was tearing itself from the dark clot of skyline in a long, thin and bloody laceration.

They had covered something close to twenty miles in the dark: down from the saddle to inspect the tracks, then gaze into the distance before climbing back atop their horses to pursue the footprints of the fleeing Bevins. Tiny spots of blood had begun to muddy the single, barefoot print the last handful of miles.

"He's hurting," Donegan whispered as they halted atop a low rise, the South Platte down below.

"Damn right he's hurting," Cody replied. "But I've gotta hand it to him. Son of a bitch is a tough one. All these miles, up and down this broken country—what with six inches of icy snow and the trail covered with cactus. Damn right Bill Bevins is a tough bravo."

There shone a glimmer of begrudging admiration in young Cody's eyes, something any man could read had he been sitting there alongside Seamus Donegan as the sun tore itself into a new day. The sky went red-orange, smearing the old snow a pale pink beneath the gray-bellied clouds hovering against the foothills.

"You want him for yourself?" Donegan asked

once he realized Cody had seen the black speck darting through the willow down along the riverbank.

Cody nodded and sighed. "Sort of a funny end to this chase, don't you think, Seamus? Me just riding down there to retake a man on foot. Not something that sounds so good when we get back to General Carr and tell him."

"Bevins ran. You caught him without firing a shot. That deserves the general's congratulations. And he's getting his bleeming horse back to boot."

"C'mon, Farley. You and Seamus ride down with me. Bastard's caused me so much trouble—I might just kill the son of a bitch if you leave me alone with him."

He saw them coming, turning to glance over his shoulder suddenly as their horses loped through the shallow snow that hugged the clumps of willow and prickly pear cactus. Bevins tripped and fell, crying out, crawling on all fours through the snow, stumbling to his feet and hobbling forward like a cripple. He was crazed, grunting like some treed animal, done in but refusing to end the chase.

"Give it up, Bevins!" Cody called out as he signaled the other two riders. All three slowed to a walk directly behind the frantic horse thief.

Bevins made some unintelligible sound as he swung around, arms wide like post oaks, crouching, stumbling backward into the snow. He lay there, heaving, his hair plastered to his forehead, rivulets of sweat creasing his beard. Cody slid from the saddle. It struck Seamus that Cody trudged over to Bevins like a man not relishing what he had been called upon to do.

"It's gone sour, Bevins," he said quietly.

With a growl, the horse thief pushed himself back through the snow.

Cody held out his hand, his right over the butt of his pistol. "Don't make this any harder'n it has to be."

Bevins moaned, sinking completely into the snow. He wagged his head, sobbing without restraint for a moment. When he had composed himself, the thief dragged one foot into his lap. Around the ankle hung the muddied, blackened remnants of what had once been a cotton foot-stocking. The sole of the stocking completely worn, it hung in tatters over Bevins's swollen, bloody foot.

"I can't go on, Cody."

Cody glanced up at Donegan and Farley for help. Then back to Bevins.

"Cactus?"

He nodded, cradling the swollen foot. "Damn thorns—lemme use your knife?"

Cody shrugged. "Sure. Don't wanna keep any man from cutting on himself he takes a mind to."

Using the point of the blade, Bevins hunched over his foot in the snow, digging at each bloody wound, cutting every thorn from the sole of his wounded foot. He handed the knife back to the scout, then held his hand up for help.

"You're a big one," Cody replied as Bevins rose beside him. "I'm thinking you better ride my horse."

"Shit, you gonna let him ride?" Farley asked, sending a spray of brown to the old snow below him. "What you gonna do—walk all the way back to our camp?"

"No," he answered. "Since you're the smallest here, I'll ride double with you, Jack."

The older man glared incredulous at the spunk of the young scout. "This is the horse the army give me, and I'll say if you ride double with me or not."

He glanced at Donegan a moment. The Irishman nodded in support.

"All right, Farley," Cody continued. "You got a choice. I'm chief of scouts for this outfit. That makes me your boss, 'cause you're riding an army horse, on army orders. You can step down and give me your horse to ride alone—or, we ride back double."

"Shit, you peach-faced ninety-day wonders are all alike," Farley grumbled. "Back in the war, why, we'd—"

"Back in that goddamned bleeming war, Farley," Donegan interrupted him, "we'd likely followed a man as good as Bill Cody into Hell and back again."

Chapter 15

Early May 1869

*B*ill Bevins caused no more trouble for Cody. But two nights later Nate Williams made good his own escape, easing into the brush to relieve himself after moon-dark, then quietly disappearing.

Donegan, Cody and Farley turned their lone prisoner over to civil authorities at Bogg's Ranch on Picket Wire Creek, more properly named the Purgatoire, which flowed into the Arkansas River upstream from Fort Lyon, where Major Eugene Asa Carr awaited the return of his chief of scouts with his favorite thoroughbred.

By the first day of May the major marched his seven companies of the Fifth Cavalry out of Fort Lyon, on orders to head north for their new duty station of Fort McPherson, on the Platte River in Nebraska. At the head of the column rode Bill Cody and his band of civilian scouts hired from the surrounding country for the coming spring campaign. Cody kept Seamus Donegan busy riding advance scout those first days of their march, steering a course past Cheyenne Wells.

Odd duck that Colonel Henry Bankhead was, when the Fifth Cavalry arrived at Fort Wallace behind the young scout, the unpredictable Bankhead swallowed his pride enough to patch things up with Cody. The following day Cody and Donegan escorted Captain William F. Brown the thirteen miles into Sheridan to purchase some supplies needed by Brown's F Company for the next leg of Carr's journey to McPherson.

Springtime on the prairie can bring about changes in the chemistry of a young man's blood, of that there is little doubt. Cody and Donegan weren't immune to the season.

Captain Brown, along with these two jolly scouts, agreed that there was better use of their time than spending it all on buying grub. Brown was soon in no condition to purchase provisions. But, taking a break during their drinking, the three provisioned as best they could and sent the goods back to Fort Wallace with the company cook. The revelers stayed behind until sundown came and the money ran out.

The next morning, Carr ordered the march north resumed. From here on the Fifth Cavalry would enter Cheyenne country, bound for Fort McPherson. That first evening's camp out of Wallace, the F Company cook stomped up to Captain Brown and the rest at their mess fire as a spring sun settled in the west.

"Captain," the cook fumed, wringing his apron angrily, "dunno what to do—can't find a trace of those damned victuals you bought yesterday in Sheridan."

Brown gazed at Cody for a moment, strangely. "Can't for the life of me figure where your victuals would be, Corporal Murphy. We bought them in Sheridan and put them in the wagon."

Murphy wrenched the apron between his hands nervously. He whispered, "Captain—ain't nothing in that wagon but a five-gallon demijohn of whiskey, another five gallons of brandy, and two cases of Old Tom-Cat gin."

Cody and Donegan howled, slapping each other or pounding a leg as they fought to catch their breath. All about them, Brown's company roared with laughter.

"Dammit, Cody!" Brown shouted above the noise. "You and that bloody Irishman going to tell me what happened?" He gazed up at Murphy, his eyes begging forgiveness of the company cook as he pointed at the two civilians. "These two are to blame! They put me in the brine in the worst way."

"By the saints, Cody—Brown's claiming we got him drunk, ain't he?" Donegan said, stomping his boot on the ground in a fit of laughter.

From the small crowd of soldiers who had gathered emerged an officer. "Captain Brown, we'll damn well trade some of our victuals for some of your . . . your provisions!" declared Philip Dwyer, commander of E Company.

"See there?" Donegan roared. "Cap'n Dwyer's here to pluck your cheeky ass from the fire, you fog-headed rummy!"

The soldiers guffawed at Brown's expense until he reluctantly smiled and wagged his head. "All right, Dwyer—we'll trade: some of your salt-pork and beans, for some of our refreshment." He glared at the two civilian scouts. "Last time I go to town for supplies with you two barleycorns!"

Cody stomped up, slapping Brown on the shoulder. "I'll damn well bet you make out better trading E Company for food than you'd done back at Sheridan bartering with that storekeeper."

Brown licked his lips, a begrudging smile growing on them. "Bet I will at that, Cody."

For days after leaving Fort Wallace and Sheridan, Kansas, behind, Brown's F Company ate every bit as good if not better than the rest of the Fifth Cavalry. Every day found the other companies bartering with Brown, trading their food for his liquor. It had all the makings of a good march north into Cheyenne country to reach the Platte River.

These would be the last easygoing days Carr's troops would share for some time to come.

"Country's thick with sign, Irishman," Bill Cody whispered as they led their horses down the bank to water the animals in Beaver Creek. They were twelve days out of Fort Wallace already. Until that morning, they had crossed not a single track.

"Carr knows it. He's posting double pickets tonight. Wants 'em doubled from here on to McPherson."

"Cody!"

They both turned to find young Major Eugene W. Crittenden halting his mount on the bank above them.

"General Carr wishes you to accompany a reconnaissance."

Cody looked at Donegan. "Must mean I don't get supper with the rest of you."

"I have some tacks in my bags," Donegan offered.

He waved them off. "So do I," and he laughed while rising to the saddle, pulling his reluctant mount away from the cool waters of the Beaver. "But if I wanted to eat hard-bread in the saddle—I would've joined the army for thirteen dollars a month!"

Cody led Lieutenant Edward W. Ward and a dozen troopers from Brown's F Company northeast, following sign of a village on the move. After casing down the Beaver more than five miles, the scout signaled the young, smooth-faced lieutenant.

"Let's halt your men here. Dismount them in that draw over there. You and me go on a ways ourselves."

"You found some evidence of the hostiles?" Ward asked eagerly.

"Not here. Up yonder a ways." He pointed over the rolling hills along the Beaver.

"You figure that's camp smoke?"

"Sure as hell ain't dust from a cavalry column."

Ward nodded without another word, turning to order his dozen into hiding before he rejoined Cody to consider the smoke smudging the far horizon.

Bellying up to the crest of a grass-covered hill, the two studied the countryside downstream, below the smoke of many fires. In the clear, pristine air of the plains, they were able to make out the gathering of hide lodges and the nearby pony herd milling in the grassy valley of the Beaver.

"How far you make it, Mr. Cody?"

He calculated. "Three miles. Not any more'n that, Lieutenant."

"I'll send word back to the general."

"Have him bring his men up quick. This is what Carr's been wanting for some time now."

Ward nodded, his lips in a grim line of determination. "We were sacked last winter when Custer and Penrose got all the action. Empty-handed for all that marching. Carr's itching to have him a shot at the hostiles."

"There's his chance, Lieutenant—yonder."

They loped back to the draw where Ward had left his men behind. Quickly scribbling a note on the small ledger he carried in his blouse, the lieutenant handed his report to his ablest horseman.

"Skaggs, take this back to General Carr. I've told him we'd wait here for him to bring up the rest of the outfit."

The solitary trooper leaped to the saddle and was gone over the hills.

"It's time for us to put a little more distance between us and that village," Cody advised.

"Whatever you advise. We'll follow," Ward replied. "Mount up, men."

The dozen soldiers were climbing to their saddles behind Cody when a shot rang out, followed quickly by two more.

"Those came from the direction Skaggs took!" Cody shouted.

As Cody brought his mount around, Skaggs himself burst over the rise to the southwest, laying low in the saddle, whipping his mount back to Ward's detachment for all he was worth.

"Get ready to stand and fight, Lieutenant!"

Ward raked the back of his hand over his lips. "We'll make a dash for it, Cody."

"You'll be damned for it, you do—and earn yourself a grave if you try to make these green recruits outrun warriors on horseback."

He glowered at the civilian. "All right, we'll play it your way."

As Skaggs reached the base of the hill and raced on, a half-dozen warriors cleared the crest behind him, hot on his tail. Screeching with blood in their nostrils, they waved their rifles and warclubs as their heels hammered the sides of their strong, grass-fed ponies.

"Dismount your men, Lieutenant!"

"Dismount!" he cried.

Skaggs skidded to a halt, leaping to the ground and sprinting the last twenty yards beside his lathered mount.

"Two squads—left and right!" Ward hollered. "Horse holders to the rear, dammit!"

Three soldiers pulled the mounts to the mouth of the coulee, where they had secreted themselves only moments before.

"Fire on my command!"

"Damn your commands. Just drop the sonsabitches!" Cody countered as he brought the Spencer to his shoulder.

The crack of his carbine served as cue to the rest of the soldiers on both flanks. Nothing pretty about it, just a lot of lead fired into the face of those half-dozen warriors.

"They turned!" one of the troopers hollered, rising from his knee.

"Damn right they did. There's too many guns here for 'em to tackle."

"Let's go get some scalps!" another young trooper shouted.

"You'll die if you try," Cody replied, stomping up beside Ward. "Likely that bunch was out hunting when they spotted your courier. Just as likely they're hightailing it back to that big village right now—with word that they can wipe out a small squad of pony soldiers if they hurry."

Ward nodded, his tongue raking his dry lower lip. "Which means we run for it?"

He shook his head. "Better you get your men into the mouth of that draw. Make yourselves a place to take a stand."

"What're you doing?" Ward asked as Cody went into the saddle, his carbine jammed into its scabbard.

"I'm riding back to bring Carr up—and fast."

"But you don't have my report!"

Cody was gone before the lieutenant's words fell from his lips. He looked over his shoulder only once as the horse beneath him found its second wind, leaning into the race. Cody smiled, finding Ward hustling his soldiers into the willow-covered coulee far behind him.

Tearing past the outlying pickets, he reined up in a glittering spray of sand made golden in the falling sun. "General! Your Lieutenant Ward is penned down. Found us a village."

"How big?" Carr came huffing up.

"Big enough to give your men a good fight of it."

"Splendid!" Carr wheeled, firing orders to his adjutant to alert the entire command. "We'll leave G and D with our train. 'Boots and Saddles' for the rest. Five minutes, Mr. Price!"

Adjutant George Price was gone to pass the word

and order the bugles blown when the major turned back to Cody. "Will Ward hold out?"

He wagged his head. "We need to cover some ground and quick, General."

"If I might make a suggestion, Cody?" Seamus Donegan loped up, leading his mount.

"What do you have to say?"

"Let Cody and me lead the first company or two ready to ride."

Carr thought on it only a moment. "Take those ready to make the charge with you, fellas. I'll follow with the rest of the outfit and support you shortly."

By the time Cody had Lieutenant Ward's detail in sight ahead, Carr and the rest of the regiment were in sight to the rear. At the moment he turned back around in the saddle, half a thousand warriors made their noisy appearance on the hills behind Ward, ready to swallow the lieutenant's men. When they spotted the advance guard under Cody and Donegan headed their way at a gallop, the Cheyenne pulled back from their attack on the dozen soldiers, allowing Ward to make an orderly retreat to join up with the rest of the Fifth Cavalry.

Carr came up with his three companies about the time the warriors reined up and turned about, intending now to make a stand of it to cover the retreat of their women and children scattering north onto the prairie. Ponies were driven ahead by young boys and old men. Women squawked at balky animals dragging travois. Children cried out, racing about on foot or plopped atop the mounds of lodge-goods heaped aboard the drags. Their escape raised a thick curtain of golden dust as the sun eased out of the day.

"General!" Cody roared as he skidded up beside Carr. "That company you sent out on the right flank is about to get swallowed up!"

Every neck craned. Rifle-fire crackled along a wide front, but no more insistent than far to the right. That growing cacophony of gunfire was all that could be heard, a thick cloud of dust all that could be seen of the action.

"Schenofsky?" Carr asked of his adjutant.

"Lieutenant," was Price's answer. "B Company."

Carr's eyes darted over the officers gathered about him. "Company A is closest. Take them with you, Cody. The Irishman too—he cut his teeth on the best horse soldiers the Confederacy could throw at him. Let's see what Donegan can do against mounted warriors!"

"Aye, General!" Seamus shouted, whirling his mount about to follow Cody.

The young scout ordered Captain Robert P. Wilson's A Company to follow him over the hill, informing the soldiers they were to follow the Irishman's battle commands.

"Just who the hell does this pompous ass think he is?" Wilson demanded, nodding toward Donegan.

"Carr wants him to pull Schenofsky's fat out of the fire," Cody replied, waving a hand to silence Donegan. "The Irishman rode with the Army of the Potomac. J.E.B. Stuart carved his initials in Donegan's back of a time—and he lived to tell of it. I'll ride with him . . . and so will you, Wilson. Carr's orders."

At the top of the hill Donegan reined them up as he quickly assessed the turmoil below. Lieutenant Schenofsky had fallen for the oldest trick in the Indian book. Following a luring, seductive decoy away from the far end of the right flank—thinking he had an easy kill. Until more than 120 warriors swooped down on his little command of less than thirty-five frightened soldiers. Cutting them off from the rest of the Fifth Cavalry, with little hope of rescue.

Most of the horses were down in the grassy sand, either from Indian bullets or sacrificed by their riders to serve as bulwarks in their desperate stand. Schenofsky clearly stood at the center of things, pistol high in the air, glancing over his shoulder at the troops on the hilltop as Donegan spread his formation for the charge.

"Skirmish—front! Left flank: out. Right flank: out! On the gallop, my command!" he roared.

Forty-five horse soldiers whipped their mounts into a wide front, sweating flank to sweating flank in a clatter of metal bit chains and a squeak of protesting leather. The horses grew wide-eyed, snorting, sensing the impending call.

"Captain?" Seamus nodded to Wilson.

"Your call, Mr. Donegan," he replied, and bowed elegantly in the saddle.

"Charge!"

Behind the civilian the soldiers streamed off the hill, like the two barbs of an iron-tipped arrow, following the mad race of the arrow-point into the fray. A flurry of dust swirled just beyond Schenofsky's desperate circle of horse carcasses. Gunshots volleyed into the yellow cloud. Then ever so slowly the firing let off as the yelling, screaming, dusty blue horsemen swept around Schenofsky's men on two sides, chasing the retreating warriors.

Donegan ordered the halt and retreat. "Cap'n, we better get back and get that unit rejoined with Carr before those Cheyenne come up in force to swallow us."

Wilson had galloped up after the soldiers were reformed in column of fours, returning to Schenofsky's ambush. He tapped the brim of his slouch hat, a begrudging smile on his face.

"My hat's off to you, Irishman. That was a pretty ride of it."

"It was at that, Cap'n," Donegan beamed, knocking dust from his patched and faded cavalry britches. "It was a damned pretty ride at that!"

Chapter 16

May 13, 1869

$\mathcal{L}$ ieutenant Jules Schenofsky saw four of his men killed when his unit was swallowed up by the decoy and ambush at Elephant Rock. Only one of those bodies was recovered. Another three soldiers were wounded in the desperate fight.

With no other casualties, Carr ordered Cody to lead two companies in the chase and until dark to keep the pressure on the warriors covering the escape of their women and children. As the sky sank to black, Cody halted the soldiers on the south bank of the Republican River.

"I'll be damned if I can't hear 'em rustling around on the other side," Cody whispered to the Irishman as they stood on the riverbank.

"You figure they're moving off?"

"Like us to think so, I'll wager."

"We can't make a go at 'em in the dark, and they know it," Seamus replied sourly.

"You find something?" Major Carr asked as he

brought his horse to a halt behind the two scouts in the deepening gloom of twilight. Only the evening star showed itself overhead.

"Your Cheyenne, General," Donegan replied.

"They make it across before dark?"

Cody nodded. "It's why they were in such a hurry and didn't put up so much of a running fight to get here."

Carr ground his teeth a minute. He studied the column coming up over his shoulder. "I can't cross in the dark, fellas. Even worse would be for me to forge across the river before the train has come up."

Cody nodded, scratching his nose. "This is a nasty bunch—been known to double back and attack at night. They've hit us and run before."

"From everything I was told before I came out here in the fifties—Indians didn't attack at night," the major said, wagging his head.

"The officers who told you that hadn't fought Injins before," Donegan said.

"What do you think makes this bunch so different than others?"

"General, these are Cheyenne Dog Soldiers," Seamus answered. "Their kind just doesn't fight to defend their families—Dog Soldiers fight simply for the love of killing."

"Then that decides it—I don't want that bunch destroying our supply train," Carr repeated. "I'll wait here until morning, when the entire unit can start off anew."

Cody wagged his head. "I agree with you on waiting for the rest of your men to come up, General— but don't count on ever finding this bunch of Cheyenne again for some time."

Carr stepped closer, the strain of the afternoon's battle showing in the creases of his dusty face. "That's maybe the first time you're wrong, Cody—but you're dead wrong just the same. I killed thirty of these bastards today. Mark my words, I'll find these Dog Soldiers again, by God. I'll find this bunch again if it takes all summer."

If it wasn't lockjaw, typhus or diphtheria, it had been worms, dysentery or malaria.

Jack O'Neill poked with an iron picket-pin at the willow limbs in his tiny fire. Remembering all the sickness of those years before the great war, when he grew up on the plantation with his white papa. In a house filled with concubines and mulatto children. Hell, even the master's lily-white children were suckled and raised by the house niggers. The man's white wife spent too much time dressing and napping and eating to be bothered with nursing or raising her own young'uns.

Too busy to keep her man satisfied as well. Jack's papa had a wandering eye, and grew partial to Jack's high-cheeked, full-lipped black mama.

"Good stock."

That's what Jack had heard the man call his mama many, many times during his visits to the slave quarters. Jack's mama was good breeding stock. It wasn't until many years later, during the war itself, that Jack learned what his mama did all those times behind the blanket partition with the white master who was his father. All the grunting and groaning.

Hell, Jack didn't do it for breeding—just for fun. It was a damp, cold, and lonely camp he had

made a day's ride west of Fort Wallace. Heading for
Cheyenne Wells and the road ranch there. Last
night he had determined he would not ride north in
search of the gray-eyed killer. Too many soldiers
and too much open territory—with Cheyenne war
and hunting parties combing it.

His plucked eyebrows had grown back, and every
day he was looking more like a freedman making
his stake on the plains. Looking less and less with
every passing sun like the mulatto turned smooth-
faced Dog Soldier running with the band now under Tall Bull.

Soon enough he could disappear into any crowd.

Jack nodded, smiling grimly as he pulled his collar up over his ears. The wind was insistent, dusting
his little fire with a spray of sparks. That wind was
all left behind in the passing of the spring storm
about the time the sun decided to fall out of the gray
underbellies of the clouds and settle on the peaks
far to the west.

He knew he was brooding on it—with a growing
despair that he had already killed twice that he
knew of, and still he had not completed his vow to
Roman Nose.

Perhaps now it would be easier to track the gray-
eyed one. Able to disappear into a crowd when it
was done.

Maybe that was something that fit like a snug
boot inside him with all the hate and loathing he
carried in a festering boil. Along with something
unnamed pulling him northwest from Fort Wallace.
They said the next fort north of here was at Julesburg, a place called Sedgwick.

But more and more Jack was thinking he should

be going to Denver City. More people. More money. And certainly more women. He had been without a woman for too long. After all those . . .

He squashed the thought of their dusky, copper-skinned limbs the way he would crack a louse between his fingernails.

Denver City was the place, he decided. If nothing else, he owed it to himself to make a holiday of it. But it still didn't explain why he felt drawn to the busy place peopled of so many white men.

Come what may, Denver City just might be the ideal place for a coffee-colored mulatto to disappear for a while, having himself a new powder-skinned chippy every night—planning what he was going to do when he finally tracked down the gray-eyed killer.

For two more long days Major Eugene Carr pushed his Fifth Cavalry behind Cody's scouts, doggedly pursuing the trail of the fleeing village down the Republican River, using every available minute of light. With the aging of the season, the sun made its appearance in the east earlier each day, easing out of the west later each evening.

As he did every morning prior to the day's march, Carr rotated his companies. On the sixteenth the major moved M Company under lieutenants John M. Babcock and William J. Volkmar forward to advance guard under Bill Cody. For the better part of six hours the forty soldiers stayed some three miles ahead of the rest of the troops, following a freshening trail.

"You care to stop the men for a spell? Let 'em refresh their canteens?" Cody asked First Lieutenant Babcock as they reached the mouth of a stream flowing from the north into the Republican.

"What's that up ahead?"

"Spring Creek, I figure."

Babcock twisted about on his saddle, quickly studying the men of Company M, dusty, sweaty and fatigued. "I suppose we should give them twenty minutes."

Cody led them down the gentle slope toward the tree-lined mouth of Spring Creek as Babcock gave orders to his second.

"Mr. Volkmar, see that two men are posted here on the high ground to watch for sign of the main column. Relieve them with two others after ten minutes."

No sooner had the soldiers dismounted and spread out along the creekbank than the first war whoop split the air.

Gunfire erupted from upstream. Over the hills poured warriors bearing down on Babcock's small detail.

"Order the men to mount!" Volkmar shouted at his first lieutenant.

Cody grabbed Babcock, whirling him about by the arm. "No! You'll never outrun these red bastards."

"There's . . . more than two hundred of them!" Volkmar shouted.

Babcock swallowed hard, his eyes growing wide as the warriors closed in. "We don't stand a chance in the saddle, Mr. Volkmar. Sergeant Payne—inform the men we'll use the horses as shields. Ring up . . . ring up, goddammit!"

The old sergeant tossed the reins to his animal to

another before he darted into the confusion, hollering his orders. "In a circle, boys! Ring up!"

Cody was pulling on his hesitant army mount with the wide streak of white running from forelock to muzzle. "C'mon, Powder Face—no time for fighting me now." He turned, shouting to a half-dozen soldiers struggling with their rearing mounts, "Close up."

"Volley fire, Sergeant!" Babcock yelled.

"Fire!" repeated Sergeant Payne.

"Let 'em reload and fire on their own, dammit!" Cody snarled at Babcock.

As the warriors swept past, they broke like the river on a large boulder, racing along two flanks of the soldiers' circle like foaming, surging whitewater. Forty guns crackled through the timber and willow, spilling three horsemen into the new green grass that waved in the spring breeze beneath an endless canopy of blue. Two of the fallen Cheyenne were dragged over the hill at the end of long, rawhide tethers tied from their waists to their ponies' necks. The third lay unmoving beneath the pounding hooves until a companion swooped by, leaning off his pony and snagging an arm.

The entire bunch was gone over the hills to north and west, their wailing cries fading beneath the midday sun.

"Get your men reloading if they haven't a'ready," Cody reminded Volkmar.

"Reload. Everyone, reload quickly."

"You think they're coming back?" Babcock asked, kneeling beside Cody, who was hunched beneath the legs of Powder Face, slamming home cartridges into the Blakeslee loading tube for his Spencer.

He snorted, feeling the drip of cold sweat down his own backbone. "Damn right they'll be back. They're just feeling you out, Lieutenant. Pushing in the edges a might. Digging for your soft spot."

Babcock swallowed slowly. His eyes raked the young soldiers in his untested command. "We're . . . soft all around, Cody."

For a moment he gazed at the lieutenant, perhaps only five or six years older than he, his eyes softening. "Then let's pray Carr brings up the rest of the unit on the double."

"We won't last long, will we?" Volkmar asked as he squatted beside Cody.

He wagged his head. "No. But we can try to fall back."

The war whoops grew in volume once more. The pounding of hundreds of pony hooves throbbed the valley floor from two directions.

Babcock strained to understand. "You just told us we didn't stand a ghost of a chance if we made a run for it. Now you—"

"We're not running, Lieutenant," Cody said, rising, slipping the Spencer over his saddle. "We'll fall back, a yard at a time. Keep the men together . . . on foot. Inside the barricade of their mounts."

The first lieutenant looked at his second. "You get all that, Mr. Volkmar?"

He nodded. "An orderly retreat it is, Mr. Babcock. Just as scout Cody has directed. Yes, sir!"

"Sergeant Payne!"

"Sir?"

"Are we reloaded?"

"Yessir," Payne huffed as he skidded to a stop nearby.

Babcock grabbed the old sergeant by the shoulder and explained the plan. "Wait till they're gone this time by."

"Fire!" Cody hollered before he brought his own cheek down on the rifle stock and pulled the trigger, feeling the powerful carbine slam like a mule kick into his shoulder. Powder Face nudged against him, frightened by the rifle fire, scared of the screeching Indians bearing down on them once more, the horse perhaps skittish most of all for the fear it smelled in its master.

Up and down the oblong ring of soldiers and mounts, the white men fired and the horses bucked and reared as arrows flitted among them, bullets hissing and whining like angry hornets.

"Now, Lieutenant!"

"Retreat!" Babcock followed Cody's instruction. "An orderly retreat . . . this way."

"Follow the lieutenant!" Payne shouted, waving his arm, letting the rest pass. He waited, watching the youngsters scurry past, each one yanking on a reluctant mount, firing after the disappearing backs of the young warriors as another wave of Cheyenne emerged out of the north.

"You coming, Sergeant?" Cody asked, stopping beside Payne.

He smiled. "We'll close the file together, you young sprout!"

Cody shoved him aside as the warriors broke from the trees.

Pict—pict—pict.

Bullets whispered past the civilian as Payne fell. Lead filling the void where a heartbeat before the sergeant had been standing. Cody was defenseless,

Powder Face rearing behind him now, pulling on his left arm, ruining his aim. The white man stood in the open.

"Get down, son—"

As Cody sailed backward in the air, he marveled on how funny it felt. The first time he had been knocked off his feet. Not really sure at first if Powder Face hadn't pulled him backward, or that the old sergeant had pushed him . . . then realizing something was dreadfully wrong with the way his head hurt. He struck the ground so hard it knocked the wind from him.

A spray of meteors cascaded before his eyes, pain welling behind them like a slow lava flow of red ice. His ears rang with a shrill whistle, reminding him of the bugle of an elk bull in the rut.

Payne was over him, dragging him up by the collar of his hickory shirt.

"Jumpin' jiminy, son," the sergeant whispered. "The rest are moving away."

"Is . . . is it trumpets I hear?" Cody asked, sitting up slowly, then turning over on his knees weakly. He felt like he wanted to heave, light-headed, and his stomach heavier like never before.

Payne put his ear to the breeze, sorting sounds. "By damn, it is! Carr's coming, young'un. We're gonna make it after all."

He stood, wobbly at first, unsure and leaning against Payne for a moment. "They're coming again —hurry . . ."

Payne nodded, staring at someplace on the top of Cody's head as he did. He reached down, untying the faded red bandanna that hung about Cody's neck. "You need something. Here, put this 'round your head so we can get the hell out of here."

Cody watched the old man spit a long stream of tobacco before he quickly lapped the bandanna around his head. It served to stop the blood dripping into his eye. Then he realized he had lost his hat. He spotted it more than thirty yards back, as the warriors screamed over the hilltop again.

He took a step in its direction.

"Leave it!" Payne shouted.

Cody nodded reluctantly, securing a second knot in the bandanna. Angrily he yanked on the rein, bringing the mount to his side as he jammed the Spencer against his shoulder and fired, then twice and a third time. Walking backward slowly, they protected the rear flank of the retreating Company M.

Through it all, every step of the way, the old sergeant at his shoulder muttered under his breath between nearly every shot.

"Jumpin' jiminy—but you're a cool one, you are. Injun bullet scratched your brains loose the way it did . . . bleeding the way you are. You're a cool one, Bill Cody."

Chapter 17

May 16, 1869

"To my dying day, Cody—I'll not forget that scene when the whole unit came up and we found you and M Company making a stand of it," said Major Eugene Carr late on the evening following the brief skirmish with the Cheyenne on Spring Creek.

Seamus Donegan sat with Cody at the fire where coffee boiled as they waited for the gray of twilight to darken into night. "You ought to hear Babcock and Volkmar go on about you, Cody."

Carr nodded, accepting a tin of coffee. "They haven't stopped talking about your coolness and bravery—especially in the face of your wound."

Cody gently touched the fresh bandage tied round his head to cover the deep furrow that marked where the Indian bullet had plowed along the top of his skull for nearly half a foot.

"If I go on this ride for you, General—I need two things."

"One is that I'm riding with you," Donegan said quickly.

Cody nodded, with a grin. "And the other is, I need a new hat."

Carr chuckled. "I'll supply you both the Irishman and the hat."

He wagged his head slowly, still aching the way it was. "Glory—but that was a damned fine hat, Seamus. Almost as pretty as my head before them red bastards tried to shoot that off."

"They nearly did, Cody," Carr replied. "We rode to the sounds of the guns as fast as I could bring up the whole unit. And as we came up, the Cheyenne broke off from their attack on Babcock. But I've got to tell you I was confused for a moment or two—seeing the Indians in retreat on the prairie beyond . . . then seeing a figure wearing what looked like a red cap rise slowly from the crest of a nearby hill. It puzzled me, because the figure wore buckskins and his long hair was caught on the breeze."

"Sounds like he was a Injin to me, it does," Donegan muttered with a smile for Cody.

Carr nodded. "When I looked closer, I could see that the figure led your horse, Powder Face . . . and I found that the figure was you, but without that dusty sombrero you're so fond of. And that's when I first spied the bloody handkerchief covering your frightful wound."

Cody stood, slinging the dregs of his coffee toward the firepit. "That hat was a favorite, General. That's why I want the army to get me another like it as soon as possible."

"When we reach McPherson, rest assured of that."

"And for my ride?"

"Any hat you want, Cody. Even mine."

"One like it will do," Cody replied. "So—you agree Fort Kearny is our best bet?"

"North and east of us, on the Platte. We've been chasing this bunch of Cheyenne about as long as we can without resupply. Fort Kearny is the closest depot. It's up to you two now."

"We'll bring supplies back for the regiment. No one else knows this country between here and there the way I do."

"And you're sure as hell not riding out of here alone tonight with that chunk of skull ridged up the way it is," Donegan quickly added.

They turned as the horses were brought up to them, and Carr took the hat from his head.

"If this fits, wear it until we get to McPherson." He reached inside his blouse to pull out a folded slip of paper. "This is the requisition I'm making on the Fort Kearny stores. It will get you what we need from the quartermaster's supplies there."

Cody patted Powder Face then hoisted himself to the saddle, feeling a bit unsteady. "We'll see you soon, General Carr."

The leader of the Fifth Cavalry saluted the pair and watched as they pointed their mounts northeast from Spring Creek.

"I wager I'll see you sooner than I imagine."

Slap dark surrounded them as they loped the first few miles, to put some distance between themselves and the regimental camp of the Fifth Cavalry.

Seamus admired the younger man who rode the piebald at his side, this Bill Cody who had fought Cheyennes that afternoon, been seriously wounded and now was taking this cross-country ride under the cloak of darkness to avoid roving war parties, as if he were the strongest man Carr had for the journey.

Perhaps he is, Donegan brooded, praying the Cheyenne were continuing their flight south and would not double back to the north.

It was well after dark, with at least an hour left until moonrise, before Seamus let himself relax in the saddle, finally believing the Cheyenne actually might be in their camp somewhere south of the Republican by now, licking their wounds and not desiring another engagement with the soldiers anytime soon. Babcock's M Company had been lucky, no doubt of that. But a good deal of the credit had to go to the old sergeant and the young scout who together had covered the company's retreat until the full unit could come up to pull their fat from the fire.

That night the pair did what to many would have been impossible—covering some fifty miles in the dark, heading by instinct and the stars above for Fort Kearny on the Platte River. Like a beacon spotted by a wayward ship on a rocky shoreline, Cody and Donegan spied the bare flagpole from beyond the rolling swell of land in the first graying of dawn that eighteenth day of May.

They were presenting Carr's request to the post commander when the sunrise gun roared across the parade.

By mid-morning the pair was leading a short procession of supply wagons from the fort, headed on a southwesterly course of interception with Carr's cavalry. The major would be continuing his march north, up Spring Creek toward the Republican.

"If I figure it right, Seamus—we'll find the general's boys camped on the creek, about fifteen miles above last night's camp."

Donegan nodded, yawning. "Where two idiots left to ride out on this ruddy fools' errand."

"Don't be hard on me, Irishman. You volunteered to come along to nurse me—but you really came along to buy yourself some whiskey."

Seamus smiled, pulling the green bottle from his shirt. "And aren't you glad I did, Bill Cody?"

"Give me a tonic, Surgeon Seamus," and he smiled. "I'm sore in need of it—and do believe my head is aching something fierce."

Cody's supply train reached Carr's camp far down Spring Creek that evening after sunset. The cheering and huzzahs for the pair who had brought in the supply train went on and on as the troops celebrated with salt-pork, beans and hard bread. Once again they had fresh coffee and were no longer consigned to boiling old grounds. Two genuine heroes who had been in the saddle for more than forty hours without sleep.

"I'll let General Sheridan know of my commendation as soon as we reach McPherson in two days," Carr said as he came up with coffee tin in hand. His nose twitched, his eyes widening. "Is that whiskey I smell, Cody?"

"Aye, it is, General," Donegan answered, standing, with the green bottle in evidence.

Carr licked his lips. "It's . . . well, by damned—let me have a pull on that, will you? It will do me some good, I'll grant you."

"My pleasure, General." Seamus handed the bottle over and watched the major pull thirstily.

He brought it down from his lips. "Been a long time, fellas. My, but that was better than I could possible imagine."

"Man can always find whiskey when he wants it," Cody said. "Especially if that man is born with a Irish nose and is named Donegan."

They had had their laugh with Carr, and wandered off to the blankets not long after filling their bellies with warm food. As it always does, the next sunrise came too early for the two who'd kept sleep at bay for the better part of two days. That reveille meant a quickened march north to the Platte River, then pointing the column west along the south bank. Again the following day Carr kept his regiment marching toward the setting sun, reaching Fort McPherson, their new duty station, near evening.

"It's about time we got here too," Donegan grumbled to Cody as they sighted the bastions of the prairie fort. He held his green bottle up in the fading light, swished the last of it around and offered some to his young companion.

Cody sipped at the whiskey, then returned the bottle.

He drank the last with a flourish, then sent the bottle sailing into the nearby Platte. "Good thing we'll be stationed near a sutler for a while, Bill Cody—for you've given this Irishman one hell of a thirst having to follow you and fight the ruddy Cheyenne!"

He was no young warrior, but nonetheless, the blood ran hot in his veins in these moments before attack.

Tall Bull glanced to the east, gazing at the brightening line stretched between the horizon and the blackness of night where the sun would emerge in a matter of heartbeats. Already the air felt warmed, if only by the prospect of another day.

Perhaps, he thought, it is the coming of battle that warms the day, the way it fires every sinew of my body.

Nearly three hundred of the finest warriors to ever fork a war-pony awaited his command. They stood in anticipation back in the timber of coulees and dry washes, behind hills in the shadows of night-going. His command would bring them roaring down on this second settlement that stained the sacred hunting ground of buffalo country the white man called Kansas.

The warriors had ridden south of the creek called the Beaver. South of Prairie Dog Creek and on to the Solomon where they had struck twice in the last risings of the sun. Raiding was good now in the Moon of Fattening as the days grew longer and warmer, as the grass stood tall and green to fill the bellies of the ponies that carried them down on these settlements.

They had been taking everything they could carry on the backs of those ponies when they left the white man's buildings burning. Thick columns of oily black smoke smudged the sky as they rode away from the reddened, naked bodies they had scalped and butchered. White-faced cattle and hogs left to bloat in the sun, arrows bristling from their ribs.

Guns and bullets, kettles and blankets. One warrior even took a fancy to a ladder-backed rocking chair and carried it off from one raid. And yesterday morning they had found a large grouping of settlers' cabins hugging the Saline River. They were close to what the white man called the Buffalo Tank, near the tracks of the great smoking horse that moved the soldiers west toward the setting sun. In that settlement one of Tall Bull's warriors had emerged from a burning cabin, holding a screaming woman thrashing at the end of his arm. She swung at him nonstop as he laughed. And she talked in some tongue that was so foreign that even Tall Bull had to admit the white man must have many dialects—perhaps as many as the Shahiyena and Lakota and Arapaho and Kiowa and . . .

This woman's tongue was strange. But she was possessed of muscle, and young enough to bear many children. Her loins would give birth to many Cheyenne warriors.

He smiled widely, glancing in anticipation at the coming light of day. To him, there was great irony in dragging these white women along instead of killing the women beside their men, who'd been left to lie and bloat in the sun near their burning cabins and butchered livestock. The women would belong to their captors, and the Cheyenne sons born of their wombs would grow to make war on the white man for many summers to come.

"It is time," White Horse whispered at Tall Bull's side.

He nodded. "Stand and give my signal."

White Horse leaped to his saddle. Tall Bull tossed him the long lance from which fluttered the hair of many who had fallen to the fighting skill of the Dog Soldier chief. The lance wavered slowly back and forth, causing a rustle along the hilltops as warriors sprang to the backs of their ponies, adjusting medicine pouches and weapons, shields and blankets.

When Tall Bull had climbed atop his pale pony, he nodded to White Horse. "It is time to rub this place clean."

White Horse volved the lance around and around in four tight circles, then jabbed the air with it, pointing down the slope.

From the throat of all three hundred sprang the cries intended to make the white man soil his pants as he lay sleeping in his warm bed, there beside his white-skinned woman who would soon lie pinned beneath a Cheyenne husband, receiving his seed, which each summer would grow into another Cheyenne warrior raised to stop the profane advance of the white man across this sacred buffalo ground.

In a wide arc the warriors swept off the hills and out of the timbered coulees, screeching their warcries as they bore down on the humble grouping of cabins and split-rail corrals that cast shadows along the Saline River of central Kansas. The first of the horsemen had nearly reached the cabins and livestock before the warriors fired their first shots.

Every bit as quickly, those first shots were answered by a few random replies from the darkened cabin windows—bright flares of muzzle-flash exploding like momentary fireflies illuminated against a summer's night sky.

The milk cows, pigs and hogs in nearby pens cried out in confusion and terror, finally in pain as the horsemen swept around them, tearing down fence-rails, freeing the animals, then having sport with the domesticated stock before each trembling beast fell kicking in its death throes.

Here and there the Cheyenne worked close-in, riding up to the small, curtained windows, smashing them with lances and rifle butts, then hurling burning torches into the dawn darkness that for a moment sheltered the white families inside. When the flames and smoke and fear grew too much to keep them inside, the settlers burst through the doors in a flurry—more afraid of the flames than of the unknown waiting in the pink-orange of dawn outside.

Some of the men fought for a few desperate minutes, aiming and reloading, shooting until overrun. Others fell immediately to bullets or arrows or club or were impaled on the long war-lance of the Cheyenne buffalo-hunting days. One man was impaled, left swinging, swinging gently on his front door.

Screaming, everyone screaming just as loud as the animals grunted and squealed, just as horrendous as the victors cried out in blood-lust as each new white victim fell onto the spring-damp soil.

From one cabin came no bright flash of riflefire. Tall Bull wondered on it. He slowly inched his pony in its direction when a pair of warriors pitched flaming brands through the window. Perhaps no one lived there in that square lodge, the Cheyenne chief thought.

Then he saw a flicker of movement, something against the darkness, a ghostlike tongue of motion against the flames leaping to secure the cabin's interior.

She burst from the cabin door, screaming, the back of her long dress aflame.

He put heels to the pony, waving off a half-dozen young hot-bloods who were headed toward the screaming woman.

Tall Bull lusted her blond hair. He had first claim to her, after all, as their war leader. He knocked her down with the pony as he swept past her, reining up in a skidding halt.

He was on the ground in the next instant, yanking the blanket from back of the pony, flopping it over the woman, slapping and smothering the flames.

Her face became a queer mix of gratitude and utter revulsion mixed with utter terror—those liquid eyes peered up at his as he fought to hold her down once the flames were out. The stench of her singed hair stunk no worse than the heavy woman smell of her.

These white women do not segregate themselves as do Cheyenne women when their time of the moon comes, he thought quickly. I must not let her touch my weapons or my war medicine while she is bleeding from her woman-place.

But he would have her now. And she would bear him many fine young sons. This woman whose man was not home to protect her, this fair-haired, blue-eyed white woman who kept screaming, shaking and thrashing as he bound her.

Tall Bull liked fight in a woman. It made the coupling that much more a pleasure.

He found himself already hard for her when he spread her white legs there in the shadow of her burning cabin and drove himself deep as she writhed beneath his fury.

Chapter 18

Early June 1869

North Platte was one of those Nebraska towns that rode the wild boom and bust cycle like a prairie tornado thundering down on a settlement out of nowhere, bringing sweet times then leaving havoc in its wake, gone as suddenly as it had made its appearance on the horizon.

Erected in that strip of land where the North and South Platte rivers joined twenty-some miles northwest of Fort McPherson, the town was originally laid out for the Union Pacific Railroad by General Grenville Dodge in 1866. With the railroad gangs, along with speculators and the assorted gamblers, drummers and whores who accompanied the rails west, North Platte grew to be quite a place for a short time.

By 1869 fame had abandoned the place, like any other homely maiden left waiting at the altar. The winds of the prairie had claimed some of the more rickety vacant buildings, toppling them. Those still left standing looked more like the gaping eye-sockets of a buffalo skeleton. Only two dozen places fronted the entire main street: a motley collection of log and clapboard buildings including the jail, three mercantiles, a bevy of watering-holes, and three hotels.

Most notorious of the three was the California Exchange Keg House, owned by Dave Perry, who advertised his offerings in the local paper, knowing how every issue was read and reread by hundreds of eager, thirsty soldiers downriver at Fort McPherson. His hotel, saloon and dance-hall proved the liveliest—the best-known of meeting places in North Platte.

"Says here in the paper that the place has '. . . the choicest brands of wines, brandies, gins, whiskeys and liquors of all kinds to be had west of Chicago.'" Captain William Brown read to Bill Cody as they eased their mounts to a halt at the rail outside Dave Perry's California House.

"Let's just hope the whiskey is cheap and the music loud."

"You aren't fixing to get me in trouble again, are you, Cody?"

Bill slapped him on the shoulder as they stomped onto the muddy boardwalk out front. "Carr didn't dare trust you to get supplies this time did he, Captain? So, we're free to drink on our own time today."

"I'm still here in an official capacity."

Cody stopped at the door, showing Brown in. "You brought me with you to help you welcome that new passel of Pawnee scouts Sheridan is sending us, right?"

Brown nodded, stopping at the bar to size up the place as Cody leaned back against the rough-hewn bartop. "Pawnee scouts, yessir. Sheridan's idea—to fight Indians with Indians."

Cody snorted. "Who's gonna lead 'em? Your army officers or their war-chief?"

Brown finally got Cody's try at humor. "Carr said I was to be on the lookout for two brothers who command the Pawnee detail: Major Frank North and his brother, Captain Luther North."

"Major and captain, is it?"

The officer waved the burly bartender down their way. "Both served with honor during the war—though neither one of 'em has regular army rank."

"But you look every inch a soldier," exclaimed the bartender to Brown. "Dave Perry's the name." He held out his hand.

"Captain William Brown, Fifth Cavalry, sir," Brown replied. He motioned to his companion. "Bill Cody, chief of scouts for the Fifth."

Cody could smell the strong stench of old whiskey on the bartender's breath. Perry's eyes were red-rimmed and bloodshot, as if he was of the kind to punish a bottle hard, day in and day out. The man moved with that kind of looseness that spoke of too much whiskey sloshing about in his ample belly. The scout put out his hand, willing to try at friendly.

Perry eagerly shook hands with Cody. "Pleased to meet you both. What you drinking today?"

"Whiskey—make it a bottle," Cody was quick to answer. He didn't like the cocksureness of the man, the way he strutted just by talking. Better to be wary of this kind, he thought as Perry turned to snatch up a bottle.

Brown laid a single eagle down on the bar.

"You'll be wanting change, Captain?" Perry asked behind that loaded grin of his. "Or, will you be drinking up your ten dollars' worth?," he asked with undisguised scorn for the young man.

Brown opened his mouth, but Cody spoke first. He wanted out of the man's way, knowing even with his few years on the frontier there were two types of drunks. The friendly ones, and the mean ones. If he did not know a man who had been punishing the bottle hard, better to stay out of that man's path.

"Keep our tab open, Mr. Perry," Cody snapped a little too quickly. The scout turned, and was about to drag the bottle and two glasses from the bar, when Perry stopped him.

"You got yourself a chip on your shoulder, I'll bet, Mr. Cody."

Bill felt the first boil of hate stirring in his belly, something simmering like anger ready to ignite. He stopped a few feet from the bar, then turned back on Perry.

"You got your nose stuck in the wrong place, shopkeeper."

"Shopkeeper, is it?" and Perry roared. A few of the patrons laughed as well. "Far as I can see, I'm proprietor of a thriving establishment, thanks to the railroad and the army." He leaned across the bar in Cody's direction. "No thanks to young jackasses like you who feel froggy enough to go spouting off at the mouth."

"Anytime you want to find out how froggy—"

"I think you both just got off to a bad start,"

Brown sputtered, coming between the two, attempting to nudge Cody off toward an empty table.

Perry kept that same implacable grin on his face as he wiped a dirty hand-towel across the rough bar. That frozen grimace reminded Cody of a rusted iron hinge no longer capable of movement.

"Mr. Cody, I imagine you're just feeling what we in the business world call the squeeze of authority."

"No—I'm feeling nothing more than the need to whip some of the smart out of your fat ass."

Perry laughed again, and when he finished, the smile had disappeared. He laid the towel down as he rumbled to the end of the bar. "For days now we've heard the Pawnee scouts were coming in to join up with you soldiers out at McPherson. Talk had it that your bunch of scouts hasn't been doing the job up to the standards of the army. I hear the Pawnees coming in to save your ass from the fire, Cody."

"No goddamned Pawnee needs to help William F. Cody—"

"Let's just sit and have our drinks in peace, Cody!" Brown lunged for the scout.

Perry was pushing his sleeves up to his elbows, past his thick forearms. "Hear it said the North brothers gonna show you and your ragtag bunch of civilian scouts how to catch some Cheyenne. About time it is too."

Cody turned, mechanically, shoving the bottle and glasses into Brown's reluctant hands, then turned back like a mainspring, lashing out with the right fist. It caught Perry square on the jaw, staggering the bar owner two steps, making him blink his eyes in disbelief.

Cody swallowed, startled that the man had not gone down with that blow, the best the scout had to give. His right hand hurt where the knuckles had smashed against Perry's cheekbone, like a mule stomped on it. A small cut had been opened there on the barkeep's cheek, the only sign of any damage to the hulking man.

The young scout drank deep of the smoke-filled barroom air as he set his feet. He knew it was bound to be a tussle just staying on his pins—realizing Perry wasn't the out-of-shape, larded barkeep normally found back with the bottles and glasses and the smoked mirror. What was beneath Perry's apron was every bit as hard as Cody's hand was sore.

He had size and strength on the young scout. Cody had only speed.

The young man ducked, driving a right into the man's belly. It was tough, but Perry still winced a bit, the wind driven from him. Cody jabbed with the left, hard beneath Perry's ribs. A second time, searching for the kidney. Then he pushed off backward just as Perry went for the clench.

The man's big hands clawed for Cody's head, raking across the long, deep scalp wound still pink and healing from the Spring Creek fight.

Cody pulled his head free, seeing stars, reeling a moment.

Perry was on him quickly. Popping a big first against Cody's jaw. A second then a third time, each sharp jab sending the young scout backward a step.

Cody felt an eye puff up. A cut opened across one cheekbone. It stung almost as much as his pride.

"You had enough, Mr. Cody?"

He shook his head, his neck feeling loosened, like thick mud beginning to set along a creekbank. Not able to hold his head up, and with it growing heavier all the time.

"Stop this!"

He heard Brown hollering, stepping in front of him. Cody shoved the officer out of the way.

"He's the one who can stop it, Captain," Perry replied.

"No need to stop," Cody said, a lip growing puffy. "I ain't pounded you into this floor yet."

Perry laughed as Cody came on, swinging, connecting at times, lunging and falling against a table as Perry stepped aside. He knew he had to control his temper—figuring that was how he would defeat the bigger man.

"Had enough yet, Cody?"

He got to his hands and knees, blood pouring from his nose and mouth, the one eye he had left to see out of glazing over. Slowly he raised himself on the table and turned to find Perry standing near.

"Had to come in here and see for myself," Cody said quietly. "Heard this place was run by a fat coward made his living off the railroad and who word has it waters his whiskey down to serve for hard-working soldiers."

Cody watched the big man's cheeks flare. Not that he had called him fat, or a coward. But to attack the man's honesty was the ticket. And whiskey was the most sensitive of subjects when it came to a saloon owner.

Perry came on like a cannon loosed from its moorings. At the last moment Cody stepped aside, foot out, fists clenched together, and chopped down on the man's neck. Perry collapsed on the table, splintering it and a chair on the way down.

He rose, even more angry as Cody backed against the bar. Perry licked at the blood leaking from his lower lip. The scout inched along the bar, feeling his way behind him. Lunging for Cody, Perry met instead a chair that split apart as it crashed against his shoulder. The barkeeper stood, massaging the side of his neck.

"You're sport enough, Cody—but you're afraid of these fists of mine, ain't you?"

He nodded. No sense in denying it. "True enough, Perry. You've hammered me like iron on an anvil. But I ain't done in."

What Perry did next surprised Cody. The saloon owner sighed, volving his neck a bit. "You punch good for a youngster without much meat on his bones. I'll bet you get good when you grow up. You may not be done—but Dave Perry is willing to call it a draw."

Bill Cody squinted that one good eye, fidgeting a moment, wary of a ruse. Perry was backing away. Some of the patrons were patting him on the back, others picking up tables and chairs and gaming chips, slowly going back to their cards. And here he stood, still flush with hot adrenaline firing his veins.

"Perry."

The barkeeper turned. "I said you should let it go, Cody."

He licked his own puffy lips. "I'll run any man into the ground says I can't find Cheyenne for General Carr's cavalry."

Perry chuckled, a wry grin crossing his face. "I'll bet you can find them Cheyenne can't you, Bill

Cody? Way you stand up and don't give in—I'll bet you can find them Cheyenne at that."

"In the name of God, General—I beg you let me ride with your men!"

Tom Alderdice stood before Major Eugene Carr and his staff officers in the rosy streaks of dawn's first light. Seamus Donegan felt sorry for the man.

"I quite understand your situation, Mr. Alderdice," Carr tried to explain.

"I can carry my own weight, General. I was with Forsyth last summer."

"Mr. Donegan told me that before he brought you here this morning."

"Then you know how I want to give them back—"

"You're distraught right now, Mr. Alderdice."

"The hell! Wouldn't you be—returning home from a trip clear down to Hays City for supplies . . . find the whole settlement wiped clean. All them bodies with arrows stuck in 'em—starting to swell up and go black. All them scalped bodies—and you can't find your wife among 'em?"

Carr backed a step as Alderdice came on. The civilian's hands were trembling, his voice rising like a man on the edge of a great precipice who knows it is up to him to jump.

"I have a full complement of scouts, Mr. Alderdice," Carr explained, his eyes saying he could find no better way to apologize.

"I'll damn well won't use up as much victuals as them Pawnee gut-eaters you're packing along!"

"Lieutenant—see that the post guard escorts Mr. Alderdice to a holding cell in the guardhouse until we are three days out."

The man's eyes grew wild, darting over the soldiers who moved forward to take him. "Three days? Didn't you understand—they've got my wife, goddammit!"

"Tom. Tom," Seamus was whispering, gripping the civilian's greasy, sweat-stained shirt as two soldiers restrained his arms. "We'll find her. Believe me—we'll find her."

Alderdice struggled, finally loosening when he discovered he could not fight his way from the three. He seemed to shrink in their arms, sobbing, the tears so long held in abeyance coming now in a gush to wash down his dusty face.

"Susanna," he whimpered, gazing up into the tall Irishman's face. "Her name is Susanna. Find her for me, Seamus."

"I will, Tom. Count on it."

"Don't matter what them red devils done to her—I want her back."

"We'll bring her back to you."

"Seamus," he said, ripping one arm free of a soldier and grabbing hold of the Irishman's wool vest. "Promise me something else."

"Anything, Tom. Just ask it."

"I can't go and do it myself," he whispered hoarsely, finally bringing his eyes off the ground. They implored Donegan. "Bring me the scalp of the red bastard—the one been . . . been . . . abusing my woman."

Chapter 19

June 1869

"*R*eally like that big son of a bitch, don't you, Cody."

He turned to find Major Eugene Carr approaching. Cody went back to currying the big yellow horse. "About the best animal I've ridden, General."

"Major North told me you took a fancy to a horse belonging to one of his Pawnees."

"Traded him for it—fair, General."

Carr moved close, stroking the animal's neck as Cody brushed a rear flank. The camp of the Fifth Cavalry bustled about them. "You name him yet?"

"Buckskin Joe."

The officer nodded. "Buckskin color, all right. Better looking than that army mule you were partial to."

A new voice came up behind them. "General Carr."

Both Cody and the major turned to find Carr's

orderly bringing up a pair of pedigreed greyhounds at the end of short leashes.

"Holloman," Carr replied.

"The dogs are ready for you, sir."

Carr took the leads. "Bring up my horse, Private. We're ready to march."

Cody smoothed the saddle blanket then cinched the army saddle on the buckskin. "You exercising the dogs today, General?"

Carr grinned within his brown beard. "You might say that, Cody. I'm bringing them along with me this morning—going to ride with you on the advance."

Eyeing him for a moment, Cody said, "Them hounds of yours any good at hunting?"

Carr took the reins to his horse from the veterinary sergeant. "Let's you and me go catch up with the Pawnees riding the point—and see just how good these two are."

"Lute North is out with them," Cody replied sourly as he settled in the saddle.

The major climbed up as well. "You don't have much use for him, do you?"

"Neither one of 'em. Made a name for themselves on the plains using the eyes and ears of their Pawnee Battalion. Just natural that I don't take a liking to folks who ride the coattails of other men."

"The North brothers have a handsome reputation, Cody," Carr commented. "I certainly hope you will continue to work with them and their Pawnees."

Cody nudged his horse out. "I won't do anything to cause trouble, General. Won't be me starts anything."

Ever since leaving Fort McPherson on this march

south to hunt for the marauding Cheyenne, the Pawnee Battalion was always the first to rise in the morning and the first to be in the saddle. Under Luther North, the younger of the brothers, the Pawnee kept ahead of the Fifth Cavalry a distance of two to three miles throughout the day, covering a wide piece of country on both flanks as well.

This second day since leaving the Platte River, Carr and Cody loped ahead of the main column to catch up with the Pawnees.

"Captain North!" Carr shouted. His adjutant, the orderly and two more staff officers rode on the major's heels.

Luther North turned in the saddle, his eyes narrowing when he found Cody riding with Major Carr. "General. You here for inspection?"

Carr removed his hat and swiped at his brow. Already the sun was growing hot, having made its appearance in the east less than an hour ago. "No, Captain. I came up here to give the dogs some exercise."

North regarded the two greyhounds. "I see. You think those two skinny dogs good for hunting?"

"I do."

North grinned, like he was rolling something around in his mind. "You think them two can catch an antelope?"

Slapping his thigh with one hand, Carr replied, "Yes—they sure as hell can."

"Sounds to me like Captain North here figures your hounds aren't up to the task, General," Cody said. He watched the growing consternation come across Carr's face.

"Suppose they show you, Mr. North—show you they can catch an antelope."

"No need to show me, General. Antelope is a fast animal."

"So is a blooded greyhound, Captain."

North finally nodded. "All right. You're on. We'll have to ride far enough ahead of the others that we don't spook any goats out there."

"Very well, Captain North. Lead on."

Cody, Carr and the major's orderly followed North. The rest of the major's staff turned back to ride with the advance guard.

"There," Cody said minutes later, pointing into the shimmering distance of the plains.

"I see him," Carr replied, excited.

"Just a lone buck," Cody said. "If we take our time, leading your dogs off yonder, down in that ravine, we can get up on him. That way your hounds will have a good jump on him."

"Splendid, Cody."

The quartet followed the course of the dry ravine for better than half a mile until they were within two hundred yards of the antelope buck. The men dismounted and bellied against the slope of the ravine to watch the show.

"Holloman," Carr whispered to his orderly, "take the hounds up the bank—where they can get sight of that buck antelope."

The orderly struggled to get the pair of dogs up to the prairie, then released them from their long leashes. He plopped on his belly to watch as the hounds started off on the lope. No sound had come from their throats.

After a moment more the antelope turned, spotting the dogs, which began baying as they closed the gap. But instead of running, the antelope bounded toward the pair of skinny, earth-colored canines.

"That damned stupid animal figures to be sociable, General," Cody whispered. "Gonna meet a couple more antelope, looks like."

"Time for us to make our show, boys," Carr said, getting to his knees then moving quickly to his horse.

As soon as the four horsemen leaped up the bank of the ravine, the antelope bounded in a tight circle and took off at full speed. By this time Carr's hounds were already running flat out. They had closed the gap on the buck in the first few seconds.

"They'll catch that antelope before he even gets started, fellas."

All four men gave a wild whoop as they hammered their horses into a gallop, following the dogs up the steep slope of a hill. By the time the horses made it to the top, Cody suggested a stop to let the animals blow. Down on the wide, dry flat below, the dogs continued their chase as the quartet watched, intrigued. In less than a minute the buck disappeared over a far hill, the hounds still some two hundred yards behind him. When the pair reached the crest of that same hill they stopped, milling about and sniffing over the ground. Then, as if in agreement, they turned and trotted casually back to the horsemen.

North had not said a thing, merely leaning forward in his saddle, watching the whole show. Holloman and Cody were quiet as well while the hounds came up. Carr stepped from the saddle, kneeling to pet the dogs.

Cody was the first to speak, sensing the major's disappointment. "General, if anything, that buck antelope is running a little bit ahead."

Holloman and North laughed along with Cody. But Carr never looked up at his chief of scouts. It took a moment before he grinned in resignation and rose.

"It looks that way, Cody." Carr climbed into the saddle. "Captain North—Mr. Cody . . . let's certainly hope those Cheyenne we're chasing aren't as successful in eluding you as that antelope was in eluding my hounds."

For better than a week Major Carr had been pushing his Fifth Cavalry south from the Platte River. Across Medicine Lake, then Red Willow and Stinking Water creeks, Black Wood and Frenchman's Fork, until they struck the Republican River. The next day, 15 June, Cody had Seamus Donegan lead the entire column into camp twenty-five miles downriver. No fresh sign had been spotted by a scout, Pawnee or white.

Seamus had located a gurgling spring near the riverbank, bringing the cavalry into camp there on the north side of the Republican. A quarter-mile below the cavalry bivouac, the wagonmaster and teamsters circled their freight wagons and unhitched their mules. Across the river from their camp and that of Cody's lay an inviting patch of tall, green grass. The teamsters waded their mules across to grass them until dark.

Several hundred yards below the camp of Cody's civilian scouts lay the Pawnee camp. Major North ordered his battalion to keep their horses on the same side of the river, hobbling them north of their bivouac and fires.

Donegan was the first to bolt to his feet at the shrill war whoop directly across the river among the mules. His mouth was still full of beans and hardtack as a crackle of gunfire and the screams of the herders split the cool evening air. Spitting his mouthful of food into the fire, Seamus wrenched up his rifle as the whole camp whirled into motion. Running blindly toward the bank, the Irishman was unable to see anything on the far bank for the thick stand of cottonwoods. To his left the Pawnees and some of Cody's scouts were running their horses into camp, shouting. He turned back, sensing the need to be mounted before crossing the river.

Cody himself was struggling to get his saddle cinched atop the buckskin in all the hubbub as Seamus leaped bareback atop his army mare. They both pushed their horses into the river as the first Pawnees dashed up, in their tongue cursing the seven Cheyenne warriors disappearing over the nearby hills with more than half of the wagonmaster's mules. One of the two civilian herders lay up the slope of the hill, where he had been scalped and quickly stripped. The second herder loped toward Donegan atop a nervous mule, careening from side to side. The man clung both to the mule and life tenaciously. Three arrows bristled from his back, quivering with every step of the mule as he approached. He tried to speak as he passed Donegan, heading back across the river. Nothing but blood came from his mouth.

Donegan reined up and watched the man reach the river, where he was helped by other teamsters splashing into the water on foot. Seamus reined about and put heels to the big mare.

Already the Cheyenne had abandoned their mules and were intent only on making good their escape into the hills to the south of the Republican. Hot on their tails were the Pawnee, shouting, scolding, shooting over the heads of the horse thieves. Cody was just ahead as North's Indians slowly galloped past him. Through the dust, Seamus watched one of the Pawnee gesture as he came alongside the white scout. The tracker then reached over and took Cody's pistol from its holster when the white man had his head turned back to find Donegan and Luther North rapidly catching up.

"Son of a bitch stole my gun, North!"

Luther North tried to laugh it off as they tore after the Pawnee. "I'm sure he'll give it back to you, Cody."

"He doesn't—he'd better plan on using it on me."

"You're taking this all a little too seriously, you ask me," North replied with the hint of a sneer.

"You can count on me helping Cody get his pistol back," Donegan growled.

North's eyes narrowed on the Irishman. "No, there'll be no trouble. I'll get the gun back, my way."

"Better keep your boys away from me, North. Doesn't seem they like me at all."

North started to laugh, but it came out hollow. "Why you say that, Cody?"

"One of them could talk a little English. Told me something as he rode by me."

"What'd he say?" North asked as the trio continued after the Pawnees chasing the horse thieves.

"Told me a bunch of his friends went south last

summer to steal some horses from the Cheyenne. But the Cheyenne learned of 'em, surrounded 'em and killed a few of the Pawnee on that raid. Your man said that riding with them Cheyenne that killed his friends was a white man . . . a white man with long hair the color of summer grass."

North flicked his eyes at Cody's long hair. "Sounds like it could be you."

"You know damned well it weren't me!" Cody snarled, about ready to reach out to yank North from the saddle.

"Man like you, North—gonna get himself in some serious trouble with his mouth," Donegan said on the far side of Cody.

North reluctantly nodded. "You're right. Couldn't been you, Cody. You're here to fight Injuns."

"You're savvy enough to know there's a few renegades running with the tribes," Seamus muttered, finding he was liking Luther North less and less the more he got to know him.

"How would you know about that, Irishman?"

He pointed high on his arm. "I took Cheyenne lead in this arm of mine last summer. Almost lost the arm for nine days of mortification. I was with Forsyth."

"Beecher Island?" North asked as they neared the spot where most of the Pawnees had pulled up.

Donegan thought he recognized a sudden, new respect for him there in North's eyes.

As the three white men reined up, the Pawnees drew back. They had been stripping two dead Cheyenne shot from their horses.

North signed and asked in English, "Where are the others?"

One of the Pawnee stepped up, a long, bloody tendril of scalp dangling from his hand. "The five ride away from this place."

North turned to the white men. "The rest disappeared on them. What is wrong with that horse?"

They turned to one of the Pawnee mounts that had collapsed not far away on the prairie, foaming at the mouth and struggling to rise.

"He dies from the heat of the chase," explained the Pawnee.

"I suppose it's a draw, fellas," Cody said, walking up beside North. "Two Cheyenne for the two teamsters they killed. So, if you'll get this son of a bitch to give me my gun back—we won't have no more blood shed."

"Is this the one took your gun?" North asked.

Cody nodded. For a moment the Pawnee glowered at the blond scout as the light faded from the sky. Grudgingly he handed the gun over to North, who passed it on to Cody.

"Why'd you take it?" North inquired.

"I had no pistol when I left camp to chase the Cheyenne," the Pawnee explained. "When I rode alongside the white man, I saw his horse was slow and would not make a good chase of it. I needed the gun and he did not. I do not need it any longer."

North translated for the two white men, then turned back to the Pawnee. "This man is not the one you saw with the Cheyenne last summer."

"We know," replied the tallest of the Pawnee. "The white man with the Cheyenne was much smaller than this buffalo killer you call Cody. And he rode in the shadow of another whose long hair was very black. His skin was very dark . . . like ours. But his hair, it stuck out from his head like wild grass."

North shook his head, explaining the Pawnee's description.

"Makes me feel a bit better—that your boys don't think I was riding with the Cheyenne." Cody sighed.

Donegan wagged his head. "Still don't explain who was, Bill. And for the life of me—sounds like one of 'em wasn't a white man at all."

North nodded. "Irishman's right. Damned well sounds like it was a nigger riding with them murdering Dog Soldiers."

Chapter 20

June 1869

"*I* damn well thought we did a good job for you, General—getting every last mule back," Luther North snapped at Major Eugene Carr.

"So I'll say it again, Captain North—you exercised no command control over your scouts," Carr fumed. "They all took off on their own—like an undisciplined mob, after seven goddamned Cheyenne. All of you! Good Lord!"

As Cody returned to the camp of the Fifth Cavalry, with North's Pawnees leading the entire mule herd and bringing the two scalps, spirits had been high. But instead of congratulating North for saving the animals and running the hostiles off, Carr loomed out of the fire-lit darkness, sputtering his dissatisfaction with the captain's lack of military discipline.

Because of that dressing down, North was growing madder by the moment. "These Pawnee aren't like your goddamned, yellow-back soldiers, General. They'll fight. Hell, not only will the Pawnee fight the Cheyenne while your soldiers cower back in some safe place—these Pawnee of mine will go out to meet the attack. Think about that, damn you! Think about the fact that my Pawnee charging across that river was the only reason you got your precious mules back!"

"Captain North—you damn well know you're close to being insubordinate."

North laughed, almost insanely; his chin jutted as he squared his shoulders, seemingly eager to provoke the commanding officer of the Fifth Cavalry. "Insubordinate, hell! You damn well know I'm speaking the truth about your soldiers."

"Captain North, I warn you—"

"Your soldiers aren't cavalry—"

"Captain Cushing!" Carr growled.

"Yes, sir?"

". . . don't really give a damn what you think, General—these Pawnee are the only fighters you've got along on this march—"

"Captain Cushing, you're now in charge of the Pawnee scouts."

"What?"

Carr ignored North, continuing to look only at the dumbfounded Sylvanus E. Cushing. "I'm relieving Captain North from command. When Major North arrives in a few days, we'll review the situation."

"You can't do—"

"I damn well can do this, Captain North," Carr said, whirling on the young man. "And, you're under arrest for insubordination. He's in your custody Captain Cushing."

"Arresting me—"

"Best hold your tongue, Lute," Cushing replied quietly as Carr turned and stomped away.

"You're my goddamned brother-in-law, Sylvanus!"

"And you're a soldier, Lute. We both knew I was a soldier when I married your sister Sarah. Now act like a soldier and make her proud."

North grumbled under his breath as Cushing led him off into camp.

The following day, 16 June, Cushing and North rode at the head of the Pawnee scouts, leading the cavalry up the Republican in search of some sign of the Cheyenne who had hit their camp the previous night. The sun was climbing to mid-sky when Luther North turned at the sound of hooves coming up from the rear at a gallop.

"Who's that?" he asked.

"Carr's adjutant," Cushing replied. "So keep your opinions to yourself, Lute."

"General's compliments, Captain!" cheered Robert H. Montgomery as he slowed beside Cushing.

"Lieutenant," and he saluted.

"General orders that you send a scouting party of your Pawnee south across Prairie Dog Creek, to look along the Solomon."

Cushing sucked at the inside of his cheek a minute, looking back at the copper-skinned scouts behind him. "Lieutenant, give my compliments to the general—but inform him that I won't be able to get these Pawnee to do a damned thing."

Montgomery appeared confused. "I don't understand, Captain."

Cushing was nettled. "Captain North here is the

only white man we have along who can make these Pawnee understand where the general wants them to go."

The adjutant smiled, then chuckled some before he reined off with a salute. "Very good, Captain. I'll pass on word to the general to that effect."

"Sure as hell hope you didn't get your own ass in hot water with the old man," North whispered when Montgomery was galloping back to the main column.

"It's the truth, Lute," Cushing replied quietly. "Carr can't ignore the damned truth."

Twenty minutes later North turned again at the sound of hooves. Montgomery was once more galloping up to the advance guard.

"General's compliments, Captain North."

North glanced at Cushing a moment. "His compliments, eh?"

The adjutant grinned. "He informs Captain Cushing that Captain North is no longer under arrest and custody. The general wishes Captain North to take his Pawnees and scout south toward the Solomon as he directed."

Cushing looked relieved.

North swallowed a bit of his pride. If Carr was doing the same, he could be every bit as magnanimous about it as well. "Inform the general that the Pawnee Battalion is moving out, Lieutenant—for the Solomon."

The following afternoon, the seventeenth, Major Frank North rode in with another two dozen Pawnee, joining the Fifth Cavalry on the march and completing his battalion of scouts. That evening when Luther North came in with his detail to report some sign of hostiles on the Solomon, he greeted his brother and the reinforcements with great cheer.

As second in command of the Indian trackers, Captain North led the way the next morning, guiding Carr's column south for the Solomon. Upon reaching the north fork of that river, Major Carr ordered a day of rest for his troops while the North brothers took their Pawnees out on a meticulous search of the countryside: Frank heading upstream, Lute riding down the Solomon.

That evening of the eighteenth the Indian scouts returned without having seen much evidence of the hostile Cheyenne. Major North's command did not, however, return to the cavalry camp empty-handed. During the day, the Pawnee had come across a small herd of buffalo. Their ponies were loaded with fresh meat intended to sizzle and drip over the mess fires as twilight sank over the rolling prairie.

The next morning found the command moving northwest, back to the Prairie Dog, then west along the creek. Major North kept his scouting parties out every day for the next week, ranging far to the north and south as Carr marched his cavalry west, continually probing the country for the hostiles believed responsible for the depredations along the Saline and Solomon. From time to time the Pawnee came across the tracks of small hunting or war parties. Still, no sign of travois was discovered.

Carr turned the command northwest once more, crossing the Little Beaver, then striking Beaver Creek, known to the Cheyenne as the Sappa. Crossing Driftwood Creek, the Fifth Cavalry moved north to the Republican, marching upriver in search of the Solomon and Saline raiders.

To Seamus Donegan it had been a march over very familiar ground. As the sun rose high each day, hanging longer and longer while summer matured and aged the central plains, it reminded him more of that march behind Major George A. Forsyth one winter gone. Covering the same ground. Looking for what might turn out to be the same bands of Cheyenne who had forced the fifty civilians to that coffin-shaped island in the middle of a nameless creek on this sun-parched prairie.

He dragged his plate of beans and salt-pork onto his lap, squatting back from the fire as the sun's final rays dressed the western sky with a brilliant orange curtain. The food no longer had any taste to it. Only something to fill his gnawing belly each evening. Like the hard bread he soaked in the hot grease over breakfast fires while the coffee boiled in the predawn darkness before Cody moved his civilians out for the day. At least he had the boiled coffee tonight—it had taste on his tongue. Something close enough to the remembrance of whiskey.

Seamus pushed the thought away and shoved a chunk of the slimy pork in his mouth. Dangerous for a man out here to be brooding so much on whiskey.

The gunshot startled him.

Hustling up, beans spilling into the dusty, sun-parched grass at his feet, he hurried off toward that single gunshot with most of the others. There was shrill shouting yonder in the Pawnee camp as he loped up.

No Cheyenne running off horses this evening. Instead, only one of North's trackers playing a bit with his pistol. The weapon still lay in the grass as the white men joined the Pawnee in a tight knot around the wounded man.

"Shot himself," Luther North explained as he turned away from the commotion. "Think I'll have another cup of coffee. Want one, Irishman?"

"Yeah," Donegan replied, following North to a nearby fire. He glanced over his shoulder at the crowd dispersing. "Shot himself?"

"In the hand. Nasty-looking wound. Frank's going to take care of it. Appears the bullet went up the man's arm—came out at the elbow with his arm bent the way it was."

Seamus shuddered to think of it. "Long and oozy wound like that—be a long time in healing."

"Here's that coffee I promised you."

They drank in silence for some time as camp settled back down. Donegan was soaking a piece of hard bread in his cup when Frank North ambled up.

"Got the Fifth's surgeon to have a look at it," he said, settling to his haunches at the fire, spreading his hands before the flames. "Damn, it still gets cold out here when that sun goes down."

"Surgeon have to take it off, won't he, Frank?"

He looked at his younger brother. "Yeah, Lute. But the sonofabitch won't let him cut his arm off."

"During the war they didn't wait for you to say yes or no," Seamus grumbled, staring at the fire and remembering the piles of arms and legs, feet and hands outside the surgeon's tents and makeshift hospitals. He shuddered with the memory.

"Enough walking wounded from that war, eh, Irishman?"

"Man went through it—he's scarred for life, way I see it. He doesn't have to be missing an arm or leg." He looked up at the clear, starry sky. "A man just had to live through it—see what we did to each other in the name of whatever we were fighting for."

"Amen," Frank North whispered. "Amen."

"They're shipping that poor bastard back to McPherson with the supply train in the morning," Bill Cody said as he came to settle beside Seamus Donegan at their mess fire.

Four days had passed since the Pawnee tracker had wounded himself. Four days of heat and maggots and blackening of the flesh along the full length of his arm. That afternoon a supply train out of Fort McPherson bearing supplies, food and forage for the mounts had appeared over the hills, guided by a detail of North's Pawnee scouts.

"How long it take 'em to get back to McPherson you figure?"

"Four—most likely five days." Cody watched the Irishman wag his head. "Shame that Pawnee won't let the surgeon near him—being nearly out of his mind now with the blood poison. Damned shame."

Donegan cut a slice from a new plug of tobacco brought in with the supply train that day. With a jab of his tongue he nestled the dark quid inside his cheek. "That arm don't come off soon, he's one man of us won't have to worry about any Cheyenne Dog Soldiers lifting his scalp."

For more than a week now the weather had been unbearably hot. Her swollen, aching feet trudged through each day's march across the trackless prairie, beneath the mapless blue of a sky unsullied by clouds hinting of hoped-for moisture.

Susanna Alderdice didn't know what she hated more. The march from dawn till dusk each day, or the nightly terror she suffered after Tall Bull's band made camp at the end of each march. She stumbled along without water beneath the blazing sun, and had to fight for scraps of food to eat because the chief's wife was jealous of the blond-headed white woman. But worse still was to dread Tall Bull each night as the stars swirled overhead, when Susanna was forced to endure the savagery of his assault and copulating.

She was reminded of the horses when they mated. The grunting. The shrill cries. It was not lovemaking with the big Cheyenne warrior. This was nothing but violence, his defiling her with his seed in her most private of places. The only time he had let her be was when she bled last month. He had been so brutal with her at first that for days on end she bled, with nothing to keep it from seeping down her leg, onto her torn stockings as she marched with the moving village each day.

He had stayed away from her, fearing the power of a woman's menstruation over his own medicine. Susanna Alderdice had gloried in that little lie, letting the brute believe she was suffering her monthly. But as quickly her joy disappeared when she realized she had had no menstruation for more than two moons now. It gave her such a galling, bitter taste at the back of her throat to think that she might be carrying the Cheyenne's child in her womb.

She turned at the sound of footsteps. Ducking beneath the protection of her arms as Tall Bull's wife rushed her, swinging a piece of firewood overhead. Battering the white woman. Tall Bull's daughter kicked and flailed at Susanna, while they both spit and hurled their curses at her.

As quickly, Tall Bull was pulling his wife and daughter from the cowering captive. He shouted at them, shoving them away, sending them off into camp.

Susanna realized her time had come. He was again sending the others from the lodge for the evening so that he could have his way with his grass-haired prisoner.

She watched the two women move slowly away as she was wrenched up, her wrist imprisoned in his grip. Tall Bull dragged her toward the doorway. It was the only time she was allowed in the chief's lodge. To suffer his abuse. He shoved her through the opening, then pulled the door-flap closed behind him.

Tall Bull tore at her ripped, dirtied clothing. She slapped at his hands, backing away around the fire. He smashed a flat hand across her cheek.

Feeling the warm blood oozing into her mouth, seeing stars, Susanna Alderdice shook her head, trying to make him understand. She began to unbutton what she had left of dignity. Rather than let the man rip the clothing from her, she would do what she could to save the dress.

There would come a day, she prayed as she lay

back upon the buffalo robes and spread her legs, watching him tug his breechclout aside and sink over her.

There would come a day when she would need this dress to wear back home.

Chapter 21

First Days in the Moon of Cherries Blackening

*H*e hated her at the same time he lusted for her with all his being. Longed not only for her white flesh, but for everything she was that he was not.

Finished with her again this night, as on so many nights past. More than two moons since he had captured her, and she still was reluctant in coupling with him.

Why was she so different than his own woman? Different than any Cheyenne woman in making love?

Several nights ago she had pushed him away and removed her own clothing, then laid herself on his bed at the rear of the lodge and spread her legs to welcome him. But it was still not as if she had enjoyed his coupling with her.

The white woman just lay there, crying while he rose to a fury of violence and lust for her and all white skins. She sobbed quietly, shaming him.

He hit her each time she did so. Hit her hard, making her eyes puffy, causing her lips to bleed. He could not help it—this that she drove him to do. What did she expect of him? He was a man, after all. And she was a woman. A white woman, but woman nonetheless.

So he cast her out of his lodge when he was finished with her. Again tonight, as he had done every night. It was for her own good, for when his wife came home, she would be angry with the white woman and would beat her. It was a shameful thing for a woman to suffer a beating from another woman, and he did not want to witness her shame. More dignity in a woman being beaten by a man.

He watched the woman drag herself away, naked and pitiful in the growing moonlight, her skimpy bundle of clothing clutched under an arm as she crabbed along on one arm and both knees. Dogs nearby were drawn to the odor she gave off—perhaps the blood, perhaps her female scent heightened by their coupling. The animals came yipping at her, sniffing at her as Susanna dragged herself into the trees, kicking, hitting, scolding the dogs that gathered, following her to her hiding place.

Turning away, he decided he had better things to think on now that he no longer had to worry about his loins. At least until tomorrow.

"White Horse," he called out. Others were with the warrior, smoking outside the Horse's lodge this summer night.

"Join us, Tall Bull."

He sat and accepted a pipe the men were smoking socially without ceremony. "It is time we talk of more attacks."

"The summer heat makes you grow restless too?" Wolf Friend asked.

"Why does Wolf Friend ask? Because he does not have a white woman to copulate with when he grows restless like Tall Bull?" joked Bad Heart.

The group laughed together, passing a water gourd around. A group of children hurried by in the deepening dark of night as the moon rose yellow as a brass cartridge in the east.

"Tall Bull is right," agreed Plenty of Bull Meat. "We must not let up on the white man now."

"*Aiyeee!* We must keep attacking until the white man and his kind are driven out," Yellow Nose said.

"What of his soldiers?" prodded Tall Sioux. "We go in search of the white man's settlements to attack . . . and still the soldiers come. It is not the earth-scratchers we must attack. It is the soldiers who winter after winter come marching to attack our villages."

"This is true," said White Man's Ladder. "The soldiers search out our villages, killing our women and children who cannot escape."

"Black Kettle lived too close to the white men," Bobtailed Porcupine muttered.

"Black Kettle is dead," Tall Bull roared. "Killed by the Yellow Hair on the Washita."

"The old men . . . the ones who act like old women, those who want peace with the white man —these are the ones the soldiers catch and kill!" White Horse shouted, his words angry. "Perhaps we should not cry for any who die, caught by the soldiers—for they were stupid not to fight back with the last ounce of their strength."

"White Horse is right," Tall Bull agreed. "We must

not just wander this prairie, staying away from the
white man. We must attack . . . and attack again.
Find his outlying settlements. Kill the white people
there."

"What of the great smoking horses that move
back and forth across the land once grazed freely by
the buffalo?" Bullet Proof asked, speaking for the
first time.

"The herds are cut in half," Feathered Bear said,
wagging his head. "No more will they cross the iron
tracks the white man has laid down for his smoking
horse."

"It is as if the white man has laid down two lines
on the prairie—one north of us, one south. The buffalo no longer move freely," said Red Cherries.

"*We* no longer move freely across the land of our
fathers!" White Horse growled.

"It was the land of our fathers at one time,"
moaned Yellow Nose. "We must not be known as
the sons who gave it away to the white man."

On the far side of camp, to the east, there arose a
commotion. Some muffled shouts and the barking
of dogs interrupted their council for but a moment.
The warriors turned back to their talk.

"Let those words rest now where your hearts lie,"
Tall Bull continued. "We will not be the last generation to ride free across this prairie. We will fight.
While other bands run away, we will fight. While
other bands tuck their tails like scared rabbits and
hide on their reservations, we will fight."

"When? When will we ride again!"

He looked at Heavy Furred Wolf, who had asked
the all-important question. "As soon as we want!"

"Tomorrow!" White Horse replied.

"Yes—let us ride tomorrow," Tall Sioux echoed.

The commotion drew his attention once more. Tall Bull turned, as did most of the others in the large ring seated in the grass. "What is this?" he asked of two young boys running up at full speed.

"Our scouts!" one of them huffed, out of breath.

"They have come back running."

"Running?" Tall Bull asked.

"They bring word of the white man."

"We will attack soon!" Wolf Friend cried in happiness.

Tall Bull grabbed the two boys by the shoulders. "What is this news of the white man? Where?"

"Pile of Bones saw the soldiers."

"Soldiers?" White Horse asked, crowding close on the two boys now.

His young head bobbed as he caught his breath from his hard run. "Pile of Bones saw them. Many. He says there are ten-times-ten for each finger on one hand."

White Horse looked at Tall Bull. "These must be the same soldiers who have been following us for more than a moon."

Tall Bull grinned, spreading his arms as he roared. "It is good! The swallows follow the hawk too closely—the hawk turns and eats the swallows up!"

"Attack!"

"*Aiyeee!* We kill them all!"

"Swallow the sparrows and spit out their bones!"

"Carr won't let you ride out with Becher's patrol, Cody?" asked Seamus Donegan as he hoisted the saddle atop the big mare.

Cody wagged his head as he tightened the cinch on the new horse he had named Buckskin Joe. "Says he wants me keeping my nose pointed north for now."

"Pawnee going to be disappointed."

The young scout sighed, smiling. "That was some show the other day, wasn't it?"

A few days before, North's Pawnees had bumped into a small herd of buffalo and killed thirty-two in a surround. Cody had then asked Frank North to hold his scouts in check while he went in to do what he did best on a buffalo pony. In a short, half-mile run, Cody dropped thirty-six bulls and cows on his own.

"From that day on, me friend, you've been some big medicine to them Pawnee," Seamus said.

"That Lieutenant Becher asked for you to come along with him and his Pawnee—said the scouts wanted you if they couldn't have me ride with 'em, Irishman," Cody explained.

Seamus stuffed a boot into the stirrup and rose to the saddle. "I'll consider it a compliment that the Pawnee want me riding with 'em when we go looking for h'athens. Watch your hair, Bill Cody." He tossed a hand as he reined away.

"Your hair just as pretty as mine, Irishman! Look good hanging from a Dog Soldier lance or lodgepole."

Seamus laughed easily as he loped over to the bustling soldier bivouac in the early light of this fifth day of July. He reported for duty with Lieutenant Gustavus W. Becher, German immigrant and war veteran in his late thirties. Major Frank North had given immediate command of fifty of the Pawnee scouts to Becher, one of North's white officers. The German officer and the Irish scout would be the only white men along on this rapid probe to the northwest.

Becher gave the order and the Pawnee column loped out of camp in an orderly column of twos.

For the better part of the morning the scouts felt their way up Rock Creek from the Republican River. Looking for sign as they probed north by west until the lieutenant ordered a ten-minute breather for the horses.

"We've seen so damned little in the last few days," Becher grumped as he settled beside Donegan in the low shade of some stunted cottonwood.

"A blessing it might prove to be, Lieutenant."

He studied the Irishman a moment before replying. "You don't want the fight that everyone says is coming?"

"I don't want to fight if I can avoid it, no. But a man must remember that what I've learned is that when you find a lot of Injin sign . . . you don't find the Injins. It's when you don't see the sign of the h'athens that a man must be wary."

Becher regarded him with a knowing eye. "Something about you, Irishman. Young as you are—but knowing savvy the way you do. Sound old, I didn't know better."

Seamus chuckled. "Just had me some good teachers took me under their wings—till I was able to fly on me own."

Becher got to his feet. "Can't help you fly, Irishman. But we do have some riding to do."

They stopped again for a brief time when the sun reached mid-sky. Miles from the next trickling creek, the horsemen quietly ate their jerked buffalo and hardtack, washed down with warm water from their canteens. From there Becher pointed his Pawnee scouts almost due north toward Frenchman's Fork, into the sandhill country that hugged close by Colorado Territory. That endless, rolling monotony of tableland reminded him of the sandhill country south along the Arikaree Fork where for nine days Forsyth's faithful had clung to hope.

Seamus had sunk so far into that warm, dreamy place a man on horseback goes to when long in the saddle beneath an endless sky, that he was unaware of the first scattering of shots. Donegan snapped awake when one of the Pawnee horses jostled against the mare in the confusion.

At the center of the melee sat Lieutenant Becher, shouting in his German-laced Pawnee. The scouts obeyed, it appeared, dismounting to split into three squads. Horse holders scurried to the rear a hundred yards, as the full brunt of the Cheyenne wave hit them.

"I say a hundred, Irishman," Becher snapped as Donegan skidded to a stop beside him, levering another cartridge into his Spencer.

"More like hundred twenty or so."

"Your eye better at this than mine," he said above the roar of the carbines. The Spencer slammed back into his shoulder.

Seamus heaved the moist quid from his cheek, his mouth suddenly gone dry and the leaf-burly grown tasteless.

The Cheyenne were sweeping over the bright, sun-washed hills in two groups that met in a sweeping arc some three hundred yards to the north.

Back they came on themselves in two rushing torrents of painted, feathered horsemen.

"They out looking for us?"

Seamus shook his head for the German. "Don't think so. Figure we just bumped into 'em." He levered the Henry and cheeked it to his shoulder.

They grew daring—he could see that. Coming in a bit closer with each run. Although there were already two of the naked horsemen stretched unmoving on the sand, the Cheyenne kept coming back for more—feeling here, then there, at the three squads Becher had ordered to make their stand.

"They'll break off soon," Donegan growled at the German. "Odds aren't good enough in their favor—and they're just as surprised as we are. Can't run us over . . . so they'll pull back to fight another day."

"I pray to Gott you're right, Irishman. We don't have enough ammunition along to make a standing fight of it."

"What'd I tell you," Seamus cheered moments later when the two swirling columns scattered over the hills to the north instead of turning to attack the Pawnee scouts again.

"By Gott, we did it! Three of them dead by my count."

"These Pawnee of yours did it, Lieutenant," Seamus said, feeling the sting of sentiment burn at the back of his throat. "For some reason they stood as you ordered—'stead of going to horse."

"To horse?"

Seamus nodded. "I'd wager it's only natural for these Pawnee to want to fight from horseback. Brought up that way."

Becher finished signaling in the other two groups.

Horse-holders stived through the sand with their wide-eyed mounts as Seamus became aware of the sun on the back of his neck once more. He dragged the greasy folds of his huge bandanna up beneath his long, wavy hair.

"Told them to reload, Irishman," Becher commented as he walked over. "You too?"

Seamus began pulling the brass cartridges from his pocket. "Where you think we are now? Colorado already?"

Becher shrugged. "Only place I know we are is on the right trail now. We're going back to bring up the main column."

"Carr will be pleased to hear of you being hit by these Cheyenne?"

Becher nodded, smiling. "Very pleased, I think. We have plenty of sign now. Good-size war party like this—painted and feathered—they were out for no good."

"Letting the wolf loose, you might say, Becher."

The German grinned even wider. "Let's get these Pawnees back to North—so I can tell Carr we've got Cheyenne wolves to track now."

Chapter 22

July 8–9, 1869

"Carr just kept staring at them footprints, like something strong came over him," Cody said to Donegan as he accepted a hot tin of coffee from the Irishman.

For two days after the Pawnees' running skirmish with the Cheyenne, Major Eugene Carr had kept his column marching northwest along the Republican River. Then, during yesterday's march, the scouts first showed the telltale footprints to Major Frank North. Not until running across a second camp with another group of footprints did North finally show them to Carr.

"The general—he finally go back to his bivouac and get something in his belly?" asked Donegan.

Cody nodded. "Only after it was too damned dark to while he walked back and forth over them prints."

"Gives me a cold feeling too," Seamus agreed. "Something I can't name, or put my finger on."

"Them prints?"

"Last two big camps we come on—this village we're trailing." He sipped his coffee awhile, refusing to gaze up into the inky sky overhead. It would only serve to darken his mood.

Cody finally spoke first as he stretched his feet out to the fire. "Did raise the hair on the back of my neck first time I saw them prints made by a woman's shoe."

"Two sets of 'em," Seamus grumbled. "Narrow . . . short little feet jumbled in among all them moccasin tracks."

Cody could see some pain glistening in the Irishman's dark eyes before he spoke. "Major's not the only one worried 'bout them women. Hell, for a time there this evening, I was thinking hard on Lulu —thanking God it weren't her with them bastards."

Seamus looked at Cody, his eyes growing moist. "It's the Alderdice woman, I know it. Tom's wife. He fought . . . with me, with Forsyth—"

Cody heard the sound snag in the tall man's throat. "I'll wager the other tracks belong to Mrs. Weichel—German woman."

Donegan set his coffee cup aside and pulled the plug from his vest pocket. From it he cut a corner with the pocket knife he kept in another vest pocket.

"I like being in camp this time of night, Seamus. Getting them soldiers bedded down and all. Prairie gets pretty quiet. Sometimes so quiet you can hear a horse fart on some bad grass he's et, maybe even hear the stars whir overhead."

"Things so damned quiet—sometimes forces a man to think on things he'd rather not," Seamus commented after a pause.

Cody could tell Donegan was not fully there with him.

"A woman?"

"What troubles a man more than anything else in his life, I ask you?" Donegan said quietly. "More than matters of life and death—it's matters of the heart, even more what a woman does to a man's heart, that trouble him most."

"Carr won't let us stop now that he's got a trail to follow."

"Forsyth was the same way—once he got the scent in his nostrils."

Cody nodded. "I think I understand how the general feels about them women dragged along with that band of Cheyenne outlaws. He asked me—and I told him. I said we don't run 'em down and run 'em down soon, that bunch we're tracking is going to fly from our reach."

"And we'll never get a chance at 'em again, will we?"

"They've turned north now. Aiming right for the Laramie Plains. From there it's a quick run to the Black Hills, sacred land of the Lakota Sioux and Cheyenne. We'll never find those women then. Be the chance of breathsmoke on a whirlwind that we—"

They both rose together at the hammer of hoofbeats. Staccato from the hills rising just past the Pawnee camp. The pair was moving when the first shrill war whoop echoed eerie and disembodied from the black of night.

Cody looked at the man running through the dark with him, certain that shrill, ghostly cry gave the Irishman willies too. With the cavalry sleeping a

mile away, at that moment it seemed they were the
only men awake in camp, heading for the dull white
of the low tents clustered where the Pawnee battalion had bivouacked. Only they—and the Cheyenne,
that is—making a second unpredictable night raid
on the forces marching under Major Eugene A.
Carr.

The Pawnee camp erupted with life. Orange muzzle-flashes flaring the night with blinding light and
the deafening racket of pistol fire. Three languages
caught in a tangled web of confusion, all smothering one another in a hodgepodge of orders and war-
cries and profanity.

Gunfire and grunts, war whoops and startled
cries from half-sleeping men all followed the disappearing hoofbeats.

Frank North appeared out of the black beside
Mad Bear, the trusted sergeant of his Pawnee battalion. At first sight of the two white scouts, Mad Bear
turned back into the dark.

"What's wrong with him?" Cody asked.

North looked after Mad Bear, shaking his head. "I
figure as soon as he found out it was you two out
here, he hightailed it back to grab his horse."

"Chasing our night callers?" Donegan inquired.

"Yeah. How many you figure, Cody?"

"Six, maybe seven." Cody asked. "Anyone hit?"

"My tent, for the most part. They came barreling
right by, firing into it. Running east to west. Fired
into Lute's tent too. Then out of camp, trying to
chivvy the horses."

"Get any?"

"Not a damned one for all their trouble," North

replied. "All of 'em tied and hobbled as I've ordered."

"Damn, but this bothers me," Luther North grumbled, appearing out of the black.

"The night raid?" Cody asked. "Injuns not supposed to attack at night."

"These do—twice now," Luther replied. "It's not only that . . ." He turned to his older brother. "Mad Bear's gone out after 'em. Says one Pawnee is worth a half-dozen Cheyenne any day."

As he said it a trio of shots boomed from the west side of camp. The four men sprinted to the sound of the gunfire, reaching a group of more than ten Pawnee scouts walking onto the prairie in the starlight. As the North brothers came up, several began chattering excitedly.

"Says Mad Bear ran after one of the Cheyenne who came through camp," explained Frank North.

"One of the enemy's ponies was hit—spilling a warrior. Mad Bear was on his way to kill the Dog Soldier when the new shooting started," continued Luther North.

"Why, did the Pawnees see some more horsemen?" Donegan asked.

Frank North shook his head. "No, says they just saw some movement out here in the dark."

After walking another fifty yards, following one of the scouts, the lone Pawnee called out ahead of them. As Cody and the rest came up, they found the tracker kneeling over a body lying among the trampled grass.

"We get one?" Luther North asked.

"Damn!" muttered the older brother as the body was rolled over.

All could see the dull brass buttons of the army blouse the dead man was wearing, the bright reflection of the blood spreading damp across his chest evident beneath the starshine.

"Shot in the back," Frank translated as the rest of the Pawnee dropped to their knees surrounding their fallen kinsman, wailing, crying out in grief.

"He wasn't killed by the Cheyenne?" Cody asked.

"They saw Mad Bear out here—chasing the damned Cheyenne—and opened fire on him—thinking he was one of the bastards rode through camp."

Seamus made the sign of the cross, a rare thing for him to do.

At that moment in the dark it struck Cody as a superstitious thing to do as well—every bit as superstitious as the way the plains Indian made his medicine over things unexplained. It gave Cody shivers standing here over the dead Pawnee, listening to the death-songs of the others.

"We're going to find them soon, boys," Frank North said quietly, turning back to camp with the other white men.

"We better," Donegan said quietly. "I feel bad blood come a'rise more and more every day. It's time we found us something more than old footprints and cold firepits."

That next morning Major Carr ordered a day's layover in camp while various parties of the Pawnee scouted the area for more sign of the Cheyenne.

"Wish we was laying to in camp, Bill," Seamus said as he refilled the loading tube on the Henry repeater.

"Wish I was going along with you, Irishman."

"Better I than you to go with Lute North's group, young man." Seamus winked and slipped the repeater into its boot before climbing into the saddle.

"He don't like me much, does he?" Cody asked, leading his big buckskin off.

"Neither do I—come to think of it!" Donegan said, then laughed easily as Cody waved him farewell, slapping the mare's rump.

Seamus joined Captain Luther North and Carr's Lieutenant Billy Harvey along with five Pawnee trackers in a small scouting party that would scour the countryside south and west of Frenchman's Fork of the Republican. After a day-long ride covering the rolling, grass-covered sandhills of the western plains, the eight horsemen had made a wide circuit back to strike the river about twenty-five miles above the camp of the Fifth Cavalry.

North called a halt.

"Your butts as sore as mine, we could do with a night out of the saddle. Ride back in the morning."

"Splendid idea, Captain," Seamus said cheerfully.

North turned to the cavalry lieutenant. "Billy—I imagine it'd be a good idea for us to ride up that hill yonder and take a look around before we go into camp."

The sun was settling amid a blazing show of red-orange as the eight worked up the slope. Near the top North signaled another halt and ordered one of the Pawnee to crawl on up to the crest, where he could have a look before the rest broke the skyline.

As the Pawnee scout made the top on all fours, he suddenly dropped to his belly. In a matter of moments he signaled the rest to dismount and join him. As the others reached the crest on foot, the sun eased beyond the western mountains, from here no more than a ragged, worn hemline of horizon.

What greeted the Irishman's eyes made the breath seize in his chest.

Less than a mile west of that hilltop Frenchman's Fork swept gently to the north. Between that bend and the bottom of the hill where the scouts lay in hiding was strung a long, wide coulee that in the spring rushed its rain-swollen runoff into the river.

But for now, moving without hurry down among the shady willow and alder and rustling cotton-wood, was what seemed like the whole Cheyenne nation on the move: mounted warriors and old men on foot, children and dogs and travois drags, while on the flanks throbbed the massive pony herd.

"You figure that's Tall Bull's bunch?" asked Lieutenant Harvey.

Luther North nodded. "None other. For some time we've figured it was his bunch been making for trouble after Roman Nose was turned good Indian at Beecher Island."

Seamus found North gazing at him. "Never thought I'd see that many Indians again in me life, boys."

North smiled in that half-sarcastic way of his. "Second time you've laid eyes on this bunch of outlaws and misfits."

"I lived to tell of the first," Seamus sighed.

"Let's pray the Irishman lives to tell his grandchildren of the second," North whispered, turning from the hilltop and signaling his Pawnee to follow him.

Seamus hung back with the soldier, watching the vanguard of the Cheyenne camp disappear among the brush and timber down near the mouth of the widening draw that met the riverbank. From where he sat, the caravan marched no more than two hundred yards from the hilltop. Many of the ponies labored under loads of fresh buffalo meat shot that day.

"They look about as ragged as our outfit," Harvey whispered.

"Same heat, same territory to cross—same goddamned chase," Donegan replied. "Times I feel like I've swallowed so much dust on this march with Carr that I could apply for territorial status meself."

Harvey nodded. "We're damned sure out of Nebraska by now, Irishman."

"Colorado?"

The officer nodded again. "Let's skeedaddle. I'm feared any minute some of those bucks gonna come riding up here to take a look around the countryside."

It struck Donegan as a more than reasonable suggestion. "Let's make ourselves small, Lieutenant."

They rejoined North and the Pawnee scouts at the bottom of the slope with the horses.

"What would we have done if they had seen us, Billy?" asked Luther North.

The older soldier thought a moment, then grinned and shrugged. "I suppose I would have said King's-X."

"A lot of good it would have done us," North replied. "We can't camp here tonight—with that big village going into camp above us."

"We have no other choice but to clear out of here quietly," Harvey suggested. "Get downriver to the cavalry to report."

North brooded on it a moment, studying the faces

of the five Pawnee. "I suppose you're right—we should report to the general."

"As much as your boys want to fight those Cheyenne," Seamus said.

The young captain regarded Donegan haughtily before replying. "I don't figure these boys want to tangle with that many warriors any more than we do."

"Like snuffing a candle in the wind, Captain," Seamus replied, for some unexplained reason feeling like he had something new upon which to hang his dislike for Luther North. The man seemed without any humor, and took offense at the smallest slight.

"You can come—or you can stay to watch the show by yourself," North said harshly before turning away.

Donegan watched North move to his horse and lead the others off before he mounted. He let the flush of anger run off his shoulders. In a way he felt sorry for this Lute North, hungry as he was to have some glory come the way of his brother and the Pawnee battalion, while Major Carr still acted partial to Bill Cody.

No wonder Luther North carried the chip on his shoulder the size of a fence-rail. Soon enough all that poison the man kept festering inside would come boiling to the surface.

It didn't really matter—before long the whole outfit would have something more to worry about than the ruffled feelings of a sour-mash civilian.

Now there was time to think of nothing more than Cheyenne Dog Soldiers—and those women's footprints in the sand.

Chapter 23

July 10, 1869

"*Y*ou gonna get my goddamned wagon loaded or ain't you?" hissed the fat mule-whacker with the rotten teeth and whiskey-stale breath.

Jack O'Neill ground his teeth, wishing it were another place, another time—and he could look down at the terror in the white man's eyes as he plunged the tomahawk into his brain.

Instead, the mulatto forced down the bile and turned back to the grain stacked in sacks by hundred-weight. The bed of the huge freighter creaked under the load as O'Neill helped the teamster chain up the rear gate.

" 'Bout time, goddammit," the man muttered, glaring at O'Neill with impunity.

Jack knew the man realized he was safe saying anything to him here in broad daylight on the streets of Denver City. The mulatto and Indian were the outcast minorities here. A man could speak what trash he dared—and a nigger, no matter a freed nigger, kept his mouth shut, he knew what was good for him.

"I ain't never gonna make Cripple Creek the way you dawdling on me, nigger."

Jack stepped back out of the fleshy man's way, marveling at the size of the pores in the whiskey-swollen nose, all scored with tiny burst veins that reminded Jack of the tracks the hens made down in the chicken yard after a summer thunderstorm back to home.

For a moment he yearned for Mama and home, then hefted the remembrance away like handling those hundred-weight sacks of feed. O'Neill watched the teamster settle with a groan from the plank seat.

"Better pick up the pace, boy!"

O'Neill turned to find the thin, bald, rail of a man with his sheaf of papers emerging from the cool shadows of the brick warehouse. He wore that look of practiced tolerance for the mulatto.

"Got three more of them wagons to load for Cripple Creek before noon. Now get your black ass moving, you want to have time for lunch."

Four smaller black men and one Chinaman worked in relay to bring the feed sacks out of the cool darkness of the warehouse. Only Jack O'Neill stood beneath in the midsummer sun, naked to the waist, his skin the color of coffee softened with sweet milk—just the way his daddy used to take it right up to that morning he marched off to the war. Down on the dock the five dropped their sacks before disappearing into the darkness. Up he dragged a bag to his shoulder, slowly kneeling to wrench a second sack beneath his free arm. That was the only way he had figured to keep up with the five of them.

They was only mindful of their jobs and families. He couldn't blame 'em. They done what the white men told 'em.

So many white men. Never had he seen so many in one place and at one time until coming here to Denver City. It had been good money at first when he hired on here down near Cherry Creek at Addison's Grain & Feed. Fair money after that first day's sore muscles. And it was only enough after the first week—he had himself a bed in a room with seven others, and two squares each day, along with some dried bread and meat broth for lunch to see him through to evening. And if he was lucky and watched his money the way he did when he first came to the plains, Jack had some left over by the end of the month to go calling on one of the powdered chippies at one of the dance halls.

Jack didn't dance with the fleshy, sweating girls. Though a white man had tried goading him into dancing for them all one time. O'Neill never went back, and steered clear of the place. He wasn't no sun-grinning, hymn-singing, foot-shuffling field nigger. Never had been. They wanted to see dancing, let 'em come out on the prairie to where Roman Nose and his earthy people roamed.

That hurt him—to suddenly have to think of Roman Nose as gone forever. All too painful and true —for he had seen the war-chief's body laid out on the scaffold, lying there for the wind and the seasons to reclaim.

The best friend Jack O'Neill knew he would ever have was a red man. Copper-skinned. And celibate to the point Jack knew had to drive Roman Nose crazy. Still, the big Cheyenne just laughed when the mulatto told him of the delicious things white women would do for money and the Indian women did for fun.

The best of friends. Roman Nose had treated Jack more like a man than any other before, or since. They had fought together. Galloping down that creekbed, racing toward the island—a vision come now before his watering eyes as clear as if he were once more riding beside the war-chief, water and golden sand-grit spraying as high as their bronzed shoulders in that morning sun.

Jack found his pace quickening as his anger and pain swelled like an overworked blister, pouring from him like the sweat glistening his dusty torso.

Simply to find the man who had killed the only friend he ever had . . .

That helped the mulatto dull some of the pain, the way the rye whiskey dulled his craving for the powdered chippies who always smelled so strongly of the man come and gone before him. He hated the women almost as much as he hated the gray-eyed white man who had killed his best friend.* Hated the women he took ravenously—because none of them were Emmy.

His eyes moistened, recalling how Emmy felt that last time in his arms, their blood mingling, pooling beneath the white girl's slashed and riven body.

He smiled, like a wolf watching a hamstrung old bull go down on the prairie.

Remembering how exquisite it was to extract so

* The Plainsmen Series, vol. 3, *The Stalkers*

much pain from the white man who had killed Jack's whore. He began to laugh right then and there beside the loading dock. Recalling how the renegade cried out for mercy—to be killed—to stop the torture that was such a delicious revenge.

As bloody and filled with gore as that torture had been for the white renegade, now Jack O'Neill realized the slow killing of Bob North was merely practice. The old man's screams, his pleading to die—all of it would pale beside what the future held.

No terror, no blood, no begging could compare with that moment to come when he got his hands on the tall, dark-haired, gray-eyed civilian scout—the killer of Roman Nose.

At dawn the morning after Lieutenant Harvey's scout had watched Tall Bull's village going into camp, Major Eugene Carr ordered his cavalry to march upriver to locate the Cheyenne trail.

Wasn't a man in that outfit didn't know he'd be going to war soon enough. Spotting the whole damned village. Even Major Royall's scout with ten Pawnee under Lieutenant Becher had run across a small war-party the day before and had a running fight with the warriors, killing three before the Cheyenne broke off and disappeared.

The gap was closing. It was only a matter of time before Carr's cavalry caught up with them.

Not that many miles up Frenchman's Fork of the Republican, Carr briefly halted his command at a site used by the Cheyenne three days before. In resuming their march, a few miles farther up the fork they came across the camp used by Tall Bull's people two nights before. The soldiers were as enthused as they were nervous. They were on a hot trail—knowing from Lieutenant Harvey's report exactly where the hostiles went into camp the night of the ninth. In a matter of a morning's march, they had closed the lead of their quarry by three days.

The major ordered camp made and the entire outfit readied for any eventuality.

"No telling what those warriors will do they find out we're breathing down their necks," Bill Cody advised Carr as they went into camp.

"Just as well," Carr replied. "I'm sending back a handful of the Pawnee and two of my men to hurry along the supply train that's due in from McPherson."

"I don't recommend you sit here like an owl waiting for your prey to come to you," Major Frank North said.

Carr considered it. "If I have no other choice—we'll make a forced march with part of the column intact, the rest waiting for resupply."

"That village finds out we're back here, they'll bolt," Luther North said, adding his pessimism.

"It's a chance I'll have to take. We're in no position to attack that village and scatter it—not knowing where our supply train is, gentlemen. I'm not going to gamble with the lives of those civilian teamsters if the Cheyenne suddenly turn about and scatter furiously. I would be signing the death warrants for our freighters."

"You might be missing the chance of your career to capture the worst outlaw this part of the country's seen in a generation," Frank North said.

Carr squared his eyes at the leader of the Pawnee

battalion. "I've considered that, Major. I'll note your exception for the record. However, I'll let others rush in for the glory. Custer and his like. As for me —I'll protect my rearguard and the civilians in my employ before I'll have their deaths on my conscience. There won't be any Major Elliotts in the Fifth Cavalry, by Jupiter!"

Cody and the rest watched Carr stomp away with his adjutant, Lieutenant Montgomery.

"He's still smoldering over last winter's campaign, ain't he?" Cody quietly asked of Donegan. "Us busting snow and our tails—coming up empty-handed while all the glory went to Custer."

"Carr's got every right to complain," Seamus replied sourly. "You heard the reports—read it in all the papers back East. That business about Custer abandoning Major Joel Elliott and his eighteen men in the valley of the Washita as soon as Custer found out his gallant Seventh Cavalry was about to be surrounded by the might of the Arapaho and Kiowa nations."

Cody nodded, watching Carr's wide back disappear among the horses and men and small, smokeless fires where the soldiers boiled their coffee and chewed on their salt-pork.

"I don't imagine Carr's the same kind of soldier as Custer," he replied, loosening the cinch on Buckskin Joe's saddle. "He's cautious, and Custer sounds full of bluff and bluster. Carr is cut of a different cloth."

Donegan snorted. "You got that right, Bill Cody. By the saints—you got that right."

Doubt nagged him as he pulled himself from her body, his breathing coming more regular, his pulse slowing.

It wasn't anything to do with the white woman. Instead, it was a doubt rattling around inside Tall Bull the way stream-washed pebbles clattered around inside a stiffened buffalo-scrotum rattle. He wanted to move the village on—but the medicine men claimed they were safe here in the narrow valley by the springs the Dog Soldier band visited at least twice each year in their migrations.

Still, the confident vision of the medicine men did nothing to allay his fear as Tall Bull gazed at the bruised white woman beneath him. She rolled to her side, pulling the shreds of her dress and the corner of a blanket over nakedness. One eye was puffing where he had cuffed her. The woman's dry, swollen lips were cracked, bloodied where he slapped her repeatedly during their coupling. Blue bruising stood out like his war-paint against the paleness of her skin.

Tall Bull cursed her—why could she not enjoy the rut as much as Cheyenne women? Before, she had fought back: crying, lashing out and kicking at him. It had been more exciting in those first days. Now, for many suns, the white woman had become a different animal—passive unlike anything he knew in the animal kingdom. It unsettled something inside him, and he resented her for it.

Not good to have this feeling about this place and the medicine men and the nearness of the soldiers . . . not good to have the woman lay beneath him, staring up at the circle of poles while he hit and bit, slapped and pinched and rutted with her.

She was not an eager partner like his wife. He cursed the white woman because she made him feel alone. Cold and eerie as he gyrated over her body, exacting his vengeance on her flesh.

He toyed with the fire smoking at his feet in the lodge lit with nothing more than the stars bursting forth at twilight through the narrow smoke-hole overhead.

Tall Bull stared at her a long time. She seemed to be gazing back at him in the dim light of the lodge. But he was sure she wasn't looking at him. Instead, she must be looking somewhere in the distance at that place she went each time he came to possess her body.

He hated her for that. If she could not throw herself into the mating like a good woman should, then at least she should fight him, just as she did the first time he spread her white legs. But something inside him told Tall Bull this white woman would never do either.

Too quickly she had learned how to hurt him.

And when Tall Bull was hurt, he hurt back.

One day he might get angry enough to kill her. When most men tired of a female prisoner, they sold her to another warrior. But he would not sell this one. She had caused him too much pain and stabbed his pride. He would kill her someday.

And if the soldiers came to rescue her, Tall Bull would glean such pleasure in driving the tomahawk into her brain. Watching the horror on her face as he plunged the blade into her head . . . wondering now if that look of terror would be any different than the fear on her face that first time he plunged his flesh within her, there beside her burning cabin.

Those soldiers gave him pause. An unsettled brooding came over him as he stared at the white woman gazing with empty, lifeless eyes back at him.

If the soldiers came—he vowed she would be the first to die.

Chapter 24

July 11, 1869

Carr rousted the men out at two A.M. They were moving at four A.M., well before first light.

No time for coffee.

Donegan listened to the grumbling soldiers and civilians in the darkness. The moon was sinking into the western quadrant, leaving enough light to march on, cutting away at the enemy's lead.

By mid-morning they had covered fifteen miles, when the column came across the camp the hostiles had used the night of 9 July. One hundred fifty miles already covered in four days of forced marches had brought them to the brink of battle.

"General—the Pawnee say the Cheyenne are breaking up into three bands," Luther North announced as he climbed down from his horse.

Carr regarded him a minute. "That's what Cody's already told me."

"With your permission, General—I suggest you put out a reconnaissance in force in three parties."

"Cody believes the Cheyenne will regroup before camping."

North glowered at Cody a moment, the turned back to Carr. "Nonetheless—we're close, sir. We follow any one trail—the other two groups escape."

"They won't escape, General," Cody protested.

"The Cheyenne're breaking up on you, General Carr—you're about to lose them," North pleaded frantically, stepping closer.

Carr appeared troubled at that prospect. He looked at Cody. "Why won't they escape, Cody? Wishful thinking?"

He shook his head. "No. They're in the same fix we are. They need water just as bad as your outfit does. It may look like they're splitting up . . . but that's just to throw you off 'cause they know your cavalry is back here. They'll regroup at the Platte."

"The South Platte?"

"'That's right, General. You get your outfit to march north from here on the double—we'll get between the river and the Cheyenne. They get there before you—you'll never catch 'em."

"What's there going to be to catch, General?" North asked. "You don't follow these trails, you don't have an idea where they're going. All you've got is Cody's word that they're pointing to the Platte."

"They've got to have water, General."

Carr chewed on his lip. "Interesting point you make, Captain North. Good point. All right—despite Mr. Cody's misgivings, we'll divide into three wings here. Captain, you and your brother will take Captain Cushing along with most of your Pawnee to scout the middle trail heading due north. Major Royall?"

The officer walked up. "General."

"Major Royall—you will have command of half our unit—companies E, G and H. Take Cody along with some of his men and scout the right-hand trail leading off to the northeast, onto that open land yonder."

"I assume you're going to lead the third wing, General?"

"Correct. Companies A, C and D. I'm taking the Irishman, Sergeant Wallace and four of the companies with me, in addition to six of the Pawnee. If nothing else, they will serve to communicate with the other two wings. I'm leaving M Company in reserve with the supply train."

Into the darkness that still shrouded the sand hills of eastern Colorado Territory, Major Eugene Carr dispatched his nearly three hundred officers and soldiers, civilian and Pawnee scouts. The sun rose over the three wings spreading out across the separate trails. From time to time Donegan watched as Carr sent a Pawnee tracker in one direction or another to make contact with either Major Royall or the North brothers.

"I can see now that the Cheyenne are moving toward the river," Carr admitted quietly to the Irishman. "Just as Cody suggested they would."

"We're in the position to flank them now, General," Seamus reminded.

He nodded in agreement, standing momentarily in the stirrups. "We come around them from the northeast—putting ourselves between them and the river—we'll have them bottled up whether we find them in camp or on the move."

"Let's hope you find them on the move."

Carr studied Donegan a moment. "Why?"

"We surprise them in camp, General—the men will fight all the harder while the women put together a retreat."

"And if we surprise them on the march?"

"They'll be running from the first shot—covered by the men only long enough to make good their escape."

"I'd rather have a fight of it, Irishman. Like Custer made of his on the Washita—I want my chance to make a fight of it for the Fifth." He fixed Donegan with his hard eyes. "I want to catch these Cheyenne in camp."

"I'll pray your boys are ready for a stiff scrap," Donegan replied as he looked away, mentally making the sign of the cross across the big dome of blue sky that had stretched over them all that morning. The sun hung white, almost at mid-sky, as hot as a blacksmith's bellows, the breeze every bit as hot as a smithy's firebox.

Less than an hour later the half-dozen Pawnee riding with Donegan began talking among themselves, pointing more frequently at the trail sign, gesturing at the skyline ahead and on the flanks. Seamus rode in among them. In sign he asked them the question troubling him.

Do we near the enemy camp?

They nodded. The Pawnee sergeant, wearing an army blouse with three gold stripes beneath his long, unbound hair, moved his hands above the horn of his saddle.

Very near, he replied in sign, then pointed off into the distance.

It took a moment to make something out of the shimmering heat rising from the rolling sand hills. But Seamus did see them. Dark, undulating forms some three, maybe four miles off. He felt the old pull at his gut, the tensing caused by adrenaline as it dumped into his bloodstream.

Those are not buffalo?

The Pawnee sergeant shook his head. *Not buffalo —Cheyenne ponies.*

I will tell the soldier chief, Seamus signed, then pulled the big mare about, back to Major Eugene Carr.

"General—the Pawnee figure it's time you should have a better idea where the village is. We've spotted what looks like the hostiles' pony herd up ahead."

"They believe we're getting close?"

"Meself even, I sense many of the smaller trails are converging," Seamus replied. "The river can't be too much farther. A handful of miles at most. There," and he pointed. "You might see the herd for yourself."

Carr shaded his eyes and gazed into the distance for the longest time. With no other sign of recognition, he glanced over his Pawnee scouts for a brief moment, then slowly pulled the steamy slouch hat from his receding brow and wiped a damp kerchief across his forehead. "Get one of the Indians to ride to Major Royall's unit. Bring Cody back. I want him to take these six Pawnee and charge ahead to find out if that is the herd or if they can see the village— or some sign of where I'll contact the bastards."

Cody rode in, received his orders and pointed his

big buckskin northwest, leading the six Pawnee in the direction he believed he would find the camp.

Carr halted his troops to await Cody's return. Time dragged itself out in the steamy heat of the plains as the horses and mules grew restless. Looking for water, wanting to graze. For what seemed like hours, Donegan had kept his eyes trained on the hills where the pony herd had been spotted. Seamus turned at the sound of a single horse's hooves.

"Donegan."

"General Carr."

"It's after noon."

"You're worried about Cody?"

Carr finally shook his head. "We haven't heard any shots."

Seamus smiled. "I don't suppose they've been swallowed up. Not yet."

"There," Carr said, and pointed over Donegan's shoulder.

He turned to see only one of the seven he had sent coming back at an easy lope. As the young, blond scout drew close, Seamus could see Cody wore his characteristic irrepressible grin.

"You found it, didn't you, Cody?"

"Just like I told you, General. Left the Pawnee there to keep an eye on things till your men come up."

Carr smiled approvingly. "I've come to trust you even more now."

Cody was clearly excited. "They haven't an idea we're about to come down on them."

Carr had been bitten by the contagious excitement. "By Jupiter—I'll have them this time!"

"There's a route—a detour. Take the command on

it through these hills . . . moving off on the right
flank. You'll skirt the village and come in from the
north. They'll never know until you're right on top
of them."

"Thank you, Cody. You've performed splendidly."

Carr wheeled his mount and was gone.

In a matter of moments the command was moving once more, just about the time the wagon train
was seen coming up from the rear. The teamsters
and mules were having a hard time budging the
bulky wagons in the soft soil and clinging sand of
the Platte Bluffs.

But now Carr had his entire force together, ready
to move in concert.

The rejoined command moved out in a clatter of
hardware and squeak of dry leather, staying for the
most part behind the low ridges and hills leading
down to the South Platte, keeping to the ravines as
much as possible, refraining at all costs from breaking the skyline.

Cody and his scouts were waiting ahead when
Carr came up and halted the long columns.

"You've got less than fifteen hundred yards to the
outlying lodges, General."

"They still have no idea, Cody?"

"You've caught them napping. Warm day like this
—most of the ponies are out grazing in the herd.
Young bucks aren't out watching their back trail.
Men back in the shade of the lodges. Children playing at the springs. It's total surprise."

They could see a few lazy spirals of smoke caught
on the hot summer breezes in the distance.

"A fairly open plain separates us from the village?"

"Good enough for a cavalry charge, General."

Carr drove one big fist down into the palm of the other hand. Then returned to his cavalry to detail the attack squadrons.

Long before marching orders were passed down through the cavalry command, the Pawnee scouts were already at their toilet, preparing for battle. First they stripped the saddles from their horses, throwing the saddles in the freight wagons. The tails of their ponies were tied up in anticipation of action. The scouts bound their long hair back and mixed earth-paint ceremonially. Weapons were polished and small knots of men smoked a bowl of tobacco together before mounting up. Many then put on a blue army blouse so that they would be easily recognizable to the young, untried soldiers in the dust and fearful confusion of battle.

Carr assigned H Company under Captain Leicester Walker to hold the left flank while Lieutenant George Price and A Company took the right.

"You are to turn the hostiles' flanks if they attempt escape," the senior major instructed his men. Carr watched them nod. "Their backs will be to the river. Let's keep it their only path of escape. Once you have secured the flanks, dash to the rear of the village and gain control of the pony herd."

As one, they turned and glanced at the herd grazing on a long, narrow bench of superb grass less than two miles on the other side of the village.

"Captain Sumner, with D Company, and Captain Maley with C Company—both of you are charged with the front of the charge. Major Crittenden will ride in command of this center squadron. Major Royall, your squadron of companies E and G will serve as a reserve immediately in my rear. Prepare for the attack."

Carr waited as the company commanders passed orders down the line and the soldiers made their final preparations for the charge. Major Frank North placed his Pawnee battalion on the far left flank, well within sight of the village, awaiting the charge. When Lieutenant Price with A Company had moved off about five hundred yards to the right and signaled that he was ready, the major rose in the stirrups. Since Price's company had the farthest to travel in reaching the village, the charge would be guided on it.

"Sergeant Major: move out at a trot."

Joseph H. Maynard turned in the saddle to give the order. "Center-guide! Column of fours—at a trot. Forward!"

The dry, hot wind picked up almost immediately, coming from the west, born out of the front range of the Rockies far, far away. Enough of a breeze that the noise of those hooves and leather and bit-chains went unheard in that unsuspecting village of Dog Soldiers. They had closed to a thousand yards, and still no sign of discovery from the Cheyenne.

Suddenly a horseman on a white pony appeared among the far herd grazing on the grassy bench, dashing off the slope into the valley, racing for the village.

"That one's seen us!" Donegan shouted into the wind.

Cody nodded. "Don't matter, Irishman—it's too late for 'em to do a goddamned thing now."

Looking over his shoulder, Seamus found Carr signaling among his immediate command. They would attempt to reach the village before the lone herder alerted the camp.

Order the bleeming charge, goddammit! he thought, the great scar across his back going cold as January ice water.

"Bugler Uhlman—sound the charge!"

It was as if Carr had perceived Donegan's plea across that distance between them.

John Uhlman put the scuffed and scratched bugle to his trembling lips as they trotted across that grassy plain toward the village. No sound came forth.

"By Jupiter—sound the charge!" Carr ordered a second time.

Uhlman gulped, pressed the bugle to his lips even harder. Still no sound came out.

"Gimme that, you fool!" growled Quartermaster Edward M. Hayes as he came alongside Uhlman, their horses bumping.

Hayes wrenched up the bugle, blowing the stirring notes.

Up and down the entire line throats burst with a raucous cheer as carbines came up and the jaded horses were urged into a gallop. Although they had been driven beyond the call of duty across the last four days, the animals answered the spurs on this last dash.

The quartermaster flung the bugle to the ground and pulled his pistol free.

That tin horn lay trampled underfoot while a dismayed, frightened John Uhlman was swept along in the final charge.

Chapter 25

Moon of Cherries Blackening

*T*hey had camped beside the upper reaches of a stream the Cheyenne called Cherry Creek, then yesterday came to this place of the springs that gurgled under the White Butte.

It was here five summers ago that Big Wolf and his family had been killed by soldiers. Through camp in a southeasterly direction ran White Butte Creek. Beside the stream stood Tall Bull's lodge.

After receiving the blessing of the shamans on this campsite the day before, the chief had turned to his people and told them, "For two suns we will make our camp here. Then we will ford the river and march north to the rock where we starved the Pawnee."

Years before, the Cheyenne had met the Pawnee in battle beneath what the white man called Court House Rock.

As the afternoon sun reached its zenith this day,

the Cheyenne of Tall Bull had little idea the Pawnee were coming to visit destruction upon them.

"People are coming!"

Tall Bull and Two Crows heard the shouts, but did not believe in any danger at first. Buffalo hunters were out, as well as hunters looking for antelope. No soldiers could surprise the village.

"There! On the hills!"

Many came out of their lodges as the shouts grew louder and more in number. Children were pointing at the horsemen riding back and forth on the far hillside. Horsemen with long hair, waving their weapons in the air. The horsemen began firing their weapons.

"Perhaps they are messengers from Pawnee Killer's Sioux war-party that has been out looking to take soldier scalps," Two Crows said, standing at Tall Bull's side.

"Yes," Tall Bull said hopefully as horsemen numbering more than ten times both hands covered the hillside, firing. "They must have taken scalps, shooting so much—"

The bullets began to whistle into camp. Whining through the hide lodges, ricocheting from iron kettles and splintering lodgepoles. Women started shrieking and children crying at the moment two phalanxes of dust-shrouded pony soldiers broke over the top of the hills.

"*Aiyeee!* Pony soldiers come behind the Indians!"

There was much confusion on what it meant— though one thing alone was certain: bullets were flying into camp. A few of Tall Bull's people already lay bleeding, calling out for help. Some lay making no sound at all.

Hooves pounded the earth. Horsemen sprinted down the hillsides from the north, east and west.

Only the south lay open to escape.

Tall Bull whirled—angry more than frightened. Not thinking of his wife and daughter. Not even thinking of the white woman. The first thing he wanted to do was kill the shamans.

In the confusion, ponies reared and cried out fearfully as the bullets slapped the lodges all about them. Men and women worked to control the animals long enough to spring to their bare backs. Most had no ponies in camp. These people tore away on foot, clutching a young child beneath an arm, snatching up weapons and a blanket or two before they fled from the village. Some toward the south and safety. Others quickly turned away to places of hiding in the sandy bluffs.

No time to tear down the lodges. Escape was all that mattered now.

As the confusion grew more mad, Tall Bull stood like a battered cottonwood amid the panic, looking for the old shamans who had guaranteed him this place would be a safe haven for his people. From his hand hung the heavy-bladed tomahawk, its graceful curve like the path the sun took from midday to sunset. In his belly the Dog Soldier chief feared this was to be the sunset of his band. All because he had listened to the old men who gazed into the bloody entrails of a badger, instead of paying heed to his better instincts.

How he yearned to kill the foolish old ones.

The horsemen were nearing the village—he had to go. No time to find the shamans. He could do so later. Plenty of time for that in the hills tonight, when the soldiers drew off.

Then he heard her voice among those crying—pitiful, pleading. Whirling, Tall Bull found her where he had tied her last night.

She had stretched to the full length of her rawhide tethers. One restraint bound a foot, another an ankle. Both securely lashed to separate tent-pegs. Again and again, like a frightened animal caught in an iron trap, she yanked at the unmoving pegs. With little strength left in her body after the weeks of her captivity, she had nothing to throw against the tough rawhide shackles.

The white woman stared up at him with those wide eyes that reminded him of an animal come to the brink, ready to chew its leg off to free itself of the trap.

He liked finding that in her eyes. Much better than the lifeless void for too long in her eyes whenever he coupled with her. This was exactly like the first time beside her burning cabin as he tore aside her dress and layers of cloth beneath, ripped down the pantaloons to expose the milk-cream flesh that lashed out at his touch.

She cowered. He stood over her unmoving. The white woman watched him raise the tomahawk over his head.

She thinks I am going to kill her now, he thought as he brought the weapon down.

Her wrist was free. A look of sudden realization crossed the bruised, bloodied face. The puffy eyes glowed with some long-lost excitement. He had not seen hope as bright as this in many seasons.

Both her hands tore at the last rawhide tether

binding her ankle. She pulled at the same time she gazed up at him, imploring him to help her. Tall Bull nodded and looked over his shoulder quickly. The soldiers were already entering the village. A flash of blond hair and a swirl of torn cloth in the distance told him the other white woman had escaped her captor. She was running for the soldiers.

Tall Bull brought the tomahawk savagely down. The iron head buried itself in the sand an inch from her flesh, severing the last rawhide tether. For an instant the white woman stared at the weapon, then brought her wide, imploring eyes to his face. He smiled at her.

Onto her knees she crawled, still unsure of her deliverance, clawing her way onto her feet with a struggle. Of a sudden she lunged to get away, arms churning, stretching, hands yearning.

On her like a coyote pouncing on snowshoe rabbit, he had the woman by her long, blond hair. A fistful of it. Jerking her about so savagely she came off her feet.

The look of fear in her eyes became real terror, like that first time beside her burning cabin.

Yet this time she watched him bring back the tomahawk a third time. From the blade to his face and back to the weapon suspended in the air.

He could smell it on her now that they were this close. For too long she had given herself up to him. Not like that first time when she had shown fear and fight—the animal odors he relished smelling on a victim most of all.

She screamed, opening a huge hole in her face as she fought against his hold on her.

Tall Bull brought the tomahawk down with all the passion he could muster.

Her warm blood and gore splattered over him as she fell from his grasp.

He left the tomahawk behind, buried to its wet, glistening handle in her brain.

Guidons snapped like angry, tormented flying insects in the hot breeze as the soldiers came on.

With ringing cheers bursting from the throats of his soldiers, Lieutenant Price performed the maneuver assigned him with precision. He turned the left flank of the enemy back on itself.

At the same time, Captain Walker's men encountered a sharp-sided ravine in making their approach to the village. That and a boggy marshfield slowed Walker's soldiers just enough from closing the gap that a few of the Cheyenne escaped into the sand hills before both Sumner and Maley raced into the center of the village.

Around the slower, blue-bloused soldiers swarmed screeching Pawnee scouts—here, then there, flitting like hawks after any target, be it man or woman. Revenge made their veins run hot.

The pools of drying blood beneath the dead and dying, like black suns.

Walker shouted to his sergeants, regrouping his men to charge after the escapees and those few ponies the fleeing Cheyenne were driving before them. Young soldiers would follow the Indians for better than three miles before their jaded mounts gave out. Four days of forced marches left little bottom in the troopers' animals.

Other squads of soldiers tore after small groups

of resolute warriors who continued to fight on foot or horseback. Retreating, suddenly stopping and turning to fire at their pursuers—the Dog Soldiers made for the grassy marsh or the sandy bluffs as pale as a white woman's skin.

A flicker of movement snagged Donegan's attention.

She burst from a cloud of dust, emerging from behind a lodge in a swirl of shredded cloth, her greasy dress and petticoats aflutter about her unbuttoned boots. Behind her came a flurry of copperskinned warriors. The closest stopped, drew back his bow.

"Get down, goddammit!" Seamus shouted. He aimed his big pistol on instinct.

As the white woman dove to the ground, the bowman lurched backward, a red blossom spreading on his chest.

As quickly, the others scattered among the lodges, into the madness of the noise and dust.

Soldiers came on Donegan's heels, leaping their horses over the frantic, screaming woman. She leapt onto her feet, dashing among the horsemen, sobbing at her deliverance, touching the hands that reached down for her. Only one soldier noticed the woman's wound, a bullet hole high in her chest. He leaped to the ground as the woman lunged for him, blubbering in happiness.

"Get her to the surgeon!" ordered an officer out of the dusty gloom.

"Yessir!"

Donegan sawed the mare's reins. She was close to done in after the hard drive of the last four days.

For the Irishman, never had there been anything like Carr's chase since that third day at Gettysburg.

But the chase was yet undone. Less than fifty yards off, a lone warrior drove four mules before him, seeking escape into the bluffs to the south of the village.

Seamus drove spurs into the mare's ribs. She responded with every ounce of her heart if not speed.

Repeatedly the warrior glanced over his shoulder as Donegan drew closer. Instead of making good his escape, the Cheyenne was more consumed in fleeing with his small remuda intact. As the white man came on, the warrior gradually realized how futile his break for freedom would be if he did not rid himself of the troublesome pursuer.

He turned and fired his old pistol at the Irishman.

Seamus immediately yanked hard on the mare's rein. She cut hard to the right, nearly going down.

The bullet smashed through the stirrup fender, grazing the meat of Donegan's left leg.

A second pull by the warrior on the trigger brought nothing but a click on an empty chamber. Tossing the pistol aside, the Dog Soldier pulled a bow from his quiver and fired the first of a handful of arrows.

Seamus ducked low along the mare's neck, hearing the first heart-wrenching, wheezing, paunch-bellied sounds from deep within the horse. Too many mounts had gone down on him for the Irishman not to recognize the oozing of life from the mare.

A third arrow *fttt-thunged* past Donegan's right ear, painfully splitting it clear to his scalp.

He sensed the sting of the warm breeze nudging

past the open flesh, at his neck the tickling warmth of blood. Seamus slowed the mare, let her stop of her own as he brought the army carbine out, flicked up the long sight, squeezed it to his bloody cheek. He held high and pulled. Opened the receiver and ejected the brass. The familiar click of the loading tube springing another round into the breech took but a heartbeat to disappear on the hot breeze that tormented his wounds.

Seamus squeezed the trigger, this time holding on the warrior's roached hair. The Spencer kicked him, the mare shuddered as the muzzle smoke went the way of the wind.

Fifty yards away the warrior reeled atop his pony, bow and arrows spilling as he slid from the animal's rump into the grassy sand, kicking up a small cloud of dust.

"You got enough left in you to get us back to camp, girl?" he asked in a whisper, laying close to her ear.

The mare's eyes rolled wild and glassy, her jaws working as if sucking for wind.

She's shot in the lights, he thought.

But the mare came around with gentle tugs on the reins. Nosing her back to the camp where the shooting and yelling had not let up, the horse faltered, stopped and shivered, throwing her head back. Then she stood riveted to the spot.

Slowly he dropped from her back and looked 'round him. Seamus threw up the stirrup, quickly releasing the cinch. The saddle and the soaked blanket came off as he fought to stand on the one good leg. He sensed his long hair sticking and tearing through the lacerated ear. Funny how such a small wound made him feel faint at times, remembering the arrow that had punctured his leg near Fort Phil Kearny.

He left the saddle and blanket behind, dragging it beneath a clump of swamp willow to hide it as best he could—deciding to come back for it later. He drag-footed it back to the mare, his grazed leg tender and burning with every gust of hot breeze. Seamus looked down at the crease in the meat of his thigh, just above the knee wounded by Confederate steel.

"I won't ride you no more, girl," he whispered to her, an arm slung over her neck. "Don't have the heart to. You been a good animal—"

Seamus turned away from the mare, unable to go on. He headed for the village and the diminishing gunfire. But the mare was beside him, her chest heaving, the bullet hole spitting froth with every breath. She shuddered and her rear quarters almost collapsed, her head weaving.

With a wag of his head and his throat burning with shame and sadness, the Irishman pulled up the flap of his holster and freed the pistol.

The mare sank with the one shot behind her ear.

Chapter 26

July 11, 1869

Not wanting to tarry long beside the mare's carcass, he headed into the village more quickly now. Dogs snarling and barking at the intruders. A few dead Cheyenne scattered on the outskirts of the lodge circle.

One of the bodies caught his attention. In a way it looked—but then it didn't. The torn dress . . . perhaps stolen from some settler during the Cheyenne raids in Kansas.

At first he could not tell—the hair looked dark, the body sprawled in the shadows near a lodge raised back against the trees. Both legs and arms lay akimbo as if struggling in death.

Was it a Cheyenne squaw, killed by one of the Pawnee? He saw what he realized was the handle of a camp axe. Perhaps one of North's battalion exacting revenge on their ancient tribal enemies. With all the blood already attracting swarms of green-backed horseflies, growing bloated and lazy as they crawled about, blackening the horrible wound that had split the woman's head from crown to bridge of the nose, exposing the crusted iron blade deeply imbedded in the pink and purplish brain.

He fought down the sharp sting of bile at the back of his throat, turning away quickly as his belly came up. He cursed himself, then cursed the killer —now noticing some blond hair strung out from the dark pool of blood. He glanced at her bloodied hands, the pale skin beneath torn wool stockings lumped around her ankles.

He was sure it was the second white woman.

In utter rage he ripped the antelope hide door from the lodge with a savage grunt and laid it over the woman's face and torso. Seamus prayed the corpse would prove to be the German woman. For now he refused to consider her the wife of Forsyth scout Tom Alderdice.

From the woman's side he had to struggle back to his feet on the tender leg. The tormenting whine of a bullet split the air beside his arm. A second whispered beside the wounded ear, causing him to duck frantically.

Renewed gunfire was crackling from a grassy ravine less than a hundred yards off. The warriors still hidden there maintained a good field of fire. They were making the most of their cover, although the great number of their shots were missing the mark, either going wild or hitting soldier horses.

"Sergeant!" yelled Donegan, wheeling, finding the soldiers charging up on horseback. The bold chevrons stood out in the yellow haze of dust and shimmering midsummer heat.

"I see the buggers!" the old file hollered back. He

waved an arm at a dozen men. "Dismount! Follow me and prepare to fight!"

Unthinking of his wounds and the flagging strength in his leg, Seamus was among them in a heartbeat, shoulder to shoulder with the blue tunics as the old sergeant led them sprinting on foot into the withering fire from the ravine. The old noncom was the first to holler, as loud as any Irish banshee, as he bore down on the enemy. Building his courage. Young soldiers and old alike came on, yelling out a common cheer. For a moment it raised the hackles on Donegan's neck as he was reminded of the courageous, mindless charge Reverend White made on the ravine beside the Crazy Woman Crossing three summers gone.*

To their surprise, up the far side of the ravine clawed most of the warriors, eager to escape. A few stalwart Dog Soldiers remained to meet the onslaught of soldiers. They only slowed the foot charge, however, one by one going down quickly under a steady, sustained barrage of carbine fire.

A handful of soldiers sank to their knees at the lip of the ravine beside the naked copper bodies, and aimed for the fleeing warriors, dropping most as the Dog Soldiers tried to escape the long-reaching riflefire.

"You look a mess, son," said the old sergeant as Seamus rose from the grass.

"It's a wee bit tender," he replied as the soldier came close to inspect the ear.

"You'll be needing some sewing done, I'd say."

* The Plainsmen Series, Vol. I, *Sioux Dawn*

Seamus gulped. "Sewing, is it? Won't have to come off?"

A few other young soldiers had gathered now, not joining their comrades in taking the scalps of the dead Cheyenne.

"I've saved worse before in my time," commented the sergeant before he whirled away. "I'll be back with my saddle-kit and we'll have you done in no time." In minutes the veteran returned, and the painful stitching commenced.

"Done yet?"

"Those britches of yours have about had all they can take, Irishman," the soldier commented as he was nearing the final stages of open-air surgery. He watched his patient's face as much as he inspected his own handiwork.

Seamus winced and bit his lip again as the needle pierced the torn skin. "You're willing to trade me, old man?"

The sergeant laughed. "Dickson it is to you, young fella. And no—I'll not trade these for them you're wearing, all patched and faded. Who'd you fight for?"

"Army of the Potomac. Then Little Phil down in the Shenandoah."

"By smoke—that was a campaign, it was!" He yanked hard on the thread, then pulled a folding knife from his pants pocket. "All neatly done, Irishman," he said proudly after the thread was trimmed. "You'll play hell keeping it clean till she clots up good and crusty."

"Here, tie this 'round me head," Donegan said, pulling the bandanna from his neck.

"Yes. This'll do nicely."

"I thank you, Sergeant Dickson."

"Don't thank me, boy. No telling but you might be able to repay me one day."

"Done and gladly!"

"Sergeant!"

They all turned to find a thin soldier loping up, his carbine slung at the end of his left arm, his right hand held up and cupped.

"Lookit this, will you?"

He held open the hand for inspection. In his palm lay the colorful oxblood and gold of a badge worn by a Royal Arch Mason. On the lower banner were emblazoned the words: WEST SPRINGFIELD, ILLINOIS.

"Where'd you come by this, Lorrett?" asked Dickson.

He threw a thumb back at the ravine. "I was looking over the body of one of the red bastards I killed. Found this."

"Took off a white man for sure," the sergeant replied.

"Bastards," muttered one of the men, his sentiment immediately echoed by the rest.

"Them Pawnee every bit as bad as these Cheyenne," said a corporal with greasy stripes on his sweat-soaked blouse.

"That's right, Walsh," replied Dickson. "I ain't seen a one of them Pawnee scouts down here mixing it up with the Cheyenne bucks like us."

"Chicken-shit Pawnee sonsabitches went after the women and children," Walsh growled. "Yellow-backed redskins . . . no one ever gonna tell me they can face the music like one of us."

As Tall Bull plunged the tomahawk down into the white woman's head, a blood-curdling cry erupted behind him.

Turning, he found his wife and daughter watching as the blood-splattered prisoner sank to the ground. They had returned for him. In his wife's hand was the halter of Tall Bull's most prized possession—his war-pony.

"You must escape!" he shouted angrily above the clamor.

"I will not go without you, husband."

"Up!" he ordered them. "We will ride!"

Tall Bull pulled his wife up behind him, then in the next frantic moment dragged his daughter of eight summers in front of him. The pony staggered as he pounded his heels to its ribs.

"Stand with me!" he shouted at the southern edge of the village where he had slowed the pony among the confused and dazed.

Already the Pawnee and pony soldiers were among the lodges on the far side of their sprawling camp.

"We go to fight another day!" Two Crows replied above the screaming clamor.

"Too late this fight!" agreed Plenty of Bull Meat.

"You are women," Tall Bull snarled. "The fight is here—it is now!"

"These soldiers are too strong . . . we are not ready!" Two Crows answered lamely.

"Go, old one! Tell the children of this day when Tall Bull stayed to fight while the rest of you ran. Tell all our people down to the lives of our grandchildren's grandchildren of this day!"

"Your words are like iron, Tall Bull!"

He turned to find Red Cherries running up through the yellow dust. Behind him came his young wife and infant. Already bullets from the far side of camp were singing around them.

"You will stay with me, Red Cherries?"

"I will fight them to my end."

A brutal sound caught in the throat of the wife of Red Cherries. "Husband, remember your child!" she screeched, holding the infant before its father.

"I do this—stand and fight—for all Cheyenne."

Lone Bear and Wolf Friend hurried up with a half-dozen others. "We should fight where we have a chance to kill many soldiers before we die."

Tall Bull nodded. "Bobtailed Porcupine has gone to the deep ravine over there."

The others shook their head in disagreement. Pretty Bear and Heavy Furred Wolf both pointed.

"Come, I know a place on the hillside," Pretty Bear suggested.

"Yes, there is room for the women and children to hide while we make our stand." Heavy Furred Wolf turned to lead them away.

Tall Bull followed, the last to follow as the soldiers slashed their way into the heart of the village on horseback.

"Take the pony," he whispered to his wife. "I am coming behind you."

One by one the tiny group entered the narrow mouth of the hillside ravine. Beneath the erosion-washed overhang of the coulee the men found places to hide each woman and child. Only then would the warriors take their places along the lip of the ravine and at its skinny entrance. Each man cut his own foot- and hand-holds in the steep sides so he could peer over the embankment in safety and fire back at his attackers.

They were discovered by a party of Pawnee nearly as soon as they reached the ravine. Cautious of the deadly fire of the Cheyenne, North's scouts dismounted at a safe distance and found themselves some cover from which they began to shoot back at the hiding place of their enemies.

Still on the sandy floor of the ravine, Tall Bull turned to his wife to say, "This is where I will die."

"We do not have to die here," she answered, more frantically. "We can run—"

Clamping his hand over her mouth, he shook his head. "I brought you and our daughter here for safety. I no longer wish to live hounded and harried by the white man and his soldiers."

"Husband—we can go far to the north with our cousins . . . live there—"

He rose, forcing her to break off her words, pulling the long, much-honed scalping knife from his belt. Without another look exchanged between them, he left, dragging his favorite war-pony behind him. At the mouth of the ravine, clearly exposing himself to the gunfire of the Pawnee, Tall Bull yanked the pony's head aside. With one brutal slash of the scalping knife he opened the animal's throat in a gush of bright blood that splattered him and the ground about them both.

The pony staggered, fighting the hold he had on it. Sinking to its rear haunches, it fought to rise, struggling to breathe. At last it sank over on its side, legs flailing for a few moments while Tall Bull raised the scalping knife high in the air. Down his arm oozed the animal's warm blood as he called out.

"Here we will die. No more do I need my brother in war—this pony. Come take me if you can, castrated women of Pawnee wombs . . . for it is here that Tall Bull welcomes death!"

Cody was among the first to join the Pawnee who were driven back from the mouth of the ravine as the Cheyenne put up a deadly fire.

He had hoped the Indian scouts would continue on, charging the hiding place, so was disappointed when they pulled back under the heavy barrage from the hillside.

For the first minutes he aimed at the heads that bounced over the lip of the far embankment, shooting from behind a low hill himself. The first few rounds he fired kicked up small spouts of earth in front of his targets, until he got the range calculated.

"Like taking fat cow and leaving poor bull, Billy," he said to himself. He licked each cartridge for luck before sending it home.

"What you got going on here?" Seamus Donegan asked as he crawled up minutes later.

Cody looked behind him and grinned. "Halloo, Irishman. C'mon, join the fun. Three shots for a dollar—just like back home where you can shoot the head off the turkey—and keep the bird!"

"How many you got out there?"

"Fourteen, maybe more," he answered.

"Damn, if that don't beat," Seamus whispered, pointing far to the right.

"They want in on everything, don't they?" Cody replied, watching Frank and Luther North gallop up, have a quick word with some of their men, then daringly race their mounts across the open plain between the Cheyenne and Pawnee positions. Bullets sang out. Puffs of rifle smoke rose over the lip of the far ravine.

"Showy bastards," muttered the young chief of scouts.

"Watch your manners, Bill Cody. Look how them two are helping you—giving us targets."

"Be damned, but you're right. I'll start on the right, Irishman. No, as a matter of fact, I want that one."

"The one shouting to the others?"

Cody nodded, driving home another big cartridge. "Bet he's chief?"

Donegan shrugged. "Don't know if he's Tall Bull or not. But he's some big medicine—haranguing the rest of 'em like that to hold out against us. You put him down, Bill—the rest will fold like a bad hand."

Cody smiled, bringing the big-bore needle gun to his cheek. "Just my thinking, Seamus."

The large, imposing Cheyenne who had been waving to his warriors whirled at the hillside, screaming out his battle-cry. As he rose from the edge of the ravine, Cody squeezed the trigger.

The big gun bruised him as it kicked back brutally.

"He's gone, Bill," Donegan whispered with admiration, slapping him on the back.

"I hit him? You see it—I hit him?"

"Blew his head off."

Chapter 27

July 11, 1869

*E*ugene Carr arrived while Cody and the Irishman were pounding each other on the back exuberantly.

By the time the major was handing his reins to one of his staff, a pair of women were signaling from the narrow mouth of the ravine. Afraid, they crouched behind the body of a fallen Indian pony, waving with a shred of cloth to get the attention of the soldiers.

"North!" Carr shouted. Frank North turned with his brother. "Get someone to talk them out of there. I want prisoners—no more corpses."

Staying back with the others behind the hillside, Carr watched as Frank North spoke in sign to the woman across the forty or more yards of open, grassy plain. He glanced at Cody. "How many warriors in there?"

"Don't know how many now, General. Maybe as many as fifteen when the shooting started."

Carr looked over his shoulder at the village, listening. "You hear that?"

"Hear what?" asked one of his staff.

"The quiet," he said, having to smile. "It's done. The fighting is over and the village is ours."

"The women are coming out," Seamus announced.

The men, Pawnee and white, civilian and soldier, stood as a pair of women leaped over the neck of the fallen pony and darted across the grassy open field. Stopping in front of Frank North, one of the two put her hands to her face and bowed her head symbolically. She gestured wildly at the ravine, then put her hands over her face again.

"What's she telling you, Major North?"

"Says she's Tall Bull's wife. He's dead."

"In the ravine?"

"Right."

"Any more?"

"All dead now."

"Take a squad in there, Major—be sure there are no snipers," Carr ordered. "Captain North?"

"General?"

"Get those women back to camp with the other prisoners."

North grinned. "They ain't both women. One's Tall Bull's daughter."

"Just get them back with the others."

Minutes later Major North trotted back across the grass field to report his findings. "I counted thirteen back in a little wash-out of a canyon, General Carr."

"That all there were?"

"No. Found seven more up near the mouth. I figure they were there to try to keep us out if we stormed the place. Two women are dead in there too."

"Fighters?"

"Looks like it—died beside their men."

Carr took a deep breath. "We've got twenty, perhaps twenty-five enemy dead back in the village."

"It's a good operation, General—even though most of the Cheyenne got away."

"Where'll they go . . . without horses, blankets and food?"

North glanced at his brother, returning from the village. "The Cheyenne will survive, General. They'll head north, find a friendly village of Sioux or Cheyenne maybe. Over time they'll reoutfit themselves and continue their raids."

"You don't sound like you think we've done any good here today, Major."

North wagged his head. "Not that at all. We've done a damned good job here. Do you have any tally going in the village, sir?"

Carr nodded, looking back across the open field as North's Pawnees emerged shouting and singing from the ravine. They brandished the dripping scalps like schoolboys coming home from the fishing hole with their catch. Each of the army scouts was hunchbacked under captured weapons and bandoleers of bullets taken from the dead.

"Yes, Major. My adjutant is seeing to a count at this time. Lodge by lodge, I want to be able to report how badly we stung these . . . these warriors."

"One thing's for sure, General," said Luther North. "This is the bunch you were wanting to get your hands on. Tall Bull's bunch of thieving outlaws."

"The two women in the village pretty well prove that," Frank North added.

Carr turned away as the Pawnee came up, not desiring to see their grisly trophies. "Tell your scouts to move away, Major. I'm still not sure yet how I feel about using Indian trackers to find and fight an Indian enemy."

"This is the first time the Pawnee have been used so effectively, sir." North waved his Indian scouts away. As a group, they ambled off on foot, talking and joking and recounting their coups.

"It's something the army will have to assess," Carr replied, drinking deep of the afternoon air. Its heat stung his lungs, shocking him. "Any of you have a canteen about you?"

While Carr drank from Donegan's canteen, Frank North reloaded his pistol. The major asked, "General, have you got plans to pursue those who fled the village?"

"You can take a company of your scouts—whatever you feel safe in taking, Major."

"I'm requesting to go along," Donegan said.

Carr nodded. "All right, Irishman. You go with Major Royall. In fact, take word to him now that I want him to have fifty men saddled and ready to ride in ten minutes. Those fittest to make the trip . . . on the strongest horses."

"What of the stragglers, General?" asked Cody.

"Aye," Donegan agreed. "There were many who had their horses break down under them."

Carr nodded. "It was a long march . . . a hard one on us all. Yes, Cody—you and Lieutenant Price need to lead a squad into the sandhills east of here. Wait until dark for any stragglers bringing up the rear. Guide them in here—the wagon train too."

Donegan left on foot behind Cody and the North

brothers. Carr waited a moment, wanting badly to go to the ravine and have a look for himself at the desperate fight that had taken place there. Instead, he admitted to himself that he would not.

Not that he was unaccustomed to the horror and gore of violent death. Too much of that he had seen already in his military career begun years ago on the plains, even before the rebellion down south.

Instead he pulled the big hat from his head and swiped a hand across his thinning hair and the receding hairline. Thirty-nine years old and he felt a hundred. It had been hard to find the stamina to push himself and his men, their animals as well, on this march. But once he had seen those tiny bootprints in the sand days ago . . . it all became so real.

No longer were these just Cheyenne he had his Fifth Cavalry trailing. Looking down at the fragments of those footprints scuffed in the sand made this band of Indians his enemy—the enemy to everything he stood for and had worked for out here for almost seventeen years.

He thought back on her painfully. Mary Patience Magwire-Carr. So far away in St. Louis. It crushed him to think either of the white women could have been his sweet Mary. He scratched his beard, fighting back the sting of tears. Once more he swallowed down the pain. Knowing this land was truly no place for her and the children.

But this is where he had to be—torn from Mary and the children. Here on campaign, happiest in the saddle. He disliked being a subordinate, and too often that dislike had shown in his dealings with his superiors. It had been his strong sense of devotion to the institution of the army, rather than the individual personalities who ran the army, that had from time to time caused Carr to run afoul of his superiors as he petitioned for arms and equipment and supplies to wage the frontier war.

In quiet moments like this, Carr dwelled on how his vigorous claims in all likelihood retarded his promotion. He knew he could be frank to the point of tactlessness.

Nevertheless, Carr remained an odd one at times, putting before all else the welfare of the men assigned him. Although only a major that summer, he was one of the few who had survived the "Benzine Board" which purged the army of its incompetents following the war of rebellion.

He strode up to his adjutant and stopped. "What have you got to report, Lieutenant?"

Robert Montgomery let the papers flutter before him. "Most of the count is complete, General. I'm waiting for the tally of stock—both horse and mule."

"Tell me the rest of it," Carr sighed. He drew himself up as he often did. Shorter than average, it was his impeccably erect carriage that made him seem taller.

"Captain Maley reports seventeen prisoners."

"The dead?"

"With the ravine fight—a total of fifty-two, General."

"What of the plunder in the village?"

Montgomery regarded his papers. "Forty bows with arrows. Twenty-two revolvers of varying conditions, and fifty-six rifles. We counted over fifty pounds of powder. Many knives and camp axes."

"Blankets and robes?"

"Yessir. Many of what I'd call a Navajo blanket. Over a thousand buffalo robes alone."

He nodded. "A large camp, Lieutenant."

"I counted eighty-four lodges myself, General. Many wickiups for the young, bachelor warriors."

It made him feel a bit better. "We've struck them a blow." Carr turned to watch the last of Major Royall's men leave camp on their weary mounts. He sighed, looking over the captured Cheyenne herd, knowing full-well Indian ponies would not cotton to the smell of his young white soldiers. There was more pressing business at hand.

"Did we find any food?" Carr asked.

"We've separated the dried meat, General. Quartermaster Hayes is waiting for you to give orders on it."

"Tell him to package what he can of it. Take it on the wagons. The men are due for a change of diet between now and the time we get to Sedgwick."

"We'll march there, sir?"

"It's closest—not that far north of here." Carr turned back to Montgomery as the last horsemen disappeared over the hill. "Tomorrow—after we bury the woman and burn the village, though. For now take word to the commands to establish a defensive perimeter and bivouac here in the village."

"You fear an attack by the survivors?"

"Not really. But, in all my years out here, fighting everything from Comanches to these Dog Soldiers—I've kept my men alive by not taking any chances, Lieutenant."

Montgomery cleared his throat, clearly ill at ease

saying what he felt he had to say. "These men would follow you anywhere, General Carr."

At that moment Carr looked at his adjutant in a new light.

Montgomery continued, "They'd do anything for you, sir. Ride into Hell and back if they had to."

"They've done just that since we started this chase, Mr. Montgomery. Tell the men I'm proud of them—*damned* proud of them."

Self-consciously Montgomery said, "Not a man who rode with you today won't like hearing those words from you, General."

"I can't tell them. It's . . . it's up to you."

"I'll let the men know how you feel, sir." Montgomery saluted and left.

Carr turned away, looking west to the far, rumpled horizon where the Rockies rose cold and keen against the summer sky.

Ah, Mary, he said to himself as the air began to cool against his bearded cheeks. *My sweet, sweet Mary—you might as well be as unreachable as those mountains right now . . . for I am feeling every bit as cold without you here with me . . .*

Seamus rolled along easily in the saddle atop a horse that would take some getting used to. Whereas the mare had been gentle and resolute, this young gelding gave hint of something that only a strong hand could control.

Riding in among the fifty soldiers and the dozen or so civilian scouts commanded by Major William B. Royall as the sun fell into the west was the only thing he could think of doing in those minutes after the short, fierce battle. Royall ordered him to stay behind, what with his two wounds.

"Begging pardon, Major—but I got Carr's orders to ride along with you. Besides, this little march will do some good, taking me mind off the ruddy wounds."

Donegan could not tell Royall or Cody or any of them that he needed this ride among all these men to take his mind off the remembrance of Liam O'Roarke and another campaign across these plains of eastern Colorado Territory almost one year gone. The same clatter of tack and weapons and drone of hooves through the grassy sandhills that had accompanied George A. Forsyth's ragtag band of Indian fighters drummed its way into the painful place inside where Seamus did his best to hide at times like these.

Best to be on the trail of the fleeing Cheyenne, better that than back in the village, alone with his memories. Struggling with the frustration—not knowing where to go but farther west to find Liam's brother, Ian O'Roarke. West now . . .

Anything at this moment to keep his mind off the thought he felt himself lashed to and bound by like a rawhide hobble.

Knowing the chances were very good that lying dead back in that village of Tall Bull's Dog Soldiers, if not very much alive and up ahead with the fleeing Cheyenne, was the nameless, faceless warrior who had taken the life of Liam O'Roarke.

Late that night of the eleventh Bill Cody watched as Major Royall led his detail back to the Indian camp. The Cheyenne had scattered in all directions like a flushed covey of quail. Royall's men returned empty-handed except for the rain and hail they brought with them.

North's Pawnees had earlier wrangled the Cheyenne herd, capturing the pride of the Dog Soldiers. More than four hundred ponies and mules Carr's troops would drive north to Fort Sedgwick.

All afternoon and through the night, troopers of the Fifth Cavalry straggled into the village on foot, having left behind any horses done in from the last four days of exhausting chase.

After breakfast around the many smoky fires the following morning, most of the soldiers gathered beside the nearby spring at Major Carr's request. Cody stood with Donegan and the scouts as the hat was passed among the hundreds. Both the soldiers and Pawnee trackers turned over nine hundred dollars in gold and cash they had found among the looted lodges.

"Last night after supper, Dr. Tesson, who is seeing to the needs of Mrs. Weichel, made a suggestion to me—something I want to put before you men," Carr told them as the morning breeze caressed the place with a hallowed sense of the occasion.

"I think his suggestion appropriate in light of the fact that Mrs. Weichel lost her husband in the raids upon Kansas made by these very warriors earlier in the year," Carr said, then cleared his throat. It was evident that he felt a tugging sentiment in the moment.

"Dr. Tesson suggested that this money be donated to the woman who defiantly survived the horrid atrocities visited upon her by the Indians who held her prisoner. Without saying more, I know every one of you men can imagine the unspeakable horrors she had to endure at the hands of her captors."

He waited in silence while the hats circulated among the soldiers.

"Our final duty this morning is to lay another poor woman to rest, here where she fell—her life given in blood to her captors."

Those soldiers who had not uncovered, quickly removed their kepis or wide-brimmed slouch hats in a nervous rustling there beneath the shady cottonwoods.

As Carr went on, from time to time uttering a phrase of his fluent French, Cody continued to gaze at the bundle near the major's feet. In lieu of a coffin, a pair of unnamed soldiers had wrapped Mrs. Susanna Alderdice in a buffalo robe and bound her securely with rawhide ropes found among the lodges. From the back of the worn Bible Carr carried in a saddlebag, he read the brief funeral service and two scriptures.

Behind him, Cody listened to the sniffles of a hundred men and the shuffling of half a thousand feet made nervous by this spiritual moment beside the spring. Men unaccustomed to showing tears wept openly as Carr ordered the body of Mrs. Alderdice lowered into a deep grave.

"We will conclude this service with the singing of 'Blest Be the Tie that Binds.' Any of you who would like to throw a handful of sod on the mortal remains of this poor woman, let him come forward in a single, orderly column as we end this service in song."

One by one the silent hundreds lined up to march slowly by the darkened pit scooped out of the grassy earth beside the gurgling spring. Each one knelt for but a moment, scooping a handful of crusty, sandy soil, tossing it upon the buffalo-hide coffin of Susanna Alderdice.

"Before our Father's Throne,
We pour our ardent prayers;
Our fears, our hopes, our aims are one,
Our comforts and our cares.

"We share each other's woes,
Each other's burdens bear,
And often for each other flows
The sympathizing tear.

"When we are called to part
It give us inward pain,
But we shall still be joined in heart,
And hope to meet again."

Thinking of Lulu and little Arta back home, safe and far away, from this dangerous land, Bill's fingertips raked across the words carved in the crude marker driven into the sand at the head of the grave. Boards torn from a hardtack box, nailed together as the last memorial to the woman who had followed her husband into this dangerous land.

Susanna Alderdice
wife of Tom
died 11 July 1869
Buried by her friends in
the Fifth Cavalry
"We knew her pain."

Chapter 28

Moon of Cherries Blackening

White Horse did not like the taste of fleeing in his mouth. Not only the taste, but the stone of a feeling in his belly that sickened him with turning his back on the soldiers.

He listened patiently as Two Crows and many of the older ones talked. It had been three sunrises since the soldiers drove his people from Tall Bull's village.

He thought that ironic, especially as Tall Bull's second-in-command. Tall Bull was dead. At least half a hundred, perhaps more, warriors dead, left behind when the village fled into the hills and Platte River bluffs. The count very well might go higher, he was afraid. But for now, no one knew for sure how many warriors they had lost. Women and children too. Many of them cut down in the first frantic minutes of fighting and flight.

How many still wandered the open prairie this

night, after all these days without food, perhaps without water . . . he found it hard to know.

Something every bit as hard to understand was why the old ones were advising that summer would soon end, and with the coming of the new season would be the death-song to their old way of life. They were for giving in and going south.

"Last summer we lost Roman Nose on what our people call Warrior River," Two Crows said to the assembled Cheyenne who had wandered the plains with Tall Bull. "This last winter, in the time of first snows, our people who camped with Black Kettle died beneath the hooves of Yellow Hair's pony soldiers. But Yellow Hair did not stop with the destruction of Black Kettle's village. Yellow Hair continued the chase through the winter and captured the mighty Rock Forehead—keeper of the powerful Medicine Arrows of our people."

"But now they live like the white man's spotted cows, kept like prisoners on their reservation far to the south of here," White Horse said when it was his turn to speak.

"I am tired," Bull Bear admitted when Two Crows did not rise to speak against White Horse. "My wife and children . . . we cannot live like this anymore. We strike back at the white man—he follows us until he catches us and drives us from our homes. We strike again—the white man sends even more soldiers after us. And each time we leave more Cheyenne bodies behind."

"So you will surrender?"

Bull Bear evidently felt the full force of White Horse's glare. He could not bring himself to look in the warrior's face as he answered.

"Too many of my friends . . . my relations—they are no longer among the living. I will go south and join Rock Forehead's people on the Sweetwater . . . perhaps Little Robe's band on the Washita. They live in peace."

"Where there is no buffalo!" White Horse shouted, startling the entire assembly gathered beneath the dark summer canopy endlessly dusted with stars like flecks of tiny foam.

"They live," Bull Bear replied finally.

"No—they do not live. And like them, if you go live south on the reservation—you will slowly die. You will walk, and you will sleep. You will eat and you will hunt for rabbits. But this is not living for Shahiyena!"

"I will go with Bull Bear and Two Crows," said White Man's Ladder.

"Go then," White Horse declared, feeling something disintegrating around him. "The rest of you who would call life on the reservation living—go with tomorrow's first light. I do not want to look upon your faces. Tuck your tails between your legs and run south. I pray the white soldiers who drove us from our village will not find you and leave your bodies to bleach on the prairie."

"We will go west before turning south," Two Crows said. "And stay away from the soldiers."

"Yes," White Horse agreed. "You should stay far away from the soldiers. For if they found you—there would be no warriors among you to fight."

"I will be with Two Crows's people," declared Standing Bear.

White Horse glowered at him. "And your heart

will not turn to water at the sight of the pony soldiers?"

"No—I will fight to protect my people."

He puffed his chest proudly. "Then stay and fight with me, Standing Bear. Come with my people . . . north—where the water runs clear and so cold that it will hurt your teeth to drink it."

"You speak of the land of the Lakota?"

"Yes. We will join them in their hunting grounds fed by the waters of the Elk River."*

"The waters are cold there."

White Horse smiled, pointing south. "On Rock Forehead's reservation the water is too warm for a fighting man to drink."

Standing Bear finally shook his head. "I do not want to have to fight for a drink of water."

"Go then—eat the white man's bacon and his flour. The heart of the Shahiyena will remain free on this prairie—wandering with the seasons as our brother the buffalo taught us in the time of our grandfather's grandfather. My heart is free."

"My children's bellies are pinched and empty, White Horse," said Bobtailed Porcupine. "We have little to eat running from the white man."

"We will find the buffalo—make meat and cure robes for new lodges," White Horse retorted.

Bobtailed Porcupine wagged his head sadly. "I cannot go on listening to the little ones cry in hunger and fear—or in missing a mother or father killed by the soldiers."

"You rode with me on every raid, my friend."

The Porcupine nodded now. "Yes, I was with you

* Yellowstone River

when we killed many of the white men building their earth houses on the sacred ground once roamed by only the buffalo. Now the iron footprints of the smoking horse cross the prairie—so the buffalo stay far to the south in the land of Kiowa and Comanche."

"Come, my friends," White Horse cheered. "We will roam the buffalo land again and live as the Everywhere Spirit intended us to live."

Bobtailed Porcupine turned slightly, only half his face shown in firelight. "I go now—to sleep, so that I can rise and be on the trail before the sun rises. My heart is heavy, White Horse. Do not hold bad thoughts against me because I wish to protect my family."

White Horse wanted to strike back with his words, but he believed the time of word-fighting had come and gone. Many others were restlessly turning behind Two Crows and Standing Bear and the others. Less than half remained resolutely behind the new war-chief of the feared Dog Soldiers.

"My prayers will be like the wings of the war-eagle over you on this trail you take south to safety, my old friends," White Horse declared in a strong voice he flung across the departing crowd.

"Know that you have brothers who will always roam this wild and untamed land like our brother buffalo. And like the buffalo, I will never be herded and penned up by the white man. When I die—it will be the free wind that blows through my bones as they lay bleaching beneath the sun!"

On the afternoon of 12 July, Major Eugene A. Carr had dispatched a ten-man detail of scouts and soldiers to ride northeast for Fort Sedgwick with his official report of the action.

Hold the train until further orders. We have captured the Dog Soldiers Village . . . All well.

With the dispatch bearers on their way, Carr turned next to the destruction of the village. When every freight wagon had been loaded with all the Indian plunder it could carry, he ordered the lodges put to the torch. He wrote:

There were 160 fires burning at once to destroy the property.

Only then did he send the order among his company commanders to begin the first of their marches that would take them away from Summit Springs. Across the next four days Carr refrained from pushing his men. Short marches were the order of the day as most of the men, and certainly the greatest number of the horses, were poor and used up.

What had raised its ugly head as jealousy the day of the battle had for those next four days become full-blown rage on the part of Captain Luther North. Despite all of North's efforts, Major Carr had continued to distrust having Indians along on his campaign. It would have taken a blind and deaf man not to realize that Carr still very much favored Bill Cody over the North brothers and their much-touted Pawnee Battalion.

Luther North was not a man given to letting go a grudge. Bill Cody and the favor Carr curried with the young scout made for many constant and growing disagreements immediately following the Battle of Summit Springs. Sharp words spoken and not easily taken back on that homebound trip spelled the end of Luther North's career with the Fifth Cavalry.

The captain resigned his commission upon arrival at Fort Sedgwick, 15 July.

"You ready to track some more Injuns?" Bill Cody asked as he walked up to the patch of shade the Irishman had found beneath a cottonwood.

Seamus pushed back the dusty slouch hat from his eyes and squinted into the sun at the tall youth. "No. Go away."

Cody chuckled, dropping to the grass beside Donegan. He leaned back against the tree and let out with a long sigh.

"Don't know what I'll do without you, Irishman— if you don't come along."

"Where you going this time, Cody?"

"Carr's given Captain Brown orders to take some companies north and feel our way around."

Seamus pushed the hat brim back and peeked out again. "Bill Brown? The bastird we got drunk in Sheridan last spring?"

"One and the same."

"What companies are you and Brownie taking out after the Injins, Bill Cody? Every one of them poor bastirds we marched in here with last week ain't fit to ride a wagon, much less straddle a horse yet."

"Carr tells me there's three replacement companies already on their way from McPherson. Due in by nightfall. He's sending home A, E and M."

"Them others what been in garrison at McPherson, eh? Maybe they'll be ready to try their hand at chasing Dog Soldiers now."

"That's the cut of it," Cody said. "You in, or have you had your fill of me?"

He laughed, easily and loud, pounding Cody on the leg before reaching over to wrap the young scout up in his big arms, squeezing Cody for all he was worth.

"You addle-brained blackguard! I'll ride with you till me tongue is swollen and there's not a drop of whiskey left west of the Missouri River. Had me fill of you, indeed!"

Seamus stood, offering his hand and pulling Cody up. "C'mon, let's go celebrate something."

Cody dusted his britches off. "I take it you're in?"

"In, by damned—or the Virgin Mary ain't Catholic."

From the bivouac of the Fifth Cavalry, the pair of them tromped up the hill to the squat fort buildings, where they ran across Captain William Brown.

"Cody. You and the Irishman just in time to buy us a drink."

Seamus eyed the cut of the short, hefty civilian at the captain's side. Though clearly not a soldier, nor at all a soldierly type, nonetheless the man wore the standard-issue, blue wool military coat. The left breast of the coat hung dripping with some twenty colorful gold medals and insignia of fraternal societies.

Donegan looked back at the captain to say, "And this time we're paying—instead of the army?"

Brown laughed along with them, then explained the joke on him to the civilian. The captain suddenly snapped his fingers, sobering. "Just remembered something I should tell you both—being friends of General Carr."

Cody went quickly serious. "He's not in trouble with the brass, is he?"

Brown shook his head. "Hell, no. The newspapers love him and the Fifth Cavalry. Nebraska and Colorado legislatures are drafting resolutions of commendation for wiping out Tall Bull's village. No," he sighed. "This is something that strikes a lot closer to home."

"Tell us," Donegan prompted.

"One of his children," Brown replied. "In fact two of his boys. Clarkey—he'd be close to three now—and very sick."

"It must be eating the man up," Cody replied. "To be out here and have your child sick like that."

Brown wagged his head. "That isn't the worst of it. The general left St. Louis just weeks after his youngest was born—young George, he is named. The boy was about five months old when . . . when—"

"What do you mean the boy *was* five months old?" Donegan asked.

The captain swallowed, eyeing the civilian. "George died a couple days ago. I was there this morning when the telegram caught up with the general."

"Carr's boy died? Of what?"

Brown shrugged. "Haven't found out. I've told you all I know from reading the telegram in his hand for myself . . . he wouldn't let it go. I just remember seeing his wife's name—Mary—at the bottom. And, one other sentence she wrote him: 'Oh dear Gen'l I wish you were here.'"

"Goddamn the way things work out for the man," Cody cursed. "We were skunked all of last winter while other outfits blundered into glory. Now here while Carr's just riding to the top of the heap—something like this comes along to kick the pins out from under him. Damn the fates anyway."

"He's heading back to be with her, ain't he, Captain?" Donegan asked.

Brown nodded. "Tomorrow. He's telegraphed Colonel Emory at McPherson requesting emergency leave. He'll go east if he gets leave or no."

"By damned—then we ought to do our best to catch those Dog Soldiers what slipped away from us at Summit Springs, boys!" Seamus cheered.

"For General Carr, by Jupiter!" Cody rejoiced, using one of Carr's favorite exclamations.

"I'm ready for that drink now, Captain," Seamus said, pointing the way. "By the way, who's your boon companion here, Brownie?"

Captain Brown stopped, suddenly self-conscious. "I'm dreadfully sorry—forgot my manners there, boys." He gestured at the squat civilian, then to the Irishman. "The tall, gray-eyed one is Seamus Donegan."

The two shook hands. Then the stranger presented his hand to the young, blond scout.

"Bill Cody's the name. Didn't catch yours."

The stranger smiled. "William F. Cody, you said?"

"That's right, sir."

"You're the one named Buffalo Bill?"

He smiled with the recognition. "By golly—that's what they've taken to calling me, I guess."

He shook Cody's hand like he wanted it to come off the end of the scout's arm. "By all that's holy—

I'm proud to make your acquaintance, Mr. Cody. My name's Edward Zane Carroll Judson."

"Sweet Mither Mary—but that's a mouthful of a name," muttered the Irishman.

Judson glanced at Donegan. "If you like, you can use the name I'm better known by—Ned Buntline."

Chapter 29

July 28, 1869

"*Y*ou can read, boy?"

Jack O'Neill looked up at the white man whose shadow had come across his yellowed copy of the *Rocky Mountain News* dated a week earlier. "I read."

The white laborer sat down on the loading dock beside the mulatto. "You ain't just hacking me, are you, boy? I mean—you really read?"

He eyed him, wishing the knife were in his hand and he could open the white man up the way the Cheyenne had taught him to use the knife. The way the renegade opened Emmy up—

Jack quickly hefted the pain of that away with a healthy draught of contempt for the man he had worked beside for weeks now. "My daddy's people taught me."

He nodded, taking another large bite of the bread loaf he ate for lunch. "I thought you was high-yellow. White daddy, eh?" When he didn't get an answer from O'Neill, the white man pressed on undeterred. "Didn't leave you nothing when the South lost, did he?"

"I like it out here."

"Shit, niggers like you thought you'd have it better when the Yankees won the war—"

O'Neill snagged the man's shirt, lifting him off the brick and plank warehouse dock. "You talk a little too much."

The man's eyes showed his quail-like fear. "Didn't mean . . . just that—ain't nothing for any of us to go back to after the war."

He let the man go and went back to his paper. His eyes were scanning the headlines on the bottom half of the sun-bleached paper as the white man self-consciously chattered on with a mouth full of his old bread.

". . . a farm and a milk cow. It's gone too—"

"Shut up," O'Neill hissed, scratching the new whiskers that itched on his cheek.

His eyes went across the words, being sure of each one. Dark letters, more bold than the others and bigger to boot, announcing the news . . . what was news days ago. He flipped the paper up— finding the date. Days old now—Lord, how it made his heart pound with something fierce and damp. Like coupling with those Cheyenne women.

FIFTH CAVALRY DEFEAT CHEYENNE
Carr's Cavalry Strike Tall Bull at Summit Springs

Bold, black words leaped at him off the yellowed, brittle page like the wings of the moths rattling at this very moment around inside his belly. He

mouthed most of them, unaware of where he sat or
the poor trash beside him as he read.

". . . Dog Soldiers driven from the village . . .
fifty-two warriors killed . . . seventeen prisoners
. . . only casualty was one trooper wounded . . .
two white women held prisoner . . . laid to rest at
the scene of the victory . . . as just compensation
for the horror of her captivity . . . returning to
McPherson . . . continuing fall campaign from
Fort Sedg—"

He looked up at the white man. Jack grabbed the
worker by the shirt again, catching him just as he
took a bite off the loaf of brown bread.

"Where's this Fort Sedgwick?"

"S-Sedgwick?" he mumbled around the bread,
swallowing, eyes glassing over with moisture as he
fought to breathe with the dough swelling on his
tongue. He spit it out, swallowing hard. "Up
north—"

"Where, up north?"

"North and east some from here . . . on the
South Platte," he answered, looking at the bite of
lumpy bread he had spit out on the yellow dust as if
he actually yearned for it.

"South Platte River."

He nodded enthusiastically, still staring at the
lump of moist dough. "You follow it—all the way
. . . can't miss Fort Sedgwick—up by Julesburg."

"Still in Colorado Territory?"

"By damned if it ain't. Still in Colorady—"

Jack stood suddenly, catching the man off balance. He fell back to his elbow on the plank floor-
ing.

"Tell your bossman the nigger don't wanna work for him no more."

"You up and quitting?"

"Just like that."

"He ain't gonna like it—here'n middle of the day."

"Tell him he's gonna have to learn to live with it. The darkie don't work here no more."

"What about your pay? You got two and a half day's coming."

"Maybe he'll give it to you, Homer."

The white man smiled, then it sank in. He wagged his head with disappointment. "Ain't likely, boy. Ain't at all likely he'll do that."

Jack smiled, thinking of what he had to do as he leaped down from the end of the warehouse dock, avoiding the moist horse apples clustered everywhere. "You're right, Homer. He'll keep my money for himself, won't he?"

"Where you going?"

"Don't matter, 'cause you don't need to know," Jack replied over his shoulder as he hurried down Blake Street, heading for the Elephant Corral, where he had been sleeping the last six nights.

That room with the seven other snoring laborers, most of them white, with one Mexican thrown in, had grown a little too close for the likes of Jack O'Neill. In exchange for mucking a few stalls, he had parlayed himself a bed of soft straw every night in a vacant stall from Robert Teats.

Damn if it hadn't beat that stuffy room with wall-to-wall bodies covered with old sweat and afflicted with britches crusted with dried urine. At least the Cheyenne knew how to live out on the prairie where the wind blew much of the stench away. And unlike the white man, they bathed.

It made him think on Tall Bull. Wondering how the big copper-skinned man looked in death. The paper had said the chief was killed by someone named Cody. And that was the man leading the civilian scouts for the Fifth Cavalry.

He remembered that much.

Enough to put it together in his mind and set his course. Feeling as if he were closing in at last on the tall gray-eyed killer of Roman Nose . . . who he knew was riding with Cody's scouts for something better than a year. This was something solid, something he could almost taste.

Snatching his few belongings and stuffing them inside the single blanket he quickly rolled, Jack slapped the stolen saddle and blanket atop the stolen horse he had ridden here to Denver City. The animal had one more journey to make for him. Didn't matter that the horse was cow-hocked and ready for pasture, he figured the animal still had enough bottom left in it for this one last, short trip north.

Fort Sedgwick beckoned.

As he left the outskirts of town, pushing along the east bank of the South Platte, Jack O'Neill was sure he could almost make out the gray eyes of the killer in the low clouds overhead that threatened to soak the land with another summer squall.

The gray eyes soon to be filled with fear.

"I'll be damned if that Buntline ain't full of talk," Bill Cody muttered as he came to a squat beside the Irishman's evening fire.

Supper over, Seamus had a kettle of coffee he had pulled off the flames. "Never at a loss for words, that one."

Cody twisted his tin cup around and around on a finger. "It ain't that he's just making conversation, Seamus—Buntline asks so damned many questions."

Donegan inched forward to splash a little cold water in the coffee kettle, settling the grounds. "What's the sort he's asking you?"

After Cody had skimmed his coffee tin through the kettle and set himself back against his saddle, he let out a sigh. "Stuff about the wagon work I did for Majors and Russell, lots of questions about the mail express I ran for a few months."

Earlier that day Captain Brown had led them down the South Platte River as far as O'Fallon's Station, where Ned Buntline hopped the train to continue his trip east. Every day for the better part of a week on the trip up from Fort Sedgwick, the soon-to-be dime novelist pressed Cody for information on his exploits and daring deeds.

"Didn't ask you anything about hunting buffalo?"

Cody snorted over his cup. "Damn if Buntline didn't like them stories—riding through 'em or making a stand of it."

The first day north of O'Fallon's Station, Cody and his scouts had finally come across the trail of the Cheyenne Dog Soldiers, who evidently were fleeing across the North Platte, toward the land of their northern cousins.

"For being such a strange sort, Buntline didn't lack for gumption," Donegan said.

"You see how he put his horse down into the South Platte all wide and high, swollen with rain?"

Seamus agreed, sipping at his coffee. "He swam the bleeming horse over like he did it every day."

"Buntline don't lack for sand and tallow, that's certain. He sure took a shine to Buckskin Joe."

"He's not only in awe of your horse, stupid. I didn't know better—I'd say the man was clearly taken with you, Bill Cody."

"Lulu and my little Arta have first call on my heart, you big Irish bastard," he replied before laughing with Seamus.

"You'll do to race that big horse of yours, you have a mind to."

Cody regarded him over the lip of his coffee tin. "You really think Buckskin Joe has the makings?"

"He's strong of leg—but what's more, he's got the right wind to make a runner. Aye, there's not many like him out here," Seamus said.

"Frank's Pawnee been licking their lips every time they come 'round him."

"You watch them, Bill. They know good horse-flesh," Donegan warned. "Nothing they'd like better than to have you wager the buckskin in a race—and lose the horse to them through some of their Indian magic and underhanded jiggery."

"You're a betting man I take it?"

The Irishman nodded. "I wasn't brought up Catholic for boon, me friend! Let's race him, what say?"

Cody thought about it for several moments, blowing steam off his coffee tin as he stared at the fire near their feet. All about them the bivouac of men and animals slowed as darkness eased down on the prairie.

"All right, Irishman—we'll race that big son of a bitch!"

For several days Captain William Brown pushed his command north from O'Fallon's Station on the South Platte, then crossed the North Platte River, where Cody had the unenviable task of reporting they were not gaining on their quarry.

"Brownie—they were two days ahead of us when we started this run. And they're at least two days head of us now, if not more."

Brown ground his teeth a moment. "Telling me we don't stand a chance of catching them?"

Cody dug a toe into the grassy sand, glancing at the Irishman. "No, we could catch 'em. Might take us until we're up on the Bozeman to do it . . . making up all the time."

Donegan cleared his throat. "They're running this time, Captain. Not like when they were with Tall Bull, taking their time."

"Irishman's right. This bunch knows the soldiers can sting 'em. They're not going to be caught this way unless we push these men and animals harder than we've been doing—harder than the Cheyenne will be punishing their own."

"Neither the men or their mounts are in that shape," Brown finally admitted. He sighed, resigned to it. "All right. Let's turn south."

"Sedgwick?"

"Yes, Bill. Makes sense—it's closest. The men are due a payday, and we can call on the paymaster there to wire duty rosters from McPherson."

"Payday sounds good, Brownie," Cody replied, winking at Donegan.

Fort Sedgwick had never seen anything like it. While most soldiers normally contented themselves with small bump-poker games, what Bill Cody and Seamus Donegan cooked up was something altogether different. Horse racing brought out the larceny and greed in everyone, soldier and civilian.

Two days after arriving at the post, giving the animals time to rest and recoup their strength, Donegan had arranged some betting sport with Lieutenant George F. Mason. So sure of his horse was Mason and his backers that a flat hundred-dollar bet was laid out on the friendly bar of Reuben Wood's place. Donegan slapped another hundred dollars of scrip down on the bar, which was quickly covered by Mason's backers. The sutler himself happily booked another two hundred dollars in side bets. Everyone wanted a dime's or a dollar's chance at winning.

Buckskin Joe and Cody had Mason's horse beat from the starting line, but impressive enough was the margin of victory that several of the Pawnee pushed through the cheering crowd, pressing around the young scout to propose a more interesting bet.

"They want to bet your buckskin against two of their finest," Frank North interpreted.

Cody glanced at Donegan and winked.

"Their ponies any good at this sort of race?" Donegan asked, his arm waving in an arc over the long oval the soldiers had laid out on the prairie not far from the squat buildings of Fort Sedgwick.

"They think they are," North replied.

Cody shook his head. "Tell them to make it four

horses and to put some money behind it. I don't want to run Buckskin Joe unless the pot's right."

North talked with the Pawnee in low tones before he turned back to the civilians. "How much money you got in mind?"

Cody drew himself up and let it go in a gush. "I'll bet all of mine if your Injuns really want to race. You gonna ante up with me, Seamus?"

"All of it?" Donegan squeaked, swallowing hard, seeing all the money flying away just moments after it had come to shower them with all its blessings. "That's bloody four hundred dollars between us, Cody!"

"My horse it's riding on," Cody replied from the side of his mouth, keeping his eye on Frank North and the Pawnee.

"But I was the one backed you!"

"I'll get you your hundred in gold—"

"It's my bloody *two* hundred in gold now, Cody!"

Cody wagged his head as North started back over from the Pawnee. "Never seen someone get hard in the way about money like you before."

"You damned idjit," Seamus hissed at Cody's ear, "neither one of us ever seen four hundred dollars at one time before."

"You got a point," he whispered as North came back.

"All right. Seems you got yourself a race, Cody. The Pawnee give you pick of their ponies—"

"Four of 'em?"

North nodded. "Four ponies—and four hundred dollars . . . against your winnings and the buckskin."

The Irishman clapped a palm against his forehead, seeing it all flying away. "Blessed Virgin Mary!"

Cody turned and smiled. "You feel the need of praying, do you, Seamus?"

Chapter 30

August 1869

Cody won the race.

But it wasn't the easiest thing to do.

The Pawnee apparently realized it was wiser not to try anything underhanded, and most of the soldiers who had put their money on Buckskin Joe gladly helped Donegan assure that no one got near the horse until the morning of the race that first day of August.

It raised a cold sweat along the Irishman's spine, he told Cody afterward, to see the way that little Pawnee leaped out first atop that high-spirited war-pony of his. But by the time the two animals were making the final homeward-bound leg of the race, Buckskin Joe and William F. Cody showed what they each were made of.

"I just let 'im have his head," Cody gushed afterward, out of breath as he reined the buckskin up in the middle of a ring of cheering soldiers. "God in

Heaven—did it remind me of carrying mail to Sacramento!"

"Injins hot on your tail!" Donegan shouted, a whiskey-thirst grin splitting his leathery face in two.

Money was being passed, backs being slapped and a few raucous songs getting ground to sand by dry throats. Then Reuben Wood, post sutler, raised his voice above the clamor.

"C'mon, boys—the sun's climbing high, so let's find us some shade and something cool to drink!"

Wood led them to the fragrant, earthy haven of his watering hole, where huge clay crocks of his special grog sweated in the heat. It was there the Pawnee turned over their wagers to Cody and Donegan. The money represented nearly half of what the Indian scouts had been paid for their services on the campaign. Yet what pained them the most was allowing the white men their pick of the horses.

First choice for Cody was the hard-boned white pony that got the jump away from the starting line on Buckskin Joe. Donegan chose a sturdy, big-headed cayuse with a wild pair of eyes that watched the Irishman's every move. More than the gleaming brown-and-white-spotted coat, it was those eyes that captured Donegan's heart. After Cody chose his second pony, Seamus picked a big-haunched packhorse that looked like she had some bottom in her.

With the condition of their throbbing skulls, neither Donegan or Cody were ready when Junior Major Eugene W. Crittenden found them sleeping off their night's revelry in the shade of a crude lean-to they had pitched against the side of Wood's saloon.

"Go 'way," Cody grumbled. His head hurt just for the talking.

"Don't you both look the sight," Crittenden replied, smiling, then went back to tapping Cody's boot-sole. "C'mon, boys. Sun's on its way up, and Major Royall wants you both at the front of the column."

"Front of what bleeming column?" Donegan asked, dragging himself off the musty saddle blanket and gum poncho rumpled beneath him.

"Oh, sweet Jesus," Cody muttered, just remembering as he dragged a thick tongue over his gritty teeth.

"You know something about this?" Donegan asked him, his voice squeaky. "What I wouldn't give for a—"

Cody was pulling on the Irishman's shirt and vest. "I forgot, dammit. Yeah," and he turned to Crittenden, "tell Royall we'll be there before the column moves out."

"What bloody column I ask!"

"The one going after some Sioux."

"Sioux is it?"

"Pull yourself together, Seamus," he pleaded. "I'm heartily sorry—forgetting to tell you."

"Tell me? Like I'm going with you?"

"Aren't you?"

Donegan wagged his throbbing head, reminded of the big bass drums the regimental bands used to pound out a stirring military air, his elbows suspended over his knees like green willow limbs. "Another ride after some red h'athens who only disappear on us like smoke on the wind . . . ghosts they are, Cody! And we'll chase 'em till we're old men. Goddammit, but I feel like a old man a'ready!"

"You look fine to me," Cody replied, yanking Donegan up to his feet, dusting him off. "Grab your gear —let's get the horses saddled."

Donegan turned at the first notes of "The General." When the bugle's final notes had drifted off, he said, "I suppose we can't let them leave without us."

"Next they'll blow 'Boots and Saddles' . . . c'mon, Irishman!"

That morning of 2 August, Major William B. Royall led seven full companies of the reorganized Fifth Cavalry from Fort Sedgwick in the absence of Major Eugene Carr. In addition to Cody's civilian scouts, Major Frank North and most of his Pawnee Battalion were entrusted with tracking the enemy. The entire outfit was rationed for a ten-day pursuit, having received word that hostiles were wreaking havoc with settlers south of the post.

On the basis of those reports, Cody led the long column directly for Frenchman's Fork. He figured he would follow it down to the Republican then work northward back to Fort McPherson over the next ten days. Some eight miles out from Sedgwick, Cody's plans changed.

"What's he saying?" he asked North's interpreter, Lt. Gustavus Becher, while eyeing the half-dozen Pawnee who had galloped back to the head of the column with some news.

"Says they ran across some lodges of Sioux up ahead."

Cody turned to Major Royall. "Put your men on alert, Colonel," he said, using the officer's Civil War brevet rank. "Looks like we're striking pay-dirt early." He looked back at Becher. "These boys have any idea what band the Sioux are?"

"Pawnee Killer's," Becher replied with a smile.

Cody thought that worthy of a grin himself. "Imagine that, Seamus. These trackers gonna get a chance at the chief that gave old Hancock and Custer himself trouble two summers back. Pawnee Killer—I'll be plucked!"

"How far?" Royall asked.

After less than two miles the advance guard came across the first sign of the village. The Sioux had been camped no more than a dozen miles from Fort Sedgwick for the past several days. But having spotted the Pawnee on their back-trail, the Sioux were at the moment covering ground.

Cody stood from inspecting the wide trail of grassy prairie scratched by hundreds of travois poles. He let some of the sandy soil slowly drop from his glove like grains through an hourglass. "Long as I live, Colonel Royall—never gonna cease to amaze me how quick those people can pack up and travel with an army nipping at its tail."

"We have a chance of catching them, Cody?"

He pursed his lips, figuring not only on what their chances were but on what Royall wanted to hear. "Maybe if we keep some of the advance guard out a little farther, rotating horses for 'em twice a day . . . we might catch up to Pawnee Killer's rear-guard by the time your rations run low."

"By God, that's good enough odds for me. Let's march!"

Cody followed the trail that led the Fifth Cavalry on a direct line, southeast for Frenchman's Fork. At twilight three days later Becher and his Pawnee rode in while Royall's troops were going into camp on the north bank of the fork. Cody took Becher along with him when he went to pass the news on to the major himself.

"Your men ready to fight some Sioux?"

That got Royall's attention. "We're breathing down their necks, is it?"

Cody nodded. "They've spotted our trackers. Yonder across the fork. In their camp, but they've busted down and are on the run already."

"Heading where?"

"South—away from us, Major."

Royall hollered at his adjutant, the camp instantly coming to a buzz all around them. "I want ten of the best men from each company—mounted on ten of the best horses each troop can muster. Ready to go to saddle in five minutes . . . better make that fifteen from each troop, Mr. Montgomery."

Cody watched the lieutenant go to pass along the orders.

"We stand a chance of catching them, Cody?"

"Slim—but making a hard run at it right now is the only chance you've got."

The hundred soldiers joined by a complement of civilians and Pawnee splashed across Frenchman's Fork as an orange ball disappeared behind the pale purple of the far mountains. The stars came out and the buttermilk-gold of the moon dressed the night sky before the trackers figured out the Sioux were sweeping back around to the northeast. Pawnee Killer was leading his village back across Frenchman's Fork.

Royall sent back a trio of riders to inform Major Crittenden of the pursuit, with orders to continue on the north side of the river until they struck the trail. The column and its supply train was to follow their trail north, wherever it led, with Royall's promise to remain in daily contact with his support.

In a big, graceful curve, Pawnee Killer's band looped northward toward the South Platte, crossing the river halfway between Forts Sedgwick and Mc-Pherson. It was near the time the Fifth made their crossing that Major Frank North rode out from O'Fallon's Station to rejoin his Pawnee Battalion after taking a short leave.

In all, Royall had to abandon ten exhausted and played-out horses in the drive his troops made coming north from Frenchman's Fork to the South Platte. He would lose another seven between there and the Niobrara River close by the Dakotas.

"This grueling chase is taking the same toll on the hostiles, goddammit," Royall cursed late one evening as his staff assessed their situation. "Forty-two Sioux ponies captured."

"We didn't capture them," Frank North reminded. "The Sioux abandoned them because they were too poor to walk."

Royall fumed a moment, then sighed. "For us the choices are more difficult, gentlemen. Appears we're not making any ground on Pawnee Killer's bunch."

"Looks like they're running north to join Red Cloud's Bad Faces for the winter," Donegan said.

"You agree, Cody?" asked the major.

"That's the safest place for them and those Cheyenne Dog Soldiers we scattered in July. With the whole Bozeman country shut off from army or civilian travel—they know it'll be a safe winter."

"What's your choices, Major?" asked Frank North.

"We're down to eating boot-leather, men. And I can tell you a lot of these men don't like the prospect of that, what with two fruitless campaigns already under their belts."

"We're in bad shape as it is—not having anything to eat on the march back to McPherson—unless we bump into some game or buffalo," North said.

Cody watched Royall wag his head. "Major, there's no other choice I can suggest than to let Pawnee Killer go this time. We can point our noses west to Fort Robinson . . . resupply there with what they can spare. Then we can limp this outfit back to our home station."

Royall stood, holding his hands over the fire. Once more it was that season on the plains. Hot enough to broil a man's brains in his hat during the day—cold enough to smite him with frostbite once the sun went down.

"All right, gentlemen. Pass the word—we'll break out at four and be on the march by five. No sense getting the men up any earlier than that: we don't have coffee left to brew."

Jack O'Neill shivered under the same cloudless sky that sucked every bit of heat out of the exhausted land.

He threw some more greasewood on the flames. He had built the small fire in a hole scooped out of the ground so that the firelight would not be so readily spotted by the night eyes of any Cheyenne or Sioux roaming this land northeast of Fort Sedgwick.

The mulatto had reached the squalid post on the

South Platte only to find that the entire seven companies of the Fifth Cavalry had moved out on campaign. Word at Reuben Wood's saloon had it that the soldiers were off chasing Pawnee Killer's Sioux northward to the Niobrara.

"That's a piece of country," trader Wood told O'Neill as he leaned over the bar in his place, lazily watching the big mulatto suck at a warm beer. "Wouldn't recommend any man riding in there alone. You riding alone, mister?"

O'Neill nodded, enjoying the caress of the ale on his tongue and the back of his throat, parched as it was.

"That bunch coming back here when they're done?"

"Not if they can help it." Wood laughed. A few others down the bar laughed with him, then went back to their own drinks. "They'll head home, likely."

"Home," he said quietly. "Where is that?"

"McPherson, of course."

"Yes, McPherson. The best way I'd get there?"

"Just stay on the South Platte—all the way," Wood answered. "You won't miss it."

"They'll be going back there, you say?"

Wood smiled genuinely. "Got to now. Colonel and lieutenant colonel of the whole damned regiment showed up there, from what I've heard. If nothing else, them boys'll come in to reoutfit and rotate units."

"Their scouts too?"

"Yeah, I suppose the scouts come back in with the unit," Wood replied. "You fixing on hiring on?"

He regarded his beer. "Might do that. Who's the leader of the bunch?"

"Chief of scouts is a fella named Cody. Rides a fast horse and likes to wager on it."

"Gimme another," the mulatto said, pushing his chipped mug toward the barkeeper. When Wood brought the mug back and set it in front of O'Neill, Jack asked, "You ever run into a tall, gray-eyed man riding with this Cody's bunch?"

Wood stood back and with a smile winked at some of the other patrons. "Run into him? I'll say. That's the drinkenest, hell-roaringest Irish sonuva-bitch I'll ever know!"

"Irish?"

"And his brogue gets thicker the more he's in the cups!" Wood cheered.

"This Irishman have a name, mister?"

"Surely do, and one I'll not soon forget. Donegan, it is. Seamus Donegan is that lucky bastard's name."

Chapter 31

August–September 1869

"Listen to this, Seamus," Bill Cody said as he loped up, coming across the Fort McPherson parade, a flimsy paper in one hand, an envelope in the other.

"You got mail?"

"It's from Lulu," he replied, excited, a vision of her shimmering before him. Cody self-consciously scratched at his bantam tuft of chin whiskers. "She . . . never really liked my beard, Seamus."

Donegan cocked his head this way, then cocked it that. "It looks awful good to me, Bill."

"You'd say that—because you got one just like it." He pressed the letter into the Irishman's hands. "Tell me what you think of it . . . smell it, by damn!"

It was late on the afternoon of 22 August. Major William Royall was reporting to regimental commander Colonel William H. Emory. The companies just in from the field had quickly handed their weary mounts over to the livery sergeant then turned out for mail-call. There was as much excitement as there was relief in the air. The regiment had not been back to their duty station for many weeks.

Seamus took the small page and envelope between his fingers. It had been a long, long time since feeling such fine paper.

"I said smell it."

Donegan did, drinking in the perfume long and deep. "My, but your Mrs. Cody uses a memorable fragrance, Bill."

"That's enough smelling now," he said, grabbing for the letter.

"What's she say?"

Cody studied the tall man's gray eyes a moment. "I . . . I'm sorry, Seamus. Damn, it was thoughtless of me to do that—showing you this letter, and you didn't get any mail."

"No one really to write to me. Not like you with Louisa and your daughter—"

"I apologize for making you feel bad," Cody said, touching the Irishman's arm.

Seamus smiled. "Let me share the letter with you. Pretend that she's writing it to me as well."

"She knows of you."

"How?"

"I told her of you last spring when I was east, you addle-brain idjit."

"You didn't tell her everything, did you?"

"About our beer heist with Hickok? God, no! Louisa is one straight-lace. Comes from quite the stiff-necked family."

"And you—Bill Cody, you just like to have fun."

He smiled back at Seamus. "Damn right." Some of the smile disappeared. "Glory, but I don't know how to feel: wanting her to be out here to share this place with me. The other part of me not wanting her to come out here with her disapproving gaze and the way she punishes me for misbehaving."

"Sounds like Louisa knows you well enough, Cody."

He finally snorted a chuckle. "Yeah, Lulu knows me. Damn, but I do miss her—trouble or no trouble that she causes me."

"When she coming out?"

"She wrote this more than two weeks back. Today being the twenty-second . . . means she and Arta are already on their way."

"Coming here? To McPherson?"

"Yes!"

"Where is she going to stay?"

His brow knitted up, his eyes darting like hummingbirds looking for a roost. "The cabin Emory's building for me isn't ready yet, Seamus." He was suddenly frantic. "What am I going to do?"

"Wait, hold on—we'll think of something."

"I can't have her sleeping on the goddamned ground, Seamus—she's . . . she's not made like that."

"Hold it—what about your friend, the sutler?"

"Bill McDonald?"

"Yes—doesn't he have a room he can let you use for a few weeks."

"Yes! Until the cabin's finished for us. They've started putting it up nearby McDonald's place . . . just past the last of the post buildings, down by his store. Splendid idea, Irishman!"

"Now that you have your mail—suppose we see about getting Donegan his whiskey. At least some ale, what say?"

Cody quickly stuffed the letter in the envelope, and it inside his shirt, nodding. "Yes, by God. We have much to celebrate."

"Home station at last, Cody. Where we won't have to worry about any bleeming Injins lifting our hair."

"You know any of 'em, Seamus?"

"It's been four years—the whole outfit's changed," Donegan answered as two companies of the Second Cavalry on detached service filed into parade formation. "Even Duncan's changed outfits. He was breveted brigadier general of the Second at the end of the war—and now in the Indian-fighting army, he's lieutenant colonel of the Fifth."

"Everything's different these days," Cody said, scratching his beard.

"I learned that lesson the hard way during the war," Seamus said. "You don't count too hard on anything or anybody—you won't get let down."

"C'mon, now—you sound like a sour apple, Irishman."

"You got room to talk, Cody." He looked over at Louisa and Arta standing across the parade, waving their handkerchiefs in farewell at Bill. "There's people who are here to see you go—folks who can't wait for you to get back."

"The leaving's hard enough, Seamus. Nothing or nobody can make it easy," he said.

In shutting off all further discussion on the subject, Cody signaled his handful of civilian scouts to fall in behind Lieutenant Colonel Thomas Duncan's four companies of the Fifth and three companies of the Second. Major Frank North's Pawnee trackers would bring up the rear of this march moving out of Fort McPherson, 15 September. Like old times, brother Luther rode along as well. Frank had talked young Lute into signing another commission with the battalion for this foray against the Sioux. With the Cheyenne all but driven from the central plains by their defeat at Summit Springs, Phil Sheridan's army had turned its attention on the Lakota bands still roaming south of the Black Hills of Dakota.

The first morning out from McPherson, Duncan strolled up to the civilians with his adjutant and orderly in tow. He saluted smartly and came to a halt, presenting his hand.

"I don't recall if we've been properly introduced or not, Mr. Cody."

"We haven't, General. This tall fella look familiar to you?" Bill asked, seeing Donegan's eyes suddenly narrow.

Duncan looked the Irishman over carefully but quickly. "Don't recall—"

"He served with you in the war, General."

Duncan regarded Donegan even more closely. Which made Seamus feel like apologizing for Cody's bluntness.

"Lots of fellas rode with General Duncan, Bill," Seamus said quietly.

"What outfit, mister?"

He held out his hand and they shook. "Donegan. Seamus Donegan. Rode with the Second Cavalry."

Duncan smiled. "Ah, now there were some riding sonsabitches from Hell."

Cody glanced at Seamus, finding him smiling just as big as Duncan.

The lieutenant colonel stepped closer. "Have you joined the Grand Army yet?"

"Beg pardon, General?"

"The G.A.R.—Grand Army of the Republic. Chapters are being chartered everywhere among Union veterans. Surely you'll join our group when we return to McPherson, Mr. Donegan."

He nodded. "I'll give it some thought, General. Don't know—"

"It'll give us a chance to talk about those campaigns against the butternut boys, Irishman." His eyes went lidded suddenly. "Why are you in this attire as a civilian? Haven't you joined regular army in all this time?"

"No, sir. I haven't—"

"Seamus here fought up the Bozeman at Fort Phil Kearny* and the next summer at C. F. Smith in the hayfield.† A year ago he was riding with Forsyth's rangers."

Duncan's scowl disappeared, replaced by a cheerful countenance. He landed a chubby hand on the Irishman's shoulder. "Seems you've still got the knack, Donegan."

"Knack, sir?"

"Just like us in the Shenandoah—remember? Always where the action was the hottest. And you, despite these worn and patched rags you wear instead of army blue—still have the knack for being in the right place at just the right time."

* The Plainsmen Series, Vol. 1, *Sioux. Dawn*
† Vol. 2, *Red Cloud's Revenge*

"Seamus might disagree with you about that, General."

"What say we get to know one another better before we put this unit on the march, gentlemen. I came over here this morning with the idea of challenging the great Buffalo Bill Cody to a shooting match."

"A shooting match?" Cody asked.

"And not only do I have the renowned Buffalo Bill, but I've got this veteran of my old outfit here to shoot against as well. What say you, Irishman?"

Seamus glanced at Bill. "I'm game. You'll shoot too, Bill?"

Cody hemmed and hawed a moment, clearing his throat. "Truth is, General—I'm embarrassed for leaving my rifle behind."

"You left it behind?" Donegan asked laughing.

"All that in leaving Lulu behind . . . I . . . it's hard enough to explain."

"Do you remember where you left it?"

"Yes, General—as near as I can recollect. Night before we pulled out, I was in McDonald's store with Major Brown."

Duncan turned to the officer. "Major Brown—evidently you had something to do with Cody here leaving his rifle behind at McDonald's store. Dispatch two riders to return to the fort and retrieve Mr. Cody's hunting weapon."

"Yes, sir, General," Brown replied, beginning to go.

"And, Major—since you're responsible for our scout's lapse of memory while you were both in the cups—I want you to loan Mr. Cody your rifle for our shooting match."

The marks were set at fifty, seventy-five and a hundred yards out against the side of a low sand-hill. Seamus used the Henry at the first two marks, but dragged the Spencer out of his saddle boot for the last mark. After the first try at the hundred-yard marks, there were only four competitors left among Duncan's staff and the three civilians. One miss and a man was out. Duncan, Cody, Donegan and a white scout by the name of John Y. Nelson waited a few moments while the morning breeze died before resuming their match.

"He's either damned good," Cody whispered in Donegan's ear while Duncan toed the line. "Or he's damned lucky."

"It doesn't matter. You might once consider losing to make the man happy," Seamus replied.

"You want me to throw the match?"

"What sweat is it off your balls, Cody? You can always say the reason you lost was you weren't shooting with your own gun."

"Yeah," he said quietly, the thought congealing in his troubled mind.

"And besides—you'll make Duncan one happy officer."

"I see your point."

"Cody!" Duncan hollered a few yards off. "Your shot. Seems I just nicked the mark. You hit it square . . . well then, you're the better shot."

Cody stepped to the line Duncan had boot-heeled across the sand, licked a thumb and rubbed it over the front blade before shouldering Brown's Spencer carbine. He took a breath, let half of it out when he heard Donegan clearing his throat behind him. The Irishman coughed again, louder.

"You fighting a bit of a frog this morning, Mr. Donegan?" asked Duncan.

The Irishman bowed his head sheepishly. "No, sir. Nothing like that at all."

Cody pulled the trigger and missed.

"Damn luck of it all," Duncan said happily, stomping up in that jolly, blustering way of his, pounding the scout on the back. "What with rest of these others out of the way—it came down just the way I wanted it when I came 'round this morning: you and me, Cody. Duncan and the great Buffalo Bill—and I beat you, by grace."

"Yes, sir—fair and square too."

Duncan grinned, squinting slightly in the growing light at the tall, blond scout. "Yes, perhaps. I'd like to think I did, Mr. Cody."

"Call me Bill."

"Bill, yes. I'd like more than anything to tell my grandchildren that of a time I outshot the great Buffalo Bill Cody."

"You just missed 'em, mister."

Jack O'Neill stood there in McDonald's store, staring at the civilian behind the bar. "They're not here? When'd they pull out?"

"Yesterday. Can't be that hard to catch up with 'em—you want to bad enough."

The mulatto's mind was awash with disappointment and yearning, after all these miles and all the days of sensing he was drawing closer and closer to his prey. He swiped at his nose then pulled out his last ten-dollar gold piece.

"Single eagle," commented William Reed, Mc-

Donald's clerk from behind the bar. "What can I do for that ten dollars?"

"Start by getting me something hot to eat and plenty of it. And bring me a bottle of something cheap and strong."

"Decided not to follow Duncan's column, eh?"

"They'll be back here, won't they?"

"All in good time, mister."

O'Neill smiled. "I'll wait. Maybe head over to North Platte. Find me something to do until that bunch gets back."

Reed nodded, turning back to the bar with a tin bowl full of steaming beans and a side of pork-fat. He cleaved off a healthy chunk of brown bread and laid it in the thick juice that raised a fragrant aroma to O'Neill's nose.

"Here you go."

"And the whiskey?" O'Neill asked, heading for a small table off in the corner by itself.

Reed brought over a bottle and glass. "Big fella like you won't have a problem finding work in North Platte. If you're of a mind to make some money while you're waiting for Duncan to come back in."

O'Neill smiled, stuffing beans into his mouth and tearing off a hunk of bread between his teeth. "Yeah, I'll just do that. Something to tide me over while I'm waiting for 'em come riding back home."

Chapter 32

September 26, 1869

Lieutenant Colonel Thomas Duncan marched his cavalry south to Medicine Lake Creek, then followed the stream down to the Republican River. It was there he established a base camp and sent out the first of the scouting parties he ordered to scour the countryside, both upstream and down.

While hunting parties from the main camp hunted among the buffalo herds to augment their daily rations, Pawnee and civilian scouts explored the territory as far south and east as the Solomon, west all the way to Fort Wallace country—intent on finding some sign of the Sioux following Pawnee Killer and Whistler.

Bill Cody sighed deeply, drinking in the chill air of a morning found on the plains in early autumn. At times such as these, that air proved every bit like an elixir. A tonic for anything that could possibly ail a man.

"Pretty, isn't it?" Major Frank North said as he came to a halt on the crest of the hill beside Cody.

"I remember some younger days spent down there along the Prairie Dog," Cody said wistfully. "Spent a long winter and early spring running a trap line along that creek with a fella named Dave Harrington."

"I knew you rode mail express across these plains," North replied. "But I never knew you trapped out here. You're a man of many facets, Bill Cody."

He smiled. "Man does what a man has to—so he can survive, running out his days."

"Seems you've always done what you wanted to, though."

"Agree with you there, Major. No sense in a man wasting his time being unhappy with what he's doing. Time's too damned short to carry a chip on my shoulder the way your brother does."

North sighed, staring into the distance. "I figure that's a big part of what has made Lute carry that grudge for you—he's never been truly happy standing in my shadow."

"Why doesn't he go off and do something all his own?"

North wagged his head. "Don't figure it, Bill. In his own way, Lute's always been his own man. But he doesn't see things like you and me."

"I've done my best to stay out of his way."

"He won't ever do you physical harm, Bill. Lute isn't made that way. He's just one to nurse a grudge till it's real sore—and he'll nurse it all his life."

"Like I said, life's too short for a man carrying 'round his own type of unhappiness."

North was quiet for some moments. His silence eventually prompted Cody to speak. "Believe I'll head back a ways, see if I can spot that advance guard of those bridge-building pioneers. Duncan will need 'em to come up for this crossing."

North slid from the saddle. "All right. If you don't mind, I'll sit here, enjoying the quiet and the view."

"Always was a pretty place," Bill said as he turned Buckskin Joe about and loped northeast in search of the cavalry column probing the countryside for Sioux.

Beneath the climbing of the morning sun he saw the dark snake of their column piercing the grassy hills burnt golden with summer's heat, in recent days kissed by the first frost come and gone like a schoolgirl sharing her first love with a wide-eyed boy.

"We'll wait here, boy," he whispered to the big buckskin, slipping from the saddle. He dropped the reins, letting the horse eat the grass that snapped and popped as the animal tore it up in grazing.

No sooner had he stuffed a slender shaft between his lips and settled back onto his elbows when three rapid shots rattled beyond the hills he had just left behind.

Without hesitation, Cody was on Buckskin Joe in a fluid leap. Leaning over, he snatched up the reins at the same moment he pounded heels against the mount's flanks. As Cody reached the bottom of the long, grassy slope, Frank North leaped against the skyline of the far hills, coming hell-bent at a lather. A puff of smoke erupted from North's pistol. A heartbeat later Cody heard the crack of the weapon.

At the top of that hill just abandoned by North appeared more than a handful of warriors.

Stuffing his reins between his teeth, Cody yanked the Spencer from its boot and levered a cartridge as it came to his cheek. One, two, then three quick shots before it was time to ride. He had spilled two riders. But in that time, at least forty more appeared on the hillside behind the six who closed on North.

Jamming the carbine back into the leather boot, he hammered the buckskin into a gallop, making a wide arc, as if he were attempting to flank the warriors; but at the last moment, in full gallop, he brought the horse in toward North on an angle. Cody wasn't able to hear the major's words. It all came out only as noise garbled among the shouts and taunts of the Sioux warriors close on their tails. North's mouth moved up and down as he drew close. They joined at a full run.

Just as Cody snugged his hat down on his head, a faint whistle keened past. A telltale sound that at the same time tugged at the hat.

"They're shooting close, boy!" Cody laid over to holler into Joe's laid-back ear. "Don't you dare let 'em close on us now."

Cody brought back the elk-handled quirt he carried around his right wrist, a souvenir captured from a lodge in Tall Bull's Summit Springs' camp. It splintered, sending a sliver of antler deep into his palm.

The hand grew warm and wet, but without much pain as he looked down at the end of his arm. The quirt hung in fragments that flopped heedlessly on the wind as he struggled to free it from his wrist.

For more than two miles they raced ahead of the screeching warriors, bullets flying overhead like angry wasps.

"Don't they look grand!" North shouted, his words gone as quickly in the breeze.

A half-mile off was the advance guard, complete with Luther North and a small company of his Pawnee scouts.

"It's our turn now!" Cody replied.

They reined up together, which caused the unsuspecting warriors behind them to howl even louder, believing they had won the chase.

"Bastards think our horses are done in!" North shouted. He immediately reined his animal in a tight circle on that hilltop, long a signal on the plains meaning *enemy in sight*.

With a wild shout and a flourish, Luther North led the two-dozen Pawnee away from the engineering detachment at a gallop.

North and Cody spurred down to meet the scouts, further drawing the Sioux into their surprise encounter with the Pawnee and cavalry. It was downright amusing to watch, as the first Sioux on the fastest ponies, who had their blood running the hottest, reached the point where they first caught sight of the Pawnee, coming strong on a collision course with them. And behind the Pawnee stretched two companies of soldiers in dusty blue.

Laughing together as they reined up, Cody and the major turned about to watch the Sioux skid to a halt and beat a hasty retreat. Luther and the Pawnee sped on past the two horsemen, hot on the trail of the warriors.

"You wanna follow along and see what happens?" Cody asked.

Frank North shook his head. "Naw, let Lute have his fun."

"Got 'em on the run now."

"They've gotta be camped nearby, Cody."

"I know—out hunting and bumped into us, likely."

"Let's go on down there and report in to Volkmar. Get his column on the alert tonight when we bed down."

Just past sunset, Luther North and his Pawnee reached camp. They had scattered the warriors, besides capturing two ponies and a mule. One new scalp dangled from a scout's belt.

Pulling out early the following morning, the column ran across the Sioux campsite beside a tributary of the Prairie Dog. Luther North and the Pawnee eagerly charged down on the lodges standing against the willows. But no gunfire erupted from the camp and no hostiles burst from the abandoned lodges.

"Looks like our Injuns scared Pawnee Killer's Injuns right on out of the country," commented scout John Y. Nelson as he came to a halt beside Major North, Cody and Seamus Donegan.

"Left in a hurry, didn't they?" asked the Irishman.

"Sonsabitches are scattering again," North growled. "Like this every time we get on a scent. Few days, the trail will all but disappear. Poof," and he gestured angrily. "They're gone like snow in a chinook."

To a degree, North was right. It was five days before any of them next saw a Sioux. And this time, it was a hunchbacked old woman.

She sat in the scanty shade of some swamp willow near Beaver Creek, either deaf or very much unconcerned at the clatter of approaching horsemen.

"I don't speak any Sioux," Cody said, reining up near the woman and turning in his saddle to signal behind. "Seamus—bring Nelson up here. His woman's Brule."

"The old one's in bad shape," Donegan said quietly as he knelt at the woman's side, looking over the well-seamed face and the lidded eyes. "They just leave her here like this?"

Nelson nodded as he went to his knees beside Cody and the Irishman. "The old ones get so old. Look at her. Doubt she's had a thing to eat in days."

"We make 'em do this—pushing the village the way we are?"

Nelson nodded. "That's likely, Irishman. A band of 'em gets on the run, they'll leave the old and the sick behind because they can't keep up. The young ones know the soldiers won't kill an old one like this—if we can keep the Pawnee off'n her."

"Pawnee'd kill her?"

"Damn right they would. Sioux scalp is a Sioux scalp to them Pawnee. Don't matter if that scalp's gray and got a couple of dry teats hanging empty below it."

"Damn but this country out here gets crazier the more I learn." Seamus dragged the canteen up and pulled the cork. She fought the hand he tried to put under her chin.

"Let her drink for herself," Nelson suggested. He spoke a few words in Lakota.

She reached out clumsily and took the canteen in both hands, really opening her eyes for the first time. It was then Seamus saw the thick clouding of cataracts over both opaque eyes.

"She blind, Nelson?"

"Yep. No doubt that's why she's here, and starving. Waiting for her time to be called up yonder."

"See what you can get out of her," Cody said. "Anything on the village."

Nelson pulled two thick slabs of jerky from his belt-pouch and laid them in the old woman's hand. She said something to him and he chuckled.

"Says she smells tobacco on me. Wants our tobacco more than our poor meat. Says white man has poor meat, but good tobacco."

"Tell her she can have some to smoke or chew when she answers your questions," Cody suggested.

With the browned stumps she had left for teeth after a lifetime of chewing hides, the old woman gnawed and sucked on the tough jerky while she conversed with the white scout. At last Nelson turned to Donegan.

"Give me some of your chew for the woman. I just found out she's a relative of my wife. More'n that, fellas—we're in the presence of Sioux royalty."

"Somebody special?" Frank North asked.

"This is Pawnee Killer's mother," Nelson replied, slicing off a thin strip of the fragrant, coal-dark plug. She promptly stuffed the tobacco in her mouth and began gumming it noisily into a moist cud.

"Where's her son gone?"

"She doesn't know for sure. Only that when he left her here three nights back, she listened to the village move off. Upstream."

"I doubt they're moving southwest," Cody said.

"I agree," said Frank North. "If anything, they'll turn north and make their run for Red Cloud's country."

"How can a man just leave his mother here?" Donegan asked, wagging his head in disbelief. He looked about, finding nothing left with the woman for her well-being.

"Says she had a little meat, what Pawnee Killer could spare when he rode off. And he left her a little gourd of water she finished yesterday."

"Just her and this greasy blanket?"

"That's right, Irishman," Nelson replied, "Seems hard-hearted to us, but it's the Indian way. Got a soft spot in your heart for the old Sioux witch, do you?"

"No," he snapped, testy as a wet goat. "Just . . . just that she's someone's mother and . . . and that red h'athen run off on her, s'all. That's what sticks in me craw like a chicken-bone."

"Column's coming up," Luther North announced, coming up easy on his horse. "Who's this?"

"Pawnee Killer's mother," Nelson replied. "You want me leave her where we found her, Cody?"

"What? And let them bloodsucking Pawnee stick a knife in her belly?" Seamus growled. "I'll have no part of that, you heartless bastirds."

Cody rose to his feet. "The Irishman's right. Let's get her packed on one of the wagons."

"To do what, for God's sake?" Luther North asked.

"Taking her back to her reservation," Cody answered.

"No better place for her now that she's bound to die out here," Nelson said.

"She don't have to die." Seamus scooted forward on his knees, scooping up the tiny, frail frame in his arms. He rose with her steadily. "I'll go down and meet the wagons coming up."

Cody and the rest watched in wonder as Donegan walked down the rise into the flat meadow filled with grass beaten down by lodges and moccasined feet. Lieutenant Colonel Thomas Duncan's troops were arriving.

"Look at the way she clings to him," Nelson said quietly. "Maybe she thinks the Irishman's her boy."

Cody wagged his head, adjusting his pistol-belt. "No. But I've a notion Seamus is treating her as good as he wishes he could treat his own mother right about now."

Chapter 33

October 28, 1869

*F*or three more weeks Duncan pushed his troops up and down the Republican, sending out scouting parties, hunting off the land, trying to catch one village after another as they scattered and disappeared from the country as if snatched off the face of the earth.

Winter was coming. The bands going south for the season were already on their way. Those planning to make the north country before the big snows came had already put Kansas Territory far behind them.

Winter's cold hand of death was coming.

The first snow was wet and heavy, coming as it did in the middle of one night when most of the men were asleep beneath their blankets and gum ponchos. By the next afternoon everything was melted and muddy and bogged down in a quagmire of cursing wagonmasters and balky mules. It was the second storm that convinced Duncan he needed to turn back home.

It was one of those plains' storms that had all the bluster of a spring blizzard, aggravated by winter's cold bite of the arctic where it had been sired. Born of the mating of wet, warm air sweeping up out of the south, tumbling and roiling beneath the frigid storm system hurtling out of the north like a hungry woman thrusting herself back at her impassioned lover, this snow had all the ingredients of a killer.

On the second day the skies cleared and the men finally ventured out from under shelter-halves and tents and the bellies of wagons to greet the sun, see what stock was still alive and to count noses. That twenty-third day of October, Duncan decided they'd had enough.

"We're close enough to McPherson—we can make it inside a week, we take our time and don't stretch out the strength of men or animals."

Five days later, as the sun heaved out of mid-sky, heading down the homeward side toward the far mountains, Cody's advance guard came within sight of the far-off bastion. Angered by an insistent west wind, the big flag snapped and protested above the home station for the Fifth Cavalry. The Irishman admitted it was a sight almost as good as laying eyes on Fort Wallace after Carpenter's brunettes dragged Forsyth's survivors out of the wilderness.*

If it wasn't Sioux, it was Cheyenne. And if it wasn't the brutal cold of a trip heading north on foot along the Bozeman Trail, then it was a sudden prairie storm that could kill a man even more

* The Plainsmen Series, Vol. 3, *The Stalkers*

quickly than the sun and starvation and despair ever could. Maybe he'd had enough, Seamus told himself—enough of the plains and these Indians. Enough of working damned hard to keep her off his mind when Jenny had made it pretty plain she preferred moving on with her life to waiting for him.

Why, Seamus asked himself, was he staying on in these parts when he should be pushing ahead?

Quartermaster Sergeant John Young turned Pawnee Killer's mother over to the post chaplain upon arrival.

"Likely he'll see that she's shipped up to Spotted Tail's agency, north in Dakota," Cody said after the civilians split off from the soldiers and dismounted on the parade.

Seamus nodded, gazing about at the pandemonium of homecoming. Officers' wives and the enlisted man's laundresses were out in force. Waving handkerchiefs and colorful bandannas, singing out the words of their favorite song: "The Girl I Left Behind Me."

"Full many a name our banners bore
    Of former deeds of daring,
But they were of the days of yore
    In which we had no sharing.

"But now our laurels freshly won
With the old ones shall entwin'd be;
Still worthy of our sires each son,
    Sweet girl I left behind me."

Youngsters wrapped against the blustery winds beat on tin pots with wooden spoons or blew on penny whistles to accompany the regimental band with every verse and chorus.

A happiness Seamus felt not a part of.

"Duncan declares Colonel Emory's splitting the Fifth for the coming winter," Cody said as they began walking slowly toward McDonald's trading post at the outskirts of the fort buildings.

"Some to garrison here," Seamus said, nodding, "the rest going where?"

"He's keeping five companies here. Six going on to Wyoming. To garrison Fort D. A. Russell."

"Damn these Indian wars," Seamus whispered under his breath.

"You want me to meet you later for a drink—wash down some of the trail dust?" Cody asked.

That brought Seamus up suddenly. "Why, ain't you coming to have one now? McDonald be expecting us come harroo—now we're back, like old times."

Cody tried out a limp smile. "I'm . . . it's not like before, Seamus. Lulu and Arta—my family is here now."

"Yes," Donegan said finally, feeling the great tug of something inside that reminded him he was without any of that family or love. Adrift on this prairie sea as he was years gone a'coming to Amerikay on that stinking death ship.

"You'll come meet them later," the young scout said, anxious to go.

Donegan suddenly felt sorry as well that he had kept Cody. "G'won, me good man. I'll share the warmth another time. Come 'round the saloon when you get the chance this evening and I'll buy you a drink in farewell."

"Farewell?"

"I've decided I'll be leaving in the morning, soon's the paymaster gets me mustered out."

"You don't have to muster out yet—I'll see to you staying on the winter—"

"No, Bill. You've had me here long enough, and it's high time the Irishman was moving on."

"We'll talk about it—"

"No, Cody. There's nothing to talk about."

"Damn you—we've a lot to talk about, Donegan. I'll see you standing at McDonald's shaky bar after sundown."

Seamus glanced at the orange orb settling to the west. "That doesn't give a man much time for saying his proper how-do to family and kin."

"Plenty time for me. Besides, I don't want you leaving, Seamus," Cody said, holding out his hand. "Not, just yet."

Donegan shook. "We'll drink our fare-the-well this night, Billy, me boy. Maybe we'll round up a few of the others to make it a merry send-off at McDonald's place."

"See you after sundown, Irishman."

He watched the young scout go, Cody's long, curly hair all the more golden beneath the afternoon sun this late autumn day. Seamus knew he'd miss the man dearly.

On instinct, he reached for the medicine pouch he kept hung out of sight inside his shirt. Before his eyes swam the face of the old mountain trapper turned army scout. In liquid remembrance of Jim Bridger.

The same two years gone since Donegan quit the Bozeman Road, bidding farewell to Sam Marr with the promise to meet him north to the gold fields one day.

"You'll never make it back," he whispered to himself as he trudged wearily toward Bill McDonald's trading store standing like an orphan at the edge of the gathering of buildings the army called McPherson. "Too much water gone under your boots."

Something more hauntingly precious than gold-fever drove him on now. Perhaps it was something that few men could really understand, never as much as they said they understood, no matter as they might try. Looking for a piece of his past, consumed with the nagging why of it all. Unable to find rest with anyone or anything until he completed the quest begun in County Kilkenny, Ireland, years before.

The familiar warmth washed over him as he closed the door behind him. All these places smelled the same: odors of men living out their days on the frontier, fragrances not all pleasant. But familiar. Stale sweat and unwashed longhandles. Tobacco smoke and whiskey spilled on bare wood. The sun's late rays shot through the two small windows at an angle that illuminated only half the room in golden, shimmering light. The rest hung back in cold shadows. The bar stood there among the darkness.

"What'll it be, Irishman?" McDonald asked as Donegan stepped up, arms burdened with gear.

"Rye, if you have it."

Plopping his bedroll and rifles off in a corner, Seamus returned to the bar for his drink.

"You'll be staying on now that the regiment's busting?"

He shook his head and threw the first shot against

the back of his throat. "No," and he wiped his mustache. "Hope to put some ground between me and this infernal prairie before snow closes travel down."

A familiar voice asked, "Where to this time, Donegan?"

He looked up, finding the old white scout, John Nelson, sliding up the bar. "Likely, Denver City holds the bait for me now."

Nelson chuckled amiably. "Ah, to be young and footloose again," he replied wistfully. "Yes, Denver City is the hive, and you young hotbloods are the drones who keep that place alive."

"What's the honey?" Seamus asked, smiling as he poured Nelson a drink from the brown bottle of rye.

"You're asking me, Irishman? Why, it's the lure of whiskey better'n you can get in a place like this stuck out here on the prairie. Maybeso—it's the lure of white-skinned women."

"You get tired of your Sioux wife, Nelson?"

"Never grew tired of her, or her widowed sisters, Donegan," and he laughed with Seamus. "They're enough to keep any three men satisfied . . . especially an old plainsman like me."

"Don't need any of that white-skinned stuff, eh?"

"No, don't need it at all," Nelson replied as a tall stranger inched up out of the darkening gloom of the barroom. "But I sure do hanker after one of them fat, powdered, flower-smelling gals a'times, I do."

"Nothing smells like a white woman," Seamus replied as the coffee-skinned black man came to a stop on the far side of Nelson.

Seamus only glanced at the stranger, but enough to measure him quickly, feeling inside he might have seen him before. Not unusual to see Negroes here on the plains. Especially here in the central part, among the forts where the buffalo soldiers of the Ninth and Tenth cavalries were stationed out across the prairie.

But the way the man kept looking at him in the foggy mirror behind McDonald made Donegan unsettled. Perhaps the man served with Reuben Waller's unit last winter and recognizes something about me, Seamus thought as he set his glass down on the bar.

"We know each other?" Donegan asked, craning his neck past Nelson.

The mulatto's face brightened with a sudden smile filled with big teeth. Everything about the man was big. He inched around the old scout and stopped almost on Donegan's toes.

"You're the Irishman they call Seamus Donegan?"

"That's right. We met before?"

He shook his head. "Never, I know of. Just, I've heard of you."

Nelson snorted, hoisting his glass filled with Donegan's rye. "Your rummy reputation is making the rounds, Irishman."

His back prickled with icy heat as he sought to ignore Nelson. "What you hear of me?"

"With Forsyth's bunch, wasn't you?"

He saw the smile there on the black man's face. Genuine enough, yellow eyes twinkling. "I was on the Arikaree Fork with Forsyth's men."

"That what the place is called? The river where we . . . where you got pinned down by the Shahiyena?"

For the first time Nelson turned to carefully study the mulatto. "Where a nigger boy like you learn a big word like that?"

He smiled, eyes flicking at the old man. "I worked hard in these parts ever since the end of the war. Picked up a few Injun words along the way."

The old scout wagged his head, as if doubtful. "No. 'Cause you say it real good," Nelson replied. "Not like no white man—and surely not like no nigger."

The yellowed eyes stayed on Donegan as if he would not be deterred, even when Seamus turned around to pour himself another glass. The whiskey was having the desired effect. His sore muscles and recently-healed wounds were numbing nicely. The empty belly hollering for supper had settled to a whimper. Across his head the troublesome apprehension was all but gone.

"It true you men killed Roman Nose there?"

Donegan nodded, watching the mulatto swim in some mist he tried to blink away. Perhaps only the remembrance of that place and Liam's death, he told himself.

"Yeah. Brave sonuvabitch that Roman Nose was," Seamus replied. "I doubt any can come close to touching the power of that bastird's medicine."

A strange look crossed the mulatto's face, something tinged with confusion. "You . . . you saw how brave he was that day?"

Seamus looked squarely at the yellow eyes, struck with how much like a wolf's they appeared. "Yes, I saw for meself how he rode down into our guns. Don't know of another man who's got that much grit." He hoisted his glass into the air and bellowed, "Here's to Roman Nose."

"Glad that murdering bastard's dead!" shouted someone from the gloom.

"Here! Here!" others hollered across the room.

Seamus continued his toast, "They don't make 'em any braver, boys."

"You saw him ride down on you?" asked the mulatto.

"I figure I got the best look at him any white man's ever gonna get," Donegan answered, then killed his glass and banged it on the bar. "Excuse me, fellas," he said, pushing himself away between Nelson and the mulatto. "Got to go use McDonald's trench out back."

"Don't spill nothing on your boots, Irishman!" sang out Nelson.

"It don't matter," Seamus replied with a grin, holding the door open a moment. "Just washes off the dust of this goddamned prairie."

He heard some chuckling trickle away as he strode off the boardwalk onto the hard, hammered earth and headed down the side of the saloon. The evening air hit him like a jolt of strong coffee. A tonic that revived most of his dulled senses.

As he stood there over the reeking slip-trench dug beneath a crude lean-to behind McDonald's store, Seamus told himself he would soon have to quit this hammering at the bottle. Unbuttoning the fly to his britches, he straddled the trench and sighed with relief. What a hammering his kidneys took in the saddle, aggravated by the whiskey he soaked them in whenever he found himself at these squalid posts strung across the central plains.

Whiskey and wandering. As he finished, Donegan looked up. The wind had picked up some, rattling along the painted canvas McDonald had tacked up over the latrine. Not far off, Seamus could make out the corner room the storekeeper had let to Bill Cody for Louisa and little Arta until their cabin was completed.

When the arm shot around his neck, clamping off the windpipe, instead of tensing up, his first instinct was to go limp against the attacker.

It was the only thing that saved the Irishman's life.

He cried out as the cold steel laid him open along the ribs as he fell against the canvas side of the lean-to. The blade tore him nearly from armpit to hip. The sudden warmth surprised him as much as the absence of real pain. He felt the blood seep instantly along his shirt, its warmth quickly going cold in the wind that slashed through the gaping tear in his clothing.

In falling, he collapsed against one of the wooden supports. Banging his head soundly, Seamus had a sudden realization that the sun must have settled far to the west, for the light was all but gone from the sky. Purple-blue twilight would hang suspended over the prairie for the next few moments, then the world would go black.

No more sun.

Only that shining black face crossing the latrine toward him, the huge blade of the scalping knife catching a glint of faint saffron light from the distant window of Cody's room. It was then that Seamus saw the knife-sheath. Fringed and covered with quillwork beneath the man's open coat.

He wondered why the mulatto from the bar was trying to kill him as he struggled to rise, his head too heavy for his shoulders of a sudden. With a pair of fingertips he touched the forehead where the skin was torn open against the timber supports as he fell. Legs going to horse-glue, stringy and without substance.

Seamus wondered why—then remembered seeing knife-sheaths like the mulatto's on the Cheyenne dead they stripped in the dry sand of the Arikaree Fork not far from the place Forsyth named Beecher Island.

He felt himself being pulled up.

Seamus twisted for all the strength he had left, his head ringing, somehow sensing that the blade was coming again.

Dragging one of the sop-rag legs, getting it in the way, he stopped the blade as it jabbed for his gut.

Not so much the meat of his leg as from the blade slicing along the big bone—he cried out in pain as he collapsed.

The mulatto's hand was in his hair, pulling, yanking back savagely—laughing about the still water being the piss and shit of white men.

Still water filled with piss and shit and a fitting place for Seamus Donegan to die.

The Irishman wanted only to know why he was about to die as the mulatto turned him over, popping his bloody head to the side.

With a gasp of shock he sucked for air when the loud report filled the canvas-shrouded latrine. The sudden light stung Donegan's eyes, blinding him.

A second gunshot, then a third.

He kept his eyes closed now, unable to take the

bright, painful light—his hammered brain unable to make sense of it. The noises of scuffling feet, the grunting, the falling throb of a body against the collapsing lean-to.

Four, five and finally a sixth gunshot.

By then they did not hurt his ears.

Seamus realized his ears were muffled from the echoing noise as some garbled voices pierced the inky veil all about him. He wanted to take his hands off his ears but his hands weren't clamped over them. Something else was atop him.

They pulled it back.

"Seamus! You alive in there?"

"C-Cody?"

"By damned!" Cody shouted, flinging his voice over his shoulder at the others. "Donegan's alive!"

Epilogue

November 10, 1869

*F*or better than a week he had stayed to bed.

First in the Fort McPherson infirmary, where his mind played every foggy, waking hour with the memory of Sam Marr.

The last few days had been suffered through in one of the three cramped, canvas-partitioned cubicles William McDonald could offer travelers passing through Nebraska Territory.

How much the smell of dried blood and sulfur and wash-water standing in the tin bowl at his bedside reminded him of the war and that hospital where he saw so many lose their arms and legs. From where he had laid, watching the surgeons and their bloodied aprons come and go, Seamus remembered the growing pile of limbs. Hospital stewards in masks and gloves, armed with gum ponchos, came once a day to drag the bloody, immobile refuse away. Perhaps those hospital soldiers buried all those arms and legs, hands and feet, in some

unmarked grave left to grow over among the battle-
fields, a fitting memorial to commemorate those
once whole who returned home after Appomattox
something less than complete.

Day after day in that narrow rope bed, Seamus
had stirred beneath his two wool blankets, sweating
with a fever—reminded strangely that he was somehow still alive. Staring at the low-beamed ceiling,
thankful that his body stretched upon the freshly-
ironed sheets was still whole. Cody brought them
each day, taking away the dirty linen. Louisa
washed and ironed a clean set for the morrow.

Bill himself visited as much as three times a day.
For the time being there was nothing much for him
to do at McPherson. The cabin Colonel Emory was
having built for the Codys was all but complete.
Lulu busied herself with sewing curtains and furni-
ture throws and talking the quartermaster out of
one wooden crate or another so that she would have
her new home furnished with planks and boxes that
would make do here far from the civilized world of
St. Louis.

For days on end his wounds seeped. Yet that was
just what the army surgeon Francis Regen wanted.
He kept them open to seep—both the leg and the
long slash from armpit to hip. Day after day Regen
came to change the bandages with Cody's help, the
little surgeon making that unconscious scolding
tone with his tongue as he worked over the crusty
wounds, pulling the cloth tenderly from every inch
of oozy flesh.

Seamus didn't need anyone to tell him how lucky
he was to be alive. Each new day came to mean one

more sunrise he did not have to face the gallows, a condemned man staring death in the face.

He had done everything he could to save his own life, and found himself wanting. It had not been enough, and in the end he needed Cody's help.

Twisting now off the buttocks gone numb, he inched to the side of the bed and sat up slowly. Behind him now were the days of healing along the muscles in his back where the mulatto's knife had opened him to the ribs. Cody told him they could see the purple-white of bone through the bunching pink of muscle as they had carried him into McDonald's. Two soldiers, the saloonkeeper and Cody himself, that night more than a week gone when the young scout emptied his pistol into the mulatto.

Not leaving any chance of finding out why he had come to kill the Irishman.

Another mystery to prick at him for the rest of his life, he brooded in those hours spent alone and immobile. Healing enough to climb atop a horse so he could hurry down to Denver City for the winter. It was all he promised himself each new day.

Bill Cody had come to McDonald's saloon as he had promised—just after sundown. To try talking the Irishman from leaving. He had asked McDonald for Donegan—was told Seamus had gone outside to do his business at the latrine. Him, and the new man.

"New man?" Cody had asked McDonald.

"A nigger. Not really—more like a high-yellow. Sounded like he knew of the Irishman," the storekeeper had explained.

By the time Cody had cleared the corner of the saloon, he had heard the scuffle. Pulling his pistol, he had stepped into the darkness of the latrine, just as the mulatto pulled Donegan's head back, ready to open his throat like a slaughtered hog.

Emptying his pistol amid the shouts of those who came running behind him, Cody had fired point-blank into the giant black man's body, hoping to drive him and the huge butcher knife off Donegan, who lay beneath the collapsed side of the lean-to.

It made for good telling—each time Seamus had Cody tell it to him again. And again. As if Donegan wanted to be sure to get it right—every detail. Hoping to fill in the aching void of that moment in his life with the recollections of others.

He had no memory of his own.

The pain and the warm. The grunting of struggle and combat, then the falling against the timber support, a falling that came a heartbeat before the first crash of thunder and bolt of blinding light, like a prairie thunderstorm's flare across the nearby bluffs.

That was all he had to hold on to—except what Cody told him.

The why was up to him to shake and leave behind.

Eventually he stood and tried out the leg again. The scabbing was taut, like the puckered, pinched and reddened skin around it, nearly encircling the outside of the left thigh. It would do to walk on the way he had been practicing the past three days, pacing up and down the ten feet in length of the tiny cubicle.

Whenever he tried to breathe deeply, the tug of the bandages wrapping his chest and belly reminded him they refused to budge. But he had healed.

And it was time to move on.

"You're ready?"

Seamus looked up to find Cody's face.

"Is the horse—"

"Saddled and watered. Packhorse too. Tied out front. McDonald and the others are out there. Waiting."

Behind Cody a throat cleared and the young scout turned, stepped aside to allow Major Eugene A. Carr into the tiny space.

"Mr. Donegan, I wanted to bid you farewell myself," he began, taking his hat from his head. He held out his hand. "You proved yourself of great service to the Fifth."

"Thank you, General Carr," he said as they shook.

He put his hat back on his head then fussed with his mustache a moment. "I'll be on my way, Irishman. Just wanted to let you know of my appreciation. And, for some reason I can't shake—I feel certain we'll see one another again."

"I don't figure on being back here for a long time, General."

Carr smiled. "Be that as it may, the plains aren't all that big, Mr. Donegan. So, till we meet again on another trail."

"General," he replied, watching the officer go.

Cody came up to the cot. "This all you have?"

Seamus looked down at the bedroll and the saddlebags beneath his heavy mackinaw coat. It wasn't much, he had to admit that. "Man don't need much where I'm going."

Cody scooped them up then moved slowly behind

Donegan as the Irishman inched his way to the door. "Where's that, Seamus?"

"Hell, in the end, Cody. Hell."

They laughed all the way down the canvas-walled hallway and out the back-door hung on leather hinges. A cold November breeze greeted him among the shadows of morning.

"I can smell Louisa's perfume on you, Bill."

Cody smiled as they shuffled slowly down the side of the saloon. "She's waiting to see you off. Little Arta too."

That made him feel sad and happy at the same time. Thinking about Jenny of a sudden—sensing the completeness Cody had in his own life.

There beside the horse and pack-animal, Seamus said farewell to the civilians and the soldiers alike. Louisa Cody pecked him on the cheek and stepped back while Cody hoisted up his daughter for a quick hug with the Irishman. Then it was time to pull himself into the saddle.

At first Bill stepped in to help, but with a stern look of admonition from Donegan, the young scout backed off.

Seamus did it himself.

Cody handed him the rope leading back to the packhorse. "You write me when you get down to Denver," he said, his hand on the stirrup fender next to Donegan's wounded leg.

"I ain't much at writing."

"Damn you—I know good and well you've written your mother every time you were back here at Mc-Pherson or Sedgwick, Fort Lyons or Wallace."

"Didn't think you paid much attention to that."

"It don't have to be much in the way of a letter—

just let me . . . let us know how you're faring, Irishman. We'll run across one another sometime soon."

Donegan smiled, something reassured inside him. "I know we will, Bill Cody." He reached down and shook hands with the scout. "You take care of that family of yours."

"You take care of yourself, Seamus."

"God bless you, Seamus Donegan," Louisa Cody sang out, waving.

"God bless you too, Louisa. See that you take care of Bill for me."

He sawed the reins aside and tapped heels. The packhorse came along smartly. There was little for it to carry—but the animal might bring a price in Denver if the need arose. And come spring, there was still that trip over the mountains into the unknown—all the way to the western sea. Looking for . . .

Seamus turned once in the saddle and looked back as he left behind the squat buildings of Fort McPherson beneath the rose of a rising sun of that November morning. Heading south by southeast along the Platte for Colorado Territory and the ten-year-old settlement sprung up alongside Cherry Creek.

Waving, he choked down the remorse of a sudden he felt for leaving. Not in leaving so soon, but in leaving people behind at all. He was always pulling away from what he knew and understood. Forging ahead into what he knew least but what drew him most, like iron fillings to a lodestone.

Liam's clue might take him far enough come spring. Eighteen and seventy it would be, he thought as his leg adjusted to the sway of the horse, and the taut muscles of his back grew accustomed to the rhythm of the saddle. He knew of nothing north of California—only Oregon country. Perhaps that alone was the pull west to find Uncle Ian O'Roarke.

But first he would winter in Denver City, working as need be to pay for room and board. The men down at the Elephant Corral might have work, even Marshall Dave Cook might prove in need of help.

There in the shadow of the Rockies he would be close to Cripple Creek and the miners who might have heard or know of the O'Roarkes. It was there in the mountains south of Denver City that the brothers had their falling out before Ian fled west and Liam began haunting the plains.

The last known whereabouts of Ian O'Roarke was the place to start—Cripple Creek.

And the only way to get there was to put one mile at a time behind him, one sunset at a time.

He looked back on the little gathering once more, feeling the pull like working the new, taut skin on his leg as he stretched it each day. The group stood there still, watching him reach that first rise in the landscape behind which he would disappear from them, they from him.

Tonight's sunset would be the hardest, he realized. It never got easier saying good-bye to friends.

But tonight's sunset would be the hardest of all.

**HERE IS AN EXCERPT FROM *DEVIL'S
BACKBONE*, THE NEXT VOLUME IN THE
ACCLAIMED *PLAINSMEN* SERIES BY
TERRY C. JOHNSTON:**

Chapter 1

Early Spring, 1871

"*B*loody right we'll share a drink one day soon,
old man," Seamus Donegan whispered quietly to
himself as he folded Sam Marr's letter and stuffed it
in one of the big pockets on his canvas mackinaw,
his heart awash wth memories of the man who had
ridden north up the bloody Bozeman Road with
him five years before.

With a sigh, he stepped down into a stream of
sunshine that poured through the breaks in the
pewter clouds like liquid butterscotch.

The tall Irishman had to admit there was something about this high country that could capture a
man's heart. Both that country down around Cripple Creek in Colorado Territory and up here in the
Montana diggings. He had left the first behind a
year before to follow the ghostly trail of his uncle
here to the gold boom towns that had sprung up
along Alder Gulch. Seamus had passed his thirtieth
birthday getting here up the backside of the Rockies.

He smiled as the sunshine warmed a freshly shaved cheek. Seamus still favored the sweeping mustaches and the long, bantam tuft sported just beneath his lower lip. The smile was as warm as the sunshine—warm in remembrance. Was a time he and Sam Marr had tried their hand getting up the Bozeman Road into this part of Montana—and both had been lucky to come through those days with their hair.

Unconsciously he caressed his fingers on the old mountain man's medicine pouch Seamus carried, tied around his neck on a buckskin thong beneath his woolen shirt, then swung into the saddle atop the ugly roan he had traded from Teats at the Elephant Corral in Denver City back in the fall of 'sixty-nine. Coming there from Fort McPherson and his brush with death at the hand of a renegade mulatto.

Seamus nodded to the owner of the shanty mercantile who also served as Nevada City's postmaster and reined up the street. Headed out of town and bound for northern California.

He had been a long time coming this far, learning this much. But he sensed he was on his last leg of a long, long journey at last. Spring was breaking winter's hold on the high passes, and Seamus figured he could be in California diggings by early fall.

What would happen when he arrived there was no way to tell. If only he could only find another wisp of a clue to the whereabouts of Ian O'Roarke out here in northern California . . .

Perhaps that fickle, fickle bitch called Fate would smile on him as warmly as the sun caressed his neck right now. It had been a long winter going here in Montana Territory. After a long winter down in Colorado as well. Both winters filled with too damn much time spent remembering faces, tastes and smells—and the touch of a certain woman who alone still kicked around inside his empty heart.

Back to the fall of 'sixty-nine he had gone to Denver City, his wounds still taut and pink and puckered. But the work he hired on to do at Teats's Elephant Corral slowly loosened up hide and sinew. Through that winter he had bedded down in the corner of a spare room at the back of a gambling hall place. Denver City was full of gambling halls and whore-cribs, and there was never any lack of something to do for a man with healthy hands and strong back in that town. Nor were there any lack of diversions for a man's purse.

The whiskey was strong—better than a man would find out along the string of posts and forts dotting the high plains where the sutlers invariably watered down their stock, stretching their profit margin.

Besides the more potent whiskey, in Denver City a man could find the girl of his liking, be she fleshy or thin, dark or pale, Mexican, Oriental or a smoke-skinned buffalo-haired chippie.

Many were the times it ate at him—this not knowing why the coffee-colored mulatto had hunted him down and nearly killed him in that stinking slip-trench latrine back of Bill McDonald's watering hole serving the frontier soldiers stationed at Fort McPherson, Nebraska Territory. If it hadn't been for Bill Cody come back to the latrine looking for him . . .

Time and again he shook off the dread of the

thought and learned to celebrate each new night he
allowed himself to share with a new chippie in a
different crib. One hurrah a week was about all
Donegan could afford dipping into his purse, what
with the way he went at the whiskey and the
women. As the months following Summit Springs
had become years now, he had noticed some subtle
changes that warned him he was getting older. No
longer did he revel in all-night celebrations, wearing down the whiskey and the women both as he
had once done. No, it was plain as paint he was
slowing. It took longer to pull himself from the
blankets the next morning when the sun came brutally calling.

As if that weren't the damnedest thing about aging now—not only were the bad times getting him
down all the more, but the good times took their toll
on him as well.

Come the spring of eighteen and seventy there in
Denver City, Seamus admitted he had his gullet fill
of it all and promised himself he would follow
down the only clue Liam O'Roarke had left of his
brother Ian. The two had their falling out in a place
called Cripple Creek, Colorado Territory.

There had been times the Irishman wondered
why he was even trying to follow the ghostly trail of
his uncle when it seemed the only one who cared
was his mother. And each time Seamus finally admitted it mattered every bit as much to him. It was
family.

Surprisingly, it hadn't taken all that long to find
some sign of Ian. A few questions asked at the marshal's office led him to track down a one-legged ex-
prospector who lived in a shanty down below the

creek. It was he who had known the O'Roarke brothers in better days.

"You do resemble 'em both, come to look at you," said the old man as he backed up to allow the Irishman room to pass into the low-roofed shanty built back into the hillside.

They both settled at the sheet-iron stove. Eventually that night, Seamus eased around to telling the man Liam was dead—buried in an unmarked grave out on the prairie.

"Heard something of that fight you had out there on the Arikaree, son," the old man admitted with no lack of admiration. "There was talk of it for weeks." He shook his head. "Must've been something—nine goddamned days. Shame though . . . Liam's gone."

Seamus found the old man's eyes boring into him.

"He was the better of the two, boy. You know that, don't you?"

He had to nod. "You're not the first to tell me."

The old man went back to gazing at the glow of the fire through the slots in the stove door. "Not that the older one was really a bad sort—just that . . . seems he was weaned on sour milk. Always took offense at everything."

"You knew them—both me uncles?"

He finally nodded. "We panned—worked the same sluice."

"Threw in together?"

"For some time, we did," he replied. "Until the woman came to mess things up."

"The woman?"

With a gap-toothed smile, he answered. "Woman

always does make for the devil with a man, don't she?"

"I suppose she does, at that," Donegan admitted. "What happened?"

"She belonged to another man. He bought her in Denver afore crossing over the hills here to Cripple Creek."

"She was bought?"

"Paid for proper—with paper money. A young thing, too. Her folks was poor-off, so they up and sold her to the fella."

"How was it Ian O'Roarke ended up with her?"

"She was tired of the beatings from the man—so cast her eye out for someone who'd help her," he replied. "Ian was there—under her spell from the start. Not that I blame the girl none. She was needing help—and that's the Bible's truth of it."

"They ran off—Ian and this girl?"

"Not before things got ugly, son. One Sunday morning, it was. The fella—this husband of hers—he found out she had been talking to O'Roarke. Others with loose jaws that liked to flap had seen 'em together a'times in secret. He come roaring in, saying she was his property, bought and paid for proper. If O'Roarke wanted her, he'd come up with the money or leave Cripple Creek for good."

Seamus wiped a hand across his dry mouth. "How much?"

"Five thousand in gold."

"That's a lot of money."

"Damn tootin' it is. Especially to buy a woman!"

"Ian have that much?"

He laughed. "Shit, son. All three of us together never seen that kind of dust in our lives!" Then he wagged his head. "Ian stood there, looking like he was figuring on it hard. Then finally told the woman to get out of the way. Up and told the gal's owner that he didn't have enough gold, but he figured there was lead enough in the pistol he carried in his belt to pay his debt."

"He killed the gal's owner?"

The old man nodded, a smile caressing his eyes. "Weren't clean, though. After he was dead that morning, friends came in that afternoon and set up a ruckus. Ian skeedaddled from town."

"How'd Liam figure in all of this?"

"All along he told his brother to stay clear of another man's woman—but Ian seemed he was bit something bad, that he just couldn't stay clear of her. Shame of it—Liam and he broke up our outfit over that woman."

"You sound like you're saying Liam wanted the woman, too."

"Liam? Shit, he wasn't the kind to get caught up yoke and traces in a woman. Not that one. He just . . . just didn't want to stir up no trouble."

"Where'd Ian go?"

"I heard later from Liam that his brother headed up to Silver Plume."

"Where's that?"

"North of here a ways."

"When?"

He thought on it, tapping a finger against his lower lip. "Eighteen and sixty."

"The woman went with him?"

The old man nodded. "Bad blood she caused between them brothers. Women just naturally have a way of stirring things up a'tween men."

"You've been a lot of help. I'll head out for Silver Plume in the morning."

"You might. Then, you might not," the old man said quietly. "No sense heading there when I heard Ian didn't stay long in Silver Plume. He moved on north with the gal, fixing to make a clean break."

"Liam ever know of this?"

"I figure he did. But I suppose he figured there was no sense in trying to mend things a'tween them. A woman can cause a deep wound that ofttimes won't heal just right—like a bad bone."

"Where'd Ian go?"

"By 'sixty-two he was pushing north to the Idaho fields. What was Idaho then—called Montana now."

"Alder Gulch? Virginia City—Nevada City—Bannack?"

His well-seamed face brightened. "Lordee! Does sound like you know of the place, son!"

"I'll be blessed!" Seamus exclaimed. "Of a time I was heading there meself. Glory . . . glory be!"

DEVIL'S BACKBONE— VOLUME 5 IN TERRY C. JOHNSTON'S PLAINSMEN SERIES— DON'T MISS IT!